MURDER AT THE LEOPARD

BOOK 1

THE VESPERS SERIES

BY R.M. VASSARI AND LUCIA OLIVIA LAMPE

Illustrations by Karolyn Walker

Maps by permission of Franco D'Angelo

Published by Vassari & Lampe, LLC

Alamosa, CO

Table of Contents

PREFACE

The political background for the Vespers Series is a cataclysmic series of violent upheavals between major European powers, including the Papacy, for control of Sicily and the Western Mediterranean. For a history of what would later be called the Sicilian Vespers, referred to in the book as the war or the uprising, see Steven Runciman's *The Sicilian Vespers* and David Abulafia's *The Western Mediterranean Kingdoms, 1200-1500* and Clifford Backman's *The Decline and Fall of Medieval Sicily*. Many prominent families disappeared through the carnage that took place in what David Abulafia calls "The Two Hundred Year War," making survival contingent on trustworthy friends and family members. We have taken liberties with some of the events and the timeline of the Vespers in order to tell our story. King Charles never took back Palermo as we have him briefly doing so in the second book. To my knowledge, he never built a warship in Trapani, but he has been documented building warships elsewhere. We have also taken liberties with the landing date of the King of Aragon to better fit the story.

Many of the main characters introduced in the first book of the Vespers Trilogy are real people who lived in the turbulent mayhem of 13th and 14th century Sicily. The personalities and characteristics given them are totally fictional. These citizens are in the pages of the notarial contracts of Adam de Citella and his son, Bartholomeus, prominent notaries in Palermo whose registers together contain over 3,400 contracts. The registers are found in the *Archivio di Stato* in Palermo written in Latin notarial shorthand. The street names, churches, neighborhoods and even the tavern names such as The Leopard and The Olive, are all taken right out of these records.

Descriptions of medieval food are also surprisingly abundant, particularly for the Mediterranean regions. Greek and Arabic influences in Sicily are especially strong and for these references, along with those of medieval taverns and inns, fondacos and the like, we have relied heavily on O.R. Constable and Henri Bresc as well as ancient narratives of classic culture, feasts and culinary instructions.

For daily life and social and political interactions we have used the works of four scholars, Pietro Corrao, Beatrice Pasciuta, Patrizia Sardina, and Franco D'Angelo. In English, David Abulafia reigns supreme as a leading scholar in all aspects of medieval Mediterranean life and Henri Bresc has written a great deal of the specifics of Sicilian life, city topography and business.

The wonderful map of medieval Palermo, altered somewhat for our purposes, is used with the gracious permission of Franco D'Angelo, whose knowledge and articles have allowed us to describe post-Vespers Palermo in detail.

Alison Daniels and Barbara Bales gave us perceptive comments on our characters. Our copy editor, Erin Smith, spent many hours perusing and correcting our book, as well as our wonderful readers – Frances McNamara, Dana Shaffer and Patrizia Sardina. But this book would never have been written without our fabulous writing group, critiquing and questioning every month. Hats off to Francie Hall, Ben Humphrey and Stephanie Kelly.

Our terrific webmaster, Jim OKeefe, designed our website (www.murder-at-the-leopard.com) and gave much needed advice in e-publishing, e-mapping and the like.

The illustrations that draw our readers further into our book were created by the talented Karolyn Walker.

And of course, a million thanks to our husbands, Bill and Bill whose support for our project was enthusiastic and unfailing, well, for the most part!

PROLOGUE
1244, The Holy Land

As the heat began to build, the four men barely glanced at each other. Soon the temperature would be almost unbearable, like standing inside a blacksmith's furnace. Dawn cast faint shadows along the desert. All that could be seen were scrubby plants and more sand, a perpetual scorching, gritty mantle without end. A soaring raptor, nearly imperceptible against the lightening sky, was the only motion. Yesterday their trembling horses had toppled from thirst and exhaustion.

Jerusalem was lost. The last desperate battle to hold the Savior's city five days earlier put an end to Christian rule in *Outremer,* and the Christian army was in disarray and flight. Four young men who began their friendship only a year ago in Sicily, bonded by excitement and hope, had become angry and cynical warriors. Their quest to serve God was over.

Pushed out of Jerusalem by a massive onslaught, the former Crusaders were fleeing like rabbits to Acre or anywhere along the sea for safety. Unwashed, starving and desperate, the sun-blistered comrades were threatened constantly by Saracen bowmen on flying horses. Grimly, they continued fighting on foot, always moving towards the sea, battling simply to endure.

Shielding themselves from the bloodshot glare of a rising sun, they slumped down onto a sand dune. One began to softly curse the searing heat when his companion put up his hand.

"I hear something."

Instinctively they froze, huddled back-to-back, swords pointing outward to strike the unseen enemy, and strained to listen. The guttural honk of camels and a slight lilt of voices drifted on the air.

Creeping forward, they flattened themselves against the sandy ridge. Peering over it, eight bloodshot eyes gazed down upon a small merchant caravan camped in a gully below. Three yawning Arabs emerged from a tent, sleepily wrapping travel-stained turbans around their heads, murmuring to each other. They wore the usual light-colored full-length kaftans, and their feet were shod in soft leather boots. Small thick rugs were shaken out for the morning devotions to Allah. Five tethered camels were grumpily rising in a rocking motion. No weapons were visible, but everyone had daggers hidden under their robes in this fiendish land.

The Crusaders watched for several minutes, then hunkered down and looked at each other. The oldest one whispered in his domineering fashion, "God has provided. We need their water and their camels to survive. They'll start the day with those jabbering prayers. That's when we hit them. Don't be merciful."

The other three nodded and silently spread out to attack their prey. Summoning their last reserves, they leaped up, howling, and charged down the hillside, falling upon the terrified travelers and slaughtering them with lethal sword strokes before they could rise. Oblivious of the blood surging into the sand, the soldiers barely paused over the twitching bodies, including one whose face still reflected astonishment. Grabbing the water bags off the startled camels, they guzzled the life-saving liquid and wiped their mouths on dirty sleeves. Sated, they grinned at each other and leisurely began to search the bags stacked neatly on the ground.

One man pulled out a small leather pouch wrapped in soft linen that clinked faintly. Greed lit his face when he spilled the contents onto the sand.

"Look! Gold!" he croaked. Four honey-colored discs etched with hieroglyphics swirled around an all-seeing eye. Impulsively, the finder of the gold grabbed one and rubbed it with a sensuous avarice, glancing anxiously at the leader, who stared at the booty with a calculating eye. The tall, quiet one maintained his usual inscrutability, while the youngest warrior only shrugged and smiled. Still, each man took a medallion and hid it on his person. Then all four got down to the business of searching for food. Finding some flat bread, olives and dates, they squatted and devoured the simple repast like a royal feast.

A whimper escaped from a nearby tent and all four leaped up, bloody swords at the ready. The oldest crusader jerked his head. Two of them crept towards the tent and then charged in. Screams were abruptly cut off as one crusader emerged, grimly dragging a dead woman. The second one stalked out gripping a small child like a wriggling puppy under his arm. Unceremoniously, he dumped the boy on the ground in front of the edgy men. The terrified lad looked at their fierce expressions and began to wail.

The oldest one rumbled, "Kill him. What would we do with a child?"

One obediently nodded; one shook his head and walked away.

The youngest, shocked, began protesting. "No! He's no more than five or six! He can't harm us. Leave him here with some food and water."

"He's still an infidel, and he'll be murdering scum like all the others soon enough," came the terse reply. "Take him behind the tent and do it." The younger man pleaded for support from his companions, but they avoided his pleading face. The boy was swept up and swung over the shoulder as the obedient one trudged away from the group.

The young crusader followed, clutching at the boy's arm and arguing. His comrade shoved him to the ground and growled, "Back off and shut up," before walking behind the tent and throwing the still-screaming child on the ground. He raised his sword. Without thinking, the young man leaped in front of the child just as the razor-sharp blade delivered the deathblow. Their brother in arms collapsed like a puppet without strings. The shaken killer quickly executed the sobbing boy and, horrified and ashamed, the survivors hurriedly divided the plunder and loaded the camels. The leader hesitated a moment. Then he dragged his friend's body over to the murdered Arabs and thrust the bloody sword into his hands. It looked as if he had valiantly slaughtered his infidel attackers before succumbing to his wounds. With empty eyes, the three men mounted the camels and rode away without looking back.

CHAPTER 1

1281, Palermo, Sicily

The tavern door slammed open and the sheriff stalked in surrounded by three hulking soldiers who glowered menacingly at the crowd. The night watchmen, all local men, slunk along behind, their authority now deflated. Abrupt silence blanketed the room. Unconsciously, people began to back away from Amodeus as the sheriff glared at each of them.

"You there," he snapped impatiently in French, pointing at Amodeus. "What happened here? And where is the body?"

Amodeus spread his hands helplessly and began his story haltingly in the foreign language. His neighbors shrank as far away as they could from the tall, impatient Angevin official whose insignia, sword and breastplate gleamed red and gold. Raynaldus and Angelica stepped forward together on either side of Amodeus in silent support. As Amodeus explained, the Angevin scowled contemptuously at the frightened faces before him, tapping his booted foot.

Before Amodeus could finish, the sheriff nodded brusquely, *"Oui, oui, j'comprend…"* and jerked his thumb towards Amodeus. Three soldiers seized him, pushing Raynaldus and Angelica aside, and dragged him towards the door.

Ysabella screamed and clung to her husband. "Wait! No! He didn't do it! You can't do that…" The sheriff spoke sharply in French and slapped her so hard she collapsed to the floor. Amodeus roared, struggling against his captors, who trod over his fallen wife's skirts, shoving him outside. Then the Angevin turned on his heel, barked more orders in French, and strode from the tavern. Raynaldus and Leo hurried behind them to see where Amodeus would be taken.

Stunned and afraid, everyone stared at the sobbing woman on the floor before Angelica fell to her sister-in-law's side, and, trembling, stroked her hair. Joanna rushed from the kitchen to comfort her friend and, slowly, the terror caused by the sheriff subsided and was replaced by anger and resentment. The noise level rose again as people shouted their dismay and anger and futilely hurled curses at the absent foreigner. For the moment, everyone was united in their disgust, whatever their private thoughts.

How had their joyous night turned to such chaos?

CHAPTER 2

"Amodeus!" called Ysabella as she bounded up the stairs and stood silhouetted in the doorway with her hands on her hips. The stern posture did not disguise her shapely form.

"Come and deal with your son. Larissa will cut off his ears if he spills any more flour in the kitchen. Why are you not out of bed yet? The workmen will be here soon, and you have responsibilities! I am going to Mass with Joanna. Hurry now!" She dashed into the room long enough to snatch up her rosary from the corner table and spied the lavender ribbons she had forgotten to tie into her gold-brown tresses. Even if no one else would see them, Ysabella knew that their color enhanced her deep-set, violet eyes, and she quickly braided them in.

Amodeus pulled the covers over his head and tried to avoid the sunlight flooding their comfortable bedroom above The Leopard. "Come back to bed, sweet. Larissa will handle the. scamp like she always does. Doesn't your husband deserve a kind word in the morning?"

"My husband has had many kind words this morning, but he slept through them all! Larissa and I have already hauled water from the well and started the soup for your mid-day meal. With any luck, the work on this decrepit old building will be done in time for us to open for Holy Week, but not if you stay in bed!" And with that, she playfully tugged the sheet off of him and swept down the stairs trailing it behind her.

He heard her call back from below and swore she could have parted the seas with her tone. "Don't forget to meet Signor Alberti today in the market! We need a good supply of cheeses, olives and dates for opening day!"

He lay back savoring his luck. Saucy and beautiful as she was now, he remembered how her unusual eyes had initially attracted him to the gangly daughter of a neighborhood tanner. They flashed blue, brown, purple, or black according to her moods or the color of her clothing. She was a little plumper since the boy was born, but her body was pleasing in all the right places and the richness of her tawny hair was as deep as ever. Yes, he had married well. And now it would be only a few more days until he officially opened his own tavern in the busy neighborhood of Palermo called the *Conciera.*

The tavern wasn't the upscale *fondaco* that his brother owned near the king's palace, but it was his – and Ysabella's of course – and their timing was perfect. Easter was five days away. The capital of Sicily would be overrun by pilgrims from all the towns and valleys of the island, not to mention visitors from the mainland and the western Mediterranean. He hoped all of them brought money to spend for good food and drink. The thud of the front door as Ysabella left roused him from his reverie, and with a yawn and a quick Hail Mary, he scrambled out of bed and threw on his tunic and clogs.

Amodeus de Rogerio was a tall, muscular man with a playful disposition and a flashing smile. His thick light brown hair and careless elegance made him instantly attractive. He had worked his whole life as a tanner in and around the *Conciera,* or tanning district. Both he and his reserved older brother, Raynaldus, had taken additional jobs, saved their coins, and invested in small commercial enterprises. Bit by bit the brothers had developed a number of thriving business concerns, a reputation for fairness, and influential connections. Raynaldus had a more serious nature. He had taught himself to read and write and became a cloth merchant. His links to local magistrates and businessmen resulted in a political appointment as the *magister di platea* of the large, influential quarter of the Seralcadio, where he lived on the northwest side of Palermo.

Amodeus's good nature and twinkling eyes initially drew people to him more than to Raynaldus. As the indulged little brother, he had taken a longer time to find the benefits of responsibility and careful decision-making. His impulsiveness once made people smile and roll their eyes. Even now as a man with responsibilities beyond those of a self-centered youth, he could still be illogical, spontaneous and gullible on occasion. But Ysabella's entry into his life eleven years ago brought out a more serious side that surprised both of them, and William's squalling appearance three years later delighted him beyond measure. To buy and operate his own tavern—a grand adventure---was the result of prudent planning. It would be the test of all he had worked for.

As he shoved his feet into his work clogs, Amodeus sniffed the yeasty smell of fresh bread that wafted up to the second floor. Larissa had taken the day's loaves to the neighborhood baker and brought them back as he still lay abed. Just as he descended the stairs William ran into his arms and begged to be swung around and hugged. It was a morning ritual between father and son. "Another year's growth, my piglet, and your papa won't be able to lift you any more!" Amodeus teased.

"I'm not a piglet," giggled William. "I'm a boy!"

"Is that true? Well, get the broom and sweep up your mess in the kitchen before you eat. Larissa has been known not to feed boys or piglets that dirty her kitchen!"

"Yes, Papa," William sighed, "but then can I go with you to see Signor Alberti? Please!"

"I think your mother and Larissa have chores for you today, and Signor Alberti is not fond of little piglets. I hear the church bells ringing now so your mother will be back. Off to the kitchen with you." And after a last hug, the boy skipped into the kitchen and Amodeus left to see Signor Alberti.

Ysabella rushed through the door moments later, put on her apron and began wrapping the new loaves in cloth to help keep them fresh. We have to plan a tasty menu to serve on opening night, she thought, mentally ticking off items in her head. The door was propped open so workmen could straggle in, and she nearly choked on all the dust as she entered the main room.

Quickly surveying the mess, she proudly congratulated herself for deciding to keep the tile floor. "But dearest, it's a tavern," Amodeus protested when they first inspected their dilapidated purchase. "We could put a cheap wooden floor in and put rushes and herbs over it, like most peoples' floors, and that would absorb food and wine spills."

"No, Amodeus, that's just it. I hate rushes and straw – they collect nasty food bits and lice. It's dirty and stinky, no matter how often you change it. Don't you see? The ancients were right – tile is easy to keep clean – just wash it and it shines! We won't have to collect straw, rushes, herbs – who has time for that? Tile is cleaner and brighter. And speaking of that, I saw some beautiful mosaics in the Cathedral last week – oh, I know we can't afford that kind of workmanship, but perhaps a simple picture or even geometric designs like the Saracens did, you know, in St. John's, when it was a mosque. I think that's so lovely and simple, too." She made a face. "Look, this room once had a handsome border around it. All we have to do is replace the broken tiles."

Amodeus thought for a moment and then smiled at his wife. "As usual, my love, you're right. I do like that idea. It's different-- something that will set apart The Leopard from other taverns. Don't drop your good ceramic bowls on it though or you can kiss them goodbye!" he smiled mischievously. Ysabella hugged her husband, standing on tiptoe to kiss his nose. God's teeth, thought Amodeus, even covered in dust with an old kerchief wrapped around her hair, she was beautiful.

Now Ysabella smiled. She had been right. Giacomo, the neighborhood tile maker, had fixed all the broken pieces and created a simple geometric pattern in reds, greens and creamy whites. The result was attractive, different and bright. And clean, too, she thought smugly. She would have to remember to get bright green paint for the door. She wanted it easily identifiable so no one could possibly pass them up! That would be a job for Nicolo. Bursting with enthusiasm, laughing and charming all she met, Ysabella still demanded and got the best from her workers and did not countenance excuses.

"Larissa, where is Amodeus and why isn't he overseeing this stucco crew? I swear, that man …"

"Now, mistress, did you not tell him to arrange for the cheeses to be delivered?"

"Oh, Mother of Mary, yes. Forgive me for my unkind thought. How could I forget? And where is William?"

"I made him clean up the flour this morning and then he was out the door like a gazelle. I wanted the workmen to teach him something useful, but he scampered off before I could speak to the foreman. That boy is well past the age when he should be handling some responsibilities. And what about his schooling? I know Amodeus has taught him his basic letters, but what about the rest? He's a bright boy. Were you going to let him grow up with no understanding of work?"

"I know we spoil him. But he's only eight years old and he's my only child. I just remember how I felt, stuck in my father's shop since I was old enough to walk, rarely getting to play outside with the other children. Sweeping floors, then learning to wait on customers, adding up sums. Tedious, even though I learned a lot. But William is so imaginative, Larissa! I don't want to stifle that! He has plenty of time to learn a trade or even the tavern business. Besides, he knows more than you think just from hanging around Nicolo and Adam. And he can say his catechism backwards and forwards."

"Well, knowing your catechism doesn't put money in your pocket! And you know from your own experience that working at a decent trade never stifled you any! You need to take charge of that boy. He's running wild in the marketplaces and makes up stories and fantasies like I never heard! And Amodeus is just as indulgent as you are!" Clicking her teeth, Larissa swept the new tile floor with vigor, shaking her head.

"Yes, Larissa, you're right. I will speak to Amodeus about sending him to a tutor or finding an apprenticeship for him after we've had The Leopard open a bit and get into a routine, but right now, we can't distract Amodeus or you and I will have even more work to do!"

In spite of herself, Larissa started laughing. She and Ysabella were more than servant and mistress; she and her husband, Mario, had watched Ysabella grow up in the neighborhood and had known Ysabella's father well. So when she heard that Ysabella was looking for a cook and serving woman, she marched in and told her to look no further. Ysabella had been delighted, but true to form, had made her prepare three separate dishes and inspected the taste and cost closely before she finally agreed. That was just the kind of thoroughness Larissa expected from someone determined to succeed, and, instead of being insulted, she respected the young woman more. Mario came to work at The Leopard, too, as a general handyman and server. They were good workers, and their devotion was obvious. It was comfortable all around, and everyone was confident that the new venture would be a resounding success.

The Leopard was in the new, rapidly expanding quarter called the *Porta Patitellorum*. Initially the area was a hodgepodge of small businesses, but now it was being reorganized and renovated. More people with money were moving in, and Amodeus and Ysabella were quick to discern the upturn. The *Porta Patitellorum* was sandwiched between the wealthy district of the *Cassaro* and the port, making it a natural pathway for people to pass through. It was also on the edge of the tanning district and next to the River *Conciarie,* areas clustered with artisans and craftsmen working the leather trade. Three major churches occupied the district's main streets. Santa Maria dell'Ammiraglio, or *La Martorana* as it was affectionately called, St. Margaret's and St. Nicholas de Burgo, were all within walking distance. More importantly, the city council often met at St. Margaret's or St. Nicholas's, meaning that if The Leopard could become a well-liked place to eat and drink to Palermo's *politicos,* their future was assured. Yes, Ysabella thought as she swept the tiles with Larissa, Raynaldus was not the only shrewd one in that family.

Also, the Great Market was down the street, where everyone went, including, she thought ruefully, her son. Young William had made the market his own, disappearing for hours into the hurly-burly of vendors and businessmen, babbling with them and bombarding them, to their vast amusement, with legions of questions about their wares, where they came from, and why they cost what they did. The vendors had good-naturedly adopted William, protected him, and, thought Ysabella crossly, fed him too many sweets. But they watched over him, and she secretly felt he was safe and among friends. For all these reasons, this growing neighborhood was where they had decided to risk their savings. Surely a clean place with good food and drink and some lively gaming and dice rooms would be a pleasant respite at the end of a long work day.

The tavern had a small courtyard in the back where it shared a well with its neighbors, although Ysabella and Larissa enjoyed their morning forays to the more public corner well to trade gossip and news with their neighbors. More heavenly to Ysabella's way of thinking, almond and lemon trees and tall myrtle bushes shaded a small part of the brick courtyard that boasted a few scattered benches surrounded by jasmine. There was even a tiny grape arbor. On a good day, their fragrance masked the stench of the tanners' refuse tossed into the nearby river.

Ysabella stood and stretched her aching back. She surveyed her new domain thoughtfully. The main room, or *buctarium,* was at least 30 feet long with benches along the walls and a hearth to her right. Tables and chairs would be scattered around as soon as she and Larissa were finished scrubbing. To her left the long countertop or *banco* would hold platters of food, wine and appetizers for her customers. The small gaming rooms were at the back on the right next to the main storage area on the left across from the kitchen. The rear door that led to the courtyard was open, beckoning Ysabella to retreat to its shady haven from the dust of the workers, but she only sighed and returned to her work.

After a minute, she and Larissa began to talk excitedly about their plans for opening night.

CHAPTER 3

The mid-morning Mediterranean sun turned the sea undulating softly around Pietro Manfredi into shards of green glass. The glare and flashes of light assailed his old eyes. Yet the man balanced himself in the prow of the ship against the swell of the waves with the straight back of a military man and stared intently southward, waiting, searching. He had kept watch on deck since first light lost in thoughts of his past, and now, his future. Dazzled by the sun, he did not see the island crest gently over the edge of the horizon.

Despite the simple belted tunic and graying hair, Pietro retained the strength in his arms and legs from many years in the saddle, riding and raiding all over Blois, Normandy and Burgundy. His demeanor was pleasant and his facial expressions mild, but it was obvious that something preyed on his mind. Even as he automatically registered the scenes around him, Pietro's eyes turned inward.

"There. Just to your left, sir," croaked the beardless and shirtless sailor coiling mooring lines into position near Pietro's feet. The man was lean, muscular and brown as shoe leather. The swift confidence of his movements easily conveyed a long life at sea. "I reckon it will be another hour before we drop anchor in Trapani—more if the harbor is crowded. And it's always crowded these days in this beastly port. Never been so drunk in my life as I was on our last trip here, so you can bet I know the best taverns in town. Come along if you want a little taste of the vine. For all the priests and church bells in Trapani, you can still find a willing woman and a tasty fish pie. Now take that battered old alehouse off the wharf, Judas's Place, for instance..."

Startled out of his reverie and wanting to discourage the man's apparently inexhaustible prattle, Pietro muttered his regrets and turned to his left as the sailor directed. No island was visible. His eyes were blurry from the long hours focused on the swales of the sea. Readjusting his position, he squinted against the glare and threw up his forearm to shade his eyes, glancing up at the lateen sail. Yes, there was a darker ripple in the flat line between sea and sky, barely discernable.

Coming home again. How would the next verse go in the ballad of his life? Would he find any measure of contentment?

As the sturdy little ship glided smoothly into Trapani harbor an hour later, just as the sailor predicted, small dhows and fishing boats darted around the waterfront. Lazy windmills near conical salt piles wafted the odor towards the incoming vessel. Pietro wrinkled his nose. The air was suddenly saturated with the smell of salt, not just the slightly salty smell of the open sea, but an oppressive and distasteful odor that overpowered one's senses and crept under the skin. The town's salt pans had made Trapani rich, but the smell invaded everyone's clothing and hair. "God's eyeballs, how could I have forgotten that stench?" Pietro wondered. "I've been too long from home."

As they approached the wharves, Pietro marveled at the men rushing from one rope to the next, twirling like shabby acrobats as they tied off one ship, pushed another away from the dock, or ran up a gangplank to shoulder another bag of grain to be carried to the warehouse. As he hoisted the rough cowhide sack of his few personal belongings and stood near the rail, the ship's captain lightly touched his shoulder. The man's hooknose and black marble eyes sat incongruously on rather plump cheeks, and bespoke uncertain parentage. A small scimitar-shaped scar just under his left eyebrow reddened as the day's heat intensified.

"Another safe passage," the captain declared in a jovial tone. "An errant storm, a broken rudder, or any number of catastrophes could have delayed us several days or sent all of us to old Neptune, but God looked down on us with favor for this voyage."

"Yes, thanks to the Virgin for our safe arrival, but also, Captain, give my thanks to your fine sailors. God does not set the sail or read the stars."

"And is this your home, sir, or do you have farther to travel?"

"My brother tends some acreage that he had from our father a few leagues outside the city just off the *Via Misericordia*. Do you know it? If I am not unduly delayed, I should arrive just as the sun sets. Will my horse be off-loaded promptly?"

"Rest assured. Livestock take first priority. The slings they ride in don't rock them to sleep like a baby's cradle, you know, but they also can't kick a hole in the side of my vessel. By the way, that's a fine animal you have, sir. I could get you a good price from the king's man here in port if you would care to sell him," offered the captain. "You would have no problem finding a horse more suitable for traveling the rough roads of this little island."

"Not in a hundred years, my friend! This stallion was a gift from a true companion and mentor, and he will sire many more just like him now that he and I turn to a more pastoral life. King Charles may appreciate this horse's many colts more than one animal alone! I hope to establish a reliable source of stock closer to home for the king, and others, of course."

"Aye, Charles will want good horses. He lusts after Byzantium, I hear. I also hear he is likely to take what he wants rather than pay for it. I wish you luck, old man." The captain strode off to bark unnecessary orders and remind his men who was boss.

A slight breeze off the hillsides carried a fresh scent of green. Yes, thought Pietro, old man indeed. I was only seventeen when I left here. That spring was much like this one, and I was a wild and impetuous dreamer on fire to free the Holy Land from the infidel. I found my way to Messina and boarded a ship to Palestine with three other young men. We would reclaim the Holy Land together and perform incredible feats of strength and cunning that would earn us an eternal place in the *chansons* of knighthood. We swore eternal friendship in the way that young men do when they are ignorant and hot-blooded.

Pietro saw their youthful idealism and spiritual dedication turn quickly to anger and cynicism after watching Christian knights fight each other for power or riches or empty titles. Incompetence and greed were rampant among the men enshrined by the Church as its saviors. He hadn't seen any of his former companions since the Fall of Jerusalem at the Battle of Gaza in October 1244. Since the long retreat. Since the massacre. That one bloody day of all the bloody days in the desert had changed his life instantly. Well, he hoped to put that incident to rest soon.

Pietro put these thoughts aside as he carefully trod down the slender gangplank and stood on the noisy and hurried pier until his horse could be coaxed down the ramp. Looking out toward Trapani while trying to avoid being trampled by dockworkers, he could just make out a landmark or two that he remembered from his youth. He could still see latticed Arabic windows and the graceful architecture that the ruling emirs had built 200 years ago and that the Christians had cheerfully re-used. Many a Muslim mosque and palace was now a church or public building in Trapani just like others in Sicily.

Trapani had grown and prospered. The port area was crowded with new buildings squeezed awkwardly in between older ones, and ships from many nations vied for good berths at the freshly built piers jutting into the bay. It seemed as crowded as Calais. Not so when he left so many years ago. Back then he had roamed two rickety piers right here for four days before finding a small ship to take him to Messina. And from there, as far as most people knew, he had dropped into oblivion.

But there were other, more menacing changes in Trapani, too. The most obvious was anchored in the harbor to the west, with laborers scurrying up and down the scaffolding and hammers ringing out across the water. A monstrous galley of enormous dimensions was rising out of the sea like an ancient god to punish mere mortals for their insignificant existence. Its two tiers of oars towered over every other ship in the harbor, domineering and arrogant in its militant supremacy. Pietro stared at it in awe; King Charles was clearly preparing for war. And someone wanted secrecy; a towering wall set on floating pontoons was being built to surround the colossus.

One would think that the opulent island of Sicily would be enough, but some men were never satisfied, especially the French. Robert Guiscard, another Frenchman, certainly hadn't been satisfied. Some translated 'Guiscard' as meaning clever, but others swore it really meant 'sneaky bastard.' That obscure Norman fought his way through southern Italy as a mercenary to eventually become Duke of Calabria and Apulia in the Eleventh Century, assuring himself wealth and power for all his days. He and his brother, Roger, then struggled another 30 years to conquer Sicily in 1071. And he would have pressed on to take all of Byzantium if typhoid hadn't killed him. Odd how a former horse thief and brigand could be transformed through folklore and ribald ballads into Robert the Wily, hero of all Christianity.

Pietro shook his head at these stories he had heard so long ago and reoriented himself. He had begun to notice how easy his mind wandered these last few years. Now, in the year of Our Lord 1281, there was no triumph in this old fighter's return--just a hope that he could live the rest of his days quietly in his childhood home.

Pietro saw his restive stallion, Nero, led off the ramp among the rambunctious and unfamiliar sights and sounds of the port. A soft cloth had been held around the animal's eyes to get him down the narrow boards without rearing or kicking. A hint of adrenalin flashed through the horse's eyes as his owner grabbed the reins, but speaking softly and stroking the blazed nose, Pietro soon had him calmed again. "Well, old friend," he said to the horse, "what do you think about the place? Let's find some food and water." The stallion nickered his agreement and carefully followed Pietro along the pier toward the main market street. It took just moments for the horse to regain his land legs, and his muscles rippled with pent up energy.

A number of market stalls hung with canopies of dingy cotton lined the cobbled street of the market. Although they looked rather disreputable, the stalls were surrounded by soldiers, sailors, merchants, mothers, and laborers intent on filling their baskets with fresh fruits, eggs, freshly plucked chickens, nuts and olives, oranges and lemons, and myriad other delicacies. A couple stalls, he noticed, had replaced the sun-faded gray awnings with brighter striped cotton in hopes of attracting more customers. He stopped at one where an enticing display of fruits and vegetables from the countryside caught his eye. He couldn't help but wonder if some of these wares were his brother's produce. After a little conversation and bargaining with the vendor, Pietro came away with a piece of flat bread, black olives, some soft cheese and apples and the directions toward a public trough for watering the stallion.

Hunger slated and horse satisfied, Pietro mounted and rode slowly toward the main road leading eastward. As he did so, a lively cacophony erupted from the slave blocks on one end of the wharf. Purchasers and sellers shouted and bargained, and the string of shackled, mostly naked humans looked miserably down at their feet. Among any such group there always would be one or two that stood stiffly upright and glared back at the crowd around them, but for most, any hint of pride or defiance had been beaten out of them long ago.

Pietro noticed white Circassian slaves, blacks from Africa, Saracens captured in skirmishes in the Holy Land, Slavs from Slavonia and Tartary, even Greeks and Spaniards who could not fight their way out of wrenching poverty. Men, women, children-- all were needed for the salt pans, the leather industry, farming and mining. Pietro found it hard to justify the vastly lucrative slave trade, but he knew society had come to depend on it. Except for an unexpected angel of mercy, he easily could have found himself among the shackled wreckage on the block. His hand unconsciously rose again to finger the cross at his neck as he moved on

Nero tossed his head and whinnied at the sheep in a nearby field, rousing Pietro from his dismal thoughts. He wanted to see his brother. Then he would think about penance. His brother Carlo, was finally giving in to his wife's oft repeated dream of a pilgrimage to Palermo for Holy easily Week, even though he should be tending his fields and orchards. Unexpectedly, the chance to accompany Carlo's little party had fallen in Pietro's lap. "Dear God", he prayed, "Let me complete this last mission so I can truly rest."

As he settled into the gentle and familiar movement of Nero beneath him, Pietro hummed a little to himself. Even though he was returning to the stone cottage where he was born, doing so was like entering a foreign land. Sicily was just as alien to him now as Blois had been. The countryside looked just slightly more familiar than the bustling place he just left. The obvious prosperity on the land was a pleasing change. There were many changes to talk to Carlo about, and he had no doubt much of it was due to the change in political regimes

Charles of Anjou won Sicily back in 1266 when his army overran weaker Sicilian and Italian forces. Some still said he personally cut the throat of King Manfred at Benevento, but Pietro, long accustomed to the behavior of princes in battle, was sure Charles had been seated safely in a luxurious tent out of sight of the real conflict. It took two more years before Charles cemented his rule by executing young Conradin, Manfred's heir, in a public square. Charles was a man who left no loose ends. It would be good to remember this if Pietro started to do business with the king as he hoped.

Charles ruled as a no-nonsense despot who demanded organization in both his commercial and military enterprises. He had had seventeen years to exert his authority across the island, and it showed. Even during his short journey through Trapani itself, it was clear that Angevin officials were everywhere, poking their long noses into any enterprise that could make their master money. Still, the unrest among the populace that he was warned about wasn't visible on the surface.

Pietro set aside his thoughts and concentrated on finding his old family homestead. As he approached the turn in the road where the little cottage should have been, he spied a well-kept stone dwelling with spring wildflowers in a pot next to the bright red door. "I don't remember the place being quite so large," he thought. "Maybe I took a wrong turn."

Then he heard the shouting. "Pietro! Pietro!" called a sinewy little man rushing toward him from a grove of orange trees. The man could have been any farmer in his drab tunic and muddy work boots, but no one but his brother would have called his name. Pietro, admittedly a little nervous about this encounter, dismounted and stood Nero, stroking Nero's nose as his brother walked rapidly towards him. Carlo's green eyes seemed to have lost a little color over the years, but the jagged scar above his left eyebrow was utterly familiar. If nothing else was the same, Pietro would have recognized his brother only from that scar. He should. Pietro was responsible for it. A rough branch opened the cut when he pushed his older brother out of a tree back in their rough and tumble days.

"Pietro!" Carlo shouted. "You've got gray hair!"

Pietro suddenly laughed out loud. "So do you!" he bellowed back. The two men threw their arms around each other, delighted to be together. Both began to speak at once, then stopped and laughed again, tears brimming in their eyes.

Carlo regained his composure and spoke first. "Praise be to God that you are home safely! We worried and worried that something would happen on your journey or that you wouldn't arrive in time. Welcome. Welcome home, *brother*!" More emotional than he expected, Pietro could only nod his thanks and mutter something indecipherable as they stepped into a spacious cottage.

"I don't remember our father's house looking this good," Pietro said changing the topic to mask his emotion.

Carlo laughed. "While you were busy collecting military honors, I married and built some additions onto the cottage. It is a little more comfortable now. You will have a bed all to yourself."

Carlo continued, eagerly telling his brother about Perna, their four children who were now married with children of their own, and his life as a farmer. Pietro looked around, expecting Perna or the other family members to emerge from a back room to greet their guest. Carlo laughed. "Perna thought she should leave us alone for awhile to get reacquainted. She's thoughtful that way. She's over at the neighbor's, at Sophia's. Sophia's the pregnant one going to Palermo's shrines to pray for a son. Perna will be home eventually."

They couldn't help smiling at each other, marveling that they were actually together. Carlo led his brother to a long oak table embellished with plain but handsome carvings, and produced a beaker of wine and wooden cups. They chattered like old crones, about old friends and new, the new lambs in Carlo's herd and the details of Pietro's voyage.

Carlo finally stared speculatively at Pietro. "What of your previous life, brother? Tell me about your wife—Julianna, wasn't it?-- and your daughter." To his surprise, Pietro's words came pouring out.

"To tell you the truth, Carlo, I was happy in Blois. Count John was a man I respected and admired. I am glad he thought of me as a friend, and I will miss him. We developed an easy camaraderie over decades fighting together. The day before I left his service we had our last meeting. I was shocked when he pressed a bag of coins into my hand. 'For years of good counsel,' he said. And I did save his life once."

Pietro paused to take another sip of the wine and a sudden flare of emotion lit his eyes. "John wanted me to help his son rule the duchy after his death, but since losing my Julianna, I just felt old and adrift. My daughter was suitably married and making a life of her own, so there was nothing to tie me to Blois. Thankfully, John understood. That's when I thought of home. I wrote to you, hoping you were still alive, and that you might want to see someone who disappeared over 30 years ago."

When he was finished, he stared at the table, embarrassed that he had been so garrulous. Carlo stood beside him, putting a hand on his shoulder in sympathy. Carlo cleared his throat and said, "When you didn't come home from Outremer, we all assumed you had been killed. No one ever brought us word, but what else could we think? We had Masses said for you every year. I could hardly believe we received a letter at all, let alone that it was from you. I ran to the parish priest to read it to me, and I immediately had him write my answer. So now you are home." Carlo enthusiastically gripped his brother's shoulders in an affectionate embrace.

Pietro drew his eyebrows together to control the tears again threatening to disrupt his composure and changed the subject. "Trapani has changed. Has Charles been good to you here?"

"Ah, Pietro, that's a long story. We'll need more wine for that." Carlo fetched another flask before settling down for a long discourse. He thought a moment before he spoke. "I have to say I haven't done badly, brother. Charles is good for business because money is his main interest. He isn't like a lot of these lords, off fighting just to fight and quarreling with his neighbors, amusing himself with women. No, he's different."

Pietro raised an eyebrow. "Then he's a good king?"

"Well, he keeps the peace, I'll give him that, and peace is good for business. But he's made a lot of new laws. We have been taxed and taxed, and his advisers are all Frenchmen. Our town council is virtually useless, a rubber stamp for a French governor who visits us much too frequently, sticking his nose into everything, and demanding more and more money. We have to get approval for everything – marriages, betrothals, land sales – it's ridiculous! And humiliating! Every single thing we do is controlled by Charles or the Church!"

Pietro listened but kept silent; he knew his brother wasn't finished. "And Pietro, we have no recourse. Oh, yes, we can go to the judges or the town council, but they really have no power – decisions are left to Charles's magistrates! Sicilians really have no authority over their own affairs. It may be different on the mainland, but I don't think so." His voice trailed off as he stared into his wine cup.

Pietro spoke carefully. "I heard he's going to war. I heard he wants Byzantium. Is that what you hear?"

"Everyone knows that. That's why we're being taxed within an inch of our lives – so he can go crown himself and be like his dead brother, that blasted Louis of France. We just want to be left alone, Pietro, to farm our land, breed our cattle, tend to our orchards, raise our families. People are afraid of him and not happy. But enough! Let's go out and tend to that beast of yours before Perna comes home to make supper."

For the first time in a long time, Pietro allowed himself to feel relaxed. As he and Carlo went out to the stables to brush and feed Nero, Pietro silently thanked God for allowing him to come home. And as Carlo chattered on about the preparations for the pilgrimage to Sicily's capital, Pietro tried not to think about what he had to accomplish in Palermo. At least for now it was not something he could share with his brother.

CHAPTER 4

Simon de Paruta paced in his courtyard garden. The scent of
lavender and jasmine drifted over the patio. The fragrance of lilies
and roses in first bloom mingled with that of herbs, but he could
not relax to enjoy this olfactory tranquility. Tomorrow, as one of
Palermo's urban elite, he would attend the service in Palermo
Cathedral to bless King Charles' new military enterprise to
Byzantium. How tedious. His bones were old and creaky, and he
knew from experience the service would drone on and on. And
seeing Roberto presiding at the altar of the imposing basilica in his
glittering robes would bring back those troubling memories.

The ceremonies were a boring and stifling obligation of his
position, but since he had become ill, his usual patience dissolved
more quickly. Simon could pretend a deep piety if need be. That
stint in the Holy Land had certainly cured him of any blind faith,
but that wasn't generally known. He went gracefully through the
motions as duty demanded. Perhaps he should feel honored to be a
Sicilian with access to the king's ministers, but he was well aware
he was only indulged by the Angevins because of his wealth and
status. He sighed.

Simon tried hard not to appear to be the decrepit ancient that his
nephews believed him to be, but all his money could not find a
physician to relieve the pains in his stomach. Lately he found
himself falling asleep off and on throughout the day, but at night
his sleep was restless. He had become more and more reclusive.
Mateo, his younger nephew, and Venutus, his long-trusted servant,
carried messages to his various enterprises and business partners
and had begun to take over the more physical aspects of the
organization. He still personally handled the more important
details of his business – silks and luxury fabrics – but he allowed
Venutus, whom he had taught to read and write, to keep the daily
ledgers, make collections from his debtors, and buy and sell less
valuable fabrics. Venutus also managed the household and slaves
and servants like a well-oiled wagon wheel. Now, of course,

Simon was tutoring Mateo in the intricacies of the business. Antonio, the older nephew, was a total disappointment. He had no head for figures and no interest in making money, just in spending it. Privately Simon blamed the boy's ineptness on the coddling he received from his mother before they came to live with him.

Pulling on his short grey beard and wrapping his cloak tighter around him, Simon leaned against a column of the portico to warm himself in the sun. He was weary. He was worried. His stomach hurt. The prospect of encountering Roberto again only exacerbated his distress. An unwelcome feeling of guilt and shame always picked at him when he thought about their past. Simon had joined three others in a brief and distasteful career as a Crusader. How carefree and fearless they had all been, never thinking past the tips of their swords. How badly it had ended. He had returned to Palermo with Ludovico but without the others.

Roberto de Scarani eventually returned to Sicily too, but when he did so, it was with the regal pomp and ceremony of a papal legate. Archbishop of Palermo, what a laugh! When Roberto sailed into the Cala, Palermo's harbor, with papal flags flying and a massive procession of clerics and aristocrats parting the crowds to lead him to the Cathedral, Simon had been aghast. My God, Roberto an archbishop! Simon had no real desire to renew their acquaintance, but his position made it impossible to avoid. Even though their first meetings were overwhelmingly uncomfortable, they ultimately came to an accommodation. They avoided each other as much as possible and agreed not to talk about the past.

Simon had not attained a highly public position like Roberto, but he hadn't done badly for himself. His home was neither the grandest nor the most luxurious in the city, but the fine details of ebony and cypress wood furniture, the tile and Carrera marble that adorned his floors and the exquisite tapestries on his walls attested to his taste and wealth. His stables housed the finest horses and his servants were the most obedient. It was the dwelling of a civilized, cultured, rich man. Perhaps if his wife had lived, the place would be warmer, more inviting. A brief thought of her crossed his mind, but he could no longer grieve. That, too, was a long time ago.

Simon's marriage to a daughter of the feudal nobility brought him a city house, a country estate and ennoblement. In turn, his father-in-law received an infusion of much-needed money to keep up his position. They both got what they wanted. Shortly after his marriage, Simon traveling to Barcelona on business, foolishly took his young bride with him. A raging storm came out of nowhere and threw their ship against submerged rocks along the Iberian coastline, bashing in the hull and throwing the screaming passengers into furious waves. His young wife and most of the others on board were lost. He survived. When he returned to Palermo, he immersed himself in his business. For awhile that provided a refuge from his loneliness and pain. Time gradually did alleviate his grief, but he also closed himself off, unable to marry again. Eventually he found it convenient to be alone, and finally he became indifferent as velvets, wools, silks and brocades consumed his life.

His natural shrewdness and tenacity served him well in the commercial arena. Yet, for all his accomplishments and refinements, he knew that Roberto, and others, had once seen him at his most vicious and desperate. Roberto remembered a much different Simon than the Palermo noble. On the other hand, the reverse was also true. Simon had seen a side of the Archbishop that he was fairly certain no one else knew about. He chuckled wryly to himself, putting his face up to the warm sun. Yes, he had definitely seen a very different side of His Eminence.

Should God grant him another year of life, he would see the culmination of his final and most dangerous venture. Several years ago while trading silks and cloth in Catalonia, he was introduced to another merchant. Ferdinand de Lerida, however, turned out to be a royal advisor and confidant of the King of Aragon using the merchant persona as a convenient cover. Simon instinctively knew there was something menacing about Ferdinand and trod cautiously around him, but he couldn't resist the man's incredible connections throughout the Mediterranean, especially when he began to make very handsome profits from their association. Inevitably, as Simon had always known he would, Ferdinand demanded payback.

Actually, the price exacted had been an exhilarating adventure. He, Simon de Paruta, a wealthy, respected nobleman, had become a spy for Aragon. Promised the power and honors he had always craved, Simon capitulated quickly. His common origins had always branded him a *parvenu* at the Sicilian court. No matter how rich he became or what titles he bore, entry into the King's inner circle, into any kind of real influence, always had been denied him. He made up his mind quickly to Ferdinand's silky proposal. He would be welcomed with open arms in Aragon! None of this pretentiousness that the French loved to harbor. Simon had no love for Charles, a foreigner. On the other hand, he had no love for Aragon either. He'd met enough bluebloods in the Holy Land to know how contemptible they could be, no matter their origin. Power, Simon reflected, was the only thing that mattered.

Now the Great Invasion of Sicily planned by the King of Aragon soon would come to fruition, and Simon would become part of the new ruling class. Privately, he looked forward to paying back some of his aristocratic acquaintances who reveled in subtly shunning him--if they were still alive, of course.

Simon limped to a cushioned bench under the orange trees, fragrant with tiny new flowers, and snapped his fingers. Startled birds flew off the branches. Venutus materialized. "Yes, Lord?" he murmured. Venutus was another treasure acquired through Simon's marriage. Quiet, unobtrusive, intelligent. Totally trustworthy. Simon had detected those qualities when Venutus was a young stable boy. He never would have noticed him if it hadn't been for his tenderhearted wife. She begged her new husband to provide for an old and faithful retainer from childhood who had become sick and disabled. His son, Venutus, lovingly cared for the old man, but they needed medicines they couldn't afford. To please her, Simon carelessly agreed. Venutus had never forgotten the kindness that enabled his father to die in comfort. Simon reaped the benefits of that unthinking nod to his wife's wishes when the young man had become his manservant. Now, decades later, Venutus was totally devoted to Simon and all his enterprises. He had become the only person in Simon's life whom he trusted completely.

Simon was feeling a bit nauseous. His stomach was acting up, but business took priority. He said to Venutus, "Fetch Ludovico the merchant. Now."

"Yes, Lord."

Ludovico Stefani scurried up the paved boulevard of the *Cassaro* behind Simon's servant. Today, as most days, he neglected to admire the elegant porticos that shaded the shops lining the street or the intricate mosaics glittering on the facades of aristocratic residences. He puffed a bit as he climbed uphill, for this most exclusive quarter of Palermo was also the oldest, an ancient site of power for Phoenicians, Byzantines, Saracens, Normans, and now Angevins, that commanded the highest point in the city. It didn't help that Simon's proximity to the twin seats of power – the Cathedral and the Royal Palace – insinuated Simon's own rise to influence. Ludovico knew bitterly that most everyday people wouldn't dare cross Simon de Paruta.

Ludovico hadn't been nearly as successful after their return from the Holy Land, although he was quite comfortable as a spice dealer. He didn't have Simon's luck in marriage. He was fond of his wife, Joanna, but she wasn't noble and did not bring any estates to their union. Secretly, he was glad of this. He much preferred his own neighborhood to this guarded, aristocratic stronghold. In the *Porta Patitellorum* he was comfortable. It was a bustling commercial neighborhood full of shops, taverns and artisans named after the *patiti* who made the wooden shoes all commoners wore. It was an old neighborhood that had expanded recently into the newest quarter of Palermo, and it was bursting was business opportunities. It was also much livelier than this stuffy, walled enclave where Simon hid out.

Ludovico walked hesitantly into the garden searching for his host. "Simon," he breathed. At Simon's frown, he hastily added "Lord", although he disliked using Simon's title. Hadn't they been companions once?

Simon beckoned impatiently. "Ludovico, I need you to do something for me."

CHAPTER 5

The pilgrims left Trapani three days after Pietro's arrival. By now the brothers were talking eagerly and telling stories that spanned more than three decades. Pietro was amazed at how quickly the old closeness returned. Perna welcomed him just as warmly as Carlo did. She was a wise and jolly woman, and a good cook. Their sons and daughters all came home to meet him, and Gino, the eldest, would care for the farm while the pilgrims were absent.

Carlo fretted as they packed their provisions. "I must say, Pietro, this young whelp who arrived thinking he could help us doesn't inspire much confidence," Carlo said nervously. "He's nothing more than a young dandy who can't even grow a full mustache! How will he help us find food and lodging on the road? Have we packed enough food? Enough blankets? I had the horses reshod and repaired the cart. With luck, and with you along, surely nothing awful will befall us."

"They all seem too young to us these days, Carlo," responded his brother. "It's likely we didn't inspire much faith in our elders at that age either. He seems better suited to sporting rings and horse races, but may prove helpful in the end." Pietro tried to soothe his brother's anxiety, although he privately felt similar misgivings about the young stranger.

"Regardless," Carlo said. "Your experience with the sword will be welcome if we should meet with brigands or thieves. God protect us! Adventures are your province, dear brother, not mine!"

Pietro smiled. "You never did wander far from home. But truly, great adventure – at least as you think of it – is found only in the fantasies of storytellers or the lies of drunken braggarts. Let me tell you, soldiering is mostly muddy and tedious. I was usually more hungry or thirsty than glorious."

Carlo saw a shadow pass over his brother's face and he turned to check the harness again, giving Pietro a moment of privacy. Although Carlo remembered an exuberant boy, the man who returned hinted of an unspoken heaviness beneath his outward cheerfulness. Perhaps he still felt the loss of his wife and hoped this pilgrimage would help lift a deep-seated burden. But if not, Carlo and Perna knew a plump widow down the lane that might one day erase those painful lines from his brother's face.

Pietro winced at the perpetual pain in his shoulder and lifted another chest into the cart. For a moment the old crusader was oppressed by the inevitable losses of life and mused on how the fates led him home to Trapani. His brother's letter had arrived in the winter as he sat by a flickering fire in Blois, after death had taken his beloved wife. Julianna had never been a great beauty, but a sensible and tender woman who made his sojourn in a foreign land more contented than he had a right to hope for. Once she was gone, however, the memory of Trapani's sea breezes and long, sultry summers intensified.

Pietro's desire to make the pilgrimage was not motivated by piety. He needed to confront one man who lived in Palermo, Simon de Paruta. How incredible that Antonio de Paruta suddenly appeared in Trapani claiming he was to escort the pilgrims to Palermo because of his uncle's distant family connection to one of them. Antonio would lead him, unknowingly, to his old enemy. Then, what would happen would happen.

"Carlo," he called, again focusing on the moment. "We must leave soon. We do not want to be on the road at nightfall."

Carlo turned and smiled. "I will do as you command my liege," he said playfully with a deep bow and hearty laugh.

Before the sun had reached midday, the small party of pilgrims set off from the crossroads south of Trapani. Their "escort," Pietro and two hired men-at-arms, rode alongside Carlo's horse-drawn cart, carrying the three women. Arturo Pandolfo and his two younger daughters were there to see them off. Arturo secretly thanked God he could entrust Sophia and Renata to his friends without going to Palermo himself. With a blessing from Father Leonardo and a few envious waves from neighbors, the group began to move. Despite Carlo's fears, they all anticipated an uneventful journey.

"When I first learned I was again with child, I immediately knew I must seek the blessing of Santa Rosalia." Sophia Pandolfo was again recounting her story to Perna as the cart rattled along. Being the impetus for this journey, Sophia claimed a certain status within the group, even though her incessant talking annoyed most of them. "With three daughters already, my husband dearly wants a son. All my prayers to Santa Lucia have had no effect; but I've been assured by people who should know that if I offer a cloth of gold to the Virgin at Santa Maria dell'Ammiraglio, and something to Santa Rosalia on Mt. Pellegrino, I will get their blessings. It is such a simple request."

"May the Blessed Virgin and the saints grant your wish, my dear friend," Perna automatically replied, having heard this many times before. She privately wondered how Sophia could go on and on about the need for a son in front of her daughter, who clearly resented it, but that was Sophia.

"Arturo said he had no time to make a trip to Palermo. You know the salt business increases every day. Oh, how I wept! I was so forlorn! Then I was angry. I could just see myself getting fatter and fatter here in Trapani, knowing we hadn't done everything possible for God to grant us this one small favor. I told him very plainly if he could not take me to Palermo, I'd find a way to go myself. That, Perna, was when I remembered I had a distant relative in Palermo, an influential one, too! Simon de Paruta!"

"Yes," yawned Perna. "We women can be very determined when we want to be."

"Well, it took me several days to remember exactly what the family connection was, and frankly, I'm sure Simon hardly remembered it himself. But I boldly wrote to him and asked his assistance on my mission. My husband thought I was daft and laughed at me. Even Father Leonardo chided me for imposing my foolishness—that's what he called it, foolishness—on an important nobleman. Actually," Sophia laughed to herself, "I never expected a reply either. And I'm so pregnant, Arturo didn't want me traveling. But when I told him you were coming with me, dear Perna, and Renata would come along to help as well, he could only sputter.

"And then, you can't imagine how surprised we were that old Simon sent Antonio to our door! I never expected to hear from him, let alone have him provide assistance in the form of his handsome nephew! Well, with all the help available, Arturo had to say yes. And you will be helpful, I know, Perna. Everyone knows you are the best midwife in the region. You have brought many healthy babies into this world."

Glancing at her daughter, Sophia was distracted from her line of thought. "Perhaps Renata should study midwifery with you. She has pretensions to be a queen, but until then, she'll need a useful skill." Renata bristled angrily at the thought. Pretensions indeed!

Antonio had arrived at their door the night before their planned departure, bearing a letter from his uncle. This onerous task of playing nursemaid to a group of penitents was excellent cover for his uncle's true purpose, but Antonio also knew it was his punishment. He had not anticipated Simon's rage when he once again he asked his uncle to cover some gambling debts. Simon then sent Antonio to help the pilgrims and to report on King Charles' gigantic warship being built in Trapani and the exact layout of the harbor facilities. Antonio resented being sent on this fool's mission. Anyone could provide the information, but he was forced by circumstance to comply.

Simon was unusually preoccupied, it seemed, with ships, shipbuilding, conditions and trade in all the harbors in the Mediterranean. Why a nobleman would care about such things was beyond Antonio's comprehension, but if he would pay Antonio's debts for now, he could talk about whatever he wanted. For the next two days, Antonio expected nothing but laboriously slow travel and stultifying, superficial conversation with a bunch of rural yokels. Still, a few days' absence from Palermo would give his creditors time to focus on someone else.

He was astonished to find in the pilgrims' party a lovely girl of fourteen. Renata had dark lustrous hair, a sun-kissed complexion, greenish eyes that looked brown in the right light, and a slender youthful figure. Who would have thought such beauty inhabited a salt-smelling hole like Trapani?

Although Renata had spoken only the most perfunctory and appropriate greeting as they were introduced, she looked boldly into his eyes. When he bent to kiss her hand she acted as though it was her due. Antonio caught a spark of interest and playfulness in her manner. Quickly plotting an amorous flirtation to help pass the days, he indulged in a little fantasy. Old Sophia was probably right about her queenly pretensions.

"Signora Pandolfo," Antonio said as they rode along, "my dear uncle briefly explained how it is that we are related, but I am not sure I fully understood. I do not remember hearing your name before." Antonio made up his mind to be pleasant to Sophia, and maybe Perna too, to keep close to The Beauty, as he privately called Renata.

"It doesn't surprise me that my name would be unfamiliar to you, Antonio," Sophia exclaimed. "My mother, God rest her soul, was a distant cousin by marriage to Simon's late wife, and no real relation to your father or mother at all. I was only a young girl when my mother learned of poor Bernadetta's tragic death. She died so young! Not even any children. My mother cried for days even though she barely knew the woman. Of course, my mother felt everything so intensely, as do I. Is it true that Simon didn't remarry even after all these years? He must have been devastated by her loss."

"Yes, Signora, it is true, although why he did not take another wife is unknown to me. He devotes himself to amassing a great fortune from the silk trade. You must know he is the preeminent silk merchant in all of Sicily and owns all or part of many other businesses. Alas, his health has been failing in the last few months and should he die, I hardly know how I would manage his many business interests and properties. If only he will live for a few more years to impart even a small portion of his great wisdom to me!"

Antonio was as comfortable with this little lie as he was with any others. He routinely liked to remind those around him of his relationship to a powerful aristocrat and his expectation of great wealth, and he easily read Sophia's gullible nature. Although Simon tended to favor Mateo, Antonio felt certain that when the time came, his uncle would have to relinquish his title and wealth to the older nephew. Surely law favored the eldest.

"Are you comfortable, lady? Would you like to stop to rest?" Sophia smiled at him and nodded. Antonio rode to the front of their little column to suggest they stop by a small stream for luncheon, and then quickly hurried back to the side of the cart to offer his arm to the women to help them down. Carlo and Pietro, riding ahead, were deep in conversation and absent-mindedly stopped where told.

While Antonio graciously assisted Sophia and Perna, his eyes kept straying to Renata. Normally, Renata would have tossed her hair and jumped over the side of the cart, but today she chose to wait demurely for his assistance. As he reached up to give her his hand, she stumbled over the hem of her gown. She grasped his arm tightly to avoid spilling out of the cart, and her cheek and hair brushed against his chest. He instantly understood that her clumsiness was no accident, and a warmth began to rise in his blood. The deep bronze cloth of her cloak accentuated the brown in her green eyes and her stumble revealed the outline of her breasts encased in a modest traveling dress. As he helped Renata regain her balance and descend from the wagon, Antonio heard her whisper, "Tonight" before she sedately joined the others for their repast.

Despite her youth, Renata Pandolfo had confidence in her beauty and a certain level of experience in seduction. She sensed Antonio's instant attraction. While pretending disinterest as she listened to Antonio's exchange with her mother, Renata carefully memorized the fine detail of his garments and the ease with which he sat his horse. Dark curls framed his angular face and enchanting smile. The rough hands and unpracticed kisses of the village boys were instantly forgotten. Here was someone who offered real possibilities—handsome, wealthy, and polite. He was clearly drawn to her. Perhaps with careful planning, she could secure an excellent marriage.

Laughing softly to herself, Renata remembered the fury on her father's face a few days before the pilgrim's party set off. He had stormed around with an apoplectic look on his face angrily threatening to send her to a convent if she did not change her ways. She easily evaded the chaperonage of her elderly nurse. She came home with small scratches on her neck and straw in her hair. She openly displayed insignificant gifts from local suitors. Her father made her accompany her mother on this stupid journey to repent of her unseemly behavior and to give the neighborhood louts a chance to cool off. But surprised by Antonio's arrival and unable to refuse the assistance of a wealthy and powerful man, he was forced to send Renata from the frying pan into the fire. Renata chuckled to herself—his attempt at punishment now appeared to be an opportunity.

The sun was dropping softly through a cloudless, tangerine sky when Pietro decided to stop for the night. Had he been riding with practiced horsemen, he would have pressed on several more miles and camped wherever a meadow presented itself. But with a pregnant woman and two old folks unused to the discomforts of travel over rutted roads, the small inn before them seemed like the best alternative. Two old hounds resting in the shade of an olive tree barely raised their heads when the pilgrims' cart rattled into the yard. A rotund little man dressed in rough homespun spurted out the door at the sound of the horses.

"Innkeeper," Pietro called as they approached the door. "We require a good meal, shelter for the night, and provisions for the horses. What can you provide?"

"Welcome, gentle people. I am Bertoli, your host." He waddled towards the group with his hands outstretched, smiling, shooing chickens with a swipe of the towel in his hands. If his large belly was a sign of his wife's cooking, perhaps the pilgrims would dine with unexpected pleasure tonight.

"My small establishment," he said with a little bow, "is at your service. We don't usually have so many people, but we can make do. If these fine ladies will share a room inside, I can offer you gentlemen a place to bed down in the hayloft. We have ample provisions for your animals and no other guests. My wife baked fresh bread today and has a delectable lamb and onion stew simmering over the fire."

The brothers looked at each other and smiled. Pietro began to dismount when Antonio's frown caught his eye. Such low-class arrangements were not at all satisfactory to him, but Pietro looked at him coldly. Wisely, Antonio said nothing and turned away. This Pietro had a sense of purpose about him, and quickly assumed the leadership of their little group. All the better for Antonio, really. Let someone else shoulder the responsibility! He could still brag about his success to his uncle. And while Pietro led, he would spend his time exchanging meaningful glances with that delightfully wicked girl and plotting her seduction. He did not expect much resistance. No dainty, reserved virgin was she! Now if he could just separate her from the others.

Bertoli's wife, just as fat as he was, rushed out of the squat little building to meet her guests. Upon seeing the pregnant Sophia, she clucked knowingly, and quickly spirited the women away to wash the road dust from their faces. She immediately began to ask Sophia questions about her impending confinement and the women disappeared into the inn in a friendly gaggle of conversation, with Renata following disinterestedly.

Bertoli led the men towards the barn where they stabled and fed the horses. Shafts of sunlight filtered through the boards of the barn, revealing an orderly row of stalls for the animals, scythes and shovels hung neatly in their corners, and a wooden ladder to the loft where they were to sleep.

As Pietro dismounted and lifted the saddle from his faithful Nero, a ray of light glinted off a circle of gold on the guard of his sword. Antonio would not have noticed if the reflection had not struck his eye at just the right angle. He looked more closely. The medallion was a golden oval a little larger than a Sicilian *augustali*. The object appeared to be engraved with undecipherable runes with a large eye in the middle.

"What is that medallion, Pietro?" Antonio laughed. "I've never seen anything like it. What kind of language is that? Where did you get it, and why is it on the guard of your sword? It surely is more valuable than the sword itself."

Pietro turned around, glaring. "The symbol is Egyptian, I was told. It's from Jerusalem and has a personal meaning for me, young man. That's all you need to know." And he resumed brushing his horse. He had no intention of telling this young dandy about the Eye of Horus, or anything else. A strange keepsake, Pietro knew, but it reminded him of the innocent hopes and dreams of a foursome, long ago, who swore fealty to one another.

Antonio narrowed his eyes at the rebuke and strode off to the inn. The simple supper and local wine was surprisingly delicious, as Bertoli had promised. Sated and fatigued from their day's journey, the pilgrims had little interest in conversation or music and retired early to their beds. Pietro talked briefly with the innkeeper as was his habit, discussing local news and politics but soon he, too, headed for the loft. The women's room had only an overstuffed straw mattress and a few wooden hooks to hang their cloaks, yet it was clean enough and smelled invitingly of fresh herbs.

Renata lay down in the room with her mother and Perna, but she made sure she had the space closest to the door. Would tonight change her future? She had never felt like this before, but she was confident of her attractions. Although they had not been able to make definite plans, she knew Antonio would be waiting for her tonight. She imagined just the right words she would say to him, how she would turn her cheek just so to display her best features, how she would imply a purity she no longer possessed. His dark eyes would sparkle as they met. His soft mouth would smile invitingly. After all, he was bit older, but really only a boy. He could not be much more experienced than she. She would act coquettishly but keep control of the situation. She wanted him to think of her seriously. Lying there in the dark under a rough blanket, she wondered that her mother could not feel her heart pounding, as loud as it seemed in her own ears. When she was certain her mother and Perna both slept soundly, she quietly slipped out into the yard.

In the loft lying on the itchy straw, Antonio had a momentary doubt about the girl as he let his imagination wander. He wondered if she would sneak away with all these people around them, but he decided she would, the little flirt. Probably looking for a little adventure in the middle of all these old people. Knowing that the creaky old ladder would surely wake someone as he climbed down, he rolled over and groaned, intentionally bumping the man next to him.

"I think I had more wine at dinner than I should have," he mumbled. "Excuse me, I better go down and clear my head. I'll check the animals and find a place to sleep below so I won't disturb you again." The only one who even looked up at him was

Pietro, who always awoke at a moment's notice. He thought fleetingly that the boy's story was a bit suspicious, but his eyes soon closed again of their own volition and he instantly fell back asleep.

Moonlight filtered through a few misty clouds. Just a half-moon tonight, but enough light to make out the shape of the old inn and the chicken coop. Antonio's natural sense of timing had not failed him. The girl was just stepping hesitantly into the yard, her cloak wrapped tightly around her. Her eyes glistened like dark emeralds. She peered into the distance, stepping delicately into the yard. Antonio glided up to her. Renata stopped short, giving a little grunt of surprise. She whispered, "Goodness, Antonio, you startled me." She glanced down demurely, smiling to herself. "I didn't expect to find anyone out here. What brings you away from your bed at this hour?"

"Those bold looks you gave me on our journey today led me to believe you have a purpose for this little rendezvous. Or did I misunderstand when you whispered 'tonight'? Of course," he smiled charmingly, "moonlight and a beautiful woman are a rather irresistible combination, no matter what the purpose."

Renata paused. A hint of uncertainty touched her now. She began to suspect she might be quite out of her depth, but confident in her charms, she pushed the doubts away and smiled. He gazed playfully into her eyes, and her heart turned over. This was a world away from Trapani and those village boys. Antonio smiled at her. "Don't you want something more from me than idle conversation?"

He reached for her and pulled her close, noticing the flush on her face in the moonlight. He stroked her cheek and slowly let his hand wander down her neck until it rested lightly on her breast. The nipple hardened beneath his palm. Renata futilely cast about for something witty to say that would stop him. All the words she had silently practiced as she lay in her bed flew right out of her head the moment he touched her face. Waiting all day for this moment had not prepared her for the actual passion now surging through her. None of the others ever made her feel so alive. With his first gentle kiss, she was hopelessly in love. With glorious desire pulsing in every part of her body, Renata quickly forgot her plot to ensnare him.

"There," she whispered. "We can find a little shelter in the cart at the edge of the yard." Renata tugged Antonio toward it. They stared at each other hungrily, and quickly made a pallet of blankets to cover the rough boards. She dropped her cloak on the blankets, revealing only a sheer shift beneath.

"Well, well," Antonio said slyly, "I see you dressed for the occasion!"

Tingling to the tips of her toes, her body rose up to meet Antonio's crushing weight. She clutched and pulled at his tunic as if she had suddenly burst into flames. Her actions now were instinctive, not practiced and measured. She demanded to be taken. If his powerful thrusts slowed even for an instant, she urged him on until she was awash in an electric storm of pleasure, and a deep growl of satisfaction rose from his gullet. Panting and dripping sweat on her taut nipples, Antonio fell down beside her. A few quiet tears slipped down her cheek, mixing with the sweat of her damp skin. In the silence between them, she murmured, "I am thinking of my future, Antonio, my future with you. My father will not refuse you when you ask for my hand."

Antonio laughed inwardly at such a bizarre notion but said nothing. Marriage---ha! Without another word, he tickled her belly, pulled up his stockings, and walked back to the barn, leaving her to clean herself and sneak back into the room with the older women.

CHAPTER 6

The next morning the pilgrims noisily prepared to leave the rustic inn. Renata lingered a bit over the wash basin making sure she was sufficiently composed to appear among the group. Bertoli and his wife had laid the table with bread and goat cheese. He offered his best ale to his guests and scurried to help load their belongings. His wife still tended to the pregnant Sophia and warned Carlo sternly not to hit all the ruts in the road lest the baby come too soon.

Blithely saying aloud how soundly she had slept, Renata climbed into the lumbering cart for another day's journey. She pointedly turned away from Antonio. It wouldn't do to appear overly smitten. Even her mother's chatter would not provoke her today. She had more important things to think about.

Pietro walked over to Antonio. "So the wine was a little much for you, hey? Was sleeping on the barn floor any better for your spinning head?" Were Antonio not the nephew of a nobleman, Pietro would have playfully cuffed his head and said a few more insults, as he had with his soldiers.

Only grunting in response, Antonio occupied himself saddling his horse and stretching the kinks out of his neck. The barn floor had been hard as rock. He had not expected such a swift or overwhelming response from that little country wench last night. The whores he usually had could barely manage small sighs of feigned pleasure. Smugly he thought how he would regale Bruno and Nicolo back in Palermo with details of his conquest. She must be touched in the head to think he wanted any future with her, but he could afford to say a few sweet nothings as the price for another night like the last. He rode with the armed men today, not looking or speaking to her. Still, he was confident she would appear in the moonlight again.

Late on the third morning of their journey, the pilgrims crested the hill overlooking Palermo's western gate, the *Porta Palacii*. The sprawling city was surrounded by a thick defensive wall with three main gates and numerous minor ones. The gate they were entering was nearest to the royal palace, hence its name. Ramshackle homes and animal pens stood outside the walls, and the travelers could see peasants tending to the livestock, driven there to feed a hungry city. Perna was jolted awake by the lurch of the cart as Carlo reined in. She gasped at the sight before her. "Sophia, look!" she breathed.

The *Porta Palacii* was 70 feet high, bristling with armed soldiers patrolling its ramparts and soaring towers with slitted windows placed at distinct intervals. Forty feet wide, the entrance contained a gleaming metal portcullis operated by huge winches. At the moment it was open, its glittering teeth suspended high, looking ready to pounce on an unsuspecting peasant. The walls themselves were thirteen feet thick, built by Roger, the young Norman king. Pietro now recognized how formidable the city's defenses were.

Sophia opened her eyes and exclaimed in excitement, "Perna! Renata! It's magnificent!" The church spires of converted mosques, the pennants flying over the royal palace, bells tolling in the cathedral and other little churches, as shops and boulevards, the huge panorama of a bustling, commercial city of more than fifty thousand people spilled out before them. The pilgrims were stunned and silent for a moment, and then the women began chattering. The men clucked to the horses, and Carlo, safely arrived in spite of his fears, smiled at the excitement in his wife's eyes.

Standing stolidly on the horizon before them loomed Mount Pellegrino, the site of the shrine of Santa Rosalia. At its feet lay the horseshoe shaped harbor bristling with the masts of hundreds of ships. Carlo could not stop himself from quietly thinking about everything that could go wrong in this huge city, and he hoped Pietro was prepared for anything.

Antonio was relieved finally to be in his element. This was his city. He moved confidently to the front of the queue and Pietro, after a brief glance at him, quietly moved his horse in behind him. Antonio led them through the *Porta Palacii*, brusquely pushing aside the pedestrians in front of him on the wide, cobblestone avenue. The women marveled at the broad boulevard with houses and shops on each side, small churches, hidden courtyards glimpsed through latticed walls, and the noise and congestion! Shaded by porticos, people sat or stood in front of the *bottegas*, eating, relaxing or arguing with the shop owners over dazzling merchandise carefully displayed.

Once I dump these yokels off at Raynaldus's hostel, Antonio thought, my little chore is over. There will be horse races all week that I refuse to miss.

The little party rode slowly through the streets, surrounded by a crush of beggars, farmers, merchants and people of all colors. Voices in unknown languages harangued passersby. Many of the buildings were two-storied, with living quarters above and shops below. Men and women clustered in front of the taverns and *bottegas*, some bickering, some resting on benches in the sun, many excitedly displaying their wares and purchases. Butcher's bloody carcasses hung in the open air with rabbits carefully laid out for inspection, octopi, huge swordfish and sardines for Palermo's signature pasta – *sarde a beccafico alla Palermitana* – sardines stuffed with golden raisins, parsley, a little sugar, pine nuts, garlic, olive oil and lightly breaded and fried, displayed for purchase. Antonio noticed their interest and explained that they should visit the *Vucciria*, Palermo's famous fishmarket, to find such delicacies.

The pilgrims passed the public baths, where the entrance was guarded by two sleepy slaves standing in its shaded portico. Their senses were overwhelmed by glimpses of courtyards with lemon and almond trees and shady benches, the smells of freshly baked bread, stews, perfumes, simmering vegetables, fresh fruit, rotting meat, unwashed bodies, animals, excrement, and the shouts, laughter and conversation carried on at an ear-splitting level. The women were dumbfounded by the theater of it all. Pietro, entering a city he visited only once more than 30 years before, felt both uneasy and excited to be back. Carlo, he noted, was nervous and sweating.

Suddenly, a swift party of three horsemen galloped up the paved street demanding right of way. People scattered to doorways and alleys, pulling small children to safety from the horses' flashing hooves. A vendor's rickety stall toppled, spilling trinkets and mirrors in the street. The horsemen never noticed. The pilgrims' cart was too big and clumsy to clear the roadway. The apparent leader, dressed in gold silks and black velvet, was forced to slow his steed and thread tightly between the cart and the stucco wall of a bootmaker's shop. He glared at the pilgrims and bellowed his displeasure.

Pietro automatically reached for his sword to confront this discourtesy. Their eyes locked, and Pietro saw only cold, steely anger. Thinking better of his instinctive urge to fight, he moved aside and let the horsemen pass. He was no longer a warrior anyway. The horsemen swept by, raising a cloud of dust around them, but the leader glanced back at Pietro with an appraising look.

"See Pietro," Carlo growled. "We'll all be killed in this place! I have no idea where I'm going; I don't even know if the sun will set in front of me or behind me. How will we ever find our way?"

"Be at peace, brother. Antonio knows a roomy hostel called The Olive. He made arrangements for us even before arriving in Trapani. He will lead us there directly. After a cup of wine, you'll feel better. I know I will. Who was that fellow, Antonio? Why does he think he can part the sea like Moses?"

"I've seen him on a few occasions with my uncle," Antonio replied. "He's a Catalan merchant named Ferdinand something who trades here periodically. My uncle usually orders people around and demands to be accommodated, but when this fellow is around, he's quite a little lamb. If you think you can chastise that fellow, wait until I'm around so I can see it!"

"You will wait uselessly, Antonio. My chastising days are over." Pietro replied tersely. If that man's a merchant, he thought, I'm a priest! Antonio turned into a quiet street and pointed towards a large pair of wooden gates that opened onto a welcoming courtyard with a fountain burbling softly in the middle.

········

Roaring into the courtyard of the large and luxurious *Fondaco dei Catalani* where he always stayed in Palermo, Ferdinand de Lerida and his men quickly dismounted and called for wine, casually throwing their reins to the stable boys.

He had arrived in Palermo several days ago in advance of his cargo
ships, shaken off the enforced confinement of a long sea voyage
and moved with purpose once again. Who was that old man with
the sword, he wondered. It had been some time since anyone had
confronted him, even in that half-hearted way. Ferdinand was a
tall, swarthy, broad-chested man in the prime of life. His short,

trimmed beard was as dark as his obsidian eyes. Remote, indifferent eyes. No one looking directly at him held that look for long.

Rushing forward, the steward of the fondaco ushered Ferdinand and his two men into the side garden, seating them at a wooden table under a shade tree. He reappeared instantly with a wine bottle and cups, and a plate of fresh fruit, bread and cheese. He bowed to Ferdinand. "Lord, I am told your cargo ships have finally arrived in the harbor. Have you brought us another shipment of that fine Spanish wine?"

Ferdinand glanced at him, a useful man, in his way. Knew the business of the port, who came and went. Nothing more than an innkeeper, really, but innkeepers knew surprising information about people. "Donato, you may send your men for the wine as soon as it is unloaded. Certainly, I have not forgotten you." Donato smiled and nodded his thanks. Snapping his fingers, he gave rapid instructions to the slave overseer, who rushed out of the garden and began bawling orders to the carters and transporters lingering near the stables.

Ferdinand had stuffed his ship with wine, cloth and Spanish horses to reinforce his merchant persona. He actually profited handsomely from his merchant ventures, regardless of the true purpose of his voyages around the Mediterranean. He could readily discuss trade routes, the newest fashions, spices or medicines with any merchant he met, however insignificant it might be to him personally. He left the actual business of trading in Palermo to his business agent, Josef, the old Jew, who knew everyone and didn't skim too much off the top.

Ferdinand politely dismissed the innkeeper and his men. He needed to think undisturbed. He recalled the brief encounter he had just had in the street. It was of no great consequence, yet he had seen the impulsive challenge in the old Crusader's face. Hardly worth remembering, he knew, since the old man had been silenced with an icy stare, yet he filed the image carefully away in case they met again. Ferdinand constantly catalogued events and faces around him, noting the comments and conversations of others, including details others missed, even while appearing preoccupied with his own agenda. King Peter of Aragon relied on his ability to report such observations; he smiled privately at the thought of their last meeting, both of them amused at his disguise as a merchant. He had cultivated this role for years, Ferdinand thought, and smugly reflected how successful he was. He fooled everyone in Palermo, even Josef. And they say Jews are clever!

Scanning this afternoon's scene once more in his mind to be certain nothing was overlooked, Ferdinand remembered the young man with dark curls. Wasn't that Simon de Paruta's nephew? What was he doing with a bunch of country folk? He would be sure to mention the encounter to Simon when they met. Perhaps Simon would know the old man with the military reflexes. The man was – or had been - a soldier; Ferdinand was sure of it. Only soldiers reached for their swords so quickly. Idly, he wondered if the nephew's devotion to dice and horse racing had turned to some more serious purpose.

············

After leaving the pilgrims at The Olive, Antonio rode further into the *Cassaro* where he made his home with his aged uncle. In a residential district glittering with palaces, Simon's edifice was still one of the most impressive. He clattered into the courtyard, threw his reins to the slave boy, and stared up at the great three-storied *palazio*. He loathed his uncle.

Sometimes he still dreamed that his mother was waiting at the door to greet him, but she had lived in Messina for some years now, and he saw her only infrequently. Antonio was nine and Mateo only four when their father was trampled by a stampeding horse in front of their parish church. In his nightmares, he still saw the horror on his mother's face when the neighbors carried the bloody body through the door. Their frantic ministrations and prayers to the saints could not save him. Only her sons, she told him later, kept her from falling apart. Antonio, rather bewildered by it all, regretted his father's death and comforted his mother, but he had never been close to his father. More pointedly, he learned to realize what the loss of a father might do to the family's fortunes or social position.

Indeed, creditors soon began demanding repayment of his father's debts. His mother had no one to assist her. A man or two made inquiries about her, but they quickly learned the family's debts were too crushing to assume through marriage. When the tears finally passed and his mother once again faced her desperate circumstances, she found herself forced to call upon Simon for assistance. She did not like Simon, but she really had no alternative. Feeling another loss, but grateful for assistance, she allowed Simon to sell her small house to satisfy the creditors, and they all moved into his grand but silent home.

Mateo was so young that he could not help quickly transferring his affection for his father to Simon. Simon, normally an austere, short-tempered man, surprisingly returned that affection and Antonio could only watch enviously as his little brother effortlessly became his uncle's favorite. Antonio could forgive his brother. He was a naturally loving and obedient boy.

Simon's gruff manner and stern voice dominated their new life, so his mother tried to remind them of his father's laugh and the playful stories told by the hearth in winter. Antonio's mother acted respectfully, tried to fulfill Simon's expectations of her, and urged her boys to do the same. Yet Antonio could sense, in his youthful way, her unhappiness and her deep resentment over their dependency. Simon felt it too, and found it at first unsettling, then irritating. Within three months he arranged for her to marry a minor freeholder in Messina. Antonio and Mateo, however, his rightful heirs, had to acquire the education and manners appropriate to young nobility. They were forced to stay.

"Come into the garden, boy," called Simon when he realized Antonio had arrived. "Mateo and I were just reviewing the qualities of Egyptian cotton. I assume you fulfilled both assignments? I will question you more closely about your observations of the harbor and the shipping after supper. For now, tell us about the pilgrims. Was that woman – Sophia, wasn't it - pleased with your service?"

"She was indeed, though she and her husband were somewhat surprised when I arrived with your letter. I don't think she really expected any response to her request for assistance. Now Sophia and her husband have nothing but the best opinion of your generosity. Still, I doubt we will hear much of them again. The husband does not wish to be beholden."

Venutus appeared with wine and almond cakes when Antonio strolled in. He fussed with the arrangements as Antonio threw himself into a chair and glowered at the servant. He despised his uncle but loathed Venutus even more. He knew the refreshments were merely an excuse to listen to the family conversation. His uncle was getting senile; he thought Venutus showed devotion, but Antonio knew better. He stared pointedly at the manservant, maintaining a stony silence, until Venutus looked at Simon.

"Let us have some privacy, Uncle."

"Venutus, you can go." Simon waved his hand and Venutus angrily left. If Simon had noticed the tense undercurrent between the two, he gave no sign.

"Really, Uncle, I want to say something about Venutus." Antonio reached for a cup of wine from the little table near his uncle's padded chair. The wine was mixed with water, he knew, since the old man could not tolerate it at full strength these days, yet he was thirsty enough not to care. "I think he takes liberties with your business, and I've noticed things missing in the past few months. That pair of silver candlesticks above the mantle in the great room? They're not there and none of the servants know anything. I think he's stealing."

Simon grunted as he shifted uncomfortably in his chair. "I know you dislike each other, Antonio, but he acts only on my instructions. He's been faithful to me for thirty years or more and I trust him. Are you sure another servant isn't pilfering? Or maybe it's your own greed for my money that makes you think ill of others. Mateo and I would like to hear what you learned and observed on this little adventure."

Antonio resisted saying more. He recognized the change in Simon's voice and knew this was his uncle's way of testing him. Simon didn't care about the pilgrims, but he was testing Antonio's self-control. Well, Mateo would find a colorful description entertaining. Mateo was the only person in the world that Antonio loved unreservedly.

Mateo at fourteen still had about him a bit of the softness of youth. His lanky frame would fill out in time, but he still stumbled over feet that were too big and pretended not to wish for a full beard or mustache to appear. Where Antonio had taken to sport and whores, Mateo eagerly embraced letters and numbers, history and philosophy. When Antonio took him along to the races or to a tavern, Antonio's friends teased the young man and tried to pull tricks on him. Yet the good-natured and smiling boy was liked by the group. He was bright, witty, and had a kind word for everyone. It was said he had a future few others could hope for.

Antonio poured himself another cup of wine, drew up his chair and launched into the story. He described the Pandolfos' house in Trapani, the salty smell that clung to everything, the countryside they traveled through, the small inns where they stayed, and the lamb and onion stew that tasted so savory. He spoke of Sophia's ceaseless chatter, old Perna's excitement at seeing the city for the first time, poor Carlo's dreadful worry, and the reunion with his crusading brother. He mentioned Renata in only the most dismissive terms, knowing he would find a better time later to brag to Mateo about her beauty and his delightful conquest. By the time the sun began to slide behind the garden wall, Simon seemed to be nodding sleepily rather than following the tale.

"I almost forgot to tell you, Mateo, about one of the most puzzling parts of this journey. This old Crusader had been in Jerusalem when it fell, according to his brother, for he would not talk of it himself. When was it? Maybe 40 years ago or more? But as brusque as he was, he did have one thing from the Holy Land that was rather interesting." Antonio fell silent as he recalled the glint of gold on Pietro's sword and thought how to describe it.

"Tell me, brother, about this thing. You cannot start a story and then break off in the middle," said Mateo reaching for the carafe and pouring. "Have another cup of wine and finish the tale!"

"Yes, yes. I was momentarily distracted. The man had a golden medallion mounted on the guard of his sword, and very protective of it he was, too! I only had the briefest inspection of it. The little golden oval had, he said, Egyptian picture writing around the perimeter, with an intricate, all-seeing eye in the middle. I asked him about its meaning, but he would say nothing. Maybe you can help me decipher the secret, Mateo." The brothers smiled at each other, Mateo instantly searching his mind for an explanation. Antonio began to explain the design to his brother and Mateo began to talk excitedly about oddities he had heard about the religion of the ancient Egyptians.

While the two brothers were involved in the puzzle, Simon shifted suddenly in his chair and instantly was alert. He tried to hide his rapt interest from his nephews by brushing away at his ear as if a fly bothered him.

"I closed my eyes just a moment, Antonio, but that little medal sounds intriguing. Tell me again what you saw." Antonio did so.

"And what of the man who had this medallion? What did you say his name was?"

"The old man was Carlo Manfredi's brother, Pietro. They say he just returned to Sicily to accompany his brother on this pilgrimage after a long sojourn somewhere in France, perhaps in Blois. He must have seen many battles. He should have exciting stories to tell. He often massaged the scar on his cheek and moved his left arm as if it pained him. I would have much more to tell you and Mateo if he had been more open, but he was not the kind of man for storytelling."

Simon froze, his eyes going dark when he heard the name. This could not be true! Covering his shock with a handkerchief, he forced a distracting cough or two and then composed his features into false calmness. "How interesting," he remarked casually, while conveying the impression of dismissing the man at the same time.

"Weren't you in Jerusalem for awhile, Uncle?" Mateo began. Simon shot him a look but forced a smile. "Yes. That was so long ago, I've almost forgotten. Mateo, I don't feel well, could you help me?"

Simon rose stiffly from his chair. Mateo leaped to his feet, and lent his arm to his uncle. Antonio stared out into the garden thinking of Renata. A soft twilight settled into the garden and the light breeze of the afternoon slowed to a puff of air now and again. He heard his uncle giving instructions, as always, as they went into the house. "Antonio," Simon rasped over his shoulder, "do not go out with your friends until we have discussed the rest of your mission. I wish to have the port information this evening after I have rested a bit."

Antonio sighed.

CHAPTER 7

Angelica de Rogerio rapidly gave last minute instructions to the slaves regarding the linens and cleanliness of the rooms for the new guests at The Olive as she hurried to the door to greet them. My, they were a dusty lot, she thought. And Santa Maria, such a pregnant one! It's a mercy she didn't deliver that baby on the road. Angelica mentally rolled her eyes as she helped Sophia climb stiffly down from the cart.

Sophia looked around as she gratefully accepted Angelica's gentle support. What she saw gratified her immensely. Everything was neat and clean, even the slaves and servants she saw. The stables were open and airy on the far side of the very large courtyard, away from the inn itself. Another side of the courtyard studded with benches, was shaded by fragrant almond trees and myrtle. Tall stone walls surrounding the complex, draped with ivy and flowering vines, muted the dust and noise from the street, although Sophia could still glimpse the soaring tower of Palermo Cathedral over one side. The inn portion was two stories high and clearly well cared for. Sophia sniffed appreciatively, smelling delicious aromas of delicate stews, freshly baked bread, and roasting meat from the kitchen. She sighed, thanked Angelica profusely and introduced herself.

"I'm pleased to meet you," Angelica was saying pleasantly as she walked the woman towards the door. The women followed haphazardly as Pietro and Carlo took the horses and cart to the stables, and Sophia began to prattle to Angelica about their plans.

"Sir," said the stable boy respectfully to Pietro, "I will take your horse."

"No, boy, thank you," answered the old soldier brusquely. "I can't sleep unless I take care of him myself--it's an old habit." His stallion nickered appreciatively and Pietro leaned against him briefly stroking his mane. Brushing his horse down, inspecting his hooves, and helping put the cart away would allow him time to gather his thoughts and outline a plan of action. He needed some peace and quiet away from those babbling women to think things over. His Julianna had never been one to natter on like these women did.

Angelica led the women into a warm, spacious room and seated them at a long table. She brought them warm damp towels scented with orange blossoms to clean the dust from their faces and hands and signaled for wine and refreshments. She missed Amodeus, her husband's brother, who had managed the hostel for years. Not only because he was so good with people, or even the work that she now had to do, but she missed his banter, his easy laugh, and his fun-loving nature. The time it took to oversee both this place and her own home! For a month now she had done nothing but run between both places, from here in the *Cassaro* to the *Seralcadi*, clear on the other side of Palermo! Angelica brushed a dark curl from her forehead and sat down for a moment with her new guests. Her extraordinary golden eyes sympathetic, she began to listen to their plans for their visit while another part of her mind drifted back to when Amodeus and Ysabella had left The Olive.

"Ysabella, why are you going?" Angelica stared, aghast, at her sister-in-law. At 32 and the daughter of a successful Catalan merchant, few things surprised her about human nature, but this had taken her by surprise. She and Ysabella sat beneath the almond trees, where Ysabella had invited her to sit down for a talk.

"Angelica, you know Amodeus hasn't been unhappy here," Ysabella began. "But even before I married him," she paused, not wanting to hurt Angelica's feelings, "he wanted to have his own place. He loves you and your son, Nicolo, and the girls, but he's just tired of not being his own man. He's always been the little brother to Raynaldus, and as close as they are, I think he just needs to strike out on his own." She raised her beautiful violet eyes to look into Angelica's lustrous gold ones. "Please understand. You know you're like a sister to me, but ever since the boys were orphaned, well, Raynaldus has looked out for Amodeus, and

Amodeus, he is a bit of a free spirit!" She laughed, glancing again at Angelica and for a moment, both of them smiled, each harboring memories of Amodeus' impulsive tendencies.

Angelica took her hand. "Ysabella, have you thought about this carefully? I love Amodeus too, but that very recklessness of his, well, you know…" Her voice trailed off as she looked anxiously at the woman next to her. "I had no idea, I mean, you and Amodeus, and little William, all seemed so happy here, and I'm worried about you not being with us. Have you planned what to do?"

"Oh, yes. Remember last year when we all walked over to the de Cisarios for that wonderful party? Well, we passed an old dilapidated tavern, The Leopard, and saw it was for sale. Amodeus went back later to talk with old Laurencio de Cisario who owns it. I think William Tallavia, Amodeus's good friend, and of course, Uncle Leo and Adam de Citella, all ended up going with Amodeus to purchase it! I think they really intimidated old Laurencio and he sold it to Amodeus for well below what he had originally been asking." She smiled at Angelica.

"Amodeus was so happy. So we've been cleaning up the place bit by bit. Hasn't Raynaldus told you? Nicolo has been helping, you know. He's been fixing up the upstairs, where we'll be living. I thought, Angelica that Amodeus and Raynaldus talked this over."

She stared into surprised eyes.

"No, Ysabella, Raynaldus usually tells me everything. He did say casually one day that Amodeus had bought some property, but he didn't say anything about a tavern." For a moment Angelica was both irritated and hurt about Ysabella's secrecy, not to mention her husband's. Then she swept that aside as both women looked at each other fondly, thinking of Raynaldus, older, protective, taciturn, and definitely one to keep things close to his chest.

Angelica hugged her sister-in-law. "I'm really going to miss you. It's been so wonderful having you here, but I understand you want your own place. Remember when Amodeus brought you home for the first time and announced that you were the one?!" They both shrieked, laughing and remembering.

"Raynaldus was stunned! He had already picked out a thoroughly respectable merchant's daughter for his little brother--respectable, fat and rich!" Ysabella giggled. Angelica smiled, too. HowRaynaldus had ranted about his brother's recklessness, turned by a pretty face! Yes, Angelica thought, he had gone on and on that night! Secretly she had been delighted with Ysabella from the start. Ysabella had spark, and personality. She was fun, vivacious, and became the sister Angelica had never had. Her mother had died in childbirth, so she never really had women around her before Ysabella burst into their lives.

In no time at all, business had picked up at The Olive. Everyone loved her; she made the clients feel special and she was a hard worker. It didn't take long for even Raynaldus, stolid as he was, to appreciate the liveliness and warmth she brought to the place. And she certainly kept Amodeus home at night! No, she had been a blessing, and although Angelica was sad to see her go, and missed her sunny smile and spontaneous laugh, she was happy for both of them. Lord, but she did wish Raynaldus would find someone soon to manage this place! Her attention was jerked back to her customers, who were asking all kinds of questions about the city. She answered their questions, and then stood up with a gracious smile.

"Well, why don't I show you your rooms, then we'll talk more about where you wish to visit. This evening, however, my brother-in-law and sister-in-law are opening their new tavern, The Leopard. I'd like to invite you to come with us there for supper, I promise you, he's got a wonderful cook, and you'll meet the rest of my family." Sophia and Perna immediately agreed, and trudged upstairs to change clothes and rest. Renata followed silently, preoccupied with thoughts of when she might see Antonio again.

CHAPTER 8

Amodeus stopped a moment to appreciate the cacophony around him and felt a swell of confidence, realizing that he had, indeed, made the right decision. Striking out on his own was both terrifying and necessary. He watched his wife, Ysabella, swish around the crowded tables on opening night at *his* place, The Leopard, teasing the neighbors and conversing readily with strangers. Adding to the festivity, many people were milling about rather than settling in one place. The aromas of Larissa's cooking wafted through the room, encouraging hungry appetites.

It was a happy crowd of locals, friends, business associates and pilgrims. Each cup of wine that was poured or coin that changed hands gave him a secret pride. Amodeus had a good cook, fair prices and fine wines, but with the added benefits of Ysabella's saucy manner and her tight fist on the purse, he knew The Leopard would have many more successful nights like this one. She had a way with people, and she certainly had a way with him! He was daydreaming a bit about her smoky violet eyes and the smell of lavender in her hair when his nephew appeared at his side.

"Uncle," Nicolo said, nearly shouting over the noise of the crowd and drawing him back from his reverie. "I never knew working so hard could be so much fun! I'll sleep all day tomorrow. How did everyone know that we opened tonight? Where have all these people come from? Did you have any idea the place would be so crowded?"

"I tried shouting from the rooftops, but your aunt made me stop – said it was unseemly," Amodeus teased. "I had to content myself with telling half of Palermo in person. I know so many people from all those years in the tanning district and at The Olive. Leo and Adam, of course, sent a few people, and Ysabella's women friends undoubtedly told the half of the town that I missed. And even though your father thinks we are taking too big a risk here, even he might have talked us up a bit. Why don't you ask folks how they heard about us as you clear their tables or pour more wine? It might be good to know if it was more than idle curiosity that brought them here."

"Yes, Uncle, I really want to know. Father said he would come by later after he and Adam finished their business. He wanted to bring Mother and the girls, too. Aunt Ysabella wants you to keep an eye on William, too. She's afraid he'll linger over his chores and scoot out the door as soon as no one is watching. By the way, we need another barrel of ale from the storeroom. Shall I get it?

"I want Raynaldus to see this crowd – to see that his little brother can be independent! You go find William and keep him close by your side. He's big enough to help out tonight. We need every hand, and he's old enough to learn some discipline. I'll get the ale. We need another cheese as well. Good thing Ysabella talked me into stocking a few extra!"

He headed to the back to fetch the supplies. On his left in the dice room, he could hear men placing bets, passing the dice, and cajoling each other with good-natured laughter. Their voices were raised with excitement, but he thought he could detect just a hint of bitterness as one or the other lost a few pennies.

Taking the key to the storeroom from an inner pocket, Amodeus realized he had not been in the room at night. They had moved the supplies during the day when there was light from the surrounding rooms. The storeroom had no window to prevent thieves from breaking in, and the flickering lanterns in the dice room and hallway could not penetrate the inky black of the hallway. He fumbled a bit with the lock in the wavering light, trying to remember where he had placed the meats, cheese, olives, ale, wine and the other commodities for his new business. Finding a barrel of ale by feel should be no problem, he thought, not to waste precious time going back for a torch. He would have to remember to hang a lantern on a hook by the door tomorrow. A satisfying creak of the door hinges signaled the door opening onto an even blacker hole than that of the hallway. Amodeus paused to orient himself.

They had been careful to leave a narrow path open straight from the door to the rear of the room, stacking barrels, crates and pallets on each side. Strings of onions, garlic cloves, and dried herbs hung from hooks in the rafters. Large jars of olive oil, barrels of preserved fish, baskets of dried tomatoes and sacks of flour were arranged under shelves holding smaller containers of olives, dried fruits, dates and pickled condiments. The storeroom gave off a scent of prosperity. He remembered storing the ale toward the back on the right and the wine on the left. Mentally congratulating himself on the fine deal he made for his wine, Amodeus moved toward the barrels in the back, but in doing so he begrudgingly acknowledged that he may have made the wrong decision about where to place things. Now it seemed obvious that the barrels should be at the front of the storeroom so he could get to them more easily. Saving a few extra steps every night would be a blessing. He would have to remember to tell Mario to rearrange things tomorrow.

Amodeus felt a little uneasy in the dark. He stepped down the aisle carefully with both hands touching the items on the sides. Just like one of those acrobats on the tightrope, he thought. Before he realized it, his foot caught under the corner of a sack protruding into the aisle, and he stumbled forward. He bumped hard against a rough pottery crock of olive oil and nearly fell to the floor. He regained his feet and rubbed his arm that scraped across the surface of the crock, but he quickly forgot the minor sting as he hefted a barrel of ale, placed a block of cheese rather precariously on top, and found his way even more carefully back into the hall. He clicked the lock back into place as the noise of the crowd called him back to his purpose.

"Where have you been, Amodeus?" Ysabella scolded. "Everyone is asking for you. Nicolo has given out the last of the ale, and I need more cheese sliced. Isn't this wonderful? I know we can make a success of this place."

"Ale and cheese as requested, my sweet," he responded laughingly. "Have you seen Raynaldus, Leo or Adam yet? Do you think they will approve?"

"Don't be so anxious, love. Of course they'll approve! Raynaldus will come around. Hasn't he always supported you in the end? Do slice that cheese for me – I'll be back for it in a few minutes." She paused, watching him turn to the counter. He had such a sweet smile. Both his manner and his appearance entranced her. With that thought in mind, she floated away again, refilling tankards and cups, serving plates of steaming stew, and scooping coins into her apron pockets.

Amodeus set the cheese before him on the countertop and reached for a knife. "Mario," Amodeus called. "Have you seen that knife I was using? I thought I set it down right here."

"I didn't see it, master. Here, use this one."

"Well, I'm sure it will turn up. Just look at this crowd, Mario. I don't think even Ysabella's careful calculations and plans could have prepared for all these people! Your wife's lamb stew seems to be quite a hit. Larissa's food is as big a draw as the wine and ale." When he last stalked out of The Olive after another argument with Raynaldus, vowing to have his own place, he truly had no expectation of such success. He often paid for his impulsive decisions, but Ysabella softened the blows otherwise delivered by his recklessness. True, she held him to account and let him know when he was being foolish, but she was fully behind this idea and together they would make it work. Now that the business was open, perhaps there would be less strain in their household.

So many had come to wish them well. There was Arnulfo and his wife who sold brassware in the market. Their son, Emilio, was William's playmate and fellow troublemaker. There was Tomaso, who lived across the street. Tomaso had dropped in on their preparations every day over the last month to keep tabs on their progress and spread the news of each little accomplishment around the neighborhood. Old Signora Benaducci had teetered down the alley from her *casalina* to stake out a place by the hearth. She regaled anyone nearby with oft-repeated stories of the old days and threatened them with the evil eye if they mentioned they had already heard the tale. Fellow tanners from his old district, customers from The Olive, weavers, bootmakers and sailors, small shopkeepers – even some Dominicans and Franciscans had stopped in to sample the wine and Larissa's delicious food.

Many in the crowd were new faces, but the city was teeming with righteous pilgrims and others. Some offered genuine goods and services, while some meant to prey on the naïve and unsophisticated. Next week was Holy Week, and it brought a welcome influx of hungry and thirsty strangers, most with coins in their purses. As with any crowd, Amodeus thought, a few of his guests tonight were probably not the honest sort they appeared to be. He would eventually weed out the cutpurses and thugs in order to maintain the reputation of his business, but not tonight! Tonight, he would even put up with Ludovico Stefani, a man he had despised since childhood.

Ysabella tolerated Ludovico because he was husband to her dear friend, Joanna, and probably, Amodeus reflected, because she was innately a good soul. For three days, Joanna Stefani had baked bread and pastries in preparation for tonight's opening. Over the last month, along with the servants and slaves, she had scrubbed walls, scraped grime from the tabletops, and chased pigeons out of this neglected building to help Amodeus and Ysabella fulfill their dreams. Ysabella trusted and confided in this older woman, and Joanna doted on Ysabella as the daughter she never had. How such a good-hearted and likeable woman could be married to that miserable old goat, Ludovico, was a mystery to him. Ludovico drank too much, was careless in business, and seemed lately to suspect everyone of ill will, not to mention his long-standing animosity towards Amodeus. Ysabella saw a pained look on Joanna's face now and then when they chatted, which she tried to describe to Amodeus, but he never wanted to hear any details.

The less contact with the old man, the better. But tonight, Ysabella had convinced him to welcome Ludovico along with Joanna in appreciation for all her hard work. They had arrived before most of the others, since Joanna wanted to help Ysabella with the final arrangement of things. Thankfully, after the briefest of greetings, Ludovico had the sense to stay in the game room away from Amodeus.

Ysabella caught a glimpse of a magnificent deep forest green cloak out of the corner of her eye and laughed. Without even looking up, she knew Antonio de Paruta had arrived. This young dandy, a couple years older than Nicolo, spent his Uncle Simon's money freely and strutted around like a peacock. She knew Antonio had a bit of a crush on her. She handled him respectfully to avoid offending Simon, but even when she was emotionally withdrawn or surly, Antonio remained convinced she couldn't live without him. Wasn't there an old Greek tale about someone who loved only himself? Antonio could be the central character! Fortunately, Nicolo had a good head on his shoulders and was not really fooled by his friend's sociable veneer. She felt pretty sure Nicolo could befriend Antonio and his crowd without getting carried away, and she agreed with her sister-in-law that he should be exposed to all types of characters now when he could learn a few lessons without receiving the hard knocks he would get later in life.

"Nicolo!" Antonio hailed. I could barely push my way in the door for all the people here." Smiling condescendingly, he added carelessly, "I did not expect to find such a crowd."

"Must be all the folks in town for the holiday," Nicolo responded as he hurried by with a tray. "There are many I haven't seen before, but they'll be getting more familiar with each other if they keep pushing each other aside and stealing the empty seats. What brings you in?"

"I hoped to draw you away from here for a little fun. Bruno has something arranged for us. I told him I would bring you along."

"You can't expect me to leave Uncle Amodeus and Aunt Ysabella to manage this crowd alone! Not tonight, Antonio. I want to stay here. Let me pour you a glass of wine, and get Ysabella to talk to you. I know she is fond of you."

"I would like nothing better!" Antonio immediately radiated a charming smile as he thought about Ysabella. This was the kind of woman you could really fall for – creamy, soft cheeks and shapely curves. Those violet eyes! And such an easy-going way about her. She would be something to come home to every night! Antonio decided to stay awhile--Bruno could wait.

The place kept filling up and the wine and ale flowed freely. Amodeus tried to keep an eye on everyone but it was impossible. Loud chatter and laughter filled the tavern. He found his gaze straying often to his wife. Once again, he marveled at the way in which she moved from group to group and made each person feel as though they had her full attention.

"William! Where is that brat?" she muttered to him as she passed.

"Aunt Ysabella! I've got him right here." Nicolo, one of her favorite people, strode over, with William trailing behind talking a mile a minute. She smiled even though she had a thousand things to do. William adored Nicolo and Nicolo treated him like a little brother, watching out for him and cuffing him on the head whenever he needed it, which was often.

"William, get some wood and keep the ovens going, so Larissa can keep the food moving," ordered Nicolo. William scampered off to collect the twigs and sticks to stoke the fires.

"Thanks Nicolo. Where did you find him?" asked Ysabella.

"Oh, the usual. He was pestering one of the merchants here. You know." Keeping track of William was a full time job. His curiosity and interest in all the exotic goods in the Great Market, his love of knights, dragons, and the like made him well known to the local vendors and merchants, who, amused by his constant questions, kept a good-natured eye on the young boy. They obligingly covered for him when Ysabella stormed into the Great Market, pretending to be ignorant of the boy's myriad hiding places amongst the stalls and goods. Once she had even found him over in the Jewish quarter, in the meat market near the Synagogue, listening wide-eyed as a solemn rabbi described how they slaughtered their animals differently from the Christians. He was a handful!

"Nicolo, I do appreciate you helping us tonight." said Ysabella softly as she quickly cleaned a nearby table.

"Oh, I thought I'd see what you needed. My father had a group of pilgrims coming in today, and they and their animals took some extra care and time, but I talked him into bringing them here tonight for their meal. Mother will be taking them to the shrines, you know. I think they want to go up Mount Pellegrino and see Santa Rosalia."

"Where are they from?" she asked as she deftly continued cleaning tables and brushing off chairs. Nicolo's father was the real entrepreneur in the family. He catered to international merchants who required a great deal more care and space than Amodeus's modest establishment could offer. But Nicolo preferred to be at The Leopard, not only because he loved his Uncle Amodeus, but also because it was like a home and not a business. During their work on the tavern, it had become the informal gathering place for the extended de Rogerio family and for their friends and neighbors who dropped in casually to view the progress and trade gossip and news.

He could usually find Leo de Iannacio here, who always had time for him. Leo treated him like an adult, and Nicolo looked up to him like a grandfather. Uncle Leo would tell him stories about when Raynaldus and Uncle Amodeus were young. His father, who not only ran a huge hostel, but also held several political jobs, was an elected magistrate, and a merchant himself, never had time to tell stories about his youth. Besides, his father wasn't exactly the story-telling type; he was quiet, reserved, politically connected and hard-working. He had a reputation for honesty and was known as someone who could be depended upon to settle an argument or arbitrate a dispute.

In fact, he often did so at a corner table at The Olive with his close friend and notary, Adam de Citella, writing down arbitration results and handing copies of the decision to each party for future reference. Nicolo thought about the old notary briefly. Adam was an immigrant from Melfi on the mainland. Adam told Nicolo that when he arrived in Palermo, he had had to renew his notarial license before the judicial council. It was actually an exciting story since Adam arrived just after King Charles took over Sicily. Desperate for literate, knowledgeable men, Adam had been welcomed for his legal expertise and was put immediately to work on the court's business, which was in chaos due to Charles' recent conquest. He told Nicolo some hair-raising stories about Charles' first days in Palermo. Although Raynaldus had apprenticed his son to the old notary, Nicolo hated the profession, sitting in an office, waiting for people to come and draw up contracts. So dry, so boring. He'd much rather be here, doing the thousand and one things it took to run a tavern, interacting with the clientele, figuring out logistics and problems of food, drink and personalities. He sighed, hoping he might convince his father to tear up his contract with Adam. Uncle Amodeus promised to talk to Raynaldus, but so far, Raynaldus hadn't budged.

"They're from Trapani, Aunt Ysabella. They'll be here soon, I'm sure." Ysabella gave him a quick smile as he moved off towards the kitchen. She shifted to a table where two strangers ordered more wine. They were rough looking men dressed in leather jerkins and well-worn boots, probably carters or tanners, but unfamiliar to her. One had curious eyes, one blue, one brown, which made her look more closely at them. The men conversed a little together, but even after a few drinks, Ysabella found it difficult to extract a smile from either of them. Like many others, they were probably just recuperating from another workday. Not everyone was an old friend. She served the wine and was moving on when someone caught her sleeve from behind.

"Raynaldus, you finally made it!" She said with genuine affection. "I knew you wouldn't keep away. Did you bring Angelica and the girls? Where are Leo and Adam? Nicolo, has been such a help tonight."

"Don't worry, little one," Raynaldus answered. "We are all here. They were right behind me, though they may have gotten lost among the crowd. I brought along the pilgrims staying at The Olive. Much more entertainment for them here tonight! You know, though, that one profitable night does not guarantee success."

"Always the cautious one, aren't you, Raynaldus? Be a dear and don't spoil the mood for Amodeus. He's determined to be independent, but when we turn that first gold ducat of profit, it will be because of what he learned from you. You know he would never say it directly, but deep down he really wants your approval. Now let me find a comfortable settle for Leo and give the girls a big hug. I'll take care of your pilgrims. Go talk with Amodeus."

Ysabella laughed to think about the tiff between the two brothers that finally led Amodeus to leave The Olive. Amodeus had worked for his older brother at his large, well-appointed hostel for years, but chafed at always being the manager, never the owner. The two personalities were definitely at odds, but Ysabella knew, and they themselves knew, that their deep family connection couldn't be broken by a few harsh words. Happily, she went to find the others.

CHAPTER 9

Laughter emerged from the back room where a few old friends were playing dice. It was a friendly game, but if you lost, none of your friends was shy about relieving you of the last few coins in your pocket. Ludovico really had no intention of being drawn into the game, but he wandered into the back of The Leopard to escape any small talk with Amodeus. Joanna's excitement about opening night had persuaded him to come along. Still, the bad blood between him and Amodeus could not be overcome by an obligatory nod of congratulations.

As Joanna became swept up in the hubbub of activity in the main room, Ludovico retreated to relative safety. He could watch the players and have a little of that good red wine, he thought, before making an unnoticed exit out the back door. His good intentions failed as he was encouraged to play by the others. As usual, one game led to another. For the first hour of play, his fortunes were looking up. The dice fell his way and earned him a small stack of extra coins that could be well used. But as he drank more and his fortunes turned, his mood became dark and his tongue sharp. His losses were mounting up to more than he could afford. He was convinced that this group of supposed "friends" was conspiring to break him. It seemed that the whole town was aware of his business misfortunes and were all laughing at him behind his back.

Antonio, too, had wandered into the game room. After a couple cups of wine and a few sweet words with Ysabella, he had forgotten Bruno's plans altogether. He thought of himself as skilled at games of chance and gambling although, truly, he usually lost more than he won. Still, the excitement of risk led him to play with abandon. With the next throw of the dice, Antonio exclaimed, "Well, Ludovico, I'm lucky again! Pay up – I don't want to wait until tomorrow for payment. From what I've heard, you make excuses rather than paying your debts. I don't intend to be another creditor on your long list."

"You little jackanapes," spat Ludovico in response. "I'm an honorable man and a friend of your uncle. Don't you dare speak to me that way!" He had loathed Antonio since Simon adopted him. What a manipulative, selfish child! How could Simon have raised such an arrogant fop?

"A friend of my uncle? Is that right? The old curmudgeon has no friends, and if he did, you wouldn't be among them! You're just another lackey for him to manipulate. Surely you've figured that out after all these years!" Antonio laughed out loud looking around the room, then down his nose at the gray-haired drunkard he could so easily intimidate. He relished the power of bullying others. Just look at how the other players moved away from them. "Now, old man, my money."

"You won't get one penny from me for the abuse you've shown me. I've listened to your drivel for the last time! I'm telling your uncle of your despicable behavior and disrespect." Ludovico, red-faced, turned to leave, pushing aside the men next to him and lurching towards the door.

"Stop, you rascal! I'll teach you a lesson you won't forget!" A flash of metal appeared from nowhere in Antonio's hand. The others gasped as he thrust the knife in the direction of Ludovico's departing figure.

A sudden hand grasped Antonio's arm and Amodeus said quietly, "Stop! Both of you! This is no battlefield, and there will be no violence in my place! Antonio, you're driving away my customers. Let's settle this like neighbors. I run a respectable establishment. Nicolo – take your friend aside before he hurts himself."

Ludovico's exit was blocked at the door by Nicolo, rushing in to help settle the fracas. The old man turned and glared venomously at those who were staring at him. "I'll pay, you little puppy! You'd be nothing if it wasn't for your uncle. There was no need to insult me. Maybe these few coins will slake your greed." With a swift movement no one would have believed such a drunk capable of, Ludovico upended his coin purse onto the table before him. A few measly coins spilled out onto the surface. One in particular gleamed in the flickering torchlight, engraved with odd symbols.

Loosing Nicolo's grip and grabbing at the luminous disk before him, Antonio clucked, "I've seen this heathen medallion before, old man. Where did you get it? Why, it's solid gold!" He held up before him a shining medallion exactly like one affixed to the sword pommel of the old Crusader he just escorted into town. That escort service was an errand of atonement for some minor deed his uncle disapproved of, but now, seeing the same strange gold piece again, it presented an intriguing puzzle. How had this crazy old merchant come by such a beautiful piece? What was the connection to the other old man?

"That's not for you, you heartless cur. Give it back to me!" Ludovico rushed toward Antonio in a panic, reaching for his medallion. He had not realized it was mixed in with his coins. He had to have it back. The more Ludovico grabbed at Antonio's raised arm, the more Antonio laughed and danced around, keeping the medal from him. Enjoying himself, Antonio tossed the medallion in the air just to watch the old man dive for it. Instead, Nicolo caught the thing and put a halt to Antonio's insulting game, pressing it gently into the old man's trembling, sweaty hand.

Amodeus stepped forward and pushed the onlookers toward the door. He declared the back room closed. He would not allow any more dice games if this were the result. Ignoring the pittance the old man had thrown on the table, Antonio, still laughing but inwardly seething with anger at Ludovico's insults, moved out into the main room with the others. This was not over, and he would enjoy every minute plotting his revenge. Antonio demanded another glass of wine, but Ysabella just shook her head and turned away from him. Antonio glowered, his face reddened with anger. Suddenly, the boy William unexpectedly materialized at his elbow, whispering. Antonio glared at him and then smiled at the message.

Looked up, he asked, "Where?" William pointed towards the courtyard behind the tavern.

Glancing around to where Antonio had been sitting, Ysabella saw William sitting there instead. She caught a brief glimpse of Antonio's green cloak swirling out the back door. Wondering, but with no time to ask, Ysabella put William back to work.

Amodeus took Ludovico by the arm to guide him out of the back room, and truthfully, to offer a little protection if Antonio was still in the main room. "Look, Ludovico, you must go home. You've had too much to drink, and so have some others. Nicolo gave you back the little medal. It's an odd thing, isn't it? Perhaps I should find you an escort to go with you a way. You've been in here a long time."

Ludovico twisted the medallion between his fingers and glared at the tavern owner. "Let go of me! I'm perfectly able to walk home by myself, thank you," he said grandly, at the same time swaying a bit and touching the edge of a nearby table for support. Amodeus hesitated a moment, but dropped the old man's arm and stalked off to his business in the bustling tavern.

Ysabella stood in the corner watching Ludovico as he staggered out the door.

"Amodeus," she said with a hint of reprimand in her voice, "maybe you should go with him. He is much drunker than he usually is, and he was so angry. Joanna would be so upset if she knew he left in such a condition. Please. He's an old man and my friend's husband, even if," she sighed, "he has become impossible lately."

"Let the old fool find his own way home. He'd deserve it if something happened to him. He's certainly tottered home drunk like this many times before. Don't you see how many people are here tonight? I can't just leave you alone."

"I just have a terrible feeling about this. It's not the same when the man is leaving your new place of business. Go after him, Amodeus. I don't want anything to happen to him. Besides, that ruckus sent some people home early. You don't want people to think we don't care what happens to our neighbors! Nicolo and I will be fine here for a few minutes. Besides, Raynaldus and Adam are here too. Please?"

Amodeus sighed. "Well, if you insist. I do have to think about the reputation of our place. I'll go after him." He reluctantly began to reach for his cloak from a peg by the kitchen door when a patron tugged on his shirt to ask a question about the fare. By the time he had heard the man out and gave instructions to settle the bill, he was at least ten minutes behind Ludovico.

"Raining," he muttered to himself as he stepped out into the street. "The things I do for love!" Raindrops slithered down his cheeks as he peered into the darkness looking for the old man, but he was nowhere to be seen. Amodeus pulled his hood around his face and strode quickly in the direction of Ludovico's home to finish his unwelcome duty.

Ludovico hardly noticed the rain as he stumbled down the street. "It's dark out, how long was I in there?" he mumbled to himself. The wall he was holding onto suddenly ended and he was grasping at nothing to keep himself erect. Tumbling over a rain barrel set out in the street, he clutched at the rim before he fell ignominiously on his face. Righting himself unsteadily, he assessed the damage. His head hurt, but no blood. His belly hurt – all that wine! Carefully balancing against the barrel, he pulled back the hem of his cloak and started to piss in the alley. He shivered involuntarily as his familiar demons of paranoia took over again. Was someone following him? He saw shadows all around him and started to shake. Someone was following him! He was sure this time!

Two men in leather jerkins left The Leopard blending in with a small group of neighborhood men just after Ludovico lurched out. They stood in the street a moment with the rain pelting down while the others scurried away toward home. A large hunk of a man and a shorter but fatter companion followed the drunken man, grinning at each other. An easy target, this one! Drunk as a lord! Push him in the gutter, hit him on the head, and take his purse, maybe even his boots. Easy as pie! Whispering, the larger man pushed his accomplice to the other side of the street to block any escape in that direction, and they both bore down on their target.

Ludovico twisted around, and seeing movement behind him, panicked. He was just about to run from the alley right into the arms of his pursuers when suddenly, an arm shot out behind him, pulling him over backward. He clutched wildly at the arm around his throat, gurgled, flailed his arms, and collapsed as a sharp blade pierced the artery in his neck. Perplexed more than anything, the thieves, approaching from behind, skidded to a stop and dropped quietly into the shadows. In the dim light from a nearby window they saw a form step over the body, give it a rough kick to be sure it didn't move, and melt into the blackness of the rain-soaked alley. The men signaled to each other, then crept up to the body cautiously, watching for any sign of movement. There was none. Blood blended with rain ran in rivulets down the cracks of the cobbled street and soaked into the dirt of the alley, hardly looking any darker than the mud around it. A long, utilitarian knife with a wooden handle lay on the cobbles. Unbelievably, the man's purse was still attached to his belt. The larger man picked up the knife and cut the purse strings while the shorter man briskly searched the corpse and pulled a mysterious package wrapped in a piece of linen out of an inside pocket.

"Halt! Thieves! Help! Help!" Amodeus ran forward, but it was too late. The thieves were already turning the corner in their escape. Amodeus reached the body and thudded down beside it, reflexively crossing himself in silent prayer. Ludovico wasn't breathing. Amodeus grabbed the old man's face and shook him hoping for any reaction, but Ludovico's body was too heavy and flopping to be alive. He reached for the man's neck to check for the pumping in the vein, but his fingers sank into a warm space that shouldn't have been there. Raindrops carelessly splattered into the fixed, open stare that looked up at him. Ludovico was dead.

At Amodeus's shouts in the street, doors and windows flew open. Torches were lit in the houses and shops. Figures ran into the dark and the rain. As Amodeus settled back in disbelief with Ludovico's head in his lap, the crowd gathered murmuring and questioning. He noticed a sharp pain biting into his lower leg and reached under himself to brush away the stone. Instead, he pulled out the knife that had been missing from The Leopard.

"Well," he thought dazedly, "I said that knife would turn up somewhere."

CHAPTER 10

Angelica put a steaming cup of tea before her sister-in-law and sat down facing her in the breakfast room of The Olive. "Ysabella, tell me everything that happened after I brought the pilgrims back last night. They were so frightened – like all of us." She reached across the table, stroking the distraught woman's trembling hand.

"Well, you remember when Amodeus brought Ludovico back?"

"Yes, I remember that," she answered quietly.

Amodeus and a silent group of neighbors had brought Ludovico's body to the tavern, followed by the night watchmen. As they stepped through the door, the noise and laughter jolted to a stop. Ysabella gasped and flung open the gaming room door, gesturing for the men to lay Ludovico's body on the table. Angelica had hurried to her side, steadying her, while Raynaldus settled the crowd and pushed them away from the door.

The initial silence burst into jabbering questions, and furious arguments. Who saw Ludovico leave? How long had he been gone? Who would want to kill him? No one could help staring at the trail of blood from the door to the gaming room. Amodeus came out of the gaming room and looked around the tavern. Friends, strangers and neighbors stared back at him, then began jostling and questioning him.

"Where did you find him?"

"Did you see anyone?"

Ysabella tenderly wound cloth around Ludovico's throat, tears shimmering down her cheeks as she thought of Joanna. Dear God, please take care of my friend, she thought. The city was dangerous after dark, especially when strangers and pilgrims crowded into town for religious days. But this was the neighborhood! How often had she run down the street to Joanna's or over to the baker's in the pre-dawn stillness or after supper? She shuddered. She wondered how to tell Joanna, who was still in the kitchen with Larissa, before the commotion made her come out to investigate. Trembling, she crept into the kitchen and closed the door.

The noise in the tavern began to subside as Amodeus held up his hand, asking for quiet. Men fell silent thinking that this could have been them. At any time thieves could lay in wait, especially for someone in his cups, and waylay them and rob them. True, people weren't usually killed, only robbed, but who knew how desperate these thieves were? Raynaldus stood partially in the shadow by the hearth, watching his brother intently.

Amodeus spoke. "One of the night watchmen has gone to the sheriff's to bring him here. I think that Ysabella is telling Joanna." A short scream from the kitchen proved the truth of his words. Sobbing and unintelligible soothing murmurs were heard. Heads bobbed all around in sympathy and some said short prayers for the dead man lying not too far away. While Ludovico was not well liked, his wife had always been a good neighbor and the crowd's sympathy now went out to her.

"How did he die, Amodeus?" someone from the back asked.

"He was stabbed," Amodeus growled. "With *my* kitchen knife, I think." A collective gasp sounded briefly. Men frowned at each other. Hit on the head with a club or cudgel was the usual thieving practice. With Amodeus's knife? Puzzled looks met Amodeus's eyes. He stopped for a moment, thought back to what he saw, then related it to his friends. He had seen two men bending over Ludovico's body, having just cut his purse, and he had shouted at them. He rushed to Ludovico's side and shouted again to wake the neighbors, who would perhaps chase after the thieves. But instead, they gathered in a hostile circle around him and summoned the authorities.

Amodeus's story finished, he walked back into the gaming room as the tavern patrons murmured over the details of his story. He carefully unwound Ysabella's cloth from the dead man's neck and stared at the wound. He felt a hand on his elbow and knew without turning that it was Raynaldus, staring at the body with him.

Amodeus gently replaced the cloth, came back into the main tavern. Some of his patrons had left, but most stayed, talking in low voices, waiting to see what the authorities would make of it. No doubt some were again pondering how fate could strike one unawares at any time. Amodeus put his arms around Ysabella and spoke to her gently as she came out of the kitchen. She nodded, dried her eyes. They were about to escort Joanna to see the body when the Angevin sheriff burst in and took Amodeus away.

....

"Oh, Angelica," Ysabella murmured, her eyes tearing. "Amodeus just went after Ludovico because he was drunk and I asked him to! I wish I never said anything! And the knife was from our tavern!" She thought back to last night's horror.

"Uncle Leo and I went to the jail this morning to take Amodeus breakfast. Uncle Leo spent some time talking with the jailers, but the sheriff refused to talk to him. They're Angevins. They don't care. They don't know Amodeus, and to them it's an open and shut case. They were even disrespectful to Uncle Leo and tried to push him out the door! It was only Raynaldus's bribes last night that prevented them from sending Amodeus somewhere worse!"

Angelica's eyes narrowed. She knew this because Raynaldus had come home, swearing and angry, and for the first time in their marriage, was unable to talk to her. Both of them were frightened and miserable. She had hoped Leo would be more successful, but apparently not.

"And," Ysabella faltered, "If they do the typical Angevin inquiry, it will be over quickly. They think they have their man and aren't interested in looking further." She wrung her hands and started sobbing.

Angelica, horrified, tried to comfort her. "We know Amodeus is innocent. Ysabella, we know that." She shook her sister-in-law's shoulders and then thought for a moment. "Stop crying! We have to help him! Ysabella, you're a smart woman and you know a lot of people. Together--you and me, Raynaldus, Uncle Leo, Adam-- we'll find out who killed old Ludovico! Listen to me!"

Ysabella stifled her sobs and clutched the cup in front of her. She raised her head and stared at Angelica. Her violet eyes were red from crying and her face was streaked with tears, but her mind began to fasten on her sister-in-law's words. Her eyes narrowed, and she hiccupped, swallowing hard as she stared hopefully across the table.

"Angelica, how can we do more than the sheriff?" she asked.

"Oh, please, Ysabella! Do they know the neighborhood? Do they know Ludovico or his business? Do they know his habits or whom he sells to in the Great Market? Do they know who lives nearby to talk to? And besides, people will talk to us! They won't open up to them. No, we have to do this ourselves because it sounds to me like they think they have the case solved. It's up to us to save Amodeus! Now, let's think what we need to do."

Ysabella, tears drying on her face, glared fiercely at Angelica. "You're right. No one will save Amodeus except us. What do we need to do?" And their heads, tawny and dark brown, bent together to plan.

··········

In a corner of the breakfast room of The Olive the pilgrims hunched around their own table, talking in low tones about last night's murder. They had only met Amodeus and Ysabella briefly in the excitement of opening night, but all of them had immediately liked the young couple and laughed at the antics of their young rascal, William. The women, glancing furtively over their shoulder to see where Angelica was, nodded knowingly at each other. See? This is what happened in the city on a regular basis. Perna, however, privately thought the dead man wouldn't be particularly missed. Hastily she crossed herself for the unchristian thought. Then she turned towards Sophia, stroking her hand. She was so far along! Not even a murder intimidated her though, as she chattered away in her usual tone. Renata did not appear to be listening.

One pilgrim in particular had been violently stunned, although his calm demeanor masked his inner turmoil. Pietro, newly arrived in Palermo, sat at The Leopard last night in shock, watching Ludovico Stefani stumble out the door. The last time Pietro saw him was the day his whole life had changed. That ill-fated crusading adventure to the Holy Land ended in disaster for all four of them. They had been so idealistic, so excited. They were going to save Jerusalem from the infidels that spring of 1244; instead they learned a great deal about human nature. He never thought he would see Ludovico or the other two again.

Pietro thought of that dusty, forsaken plain in the Holy Land. By rights, he should have died there, as so many others had. Too many were needlessly cut down by the swords of the Saracens, or even worse, the stupidity of Christian barons or by thieves or murderers professing to be Christian. At first he had not known how he arrived in the camp of Count John of Blois. The pain brought fleeting but horrifying pictures to his dreams. In the lingering days of his recovery, remarked as a miracle by some, he eventually sorted those pictures into a coherent story of events he now had no real desire to remember. A searing shame deep in his heart led him to say nothing about those events to his rescuers, a group of French knights. Let them imagine what they might.

Once he healed reasonably well, Pietro pledged himself to Count John's service in return for his rescue. Hoping to leave the piercing memory of his betrayal in the dust of Jerusalem, he willingly sailed for a distant land among men he did not know and whose hearts he initially could not read. It seemed at the time like sailing off the edge of the earth. The long journey to Blois in France allowed him to observe the man who saved his life. What he saw impressed him enough to offer his service and his sword to a man who was taciturn but fair in judgments and thoughtful in speech. Pietro was content in his choice, although the burden of how he was separated from his three companions was upon him, even then. To forget, he made himself indispensable to his new master, and eventually rose high enough to earn a commission, rewards, security, and occasionally, his lord's ear. Blois became his dwelling place, although never fully his home. He met Julianna there, and the years with her brought him the peace that most warriors only dreamed of. The thought of returning to her smile and warm hearth sustained him in battle, and eventually it was his only goal during the long marches and rough nights of military campaigning – at least until she was gone.

How strange it was. In the many hours traveling to Trapani, he thought about his deeply personal mission of penance and restitution. He had not envisioned this rather pitiful pilgrimage as his pretext for once again entering Palermo, but it allowed him a cover for his plans. But he had never been prepared to see Ludovico again. Especially since he once swore that if he ever did, he would kill him.

....

Raynaldus, Leo de Iannacio, and Adam de Citella were listening gravely to three men in another room of The Olive at the same time Angelica and Ysabella were planning their investigation. Raynaldus steadily watched the merchants' eyes as they told him their suspicions about Ludovico's latest deceits, which, they declared, had been going on for months. All were angry and bitter.

"Raynaldus, several times the Master of the Market has caught Ludovico with false weights. Occasionally, he sold Cyzican alum, the cheapest kind, as rock alum from Karahisan, which, as you yourself know, is the best. The cloth merchants are furious; everyone needs alum to fix the color infused into their cloth.

Ludovico's thievery made some of their cloth virtually worthless. And some of his 'exotic herbs' were nothing but oregano and basil, dressed up with some kind of minced myrtle leaves. And that's just what we caught him at. God only knows what else he's been up to!" said Iacobus Aldibrandini, the richest of the three merchants.

Raynaldus looked at Leo, who stared back impassively. His old friend and notary, Adam de Citella, recorded the distressed merchants' statements. Leo, Adam and Raynaldus had heard these complaints for months about Ludovico, and Raynaldus, as *Magister della Platea* and in charge of the commercial activities in the Great Market, had quietly been investigating the charges along with the Master of the Market.

"Gentlemen, you won't have to worry any more about Ludovico's questionable business practices. He was murdered last night after leaving my brother's tavern. We suspect thieves, but there may have been another motive."

The three merchants glanced at each other, registering varied degrees of relief and false sympathy on their faces.

"Raynaldus, I'm not sorry to see him go. He's been making us all look bad to the international traders and other island merchants with his dishonesty," said Angelo Confalano after a moment of silence. "We've all lost money and business because of him. And he's not a pleasant fellow to deal with either. Good riddance, I say."

Raynaldus looked intently at each of the merchants. "Can I assume, then," he said gratingly, "that none of you had anything to do with this?"

Leo and Adam, surprised by their friend's blunt question, turned watchfully to gauge the merchants' reactions.

"No, Raynaldus, we did nothing to Ludovico. He was a drunk and a dishonest man who probably got what he deserved. But do keep us informed," said Iacobus, smiling slightly. "After all, we can't have thieves running around killing merchants, can we?" With that, he stood and abruptly gesturing to the other two, stalked out of the room, leaving Raynaldus rubbing his nose and staring after them.

CHAPTER 11

As soon as the merchants left, Angelica swept into the room pulling Ysabella with her.

"Raynaldus," she began, "Ysabella and I have been talking. That sheriff isn't going to do anything to save Amodeus. He thinks he has his man!"

Raynaldus glared, still remembering how they were treated, and Leo and Adam both scowled. They sat down together, hands on the table, everyone tired, angry and anxious.

"Raynaldus," Angelica said firmly, "we must take matters into our own hands. We need to investigate what happened last night, or Amodeus will hang." Ysabella stifled a cry and pulled herself together, her face still wet with tears. She leaned across the table and asked each of the men, "Will you help us find out who killed Ludovico?"

Astonished, the men all began to talk at once. "We can't take justice into our own hands," said Adam decisively. "Let the authorities handle it. We know Amodeus didn't do it, and we can bring witnesses to the quarrel Ludovico had with Antonio. Mario can testify that the knife was missing from the tavern quite early in the evening. I think we should avoid antagonizing these Angevins or drawing too much attention to ourselves, especially with tensions running so high."

"But Adam, they don't care! They think my husband did it! He was found with the body, and the knife was underneath him! Why should they look any further? They didn't believe Amodeus when he told them about the two men bending over Ludovico even though his purse was stolen – gone, the purse strings cut! Obviously Amodeus didn't steal it. It wasn't on him, and he knew from the dice game that Ludovico had no money! As if he'd steal anyway! They're not even looking at the facts, Raynaldus! No, we have to do something or ... "

"Ysabella, this is no matter for a woman. And you're foolish to think so." Adam frowned.

"Wait, Adam," interjected Leo. "I thought about this all night and actually, this morning when we went to the jail, I could tell the authorities weren't planning to pursue this further." He looked around the table sternly, "I think Ysabella has a point. We need to figure out what happened and start talking to people – neighbors, friends, business acquaintance--to re-trace Ludovico's last days. We also need to find out from everyone who lived on the *Via Calderai*, the route that Ludovico took home, to see if they saw or heard anything. We know Amodeus didn't kill him, so it must have been someone who, well, he has enraged. Or," Leo paused for a moment, "even defrauded."

Everyone started arguing vehemently.

"Wait!" Raynaldus shouted. "Let's do this logically." The others stared at him. Unexpectedly, Raynaldus's eyes filled with tears. "He is, after all, my brother, Ysabella," he said softly, covering her hand with his. Ysabella nodded mutely, momentarily shaken by his unusual display of emotion. Leo nodded ans rose from the table. He began walking around the room, his mind racing with ideas, like a horse around a racetrack.

"First," he began, "we need someone like Raynaldus or Adam,"-- he turned to look at each of them briefly-- "to go to the sheriff's office and find out how much time we have before they hang or move Amodeus. He paused, putting a hand on Ysabella's shoulder for a moment, and continued walking more slowly. "Because Raynaldus has influence and Adam has been connected to the judiciary as official notary for many years, they should visit everyone who has any influence to bring some pressure on that sheriff." Everyone nodded. He found all four faces turned to him like flowers towards the sun.

Ysabella hesitated but spoke up firmly. She would normally look to the men to make decisions, but this concerned Amodeus's life. "Someone needs to send a message to Simon de Paruta to tell him about Ludovico's murder. That argument between Ludovico and Antonio last night was ugly. I'm sure Antonio wouldn't do murder, even though he is a sneaky thing, but he will need to be questioned. I don't know exactly when Antonio left, but maybe he knows something, and it would be a courtesy to Simon to relate the entire story, especially as it relates to his nephew."

Raynaldus stood up. "I think Ysabella's right. Adam," he turned to the old notary, "would you come with me now?"

Adam could only shake his head in wonder at this unlikely scheme. "I don't agree, Ysabella. I know how important it is – to all of us – but really, what can we do? If the sheriff is as sure as you say he is, no witness is going to change his mind. Many Angevins seek me out to write up their contracts, and I work at the court regularly. I'm not sure I can afford to be seen as directly opposing the authorities."

Ysabella sucked in her breath. Raynaldus, a restraining hand on her back, said, "I understand your position, Adam, but I think Ysabella's right. Your connections at court and among the officials could be valuable to us. We'll need to know what they're thinking and how soon they will feel forced to act. Adam, my friend," he turned to the old notary, "surely a few discreet inquiries would not mark you as a traitor. Would you at least come with me to see Simon de Paruta?"

The room was silent until Adam grudgingly agreed. "I can at least do that much, Raynaldus."

Returning to his usual brisk manner, Raynaldus turned back to his wife. "My dear, I must leave The Olive in your hands for now. And perhaps," he said thoughtfully, "I don't know, but do you think any of the pilgrims saw anything useful last night? I'm not

sure what, but it might be helpful to talk to them anyway."
Angelica rose, put her arms around his waist and her head against
his chest. He buried his face in her hair for a moment and then
gently kissed her forehead. With his eyes, he motioned Adam
towards the door. As they were leaving, Adam turned to Ysabella
to say they would return as soon as possible after talking with
Simon.

Ysabella was still shaken by Adam's outburst. She looked to Leo
and Angelica as if she would dissolve into tears again. Instead,
with some of her old decisiveness, she said, "Raynaldus has a
point. Let's make sure your pilgrims are fed and comfortable,
Angelica, and see what information we can get from them in the
process." Angelica nodded and led Ysabella to the kitchen to
gather breakfast for the pilgrims. Leo set off on his own mission to
see his cronies in the marketplace and to begin retracing
Ludovico's activities.

··········

Simon de Paruta was so weak most days that he could barely walk
from his office to this sunny spot in his garden, but today was one
of his better days. At least until he received word about
Ludovico's murder. Shaken, he called Venutus to bring wine. He
thought back to the last time he saw Ludovico, remembering how
angry he was at him, and remembering who else had commented
on Ludovico, as well. Had it only been yesterday?

Had he been able, Simon would have been pacing in utter
frustration when Ludovico arrived, late as usual. He was testy
with the old fool. "I am a busy man, Ludovico. I've called you
here on an important matter and you fritter away the time, as
always. I'm expecting another visitor soon, someone that I cannot
keep waiting as you have kept me."

Ludovico only stared at him grimly. He was in no mood to be
upbraided, and he, too, had better things to do than dance around
some self-important boor like Simon. He sat down sullenly, eating
a few grapes from a near-by plate.

Simon stared down impassively at his former friend, composing himself. "Ludovico," he began, sitting beside him, "How are you attending to business? I've heard rumors that you have been spending most of your time in the taverns and driving away your customers by your drunkenness. Is this true?"

Ludovico glared at him. "How I handle my affairs is none of your concern, Simon. I didn't come here to be scolded like a child." Simon was like everyone else. He professed to be a friend then stabbed him in the back on the slightest pretext. "Why did you call me here? Just to say that? Well, if that's all, I need to be going. As you say, I have business to attend to," he snapped.

Realizing he had made a mistake in being so abrupt, Simon softened his tone and said, "Forgive me, old friend. I should not have spoken so harshly. I haven't been well lately and even my nephews tell me I've been cranky." He smiled at Ludovico, who stared blankly back, no longer belligerent but not especially mollified.

"Ludovico, someone from the past has returned from the dead. Pietro Manfredi arrived in Palermo yesterday. My nephew was with him. Antonio saw the medallion--our medallion, The Eye of Horus. He arrived with a group of pilgrims from Trapani, one of whom, I believe, is his brother. His appearance may have grave consequences for us both."

Ludovico was stunned, unbelieving. Pietro! His head began pounding again. He stared at Simon, confounded. Simon told him Antonio's story about the old Crusader and the medallion affixed to his sword. As he spoke, they both felt the sand in their eyes, the heat of the desert, the despair and hunger on the long retreat from Jerusalem. Details came back unbidden that they both had tried to forget. They stared at each other bleakly, all differences momentarily forgotten.

"This person must be an impersonator. No, Simon, Pietro could not be alive. Who knows how many such medallions were sold by the Arabs back then? I can't believe it."

Simon spoke slowly. "I've considered all that, Ludovico. Believe me, I've thought of nothing else since Antonio described this little band of pilgrims to me. He described the Crusader in detail and I swear, it sounds like Pietro. Also, remember, he was from Trapani. This man answers to the same name. But you're absolutely right--we need to be sure. That's why I called you here. I need you to confirm that he is, in fact, our old acquaintance. Antonio could only get a few parts of his story. He has been fighting for some noble in France all these years. His wife died, his daughter is married, and he returned to live with his brother in Trapani. It sounds like Pietro. It's a plausible story. I don't know how he survived or how he got out of the Holy Land. He's not a Palermitano, so we probably wouldn't have heard if he survived.

Simon gripped Ludovico's arm. Ludovico winced. For a sick man, he was still strong. Or perhaps it was desperation. "Ludovico, he's staying at The Olive. You know the place, Raynaldus de Rogerio's hostel off the Ruga Marmora. We need to find out why he's here. Can't you visit the hostel to sell spices or something? You must get a good look at him, and then we'll know for sure."

Ludovico started laughing hysterically. "Simon, he'll know me, too! What should I say to him? Pietro, I'm so happy you're alive! We thought you died! No, I don't think this is a good plan at all. It's dangerous. For me. For you. It's crazy."

"Ludovico, if you cannot go into the place, just wait near the entrance and wait until he comes out. Get a good look at him. He's not the type to linger in the garden or over meals. He'll leave the hostel on some errand or other, and you can come directly here and report to me. Then we'll discuss what to do. And if he's not at the hostel, there's some woman in the group who chatters like a magpie. Maybe you can find out more about him from her."

Ludovico stared at him. "No, Simon. I'll be taking all the risks. You sit here, safe and sound in your palace!" He scowled, looking at the floor and then glaring at Simon.

Simon smiled and put his hand on Ludovico's knee. "Ludovico, I'll make it very worth your while. Although," he added, "this is something that benefits you as well. I am completely aware of the danger, yes, you're right, the danger of your mission. But only you or I can identify him, and I, well," he looked down at his legs, "I'm not very mobile these days." He tossed a bag on the table between them, watching Ludovico carefully.

Ludovico's eyes glittered at the thought of payment. He needed money desperately. Someone had to identify this man, but he fervently prayed it would not be Pietro. He didn't really understand how it could be. That made up his mind. How could it be him? He sat still for a few moments, turning things over in his mind. He didn't like Simon's plan, but he couldn't think of anything better. He took the purse.

The clatter of hooves in the courtyard startled both men. Venutus hurried to admit a tall, hawk-faced man dressed in black and gold. "Ah, I see you have a guest, Simon," he said smoothly. "I'll take a walk in your lovely garden …"

"No, no, Ferdinand. Our business is concluded, and Signor Stefani was just leaving. Ludovico is an old acquaintance and business partner. We often talk of shipping arrangements, the latest taxes Charles imposes upon us poor Sicilians, that kind of thing. Ludovico, may I present Ferdinand de Lerida from Barcelona."

Still flustered by their previous conversation, Ludovico muttered a greeting and nodded. Ferdinand nodded back coolly, noting the man's lack of composure. He could smell a vaguely sour stench of wine on him, and at this time of the morning!

"Simon. Lord," he added hastily because Ferdinand's cold black eyes made him very aware of his status, "I'll get back to you on the business we discussed."

"Yes, Ludovico, I would appreciate that," Simon inclined his head toward his servant to show the man out.

"Simon, how is your health?" asked Ferdinand pleasantly.

··········

Angelica and Ysabella hurried into the breakfast room bearing wine, fresh bread, and bowls of fruit. The pilgrims, quiet and talkative by turns, fell silent at their approach. But when Angelica and Ysabella, bravely smiling, sat down with them, they all began to talk about last night's events. They murmured expressions of support for Ysabella.

Talkative Sophia Pandolfo, hugely pregnant, was the first to comment. Turning to Ysabella she announced, "I only met your husband briefly, my dear, but I'm quite convinced he didn't do this horrible thing. How we can help? If you need someone to look after William, I would be most happy to do so." Ysabella smiled but gratefully demurred; Sophia had no idea what she would be in for!

Her palms down on the table, Ysabella surveyed the small group – Sophia, who had come to Palermo for Santa Rosalia to bless her with a boy child; Sophia's beautiful but sullen daughter, Renata; Carlos and Perna, and Carlos' taciturn brother, Pietro – who all looked back at her solemnly. "I appreciate your kindness, and I'd like to ask you all some questions about last night. Did you see anything that you think might be helpful?"

After a thoughtful silence, they all turned to Renata, Sophia asking her sharply, "Did you see anything when you went chasing after Antonio? How long were you with him?"

Antonio! Ysabella was taken aback. Was there something more than the argument that involved him? Ysabella leaned a little towards Pietro who frowned in silence. "Sir, did you see anything that might help us?"

Pietro stared into her violet eyes, remembering Julianna for a moment and sincerely wishing he could help her. He shook his head and then got up and walked out. He knew Amodeus didn't kill Ludovico, because he had slipped out of the door after the old drunk. But he couldn't tell Angelica or Ysabella that without betraying his own purpose. And he was sad about that.

CHAPTER 12

"Josef, listen." Ferdinand snapped his fingers to regain the man's attention while Josef watched the stevedores unloading wine and silks from one of Ferdinand's galleys in the harbor.

Josef sighed. The Catalan could certainly be condescending. If he didn't pay such a high commission and have goods of such high quality, he wouldn't bother with him; but the few extra coins he was able to pocket from the resale of those goods made him choose to put up with his arrogance. Josef inclined his head respectfully as Ferdinand went on.

"I've received some very interesting information about King Charles' ship in the Trapani harbor. I was just wondering…" Ferdinand turned to pace the stone wharf as he and Josef began discussing Trapani and King Charles' ships. Absorbed in their conversation, they did not notice Antonio de Paruta emerging from one of the run-down taverns after having visited one of Palermo's more interesting waterfront treasures, Fatima. He spotted Ferdinand and Josef strolling towards him, deep in conversation, and ducked back into the doorway.

"Ah, yes, Charles' ship," Antonio heard Josef saying to Ferdinand. "My nephew is one of the boat wrights building that warship. Yes, she's quite incredible, isn't she?"

Trapani. He had just seen the very ship and made a report to Uncle Simon. What did this arrogant merchant care about a warship in Trapani? Antonio edged closer as the men conveniently sat down on a bench in front of the tavern. Antonio's eyes widened in surprise as the conversation progressed. Why, all that information about the ship and the harbor – he had just given all that to Uncle Simon! Had Uncle Simon then relayed it to Ferdinand? Why? Why would he care?

Antonio frowned, puzzled, but soon gave up. He had other things to do today, but he was curious. Softly, he closed the tavern door and went out the side door. He didn't want Ferdinand to guess that he had been eavesdropping on his conversation. Ferdinand straightened up suddenly, hearing the door close. Ever alert, he quickly looked around and saw the back of a familiar figure stealing down the filthy alley. Simon's nephew, he concluded. What had that whelp heard? Did it matter?

The two men finished their conversation, stood and stretched. Ferdinand idly asked Josef about business. He didn't really care about the details. He just wanted to end their conversation on a pleasant note, having picked up some additional information on the warship. He needed to go somewhere and think. Josef's last comment, however, made his head jerk back. "Ludovico who?" he barked.

"Oh, I think you met him recently," Josef said, surprised at his sudden intensity. "Ludovico's an old business friend of mine from way back. Someone murdered him last night."
Ferdinand just huffed in disguse and said goodbye abruptly, leaving his business agent standing on the wharf. Josef, used to the man's brusqueness, thought nothing of it.

Ferdinand filed away the murder to think about at another time. He returned to the fondaco where he donned less flashy clothing. Antonio was the pressing issue of the moment. He needed to find him, watch him, and make up his mind about him. The boy could tie Ferdinand and Simon together. If he knew only about their commercial dealings, it wouldn't be a problem, but he may have heard more than he should about the warship and Charles' military intentions. Was he stable, or not? He didn't like what he saw today, Antonio skulking around. It looked as if he were spying on him.

Putting on a hat that hid his face, Ferdinand walked towards the *Cassaro* from the port, a healthy walk that gave him time to think. His concentration was so intense he barely noticed the cacophony of the marketplace: spice vendors, arguments over prices at the horse and sheep stalls, bargains trumpeted by hoarse-sounding cloth merchants, the dazzling jewelry displayed, the chisels and hammers of the tile makers, or even the distasteful smells wafting from the butchers and tanners. There were several loose ends he needed to tie up. He could see Simon wasn't going to last long, and he would need a replacement here in Palermo. Could that be Antonio? His informants had been contemptuous of the swaggering youth. To a man, they told Ferdinand of Antonio's brash personality, his gambling debts, his fondness for drink and whores and his chronic shortage of money. That might make a man desperate and willing to do anything, but no, he was too cocky, too shifty and sly. That one could never be trusted.

Ferdinand had briefly entertained hopes that Simon's associate, Ludovico, might be a suitable replacement, but that was before actually meeting him. A clear disappointment, obviously a drunk and unreliable, he thought angrily. And now it seems, suddenly unavailable. He smiled to himself and strode off towards the *Cassaro* to Simon's house. Who could he get to replace Simon?

"You! Where's your master!" Ferdinand arrogantly spoke to Venutus.

Venutus hardly recognized this man in ragged clothing, but his demanding tone and steely eyes quickly identified him. Angrily, Venutus lowered his eyes as he responded. "Lord, he's in the garden."

"Well, fetch us some wine," grunted Ferdinand.

Bowing only enough for propriety's sake, Venutus waved him towards the garden and turned away. Simon looked up at the intruder, mildly annoyed. He was so volatile, this Ferdinand. What now? Venutus quietly reappeared with wine, cheese and olives that he placed carefully on a small inlaid table.

Ferdinand sat down, looking at Simon. Simon stared steadily back. "Well, what is it?" he asked. "Nice clothes, by the way."

Ferdinand scowled. "I wanted to discuss your nephew, Antonio. I think he has been following me. I caught him spying on me at the harbor but he scurried away before I could confront him. Any idea what he is up to?"

Simon raised one eyebrow and scowled. "I have no idea. Why would he do that? Antonio has no interest in business and is a constant disappointment to me. Perhaps you were mistaken."

"No. That green cloak of his can be seen a mile away. And, by the way, I saw someone sneaking after Antonio, too. It appears he has a follower of his own. Unpaid creditor, perhaps?" The Catalan smirked.

"Who would follow Antonio? It's preposterous."

"How would I know what goes on in Palermo? But your boy must have enemies. I don't want any interference, Simon. Do you know everything your nephew is up to?"

Simon sat very still. That fool, Antonio--toying with Ferdinand. What an idiot! Was Antonio really too stupid to realize how dangerous this man was? He looked placidly back at Ferdinand. "I don't have the foggiest idea, Ferdinand. As if I would know every footpad in Palermo."

He knew the old man was lying. As his black eyes bored into Simon's, Ferdinand merely waited to see if intimidation would make him squirm. Simon remained aloof, chose some olives and sipped his watered wine. He looked directly at Ferdinand. "Well, Ferdinand, I can tell you were unhappy with Ludovico as an associate of ours. You, um, didn't trust him. Did you know that our friend was murdered last night?"

Ferdinand smiled. "Yes, I heard of it from Josef the Jew. What a pity."

"You didn't have anything to do with that, did you?" Simon asked in a falsely casual tone, his heart racing. He felt sure Ferdinand was involved somehow in Ludovico's death. Just the contempt shown by the Catalan toward the man at their recent meeting made him suspicious.

"Really, Simon. What you don't know won't hurt you," Ferdinand quipped. "But Antonio is very much alive, and he may be a threat to us. He's a little sneak, you know, and I think he knows more than he should. Is he truly any risk?"

Simon stared at the Catalan who suddenly seemed even more sinister than usual in the soft Sicilian sunlight. Antonio was proving to be a problem. Lately Simon had wondered how much his nephew had seen and heard, and once Simon actually caught him looking through his papers, as if he'd be dim-witted enough to leave anything important lying around.

"In truth, Ferdinand, I've never cared for the lad. He's devious and likes to talk, a braggart really. Trustworthy? Not at all. I think he listens at keyholes, but I doubt his ability to put anything he may have heard to use. But," and he raised his eyes to heaven, "he's my sister's son. What can I do?"

"Well, Simon," Ferdinand said gravely. "These things have a way of working out."

·········

Angelica and Ysabella sat quietly in the breakfast room after everyone else left. "What do we have?" Angelica asked briskly.

"Pretty much nothing," Ysabella answered, "but remember Amodeus saw two men bending over Ludovico, and Ludovico's purse was missing. Anyone at The Leopard last night knew about the fight between Antonio and Ludovico and that Ludovico had no money, so why would Amodeus intend to rob him? It doesn't make sense. And where is the purse? It wasn't on Amodeus. See, Angelica, the magistrate is not thinking logically."

"We do have something that might be helpful. Carlo mentioned seeing you serve two men last night at a corner table. He noticed they kept to themselves, but when the tanners left right after Ludovico staggered out the door, they got up, too, trying to blend in, but he's pretty sure they didn't look like tanners. Do you remember anything about them? Can you even describe them?"

Ysabella pictured the table and the two rough men sitting there. They were just like so many who were there last night, drinking, talking. But, no...they weren't talking. They weren't even doing much drinking. They were watching everyone else. "I don't remember much about them. They looked like a lot of the other men who stopped in after work to have a drink and relax. One was tall and the other shorter and portly. Their boots looked old and worn. Why would they by important?"

"I don't know. It was just something Carlo noticed. We'll have to think about that later."

Ysabella shook her head and smiled sadly at her sister-in-law. "I'm so tired right now, I really can't focus on puzzles. Maybe I'd better get some rest."

Both women turned as they heard a discreet cough behind them. Sophia Pandolfo waddled slowly towards them, her pregnancy clearly slowing her down. She sat down again and looked directly at Ysabella. "There is something else I saw," she said hesitantly, "but I didn't want to mention it in front of the others."

Ysabella's fatigue was immediately forgotten as they turned questioning faces to the woman.

"After the drunken man staggered through the room and went out... Ludovico, did you say? Well, Carlo's brother had been sitting next to me. He made a strange noise in his throat when he saw the man, so I looked at him. He was pale as a sheet, and he was staring at the door. Then he just got up and left. That's all I know. He didn't say a word to anyone, but of course, people were so excited by the commotion and talking about Antonio and his behavior, I don't think anyone else noticed."

She looked at the women and said quietly, "He's Carlo's brother. They've just been reunited. He is a sweet man, quiet. Perna is my best friend. I just didn't want to say anything in front of them. You understand?" She rose awkwardly from the bench and left the room.

"I thought his face looked strange this morning," Ysabella said. "So he followed Ludovico outside. Why didn't he tell us that when we asked?"

Angelica could not explain.

Ysabella jumped up with renewed energy. "Well, I'll think about this at The Leopard. I'm determined to keep it open, even without Amodeus around. Why not? I'm not going to let people think we have something to hide! I might hear something useful from our friends and customers. And well," Ysabella bit her lip, "if I don't have something to do, I'll go crazy. I have Larissa and Mario and two slaves. William is young, but he can help, too."

Knowing Ysabella, Angelica was not really surprised at this announcement. "I'll send Nicolo over to you as soon as Raynaldus and Adam return. I have plenty of help here, and he likes to help you. Later we'll sit down and decide what to do next. Do get some sleep, if you can."

Ysabella smiled and left. Angelica was like a big sister – bossy, protective, but comforting, too.

She walked slowly back to The Leopard, mulling over the few facts they had and thinking the day couldn't possibly get worse.

She was wrong. Larissa met her anxiously at the door. "Ysabella," she began hesitantly, looking down at the floor.

"Yes," Ysabella snapped at her friend but then sat down abruptly. "I'm sorry, Larissa, what a day this has already been. What is wrong?" she said more gently.

Larissa still looked at her feet. "It's Signora Joanna. She asked me to tell you that she won't be back here for awhile. She, well," the cook trailed off uncertainly, "she asked that you please don't come to her house."

Ysabella stared at her, eyes wide, her mouth dropping open. "Oh, Larissa, she can't possibly think Amodeus had anything to do with Ludovico's death! She knows Amodeus better than that! She knows I sent him after her husband because he was so drunk I thought he'd fall over and pass out!"

"Mistress, she's probably in shock, not thinking clearly. When she settles down, she'll see the light. She's a very levelheaded woman, after all. Don't worry. We know the master didn't do it, and she knows it too. She's just upset."

Ysabella thanked Larissa dully, thoughts whirling like squirrels in a cage. Her dear friend, Joanna, someone she thought she could lean on, but well, what did she expect? It looked so horribly obvious. Anyone might think Amodeus had killed her best friend's husband.

. . . .

A small noise made Simon look up; it was only his faithful Venutus, who asked if he needed anything.

"Venutus," Simon began carefully, "when Ferdinand de Lerida was here …" His voice trailed off.

"Yes, a most unpleasant man, if you will permit me to say so," answered Venutus.

"You and I have no secrets from each other, Venutus," Simon growled, "and yes, he's unpleasant and dangerous. We know he's Aragon's assassin."

More softly, he whispered, "And we've always kept an eye on him when he's in Palermo, haven't we?"

"Yes, master."

"Find out where he was last night."

Venutus inclined his head in acknowledgement. "Do you think it was he who killed the old merchant, master?"

"I don't know. I know he took an immediate dislike to Ludovico. He didn't like us using him as an informant because of his drinking, too unstable he said, and I agreed. But who would want to kill him? He really knew very little, as I assured de Lerida. I don't like this. We need to know what happened." Abruptly he asked, "What do you think, Venutus? Did Ferdinand kill Ludovico?"

"I think it's very possible, master. That man is no stranger to murder."

CHAPTER 13

Raynaldus and Angelica arrived at The Leopard in a flurry with Nicolo. Larissa and Mario waited on customers who drifted into the main room of the tavern. He immediately helped them serve a group of hungry pilgrims chattering in amazed voices at the relics of the nearby churches of St. Francis and Santa Maria dell'Ammiraglio including body parts of saints and, as one dumbfounded devotee stuttered, a piece of Mary's cape.

Ysabella barely heard the conversations as she served drinks to some thirsty merchants, her smiles less brilliant, her manner more subdued, exposing her inner anxiety. She herself had been at Mass at dawn this morning, praying earnestly to the Virgin for her help. As she glanced over at the table of satisfied seekers still discussing their *peregrinage* of churches, she couldn't help but wonder if the Virgin had listened to them more than her. Sighing, she finished with her customers, wondering how Amodeus was sleeping. She stifled the sudden upswelling of emotions and doggedly began wiping down the tables.

In a private room at the back, Raynaldus and Angelica joined Leo and Adam, talking quietly and waiting until Ysabella could spare a minute. She crept in, fell into a chair and asked tiredly, "Well, what have we learned?"

Raynaldus coughed a little, but Leo spoke first.

"Raynaldus and I went to see the sheriff to find out how much time we have to find Ludovico's killer. The sheriff was rude, but one of our friends must have gotten to him because he promised to hold Amodeus locally until the *iudice* will meet in a court session one week from tomorrow. We have no more time than that.

"Of course," he added hastily, "that doesn't mean they would find Amodeus guilty when they hear the case. After all, they are our local judiciary. But we can't be sure of that, especially with the sheriff testifying." He paused to gauge their faces and continued.

"Now," he beamed, "I have some good news! Ysabella was right in sending us to the market. William and I," and everyone smiled, "found out something very interesting today. I happened to spend some time talking with Josef the Jew. Josef told me that the day before Ludovico was murdered he met him coming out of Simon de Paruta's house. Ludovico seemed distressed, but kept the conversation on inconsequential subjects. Ludovico showed Josef a beautiful ivory comb inlaid with tortoiseshell he had bought for Joanna. Ysabella, do you know if Joanna got her gift before the opening? Did she say anything about it?"

"No, she didn't wear it or mention it that evening."

"Then Ludovico must have still had it on him when he died. Today Josef sent me to the shop where Ludovico bought it, so I have a detailed description. That comb was found today in the Great Market in the stall of…let's say…an old acquaintance. In exchange for a small sum of money and the promise of no nosy magistrates, he readily told me everything he could."

He smiled a rather self-satisfied smile as all eyes were now fastened on him, Ysabella in particular staring intently. He continued. "The merchant bought the comb from a whore whom he sees around the market on occasion. He thinks she lives near the port but can't really say where. He has no idea what her name is, but he describes her as fairly young, maybe 20, with brown hair and brown eyes, like a thousand other women in Sicily. But he did say one thing that might help us find her. She has a small limp. He paid her only a pittance of what the comb was worth and she disappeared. We need to find that woman."

Ysabella spoke up excitedly. "But Amodeus didn't see a woman that night; he saw two men. She must have gotten it from one of the thieves! Was she alone when she sold it, Leo?"

"Yes, unfortunately. No one, man or woman, was with her, according to my informant," Leo said regretfully.

"All right," said Ysabella. "That's definitely progress. What else do we have?" Angelica nodded to Raynaldus, who quickly summarized what he had found out about Simon and Ludovico and his interview with Antonio, and finished with Sophia's information regarding Pietro. The group was surprised to learn that Pietro had a medallion with an odd inscription that seemed to match Ludovico's. "I tried to find Pietro Manfredi later on this afternoon," said Raynaldus, "to ask him to explain these things, but he never returned to The Olive. I'm sure he'll come back tonight some time, and then we'll sit him down and get some information from him. What is it, Leo?" he said frowning.

Leo wrinkled his forehead and turned to Adam. "Do you remember, Adam, when Ludovico returned from the Holy Land?"

Ysabella and Angelica gasped; Raynaldus let out a short laugh. "Ludovico? In the Holy Land? Doing what? Selling spices?!" Chuckles erupted around the room, even Larissa, clearing the table, could not help but smile.

Adam spoke up. "Ludovico, when he was very young, went to fight for Jerusalem as a Crusader. And as Leo has reminded me, he went with another young man, Simon de Paruta. When they left, of course, they were just two young men who went off on Crusade, not the successful merchants we know today. I had totally forgotten about that until now. When they came back... yes, I remember when they returned. I think it was in 1244 or 1245. I remember because it was the year I had to re-apply for my notary's license. They were both changed men, I can tell you that. I had forgotten about that until tonight."

Raynaldus was so surprised he was silent. Leo had taken Ysabella's hand, who sat stunned by the information. She had known her friend Joanna for years, and she had never said anything like that about Ludovico! So, what did this mean?

Raynaldus cleared his throat and put his hands on the table. "So, now we have Pietro Manfredi, who admitted he was in the Holy Land and who has this medallion on his sword hilt. Then Ludovico comes up with the same medallion. This was confirmed today by Antonio when Leo and I interviewed him at Simon's."

He looked at Leo. "Did they all go together to the Holy Land – Pietro Manfredi, Ludovico and Simon?"

Leo shrugged, glancing toward Adam for an answer.

Adam thought a moment. "I don't know, Raynaldus, I don't remember three of them, I just remember Simon and Ludovico left. I didn't know them that well, but I remember distinctly when they returned because they both had money and immediately set themselves up in trade. Simon favored silk and the higher end of the cloth trade. Ludovico was a spice merchant. That's why I remember when they came back. I myself was just starting out then and they gave me some business writing up contracts."

Leo sat at the table silently. Was now the time to mention what he knew about Ludovico in his youth--how he had been in love with the mother of Amodeus and Raynaldus, and apparently, as he recalled, that affection had been returned? Right now, that didn't seem too relevant. He decided to keep that information to himself. And wasn't there someone else who had left with Ludovico and Simon? Someone who wasn't Pietro Manfredi, but someone whom he couldn't quite remember either. It was so long ago.

In the meantime, Ysabella began talking excitedly. "So we know that Ludovico and Simon de Paruta went crusading together. Perhaps they met Pietro Manfredi somewhere in the Holy Land. Somehow they're all connected, but why that would have anything to do with Ludovico's murder?" She looked around, but everyone seemed as mystified as she was.

"So that means that our best lead is to find the whore, right?" Angelica agreed softly and the men all rumbled their assent. "Well, that's something to do for tomorrow, then."

The men glanced at each other surreptitiously. Ysabella clearly had no idea how difficult that would be – there were hundreds of whores just at the port alone.

She jumped up, re-energized by the information and by forming a plan. "I need to get back to the tavern. I think Nicolo and Larissa and Mario and I can handle the business tonight. Some of the neighbors aren't coming back. I think they're a little frightened by what happened, but there are plenty of pilgrims and others out there that are hungry and thirsty. I'm keeping The Leopard open and it will be successful, too!" She tossed her head resolutely, smiling at her extended family, and walked back into the main room.

As the door opened, the chatter and clatter told the family that, at least for tonight, Ysabella and The Leopard would definitely be busy. Thoughtfully, they all made their separate ways home, reminding each other that they would all meet tomorrow at the church of St. Margaret's for Ludovico's funeral.

By the end of the evening, Ysabella was exhausted. Mario was cleaning the tavern as she and Larissa washed the dishes, cups and bowls heaped up in the kitchen around them. Nicolo had gone home an hour ago. It had been another successful night at The Leopard, but Ysabella and Larissa both noticed that most of the customers had been strangers. Where were their friends and neighbors?

"Larissa, do you think people are frightened to come here because of what happened to Ludovico?" fretted Ysabella. She turned to her servant who had lived in the neighborhood all her life.

"Perhaps, mistress. Don't worry, they'll come around soon. There isn't a more comfortable tavern in the neighborhood, and besides, they'll all be curious about what's happening. I'll put the word out tomorrow, and believe me, we'll have faces we know in here tomorrow night! How was the master tonight?"

Ysabella and Raynaldus had taken Amodeus his dinner earlier in the evening. Raynaldus visited him every day. When Ysabella had asked to accompany him on his daily visits, he refused, saying that a jail was no place for a woman. But tonight she had persuaded him. Despite her irritation, Ysabella was touched by his devotion, seeing a side of him that she hadn't appreciated properly. Because he was there, she had remained fairly quiet during the visit, but at one point, she asked Amodeus again why he disliked Ludovico so much. The answer was a stony silence. Angry, her anxiety mounting, she decided to return to the tavern, leaving Raynaldus to talk with his brother.

As she was leaving, she paused at the cell doorway. "My love, I have never badgered you about that before, but, you know, your life may depend upon telling us. At your trial they will ask you because it's common knowledge. What will you say to them then that you won't say to us now?" Amodeus's eyes widened, but he remained silent. Ysabella swirled out the door, leaving the two men staring at her skirts brushing the ground. She ran back to The Leopard, heading straight for the kitchen.

Mario put his head in the door. "We'll need to check the storeroom tomorrow in the daylight and take inventory. We'll probably need to restock."

Larissa nodded and turned to Ysabella. "We'd best plan to go to the market tomorrow, and Mario and William will need to fetch wood. I think some chickens, and perhaps a piglet. And what about dropping off our grain to the miller's as well? He can grind it while we're at the market, and we can pick it up on our way back so we can bake our bread and pastries."

Ysabella nodded as she slowly took off her apron. She walked out to the main room of the tavern, now swept clean of food bits, dirt and debris. Mario was just ending his last job – washing the tile floor with fragrant lemon water. Ysabella patted his arm and told him to take his wife home. Larissa came out of the kitchen, surveyed the tavern with a skeptical eye, wiped off the counter for the last time, and hugged Ysabella. They left to go home, two doors away. Ysabella shut the door behind them, locking it and pushing the long wooden board across it. She dragged herself upstairs to look in on William, who had thrown himself onto his bed hours ago, exhausted by his day in the market and all the excitement. He was sound asleep, still dressed, his arms wrapped around a pillow. Ysabella tenderly drew a blanket over him, ran her fingers through his hair, and kissed him goodnight. He never stirred. In her own room, she absently picked up clothes and hairpins, shifts and stockings strewn around.

She sat down on the bed, thinking about Amodeus. "I will not cry," she told herself fiercely. "My god, I do miss him." She undressed and crawled under the covers, but tossed and turned, thinking about her husband. Finally, she got up, went into William's room, and curled around him, savoring his warmth. She fell asleep as quickly as her son had.

It was a bright, sunny morning, not at all suitable for a funeral, thought Ysabella. Larissa and Mario were waiting patiently for her outside but she still dawdled, dreading to see Joanna. Had she lost one of the few close friends she had? Today would be the day to find that out, she supposed. She pinned her silk scarf over her head, subduing her golden-brown tresses underneath. William was overjoyed to be with Nicolo, who had solemnly asked him if he would help bring back supplies for his mother's tavern. Equally grave, William nodded and the two left to commandeer more wine, ale, cheese and meats. The boy missed his father so much that Ysabella thought it would be better if he didn't attend the funeral, despite Angelica's advice. The three walked quickly to the parish church of St. Margaret's.

St. Margaret's was in the parish of the *Conciaria,* the tanning district where both Ysabella and the de Rogerios had grown up.

Magistrates and civil authorities often met in its cavernous apse, as well as the district's men to vote on local issues such as maintaining the night watch, garbage and manure pickup, and water issues. Ysabella loved the old church. Here she had met Joanna when she was just a teenager. The older woman had taken the motherless girl under her wing, showed her how to properly bake bread, sew a straight seam, how to make proper herbal infusions for aches and pains, and the thousand other things that girls' mothers do. So while Ysabella's father taught her enough letters and arithmetic to help in his tanning shop, Joanna had become almost a surrogate mother. As Ysabella grew older, that relationship subtly changed into friendship, something Ysabella fervently prayed would not end.

The three stepped into the gloomy expanse of the dim church, knelt and crossed themselves, then proceeded up the aisle. Raynaldus and Angelica, Adam and Leo, and several of Ludovico's acquaintances were already seated. The pilgrims from The Olive tactfully sat a few rows back. Joanna sat next to Angelica, silent and upright. Ysabella, Larissa and Mario slid behind them and just for a moment, Ysabella gently put her hand on Joanna's shoulder. She felt the older woman stiffen, but her fingertips lightly grazed Ysabella's. Ysabella closed her eyes and said a prayer of thanks knowing there was forgiveness in that touch.

After several moments of silence, the parish priest appeared. Everyone bowed their heads to begin the prayers, but an odd squeak suddenly echoed in the vast chamber. The priest gasped and fell silent. The parishioners looked up, surprised to see the Archbishop of Palermo striding through the sacristy door in full regalia. He stopped before the parish priest. Father Barzini knelt to kiss his ring, and as the astonished audience watched, the Archbishop bent down to whisper in his ear. The priest's eyes widened, but he nodded shakily and stepped aside. The Archbishop of Palermo began to preside over Ludovico Stefani's funeral mass. He performed it swiftly but gracefully, and then, with a swirl of his robes and a nod to the widow, he was gone.

The crowd sat for a moment, stunned, and then everyone began talking in low, excited ripples. Raynaldus leaned over Angelica and stared at Joanna, whose surprised eyes were enough to tell him she was just as amazed as everyone else. When Ysabella sat down next to Joanna, Raynaldus stood to look around at the congregation. Pietro Manfredi with the pilgrims in back was staring straight ahead. When Raynaldus touched his arm, he flinched and turned unseeing eyes in his direction. Clearly he had been lost in thought. Bending over the old crusader, Raynaldus whispered something to him, and they walked together out the cathedral doors.

CHAPTER 14

Ysabella, Angelica and Joanna sat inside the church with their arms around each other, alternately laughing and crying.

"I knew Amodeus didn't kill Ludovico, Ysabella, I knew it. I was just so confused, and it happened so suddenly, and …," Joanna held onto Ysabella tightly, imploring, and whispered, "I hope you can forgive me."

Ysabella, her eyes shiny with tears, just nodded and hugged her. Angelica was also smiling and crying at the same time. The three women walked out into the sunshine together, absorbed in their reconciliation, never noticing the two men intensely locked into a battle of wills under the church portico.

Raynaldus's eyes were steely as he patiently, but with escalating hardness, asked his questions. Pietro, given his decades of fighting, did not wilt immediately under the man's anger. Calmly he explained to Raynaldus that he had simply gone out for air that night and did not follow Ludovico. Yes, what a coincidence that their medallions were the same. Really, though, trinkets were sold all over the Holy Land. Well, if Raynaldus had been there, he would know that. No, he had gone the opposite way from Ludovico and hadn't seen a thing.

Frustrated, Raynaldus nodded curtly and joined Leo and Adam, tersely repeating the conversation. The three men looked speculatively at Pietro, who merely spun on his heel and walked away. After a brief conversation, Raynaldus and Adam marched firmly down the street, heading for Simon de Paruta's house.

Leo watched them walk away and then approached the three reconciled women to ask if they needed an escort home. Angelica graciously accepted his offer. Joanna intended to stay with her at The Olive for several days. Ysabella, relishing the relief she felt, rejoined Larissa and Mario to make their way to The Leopard.

"Santa Maria," said Larissa, crossing herself fervently. "I never thought I'd see His Eminence doing something for old Ludovico. What in the world was that about?" Mario was just as bewildered, but rather than discuss it with women, deposited them at the door of The Leopard, and headed off to the Great Market to bring back supplies.

Ysabella fetched two cups from the kitchen shelf, grabbed a small *botti* of wine, and sat with Larissa under the shade of the lemon trees in the courtyard. Larissa was still babbling on about the Archbishop. Ysabella, frowning, wondered why such an important man would do such a service for a person such as Ludovico. She idly traced patterns with her toe in the dust and shook her hair free of its silk scarf. That reminded her of Joanna's comb. Suddenly clutching Larissa's arm, which momentarily silenced the woman, Ysabella said excitedly, "Larissa, we need to find that whore. Now."

Larissa could only stare at her in shock. "Mistress, do you know how dangerous it is to go to the port? Why, that's a job for the men. Are you crazy? It's no place for a decent woman, I can tell you that!"

"And jail is no place for a decent and innocent man, Larissa, I can tell you that!" hissed Ysabella. Larissa rolled her eyes and edged away from Ysabella, who only smiled brightly and coaxed her closer.

Larissa narrowed her eyes as she listened to a plan that, in her mind, was totally insane. Dangerous. Ridiculous. "No, mistress, if you want to find that woman, you need to tell the men."

"Really, Larissa," Ysabella pleaded, "In her position, would you talk to a bunch of men who were trying to bully you into answering questions? Of course not...would you?!" Larissa shook her head warily but remained unconvinced that she and Ysabella should go down to the port.

"You know what happens to women walking around by themselves," she glared. "And no decent woman does! What can you be thinking? It's too dangerous."

A sly look came over Ysabella's face. "You don't think I haven't thought about that, do you? I know it's dangerous, but think, Larissa! If she thinks we're, well, sort of like her, wouldn't she be more liable to talk to us than to someone like Raynaldus or Leo? Can you imagine opening up to those two?" Even with the seriousness of the conversation, they both giggled at the thought. "Larissa, she'll talk to us. She'll talk to me if she knows my husband's life is at stake! Please, let's try this. The men would only frighten her!"

Ysabella hesitated before continuing. "And of course, we will go prepared." Slowly out of her boot she drew a wicked looking blade, small, but sharp. "I'm not a tanner's daughter for nothing, Larissa. I know how to use this."

Larissa's eyes were as big as bowls, but after a moment, she pulled her own knife from a hidden pocket. "Yes, every woman who has to go out to draw water, go to church or to the market, knows how to use a knife; we don't often have escorts like rich women have."

Ysabella stared at her and burst out laughing. Larissa frowned. "I still don't think going to the port is a good idea, mistress. But if you're determined, well, I won't let you go alone. I think you're right about her not talking to the men, but," and her eyes clouded, "how would we find her?"

"We'll just ask!" Ysabella said blithely. She's young and has a limp. Surely most whores don't limp! Come on. Let's do this in broad daylight; it has to be safer than at any other time. And we need go before Mario or anyone else gets back and tries to stop us."

Ysabella ran upstairs, flinging clothes aside until she found what she wanted – two stained smocks and old kerchiefs -- which she brought down into the garden. The two of them smoothed down their old clothes as Larissa continued to grumble. With a final nod of resolution, the two women slid their knives back into their boots, tossed back their wine, and walked arm in arm out of the garden towards the port.

....

Raynaldus stalked over to Simon de Paruta's house, his mind whirling with the Archbishop's surprise appearance and Pietro's smooth but definite elusiveness. He stopped outside of Simon's *palazzo* to think about what he would ask. He stepped through the gates and knocked on the ornate doors. Venutus answered immediately and smoothly asked him in, hiding his surprise at the man's second visit. Was this official business, magistrate? Raynaldus, already irritable, snapped "It is a murder investigation. Is that official enough?"

Raising an eyebrow, Venutus disappeared down the hall to announce him. After the steward knocked discreetly on Simon's office door and entered, Raynaldus could hear raised voices that became abruptly silent. A few minutes later, Ferdinand de Lerida smoothly swept past Raynaldus on his way out. Venutus ushered Raynaldus into the old man's chamber. As Simon greeted him, Raynaldus asked bluntly, "Who was that man who just left, Simon?"

Simon anwered shortly, "A Catalan merchant I trade with. His name is Ferdinand de Lerida. Do you know him?"

"No. He is a stranger to me. Simon, I'd like to know about your long association with Ludovico Stefani." Raynaldus seated himself without being asked, and looked directly at his host. "Especially about your adventures in the Holy Land."

Simon caught his breath but maintained a calm façade. He had expected this at some point. Ludovico's heavy drinking almost guaranteed something like this. Playing for time, Simon idly drummed his fingers on his desk and asked Raynaldus innocently, "What makes you curious about that, Raynaldus? I thought perhaps you'd come about Antonio."

"Ah, yes, your nephew. We'll get to him later. There seems to be a little problem with his alibi."

Simon glowered at the magistrate. "A problem? Some little slut who thinks she can get money from him? You must be joking, Raynaldus."

Raynaldus smiled coldly. "Well, the problem seems to be Antonio's, Simon. The girl admitted they spoke, but very briefly, not to mention very rudely on your nephew's behalf, I think, and," he looked casually at his fingernails, pausing a moment, "there seems to have been plenty of time for Antonio to have run after Ludovico. After all, he was drunk and old. Who saw your nephew after this girl did?"

Simon clenched his jaw. "I don't know what you're up to, but I can guarantee you that my nephew did not kill that old fool. You'd better reconsider if you think I'm giving him up without a fight!"

Raynaldus waved his hand in the air, dismissing the subject, and leaned forward in his chair. "Let's talk about your crusading days, shall we?" He glanced at Venutus, still arranging wine and fruits at a side table, and paused deliberately. Venutus felt the eyes on him and slid quietly from the room. As he opened the door, he came face to face with Antonio leaning casually against the doorjamb. They stared at each other for a moment, and Antonio backed away. Venutus closed the door staring at the youth's retreating form.

Antonio was disgusted at being forced to stay at home. Renata's story to Angelica had made it seem like he was the killer! He wanted to throttle her. Maybe he should pay her a little visit. No, not a good idea; she was clearly angry with him. He had acted a little hastily. Perhaps he needed a go-between, an intermediary who could calm her down and talk to her. He stalked over to the stables and ordered the groom to saddle his horse. He'd go to The Olive and coax Nicolo into talking to Renata. Nicolo's obvious interest in her flagged when Antonio bragged about his exploits with her, but Nicolo would help him--he always did. Nicolo's charm could get Renata to change her story. The groom brought the horse and Antonio leaped into the saddle and peppered the man with dirt from his horse's hooves.

As Antonio thudded into the courtyard of The Olive, he could see that it was quiet. Perhaps Nicolo was gone and he could talk to Renata himself. He walked into the hostel to find Angelica and Joanna drying herbs underneath the open window.

"Before you even ask, Antonio, Nicolo is not here. I think he went to the Great Market." Cockily saluting the women, he turned his horse around and cantered down the Via Marmora towards the gate leading into the Porta Patitellorum. Antonio pondered the tidbits of information he had gathered. The Archbishop had appeared mysteriously and said the funeral mass at Ludovico's funeral! And Mateo said he had a ring made of the same medallion as Ludovico's. What connected these men? And how did they connect to his uncle, who had been in the Holy Land with Ludovico! Ludovico Stefani and his Uncle Simon – crusaders! That had actually stunned him! He would never have thought it possible! So his uncle must have had a relationship with Ludovico beyond the business one. Was that important?

His thoughts were interrupted when he spotted his friend as he walked his horse towards the fountain in the center of the market. "Nicolo! Nicolo!" he shouted. Nicolo grinned and waved, holding up a finger indicating to wait a moment. He completed his transaction and then said something to William at his side, who ran off.

Nicolo ambled over to Antonio, slapping his thigh and looking up at him. "I thought you were under house arrest," he teased.

Antonio's face darkened for a moment and then he laughed. "Let's go have some wine, Nicolo. I need to ask you a favor," he said candidly. Nicolo nodded, and indicated a wine shop at the end of the small *darbum* or dead end alley, to their left. Antonio dismounted, tied his horse to the fountain, and together they strolled over to the tables and chairs spread out in front of the shop. Antonio called loudly for wine. Neither of them noticed the tall, swarthy man sitting inside the wine shop under the open window, listening to everything they said.

"Nicolo, I've had quite a morning, a morning that could mean life or death to me!"

Nicolo smiled, used to Antonio's hyperboles. "What do you need, Antonio?"

Antonio gulped some wine and told him about Renata and the night of Ludovico's murder and how she was trying to implicate him. He told him that Mateo, who had delivered a message for his uncle, had spied a ring on the Archbishop's hand that looked like Ludovico's medallion. He told him about his uncle and Ludovico going to the Crusades.

When he was done, Nicolo frowned. "What does it all mean, though, Antonio? I can understand that Renata may have been confused about how much time you spent with her that evening, but this business with the Archbishop. And your uncle and old Stefani crusading together? That's rich!" Nicolo started laughing, and both of them sniggered, thinking about two old men as swashbuckling crusaders.

"No offense to your uncle, of course," Nicolo added hastily, grinning.

"No offense taken!" Antonio said airily. "It's all a very mysterious business isn't it? That medallion keeps popping up all over. Now, would you be willing to find out if Renata will tell the truth? I know she won't want to talk to me," he leaned over the table confidentially, "because actually, Nicolo, I was very blunt about not wanting to see her again. I mean, after all, what kind of a loose woman must she be anyway?" He drank more wine and looked at Nicolo expectantly.

Nicolo hesitated, thinking, not for the first time, how conceited Antonio was and feeling a need to defend the girl for some reason. "I'm sure she is angry with you for taking such advantage of her, but I'll talk to her," he said shortly.

"Splendid! Nicolo, you are a great friend to me! You always have been! I'll talk to you tomorrow. I'd better get back to the house. The old man will have a fit if he finds out I left, although he might be happy that I am taking matters into my own hands—well, in your hands, I guess. Look, you said your family was having dinner at The Leopard tonight, right? Why don't I drop by and you can tell me what she said." Nicolo nodded and stood up, looking around for William. Antonio walked back to the fountain, mounted his horse and rode away, satisfied with himself. The man inside the wine shop was equally satisfied.

CHAPTER 15

Ysabella and Larissa walked down the *Via Materassai* towards the port. Shops and vending stalls lined the street, slowing their progress somewhat as the women inspected first one, then the other. Remembering their business, however, they ignored the latter stalls and kept on. Men glanced appreciatively at Ysabella; even her dowdy scarf couldn't hide her tawny hair, and when she glanced at them, the smokiness in her violet eyes produced even more admiration. Larissa grabbed her arm, hurrying her along.

"Come on, we don't want to attract any attention."

The two women hurried on towards the port. They stopped in front of St. Iacobus, the church of the Genoese merchants, uncertain where to proceed. The area naturally smelled of fish. The cacophony was louder, the men rougher. Larissa pulled her into the church, where they hastily sank onto a bench.

"I'm not sure about this, mistress. This is beginning to scare me," Larissa said frankly. "We've been getting too many stares, and the men are getting rougher looking. These aren't gentle merchants, they're sailors and stevedores and wharf rats. I'm not sure we should go on."

Ysabella stiffened. "Larissa, we can't give up now! Amodeus's life depends on it! You agreed that she won't talk to the men! We've come this far. It's broad daylight and truly, nothing has happened, despite the weird looks. There are plenty of people around, women too. We'll be fine. I just don't know exactly where, well…where to find a whore. I don't know where she would be, exactly, do you?"

A small laugh and a discreet cough behind them made them turn around. A ragged woman leaning on a cane stared at them. "Excuse me. You're looking for a whore? What would two women like you be doing looking for a whore?"

Ysabella blushed, embarrassed. "Yes…I, um…I'm looking for my sister! She ran away from home! We can't find her, but we heard that she's at the port! We're afraid she's running away with a sailor and I have to stop her. I love her, and I need to find her!"

The woman looked at her, amused. "Same old story, I see. Well, I can show you where your sister might be. I don't know if you'll find her, but there's a certain area where the 'ladies' stay. Are you sure you want to go down there?" She glanced at their clothes, at Ysabella's fine leather belt, at the silk scarves, once expensive even if now faded.

Larissa's eyes narrowed as she met the stranger's eyes. "Yes, we're sure."

The woman moved back abruptly. "Well then, follow me." She swept out the door, and the two women stared after her.

Larissa whispered, "That was a good story." Ysabella squeezed her hand, and they both hurried after the woman, who was just turning a corner.

Intent on following the woman, they hardly noticed how poor and decaying the houses were becoming. People were lying in the alleyways or leaning against dilapidated doorways, staring at nothing. Men stared at them boldly, some even touching their dress or scarf. Ysabella and Larissa hurried on, snarling at anyone who came too close.

The woman stopped several blocks from the church within sight of the harbor, and turned, waiting for them. She waved her hand to her right, indicating a rabbit's warren of alleys and tumbledown huts and buildings. "There's where the port whores are. Be careful, and I hope you find your sister." She left the women huddled under the eave of a decrepit tavern.

"What do we do now?" Larissa faltered. "Just hail everyone coming down the street and ask them if they've seen some whore?"

Ysabella hesitated, uncertain and afraid. "I don't know, Larissa." They clutched each other's hands uneasily. "Do you think we should ask at the tavern here?"

"No!" Larissa said scornfully. "That's where men that visit those kinds of women hang around. We'd just be asking for trouble!"

They were looking at the tavern door when it suddenly opened. A well-dressed man stepped out. Seeing them, he raised his eyebrows and swept his hat off his head, addressing them politely.

"Ladies, may I help you? You seem out of place here!" And he cocked his head, smiling.

Ysabella heaved a sigh of relief. Surely someone so well dressed would assist them. Eagerly, she nodded. "We're looking for my sister. Someone told my family she was here, well, around here. She's brown-haired and has brown-eyes and walks with a slight limp. She's only 20 years old. We think she ran off with a sailor! I'm just trying to bring her home. Will you help us?" She looked beseechingly up, putting a hand up to tuck back a stray, lustrous lock of hair.

The man stared at her appreciatively. "Your sister?" he asked politely.

"Yes, my sister. Do you think you've seen someone like I described?"

"Yes, I believe I have. Only this morning. Let me think where." Ysabella's eyes widened, and she glanced out of the corner of her eye towards Larissa.

Larissa gave a little shrug and asked the stranger, "What are you doing here, if I may ask?"

"A good question, mistress," he answered gravely. "Actually, I am a Florentine, as you might guess by my attire," he put out his hands and indicated his clothes. "I had some business to transact at the port and I too, am looking for something a little, let's say, unusual. I had hoped to find it in this hovel," he nodded contemptuously towards the crumbling tavern he had just left, "but such was not to be the case. Now I thought I would return to my ship," he waved towards the harbor and try again somewhere else." His manner became brisk, "But let's see what we can do for you. You should really not wander around here. It's unsafe and there are unscrupulous men around. Shall we try to find your sister?"

He offered an arm to each woman. Hesitantly, they accepted it, Larissa with a little shrug, Ysabella with a short nod. "I think I saw such a young woman on the next street over. Shall we?"

The three of them paced sedately across to the lanes lined with hovels and huts. With every step, Ysabella felt her stomach muscles tighten. What kind of woman could live here in this filth, with these people? Shadowy men and women, old and young, ragged, angry, desperate, glimpsed through windows and doorways, some lying or sitting in the alleys, all of them dirty and gaunt. Ysabella shivered, causing the man to glance down at her kindly. "We won't be here long. I think she's at the end of this alley. Be careful where you step."

He shepherded Ysabella first, then Larissa, to an open doorway at the end of the alley. The women hesitated, gripping each other's arm. Ysabella stepped forward and peered into the dark, smelly room. Behind her, she heard a grunt, then a thud. Whirling around, she saw the man put a small club back into his belt and step over Larissa, who was now lying face down in the alley with her hands flung out. Horrified, Ysabella stumbled over the threshold and backed up until she could go no further. Her back hit the wall and she cringed while the man gently closed the door, lit a dirty rag for a torch, and put it in an equally filthy bowl on a table. In that flickering light, he appraised her frankly.

"Well, I told you I was looking for something a little special. I think I've found it. What beautiful eyes you have! And clearly, what a foolish family to let you come down here alone. How lucky for me!" He moved toward her, taking the club out of his belt and rubbing it on his leg suggestively.

Ysabella whimpered and sank back onto her heels, pressing her back against the wall. Why had she done this? What was wrong with her? Why hadn't she listened to Larissa? And Larissa, God's Teeth, was she dead or still alive? Shaking, she put out a hand, the palm turned toward him. The man laughed and walked toward her until her palm touched him.

"Please," she begged, "don't hurt me. I'll do anything you say, just don't hurt me." Eyes glittering, he nodded, offering his hand to help her up. She rose gracefully, holding his glance with her own smoldering eyes, and watched with satisfaction as his expression changed to one of utter surprise.

"I'm a tanner's daughter, and I know how to use a knife," she whispered. She pulled out the blade that she had buried in his stomach and stabbed him again under the armpit, causing the club to clatter from his nerveless fingers. She pushed him away, but he wasn't done with her yet.

Roaring, he grabbed her hair, spouting blood and moving so quickly the knife ripped out of her fingers. She kicked and struggled. He threw her against the wall, knocking the breath out of her. Suddenly he screamed, a high-pitched scream, and tried to turn around. Stumbling, he crashed down, hitting his head on the corner of the table and spilling the lit rag. Larissa, blood running down her face, kicked his head and stooped to take back her own knife.

"I told you, mistress, everyone should have a knife if they're going to be out without an escort."

Ysabella clutched her friend to her, thankful she was alive. She stamped at the burning rag and scrambled across the floor to find her knife, slipping it back into her boot. They both glanced at the body, kicking it reflectively, and pushed open the door grateful for the sun's warmth.

"I think I've had enough adventure for one day," Ysabella murmured as she examined Larissa's head. "Here, I'm binding this up with your scarf. Let's get out of here." Together, the two women ran out of the alley, surprising the lethargic drunk lying propped up against the building. They picked their way through the lane, looked around to get their bearings, and ran towards the port. No one made any attempt to stop them, and, bleeding and disheveled, they marched into the office of the *Maestro Portulano*, whose astonished face Ysabella still remembered years later with a smug satisfaction.

"Sir, I just killed a man. A piece of filth who says he was a Florentine. I don't know what he was, but he attacked me, hit my friend here, and I demand that you send a messenger to my brother-in-law and my uncle. Their names are Raynaldus de Rogerio and Leo de Iannacio."

Ysabella and Larissa sat down in front of the confused magistrate, and offered her blood-stained knife for his inspection.

....

Raynaldus stomped into the private room at the back of The Leopard, roaring his anger. Leo, secretly amused but relieved that Ysabella and Larissa were actually safe, followed him. Mario hurriedly brought supper in for his wife and the family. Angelica, Joanna, Nicolo and Adam trooped in carrying utensils, plates, and platters. Ysabella and Larissa entered last, triumphantly and audaciously seating themselves at the foot of the table.

"You could have been killed! Or almost as bad! What were you two thinking? I can't believe it!" Raynaldus ranted on and on as Angelica and Joanna bathed Larissa's wound and brushed out Ysabella's hair. They had changed their dresses and tried to be presentable. The whole family was astonished, worried, appalled, but overall, grateful they were safe.

Angelica walked over to Raynaldus, putting her hand on his arm. "Husband, calm down. We need to discuss what's happened here. Stop shouting and, as you say, let's be logical. Let them tell the story!"

As it turned out, Ysabella and Larissa had found the whore. After pouring out their story in excited, incoherent bunches to the *Maestro Portulano*, he dispatched a messenger to Raynaldus and Leo and took some armed men to the hovel, following the women's directions. To their surprise, they found the body exactly where the women said it would be. Bringing it back to the enclave, they laid him out and inspected his purse.

"The man was no Florentine either! He lied!" declared Larissa, making everyone smile at the understatement. "He was just a well-dressed thief and thug!"

The *Maestro,* reassured as to their identity after the messenger had returned, breathless, with Raynaldus and Leo on his heels, informed them that a woman had been found that morning. Dead, unfortunately. Young, brown-haired, brown-eyed, said to have a limp, but with a terrible necklace around her throat. Someone had garroted her, quickly and precisely. Raynaldus heard the pronouncement with amazement before he hustled the two women out of the magistrate's office, leaving Leo to thank the man for his messenger and for detaining the ladies.

"Well, we found her, sort of!" Ysabella yelled defiantly at Raynaldus.

Adam and Leo, now that she was safe, were smiling broadly.

"Yes, you certainly did," Adam stated mildly. "Now, where are we here? Time is running short and as entertaining as this has been, we need to sit down and reassess where we are." That pronouncement sobered everyone instantly.

Ravenous, the two women fell to eating, while everyone around them discussed the new information that had come their way. The first announcement involved the Archbishop of Palermo. That he had officiated at Ludovico's funeral Mass baffled and amazed everyone, but Nicolo's information stupefied them.

"Yes," Nicolo declared, looking around the table. "His Eminence has a ring on his right hand, the same medallion as the old crusader and Ludovico!" Mateo de Paruta saw it when he delivered a message from Simon to the Archbishop."

Raynaldus looked up sharply. "What message was that, Nicolo?"

The young man shrugged. "I don't know, Father, Antonio just told me that Mateo had delivered a message from their uncle to the Archbishop yesterday. That was when Mateo saw the ring." Leo rubbed his chin. Adam looked up at the ceiling speculatively. What was going on? This seemed to be so far beyond the murder of a drunk, old merchant.

"Antonio also told me something else, but I'm not sure it's important." Nicolo paused. Even Larissa and Ysabella raised their heads from their plates and looked at him. "He told me he had followed that Catalan merchant, Ferdinand de Lerida. He overheard Ferdinand and Josef talking about King Charles' warship that he's building in Trapani, ships and harbors. He said his uncle, Ludovico and Ferdinand, had all talked in detail about those kinds of things a lot lately, but," he said lamely, "I'm not sure if it's not just merchant talk. Antonio wasn't sure either, although he did say he thought it sounded more military than commercial, but that's just Antonio talking." Nicolo trailed off and looked expectantly at his father.

Raynaldus was listening carefully, his mind racing to consider the information his son was telling him. He smiled at Nicolo and strode over to put a hand on his shoulder. "Thank you, my son. I don't know what it means either, but I have a feeling, too, that it's important. I just don't know why right now."

Nicolo turned to Ysabella. "Should I check on the tavern supplies and see who's out in the main room?"

Ysabella nodded gratefully, and he walked rapidly out the door. She could hear him greeting customers and relaying dinner orders to Mario, who was temporarily the cook in place of his bruised wife. She carefully put down her chicken wing, wiped her chin, and looked around. "We know more now than we did yesterday. We know that Simon and Ludovico and the old crusader and maybe even the Archbishop were in the Holy Land together. Does that have anything to do with Ludovico's murder? Could one of them have done it? If so, why? That was so long ago. If something had happened back then, wouldn't Ludovico have been killed long before this?"

Various heads nodded at her logic. She continued, thinking it out slowly for herself. "So maybe the Archbishop was just presiding over a Mass for a long-forgotten old friend. That's possible, isn't it?" Shrugs and other innocuous body movements could be seen around the table.

"And then Antonio and Renata." She looked at Angelica. "What is Renata's story now? Is it the same one she told the magistrate earlier?"

Angelica sighed and rearranged her skirts. All eyes were on her. "Renata told me that she had fallen in love with Antonio on the way from Trapani to Palermo. She believed he felt the same. Of course, he didn't, and he took advantage of her. She's devastated and ashamed and she told the magistrate he was with her for only a few minutes to get back at him."

Angelica looked around the table. "She told me this afternoon that he was really with her for at least 20 minutes, none of it pleasant; but nonetheless, if that's true, he couldn't possibly have had the time to run after Ludovico and kill him."

Raynaldus pursed his lips and blew out a breath. "Well, as much as I detest him, I never thought Antonio would do something like that. So we're back to square one. Pietro Manfredi is not forthcoming with me, but there's nothing I can do about it. I can't arrest him or force him to talk to me. He knows something but I don't know what. He also knows about the past in the Holy Land, but he isn't talking about that either. I don't know what to do with him. In spite of all that, I like the man, but damn, he's not helpful. That's a fact."

Leo spoke up. "Now, aside from being a sneak and a spoiled brat, why would someone like Antonio take the time to follow this Ferdinand? That doesn't make sense to me. We need to know more about this Catalan."

Angelica spoke up. "I don't know, Uncle Leo, but I can offer one suggestion. You know I am a *Catalana,* although I've lived here so long I almost forget that myself! Why don't I ask among the Catalans in the community, especially at the Fondaco, and see if anyone knows anything about him. Uncle Leo, you are good friends with Josef. Ask him what he knows, too."

Raynaldus nodded at her approvingly.

"And Adam, you have so many contacts in the notarial world. Surely, as a merchant, he has to execute contracts. Can you see what kind of goods he deals in, who he deals with, that kind of thing? He certainly seems to keep turning up, so we should at least know something about him."

The men nodded, and Ysabella beamed at her sister-in-law fondly. If her sister-in-law had been with her and Larissa this afternoon, she would have torn that man apart! Although, she thought smugly, she hadn't done a bad job herself. Guiltily, she turned towards Larissa. Her servant and savior sat in the corner, snoring in her chair.

CHAPTER 16

Ysabella motioned to her brother-in-law, indicating the sleeping woman behind her. Facing his family members at the table, Raynaldus asked if there was anything else to discuss. A soft chorus of negatives made him smile. He stepped over to Larissa and gently picked her up.

Angelica opened the door.

"Raynaldus, put her in my bed upstairs," whispered Ysabella. Following him upstairs, she tucked Larissa in and tiptoed out of the room. Raynaldus put his hand on her arm.

"Sister, I know your only thought is to save Amodeus. But please, don't do something like this again. If other women think they can do something like this ... you came back alive but you were lucky. Others might not be. Please – think before you act, I beg you." And he turned and clumped down the stairs.

Adam and Leo were having a quick glass of wine before the fire before ambling into the night.

Ysabella came slowly down the stairs, frowning at Raynaldus's admonition; she then turned doggedly to business in the tavern. She and Nicolo conferred over the counter near the kitchen and watched in satisfaction as customers, both familiar and unfamiliar, wandered in to eat and drink. Larissa was right--people were coming back. Several neighbors came up to her, squeezed her shoulder or her hand, and asked quietly about Amodeus and news of the investigation. Aunt and nephew began to weave through tables and chairs that were rapidly filling up as the aroma of Mario's cooking wafted through the tavern. Low rumblings of conversation and soft hoots of laughter reassured Ysabella that tonight would be another good night at The Leopard, making her heart ache even more for her husband.

Nicolo watched his aunt shove aside her fatigue to flit about The Leopard as if propelled by an incubus. She smiled at her patrons, but in the dim light shed by the fire in the main room, some noticed how her usually glittering eyes were now a deep, murky grey, shadowed by fear.

Antonio tramped in an hour later, stopping short inside the door. He found a roomful of talking, laughing people eating and drinking with gusto. Ysabella, moving through the crowd, was talking and serving her clientele with what looked like her usual verve. Antonio frowned a moment. He really thought that the tavern would be quiet and gloomy, Ysabella probably needing some of his comforting and understanding presence. Well, he'd have his little chat with Nicolo and find a 'comforting presence' for himself elsewhere.

"Antonio!" Ysabella waved at him. Why she was so stubborn, refusing to let her men folk take over, Antonio didn't know. Ysabella wasn't sure herself, but this afternoon's near-disaster had left her feeling curiously powerful, no longer a bystander in the efforts to get her husband out of jail. No matter what Raynaldus said. She was tired but determined. Seeing she was busy, Antonio simply flapped a hand and threaded his way through the crowd to Nicolo at the counter. He automatically poured the cup of wine Antonio would want.

"Nicolo, did you get a chance to talk to Renata?" Antonio asked, holding his breath.

"Actually, I didn't, Antonio," watching his friend's face fall. "But my mother did, and she changed her words, saying now that really you spent about 20 minutes together. If she is telling the truth this time, no one thinks you had time to run after old Ludovico and kill him."

Antonio blew a pent-up breath out of pursed lips, surprised at how relieved he felt. He wrapped his beautiful green cloak around him and grinned. "I think our friend Bruno has something going on tonight, so I'm off." He looked around speculatively.

"I'm glad to see things are busy here, what with everything going on." He looked straight at Nicolo. "I really am," he said quietly.

Nicolo smiled at his friend's sincerity. "Well, so am I. Check out the dice room on your way out. I think there's a game going. Give my regards to Bruno and the boys. As you can see, I am needed here tonight."

Antonio wandered back into the dark hallway leading to the game room. He heard shouts of exhilaration and groans of dismay, but for some reason he did not understand, the thought of entering that room again was a bit repulsive. He laughed at himself for such a silly notion, but still decided not to play. He pulled his cloak a little tighter around him and continued toward the back door to slip through the courtyard and get back to the street through the alley.

As the evening wore on, Ysabella's activities during the day began to catch up with her. Pausing for a break, she ran upstairs to check on William, curled around his pillow, his little wooden sword askew on the floor where he had dropped it as sleep overtook him. She peeked in on Larissa, snoring gently in her bed. Ysabella sat down beside her, stroking her hair, thinking about how much their relationship had changed in such a short time. Initially, Larissa was merely a neighbor looking for work in the new local tavern. Ysabella had known her for a long time through the neighborhood, St. Margaret's, and the local markets, but it was no more than a friendly acquaintance. Now they had experienced something together that drew them into a closer relationship.

She thought more about the women friends she was coming to know better now that a crisis affected them all – Larissa, Angelica, and Joanna. Angelica was like an older sister, well, sometimes a mother. Angelica liked to fuss over her. Joanna fussed just as much, and Ysabella secretly basked in their attentions.

Lately, however, this murder investigation, of all things, brought out other sides to their characters, and to her own, that she hadn't really been aware of. Before this, she would never have considered going to the port as she had this morning. She would never have kept The Leopard open without Amodeus, and she would never have directed Raynaldus and the others as she was now. Was this a newfound strength or just desperation?

She found herself mulling over the information they had accumulated and puzzling over how the pieces fit together (not very well at this point, she thought ruefully) but thinking logically in ways she hadn't considered herself capable of before. Even the men in her family – Raynaldus, Adam, Leo – seemed to be looking at her differently. She had always considered herself resolute and practical, but now she was acting like a decisive woman of action, capable of a cold logic she didn't know she possessed. And she was also a killer. That stopped her. She crossed herself fervently, tears suddenly spilling down her face. Yes, he had deserved it and she was only defending herself, but what kind of woman could so coldly take another's life?

Even Angelica and Larissa were doing things they hadn't done before. She was seeing a side of Angelica that she always knew was there, but channeled differently. That take-charge decisiveness of her sister-in-law that at first had secretly intimidated her had really come to the forefront in trying to find Ludovico's killer. She seemed so confident about going to talk to her Catalan friends about that arrogant merchant, Ferdinand whoever. And she had confronted Renata and gotten information from her, refusing to let up until she got what she wanted. Yes, this whole business was bringing out surprising talents from everyone. Even Larissa! She looked down at her friend, sleeping, and silently blessed her for saving her life, or at least her virtue.

Back downstairs, Ysabella found the tavern was beginning to empty out. She was relieved; her small reservoir of energy was spent. Perhaps sensing that their hostess was winding down, the few men left in the dice room began to leave, some smiling, some grumbling, but all relatively good-natured. She watched as the rest of her guests called goodbyes and put on their caps and cloaks. She saw her neighbors to the door, murmuring goodnights and thanks, and closed and locked the door behind them. Nicolo was clearing trenchers and mugs from the tables, and Mario was already scrubbing pots in the kitchen. She grabbed a broom to begin sweeping up, but had no heart for it. Turning to Nicolo, she said tiredly, "You know, I have a bit of a headache. I think I'm going to sit outside in the courtyard for a few minutes, get some fresh air, and just unwind. You and Mario can leave the rest until tomorrow."

Nicolo smiled. "I wondered if you would ever stop. You've had quite a day, Aunt Ysabella."

She flashed a sardonic smile at him. "Yes, I have, haven't I? I think it's catching up with me." She poured a glass of her favorite red wine, savoring its tart pungency, and walked slowly towards the courtyard, thinking about Amodeus and anticipating the relaxing aroma of lavender and sage. She pushed at the door but it barely budged. Frowning in exasperation at one more complication in her day, she set the wine on a nearby shelf and used both hands to shove harder. It moved barely an inch, letting in a wisp of cool night air laced with the coppery taste typical of the river into which the tanners dumped their refuse.

"Nicolo!" she called, "Something's blocking the door! Come help me, please?"

Nicolo was just fastening the pin on his cloak to leave the tavern when he heard his aunt call out. He hurried down the dark hallway to see for himself what the trouble was. He stepped in front of Ysabella and put his shoulder to the door as any young man would, but only managed to move the door a foot. "Don't worry, aunt. I'll go out the front and through the alley. I can kick aside whatever is blocking it and open the door from the outside. Just wait a moment."

Ysabella took up her glass and sipped a little wine, tapping her foot in frustration. She heard Nicolo's footsteps echo through the silent tavern as he went to the front door, and she heard the rasp of the key against rough metal. A few moments later, the creak of the hinges on the gate to the alley indicated his arrival, but Nicolo's footsteps thudded to a halt before the halfway open door.

"Well," Ysabella said crossly, irritation replacing her anticipated relaxation. "What is it?"

Nicolo didn't answer. Ysabella stuck her head out the door. In the wavering light of the torch Nicolo carried, they both stared at the body of Antonio de Paruta, sprawled awkwardly on the paving stones of Ysabella's courtyard. Ysabella screamed, and Mario, running from the kitchen, barely caught her as she fainted backwards in the hallway, her wine glass crashing to the floor.

CHAPTER 17

When Ysabella's eyes fluttered open, she was lying on a bench in front of the fire, Larissa anxiously bathing her face with cold water. William, awakened by the screams, sat cross-legged on the floor grimacing at his mother with tears spotting his smooth cheeks.

"Lie still," her friend commanded gently.

"Larissa, what … was that Antonio?"

"Yes," Larissa said grimly. "Bodies piling up all over the place. Nicolo ran to get Raynaldus, and they are standing guard in the courtyard. The night watch was notified, and the sheriff will be here soon, I'm sure."

As she spoke, the front door opened and in strode the *magister xurte*, as expected, followed by his retinue of armed men. He stood motionless for a moment, looking down at the frightened women, and snarled something in French. Larissa pointed wordlessly to the back of The Leopard, and he marched down the hall where the back door was now standing wide. He snarled again as he crushed a piece of the wine glass under foot. Raynaldus approached the sheriff while Nicolo held a torch near the body trying not to step in the black puddle of blood already drying in the night air.

Raynaldus led the official to the body and they deliberated in low tones, the sheriff impatient and condescending. The inert lump still lay near the door like a lost rag doll, motionless fingers poking out under the tablecloth Mario had respectfully draped over it. The sheriff walked over to Antonio's corpse, lifted the tablecloth, and examined it perfunctorily. His back rudely turned to Raynaldus, the sheriff began speaking again in French.

"Stabbed in the neck, bruises around his throat," the sheriff said casually. "No marks on his arms or hands. Probably never saw his attacker."

He turned and stooped, looking carefully at the young man's fingernails. "Nothing," he muttered softly, glancing up at Raynaldus. "No fabric, no buttons, nothing to help us here." He let the hands drop to the ground.

Raynaldus looked away for a moment, then cleared his throat and addressed the angry sheriff. "I suppose someone should go immediately to Simon de Paruta's house and inform him."

"Yes," the sheriff sneered. "You may accompany me if you must. I don't suppose you have any idea who would do this." His voice lifted insultingly in a question, but he really didn't expect Raynaldus to answer.

"Well," Raynaldus said ironically, "we know my brother didn't do it, don't we?" And enjoying the surprised look on the sheriff's face, he turned on his heel and went back into the tavern.

He stopped by Ysabella and Larissa, who were talking softly with Leo who had arrived just after the sheriff, and squatted in front of Ysabella. "Are you all right, sister?" he asked her gently, taking her hand. Ysabella only nodded wordlessly.

"I'm going with the sheriff to tell Simon. His men are removing the body. Leo, please stay here with Ysabella. Mario and Nicolo will stay with you and Larissa, too." Leo helped Ysabella off the bench as Raynaldus trailed out the door after the official.

After the men left, Leo and Ysabella sat silently at a table. William snuggled against his mother, falling asleep again in the warmth of her embrace. Larissa set cups and wine in front of the somber group. Ysabella was the first to speak.

"I thought," she said slowly, "that Ludovico had been killed by thieves. I'm still not sure he wasn't. But this. Who would kill Antonio, even though," crossing herself and thinking it wasn't good to speak ill of the dead, "he wasn't that likeable? And we know he's been following that Ferdinand person, and there's that odd medallion that keeps popping up. None of it makes sense."

Larissa looked at Leo as if seeking permission to speak. "I don't know, mistress, but I'm afraid of what this will do to the business here. The Leopard will begin to get a reputation where people are murdered and no one will want to come here. The sheriff may even try to shut it down. Then what?" Ysabella's eyes widened in acknowledgment of her friend's logic.

"I don't know, Larissa, but you're right," she said helplessly. "None of this is our fault--what can we do? Still, our customers came back after the first murder. Why wouldn't they come back after this one?"

Nicolo and Mario plodded into the room and sat down at the table. After helping the sheriff's men move the body and scouring the blood from the stones by torchlight, they were both tired and short-tempered. Hearing Ysabella's question, Nicolo spoke up.

"Aunt, I don't know what's going on, but we're all staying here with you tonight. I don't think you're safe here anymore. Could someone resent you or your business so much that he is killing customers to drive you away? Could that be the motive, while the Crusader story is just a coincidence? I know there was some connection between Ludovico and that Pietro Manfredi, but what would some piece of ancient history in a far away place have to do with two murders now in Palermo?"

"I'm convinced there is a connection," Ysabella responded. "If someone wanted to drive us out—though I have no earthly idea who that might be--they had many weeks before we opened to set a fire or steal all our supplies without killing anyone. This isn't about us, I'm sure. But the medallions certainly suggest a connection no one will talk about. Joanna said Ludovico never mentioned Pietro to her as either friend or enemy, so what connection could there be, other than that they seemed to hate each other?"

"Well," Leo said briskly, "it will just be a matter of time to find the men who were associated with the dead whore. The *maestro portulano* thinks he might know what they look like, and he's scouring the city. Especially since," he grinned, "the two respectable ladies involved just happen to be related to a magistrate."

The wry comment temporarily lightened their somber moods, but Leo continued. "Your attacker was not one of the thieves, as far as we know, but by now the story of your assault has spread to every corner of that district. Someone will slip up or identify the men we are looking for."

Ysabella shifted restlessly, glowering at her wine glass. Chewing her lower lip, she said, "Unless they've left town, those men can't really hide for long, as you say. Perhaps they can give us a clue as to what really happened that night with Ludovico. And that might lead us to whoever killed Antonio. "

Larissa nodded and stood up. "Thank God no one here was harmed, but finding the killers will wait until tomorrow. It has been a long day, and I think everyone should think about getting some sleep. Nicolo and Leo will take William's bed if William can be tucked in with you, mistress. Mario and I will make a pallet on the floor." Overwhelmed by their fatigue, the friends could only nod their agreement. Hugging or touching each other briefly, Nicolo carried William upstairs, and Leo straggled along, but Ysabella sat for a private moment by the fire.

·········

Ysabella's eyes flew open at the sound of a terrible racket. She must have nodded off. Someone was hammering on the door! Fearfully, she crept over to peep through the window. Angelica and an armed guard stood in the street. When she saw Ysabella's movement, she called, "I had to come. Let me in." Ysabella fumbled with the lock before she could admit her sister-in-law. The guard remained outside.

"Oh, sister, I came as soon as I could. How dreadful!"

"Yes, shocking, but we weren't harmed."

"It has been such a long day. I have learned some things about the Catalan. They say he is a spy."

"Angelica, that man keeps popping up. What role does he play in this? It seems to be only a local matter, nothing for foreigners. We need to find out more about him. Leo is asking about him in the market and should learn something more tomorrow. I want to talk to our neighbors--maybe they saw something. And of course, I want to make sure everyone knows The Leopard is still open." Ysabella stopped, staring at Angelica's sudden grimace. "What, dear?"

Angelica hesitated, but plunged ahead. "Ysabella, do you feel safe here? Do you want to come with us to The Olive until this business is resolved? She took Ysabella's hand, stroking it. "I'm afraid for you. And you have William to think of, you know."

Ysabella laughed. "I'm perfectly fine, *cara mia*. Uncle Leo, Mario and Larissa stayed with us last night and we all slept like lambs. We'll be fine. But I'll keep your very generous offer in mind." Ysabella stood up, shook some crumbs from her dress, and smiled down at a frowning Angelica.

"Then I'll say this openly, Ysabella. We love you. Your family and friends are supporting you, but *you* must think of others, as well. If something happens to Amodeus, God forbid, then you are the only one left to take care of William. And if something happens to YOU, then who will take care of your son? Have you ever thought about that?"

Ysabella just waved her hand in a dismissive gesture. "I AM thinking of everyone. I do nothing but think these days."

Angelica continued, "No, Ysabella. Listen to me! I don't mean to be cross, but you've only been consumed with how others may be of use to you. You haven't given a thought as to how this might affect us or The Olive. Our reputation is the least of it, but my husband and my son are spending hours and days over here, which takes them away from their responsibilities and their lives – and away from me. Thank God you aren't alone in this, but not being alone also means you must consider what it's doing to everyone else."

Ysabella slammed her hand down on the table, blazing at her sister-in-law. "I can't believe you're worried about yourself when your own brother-in-law--and my husband—could be hanged for something he didn't do! Are you telling me you aren't going to help me anymore?!"

Angelica slammed her hand back in response. "No, I'm not telling you that. I would never not help you. But I am worried about myself, my family, and about you and Amodeus, too. Even about Leo and Adam. We're all affected. I just want you to think, and to consider us sometimes instead of just barging ahead and doing whatever you want."

The two women glowered angrily at each other. The men moving around upstairs had gotten very quiet. Ysabella was the first to look down. She caught her breath and looked over at Angelica, whose golden eyes were practically sable with fear, anger and worry. Ysabella grabbed Angelica's trembling hands. "No, I wasn't thinking about you. You're right. I wasn't thinking about you and Raynaldus and Nicolo at all, just about me. And my troubles. And how grateful I am that I have all of you. I'm so sorry …" and both women burst into tears and hugged each other fiercely.

"Look," Angelica sniffled, "this is affecting all of us. That's all I'm saying. Just think about coming and staying with us. Think of what I said, please? I have to go home." And with that, a little overwhelmed, she stood up, heaving a sigh of relief. Signaling to her guards, she ran out into the darkness after a hug and a flurry of goodbyes. Mario cautiously came downstairs, looked at Ysabella, who smiled wanly at him, and put out the torches in the tavern. He made sure the doors were locked as Larissa laid a comforter on the cold tile floor.

··········

"Simon, I'm sorry to wake you in the middle of the night with such terrible news," Raynaldus said gently after the sheriff had made a curt announcement and left with no further word. Simon's head was in his hands; servants were hovering, frightened and surprised. Venutus, as usual, was silent and efficient, bringing warmed, spiced wine to his master and quietly waiting for instructions. The odor of cinnamon drifted across the room belying everyone's dour mood.

Simon lifted his head, his expression anguished. "Raynaldus, do you know---- have you any idea, who could have done this?"

Raynaldus shook his head. "But we'll find out, Simon, we'll find out. The sheriff's men will be bringing his body here soon." Then he quietly shared what little information they had. Simon groaned, half-rose, then fell heavily back into his chair. Venutus rushed forward to settle his master, putting an end to any further conversation. Raynaldus respectfully left the room, and a scowling Venutus followed to usher him to the door. As they walked to the entrance, Mateo rushed by and flew into Simon's office.

"Venutus," Raynaldus questioned, "You know this household. Are you aware of anyone who wished Antonio harm? Did you hear anything that might be helpful? Was someone threatening him? Were creditors getting rough with him?"

Venutus hesitated, looked down at the ground, then at Raynaldus. "I know, Master de Rogerio, that he had many creditors and possibly some can be rather rough in their ways. But I think ..." He stopped, not sure what to say. Raynaldus waited patiently, sure that this trusted servant knew something but was struggling with his loyalty to Simon.

"Come, Venutus," Raynaldus said, taking his arm and walking him outside. "We need to know everything if we're to find this killer."

Venutus looked steadily at his inquisitor, shadows from the palace torches flickering across his face. "Antonio had been following this Ferdinand de Lerida, a business associate of Master Simon's. I don't know why. He's a Catalan and a dangerous man. There are rumors about him ..." his voice trailed off. Raynaldus waited again for the servant to continue. Sometimes it was better to let people ramble than interrupt with questions. He frequently got more interesting information that way.

Venutus cleared his throat and continued. "Signor de Lerida came to the house, angry, and demanded from the master to know why Antonio was following him. I don't know what was said after that. As I said, he's a very dangerous man. Is there anything else? I need to return to the house." Venutus glided away before Raynaldus could dismiss him, gruffly assigning a slave to accompany Raynaldus through Palermo's dark streets.

Mateo lay on his bed sobbing. His best friend in the whole world, his adored brother, gone. Uncle Simon had hugged him and spoken some words instantly forgotten, but Mateo knew his uncle wouldn't grieve for Antonio like he would. Who would do such a thing? Just yesterday they were laughing together, picturing Uncle Simon, Ludovico and the Archbishop swinging their swords and galloping across the sands of Outremer together. Antonio had been so surprised by Mateo's glimpse of the archbishop's ring. Mateo remembered feeling proud that he had shared something that seemed important to his older brother. Did his brother's death have something to do with that medallion? Or even more frightening, with the Archbishop?

CHAPTER 18

The next day as the parish church bells were ringing, Adam and Raynaldus arrived at The Leopard. Despite the early hour, they noted gratefully that at least a few people were eating and drinking and lounging inside the tavern. Not everyone had been scared off from The Leopard. Ysabella and Larissa were in the kitchen, cooking and talking in low tones, still subdued by last night's events, but momentarily distracted by the customers and friends. Leo, still yawning, sat in a corner with fresh bread and oranges before him as Nicolo resumed his role as host.

Raynaldus and Adam sat down at Leo's table. Raynaldus pulled off his boots and put his feet up, telling his companions about his trip to Simon's and Venutus's story about Antonio following the dangerous Spaniard for some reason. "Well," he mused, "perhaps it's time we look into this Signor de Lerida. What do you think, Adam?"

"As I have told you before, my friend, I still think we should leave this whole investigation to the authorities; but if you are determined to pursue this on your own, I'll talk to the other notaries. Lerida's a merchant--he must make contracts. I'll find out who he deals with, what he buys and sells. See if we can get an idea of what he's about. I think I remember," Adam said, stroking his chin, "that Josef the Jew is his business agent. I'll talk to him." Adam conveyed doubt with every word, but Raynaldus just nodded and closed his eyes.

While the few early customers focused on breaking their fast, Nicolo had lingered near the table listening to his father's conversation, but he could think of nothing to add. As the group fell silent, lost in their own thoughts, Nicolo too fell into a reverie, forgetting his duties. An image of Antonio's buoyant entrance to the tavern the night before, artfully moving in just the right way to display the luxurious cape everyone envied, flashed in his mind. He was just about to grin at the thought when it was replaced by the horrifying grey and bloodless face of the same eager youth later staring blankly at the stars. But, no--it wasn't quite the same figure, he thought. What was wrong with that image? It took him a few moments to realize that the emerald cape had disappeared from the body. Did someone want that garment so badly that he was willing to kill for it? Or did someone else come along after Antonio was dead and take it, hoping to be able to clean away the bloodstains? It was an odd thing to be stolen. Anyone who dared to wear it would be instantly suspected. Still, he would tell his father. Maybe the littlest detail was important.

Leo tugged at Nicolo's sleeve, startling him. "Where are you, young man? Would you kindly bring me some cheese to go with my meal?"

Embarrassed to be caught so inattentive, Nicolo gave a hasty response and went off in search of Leo's favorite soft cheese mixed with nuts and berries, knowing that Ysabella concocted this delicacy just for Uncle Leo. He found the crock on the back shelf and was just turning back to Leo when he bumped into someone surprising.

"Mateo! What are you doing here?" Nicolo hugged the young man who looked nearly as lifeless as his brother had. "Have you eaten? Father's over there if you'd like to join us," and pointed over to the corner.

Mateo smiled but declined. "I came to see you, Nicolo. I know you were his friend. I'd just like to tell you something that Antonio and I had talked about before he, well…" and he delicately turned away, temporarily unable to speak.

Nicolo waited respectfully before saying, "Anything, Mateo. Just give me a moment to finish this chore. Why don't I bring something out to the garden and we'll sit out there?"

Mateo nodded and went toward the back while Nicolo set the cheese in front of Leo and patted the old man's shoulder. He wanted his father to talk with Mateo, too, but Raynaldus seemed to be taking a little nap. Stealing away quietly so as not to disturb him, he joined Mateo out in the garden, gingerly stepping over the flagstones where he had found Antonio's body. He wondered if Mateo would be comfortable here, but the youth did not seem troubled. In the bright morning sunlight, Nicolo could pick out a few dark spots they apparently missed in the late night clean up.

"I am so sorry about your brother, Mateo. We will all miss him, as I am sure you will. What was it you wanted to talk about?"

Mateo hesitated, holding back tears. He told Nicolo about seeing a medallion in his Uncle's possession that looked exactly very much the one that Ludovico and the old Crusader both had. Antonio had described the oval so clearly that he was sure it was the same. Most surprisingly, he also had seen the same gold piece made into a ring worn by the Archbishop.

Nicolo was surprised, but asked Mateo, "Well, why would Simon have such a thing? I mean, do you think the medallions have anything to do with why Antonio was killed? Surely Simon could not have had a hand in it. You know," he said hesitantly, looking away from the boy, "Antonio had a lot of creditors that he treated shabbily, not to mention other people who were not fond of him."

Mateo nodded. "I understand what my brother was, but he had those creditors for a long time. Why kill him now? Why not just go to my uncle if they were so angry or desperate to be paid? My uncle would rant about it but eventually pay because he wouldn't want the scandal."

Nicolo's eyes narrowed. He looked at Mateo appreciatively. "You're right. I hadn't thought of that. So, are you saying, then, that Antonio may have known something about the medallions or guessed at some connections between these men that resulted in his death? What do you think he found out? Did you ask your uncle about it?"

"Uncle Simon just said it was something they all picked up in the Holy Land together, a trinket that was common there. I think he told that to your father when he came to see him, but I don't think your father knows that the Archbishop has the same medallion. I carried my uncle's message to the Archbishop and told Antonio about his ring. I can't help thinking it may be important, but I don't know how. If it were just a common trinket like he said, why has no one seen one like it before? Many of the confiscated riches of Outremer show up in a trading port like Palermo. Nearly anyone who went there could come back with a medallion or jewels or something to sell. And how did a man so high up in the Church get one? Was he in the Crusades, too?"

Nicolo raised his eyebrows. "You're not saying, are you, that you think the Archbishop of Palermo is involved in this? That's preposterous, even though now that I think about it, it was definitely odd that he came to Ludovico's funeral Mass. In fact, you saw him there. Hmmm…" Both young men thought about that for a moment.

Mateo spoke first. "I can't imagine the Archbishop killing anyone, Nicolo. That just sounds so crazy. But I can't get it out of my mind that old Ludovico had this medallion, the old crusader comes to town with one like it, I see Uncle Simon's medallion, and then the Archbishop's. That piece connects four men. I don't know… It just doesn't seem so random, do you think?"

"Mateo, I'm wondering now about Signor Pietro. He's clearly a fighter. I've seen his sword with the medallion in the pommel, and it's obvious he knows how to use weapons. Knives, I'm sure. I haven't paid much attention to him, but I wonder if I should start?"

Mateo shrugged helplessly, his face clouded, and tears welling up. "I don't know, Nicolo. But Antonio died and maybe this is a piece of it. How could something from so long ago be so important now? It's just all so crazy!" They were both silent, letting the soft morning breeze feather over them.

Finally, Nicolo stood up and Mateo followed. They trudged back into the tavern, first checking on Raynaldus, who still had his eyes closed, his food and drink untouched. "I'll tell him as soon as he wakes," Nicolo said as he walked with Mateo out to the street. "Thank you for bringing this information to me. I don't know what it means either, but one thing is sure. If having this information killed Antonio, you must be very careful not to tell anyone else that you know. I don't see how this could be dangerous, but if it is, please, don't say anything to anyone. And come to us at any time. You know we are your friends."

Mateo's brow furrowed and he watched the toe of his boot draw little circles in the dust. "I never thought about that, I mean, that they might kill me too. I was thinking about Antonio. I'll be careful, I promise. And I'll be sure that Venutus is with me if I go out. If I think of anything else, I'll come back. You're staying here for a few days?"

Nicolo gripped the boy's arm. "I think Aunt Ysabella would like the company, and William needs extra attention. I can put off my studies for a while to help out. You know I'm not enthused about notary work, anyway."

The young men parted, waving to each other, as Nicolo watched Mateo run up the street. Interesting information, but was it even important? Nicolo gave up and went back into the cool darkness of The Leopard.

··········

Ferdinand de Lerida lounged in the shady back courtyard of the *Fondaco dei Catalani*, eating grapes and bread dipped in olive oil. He squinted into the warm Sicilian sun through the lacy canopy of the courtyard's trees and heard the sweet singing of birds in the branches. The manager of the hostel had just brought a message informing him of Antonio's death. He wondered what that news would do to Simon. Simon would soon be dead, too, from whatever wasting disease was eating away at him. He had to give the old man credit. He was impressed with how Simon had managed their most successful duplicity over the years. The old man could weasel information from the most reluctant informants when he put his mind to it. Some coin here, a favor there, even a threat of implication in scandal—Simon employed all with equal refinement. And his network of informants rivaled that of Ferdinand, himself. It seemed he knew something about everyone in Palermo, either prince or pauper. Yes, the old man had been valuable, but now he must be replaced.

Fortunately, before he died, Antonio had brought back interesting details about the massive trireme that King Charles was building in Trapani. The arsenal in Trapani was one of the three major shipyards in Sicily, smaller than the other two in Palermo and Messina, but still able to accommodate such a big building project. The Trapani shipyard had been expanded, and now it was being walled off from prying eyes. Ferdinand could understand why and he appreciated the bribes that Antonio had spread around to get a look at the huge warship that, if his plans went accordingly, would soon be no threat to his sovereign, the King of Aragon, or anyone else.

Everyone knew Palermo's harbor was protected by *La Catena*, the monstrous harbor chain that could be stretched across the mouth of the *Conca d'Oro*, to prevent enemy warships from landing. That had been a Greek invention, perfected by the Arabs, who were clever with machinery. Immense winches on each side of the harbor, pulled by huge draft horses, stretched the chain across the port. It was a miracle of military engineering. Probably child's play for the Greeks, Ferdinand thought, remembering an amusing story about the First Crusade.

When the French first arrived in Byzantium on their way to the Holy Land, the emperor had received them in his famous throne room. Incense swirled around the base of his throne as the Crusade leaders filed, amazed, into the glittering room studded with gold and jewels. Then the throne began to rise, slowly and majestically, causing the barbarians to drop astonished to their knees. Ferdinand laughed softly as he thought about it. Educated men, men living in the Mediterranean world, had known about mechanics for centuries. What a picture that must have been! Those idiot Franks actually thought the Emperor's throne was raising by magic!

As entertaining as this story was, Ferdinand turned his thoughts back to Simon's present intrigue. The machinery for the harbor chain, of course, was heavily guarded by royal troops specially selected for loyalty. No one was allowed near the facility except the king and his highest advisers. Even the workmen were escorted by a guard when making any adjustment or repair to the mechanism.

Simon, however, had managed to bribe one of the engineers. Somehow, he had found the man's weakness, something that had required a great deal of money and made a desperate man turn traitor. It had taken a long and delicate negotiation, but money, of course, was one of the least of Simon's problems. Eventually, he had turned the man. And when the King of Aragon sailed his war fleet into Sicily, the chain that had stopped countless armadas would be down, useless. Yes, Ferdinand had a great deal of respect for Simon.

Of course, they would all die for this if they were found out, and not in pleasant ways either. Simon might be taken by the hand of God at any time, but Ferdinand had many more valuable years ahead. He would have to learn the name of the engineer and pay him a visit. He wanted to be sure the man knew that the plan would not end just because one old man had died. Perhaps he should visit Simon today—it would be proper to offer condolences, but no, perhaps tomorrow would be a more tactful time.

He got up, stretched, yawned, and was about to saunter into his rooms for an early siesta when one of his many informants sidled into the courtyard, bowing and scraping reminding Ferdinand of a pig snuffling for truffles. Glancing at the filthy ragamuffin, Ferdinand stifled another yawn and growled out, "Yes, what is it?"

"Lord," said the dirty apparition, bent so low that his nose nearly touched his knees, "someone has been asking around about you. You told me to come straight to you if this ever happened."

Immediately Ferdinand lost his languor. "Who is this 'someone'?" he asked softly. When his informant made no answer, suddenly Ferdinand clutched the man's rags and lifted him up with one arm. "Who?!" he shouted.

The man, terrified, suddenly looked into Ferdinand's hawk eyes and began to stammer. "I…I think …

"I don't pay you to think! I pay you to bring me information! Who is it?" he roared.

The beggar squeaked and then began coughing as his feet slowly left the ground, hoisted higher and higher by a fuming Ferdinand. "Lord, please," he gasped. He cried out as Ferdinand casually dropped him in a heap to the courtyard paving stones.

Choking on his words, the informant said meekly, "She's the wife of a local magistrate, Raynaldus de Rogerio, the owner of a hostel in the Cassaro. She's a Catalana. Her father was the merchant, Raymund de Bareljo. Then she married Raynaldus. She manages the hostel and they live in the Seralcadio near the Church of the Venetians." He coughed, spit, and started to crawl away.

Ferdinand barely noticed him. Why would someone like that be asking about him? "You, dog! Get back here. Find out why she's asking about me. What is this about? Who's talking to her? I want answers by sunset. If I have them, my friend," he smiled dangerously, "I'll pay you double your rate. And find out about her husband, too."

"Yes, lord! I will find out!" and the beggar scrabbled away, eyes glistening at the thought of imminent funds. Ferdinand didn't even watch him leave. Instead, he returned to his room. All thoughts of a nap evaporated. The name of Raymund de Bareljo rang a bell, but for the moment, he couldn't place him. Probably nothing – some transplanted Catalans sniffing around hoping for a deal on something. He'd think about it, but at any rate, he'd know by sunset what was going on.

CHAPTER 19

That same morning, the pilgrims at The Olive all bustled down to an early breakfast, chattering and excited about touring Palermo's shrines. Today was the day Sophia would lay a gift at the feet of the Virgin Mary and, perhaps, be blessed. Tomorrow she would climb Mount Pellegrino to the shrine of Santa Rosalia and do the same thing. Then, triumphantly, she would go home and produce a bouncing baby boy for her husband. Wrapped in these thoughts, she was oblivious to Angelica's obvious lack of sleep and the silence of the usually talkative servants. The other pilgrims were equally preoccupied. Renata, having unburdened herself to Angelica the day before, was the only cheerful presence.

The pilgrims had been fed and were ready to go. "Good morning," they all chorused at their hostess's appearance. Plastering a smile upon her face, Angelica turned to her servants and rattled off instructions for transporting their party and supplies around Palermo for the day. There were special considerations for Sophia and her pregnancy, and she consulted with the mother-to-be before she strode into her kitchen to give final instructions. The old crusader, she noticed, was already gone; thus only Carlos and Perna, Sophia and Renata were going with her. She would take a strong retinue of her own men. She didn't know if the family was truly in danger, but she did not intend to take chances. The hired guards who had arrived with the pilgrims were quietly instructed to stay at The Olive and stay alert. They nodded gravely, appreciative of not having to tramp around to shrines all day listening to women's chatter.

At the breakfast table Angelica explained that, as a Roman, Greek, Muslim, and now Norman capital city, the number of shrines and churches in Palermo was overwhelming. Each regime had built its quota of holy places. Since Sophia was most interested in requesting help from the Virgin Mary, Angelica suggested that they see her most prestigious sanctuaries and chapels. After tomorrow's expedition to Santa Rosalia, if further prayers were needed, perhaps they could follow up with the Churches of San Giovanni dei Lebbrosi, San Francisco and San Domenico, or Santa Barbara and Santa Margarita later in the week. She understood that this might be the ladies' one and only journey to Sicily's most beautiful and largest city, and that they intended, as much as possible, to take the fullest advantage of their spiritual odyssey. Ttheir itinerary would begin with an exploration of the nearest shrines, stopping for a refreshing repast at La Martorana, whose cloistered nuns prepared the unique and delicious almond paste marzipan known as *pasta reale.*

Angelica arranged for Sophia and Perna to travel in a comfortable wooden cart enclosed with muslin curtains which enabled the soft breezes to cool the women within while, at the same time, shield them from the sun. Only the main avenues of Palermo's five quarters were shaded by elaborate wooden canopies built by the ingenious engineers of the Islamic Caliphate. Carlos rode behind the slow-moving cart while Angelica and Renata, wearing broad-brimmed hats, rode sidesaddle on docile palfreys, all surrounded by guards. Today Angelica was grateful for her guards. Holy Week had brought throngs of pilgrims into the city and the men would save her little band from being pushed and shoved by the surging masses.

Such entourages were not unusual. Aristocratic women often rode through the city concealed from plebian eyes and surrounded by watchful armed chaperones. Maids or menservants descended from such carts to conduct their mistress's business and to make purchases while occasionally curtains parted so that curious ladies could drink in the odors, colors, sights and sounds of the cacophony which arose from the politics and business conducted in the streets at ear-splitting levels. And no matter how often the street sweepers swept and washed the cobbled main boulevards, there was no getting around the odiferous smell of freshly dropped horse dung and general garbage that people casually pitched into the streets.

Angelica, however, as a merchant's daughter, was used to it all and generally enjoyed her forays through the city although, as a wealthy man's wife, Raynaldus always made sure she traveled with protection. Angelica smiled at Renata, who had donned the pale blue gammura for the occasion and wore a dainty pair of gold earrings peeking out from below her coif. Clearly, Renata also enjoyed being out, and she obviously knew how to ride a horse. Since their talk, Angelica found herself liking the young girl. Away from her mother, Renata was lively and amusing with a droll sense of humor. She had a knack for telling funny stories, and her beauty distracted people from realizing how intelligent she was. Intelligent except for that foolishness with Antonio, Angelica remembered, but many a country girl had to learn the hard way. She was thinking about that when they approached their first destination.

Her little band had picked their way slowly through the crowded, narrow streets to arrive at San Giovanni degli Eremiti. The five dusky red onion-shaped domes of the Church of St. John of the Hermits and its luxuriant gardens were a feast for the avid eyes of the pilgrims. As her entourage slowly disembarked from horses and carts, Angelica entertained them with the history of the monastery.

Converted around the middle of the 12th century by the Norman King Roger, the original building had first been a sixth century Gregorian monastery dedicated to St. Ermete, then an Arab mosque that, along with San Cataldo, more recently reverted to Christian churches. Orange and lemon trees, sweetly scented lavender and mimosa surrounding stately palms, provided shade within the gardens and framed the walks as Angelica's humble petitioners filed into the cool, dark interior. Tactfully allowing Sophia and Perna privacy at the altar, Angelica and Renata, with two of their guards, stood quietly in the transept. Completing her prayers and making a suitable offering, Sophia waddled outside, Perna close behind. They were fanning themselves as they paused in the tranquil gardens to sit on the stone benches and enjoy the near silence provided by the lush foliage and dense stone walls.

Without hurrying her charges, but without letting them waste time, Angelica guided them back to the cart and horses. She quietly told them about their next stop, the Church of Santo Spirito just outside Palermo's walls. Threading their way through the *Porta Judayce*, they quietly traversed Palermo's sprawling Jewish sector, the pilgrims gazing curiously at the mysterious neighborhood around them. Angelica informed them that although many of Palermo's Jews lived in this part of the Albergheria, they were free to live anywhere they pleased. Josef the Jew, for instance, with interests in the trade at the port every day, lived just a few blocks from the offices of the *maestro de portulano*.

They passed the main synagogue, a beautiful imposing structure of marble, mosaics and timber, where men in long side curls waved their arms and argued Talmudic subtleties. Perna gasped as they next passed the Jewish market where voices raised in Arabic and Hebrew harangues mingled harshly. Most of Palermo's Jews had emigrated from the Maghrib, or northern Africa, and thus spoke Arabic as well as Hebrew.

As they exited the quarter through the tall, stately Gate of St. Agatha, Renata joined her mother and friend in the cart where the women talked excitedly of all they had just seen. Angelica rode with Carlo, discussing the history of Palermo and of Sicily. Riding through orchards, they soon came upon a humble church built by Cistercians more than 100 years before. Angelica helped the women from the cart, gaily informing them of the Sicilian attachment to this church.

"For as long as I can remember, all Palermitanos and often Sicilian pilgrims, gather in the square of Santo Spirito for the Vespers service on Easter Monday. It is a unique custom, yes, but a social and religious occasion not to be missed." Shrugging and smiling without fully understanding the importance of such a tradition, the pilgrims entered the church, again allowing Sophia and Perna their privacy in front of the altar.

Angelica lingered only briefly, letting the rest of the party keep an eye on the two women while she briskly re-inventoried the drinks and refreshments packed in the women's cart. Detaching one of her guards, she instructed him to precede them to their third station, the Church of Santa Maria dell'Ammiraglio, or as it was affectionately known by the locals, *La Martorana*, taken from the pious founders of the original Benedictine convent founded there in 1194. There they would stop for a mid-day repast and sample the nuns' delicious *pasta reale*.

The pilgrims emerged respectfully from Santo Spirito. The warmth of the Sicilian sun and being surrounded by the ever-present fragrance of orchards and gardens imparted a lassitude among the pilgrims. Angelica noted especially that Sophia, carrying her extra burden, seemed suddenly fatigued. Approaching her, she put her arm around the woman's shoulders and whispered, "Sophia, at our next destination you may sit for awhile and we will have dinner."

At the idea of food and drink, Sophia perked up and nodded vigorously.

As Angelica carefully handed her into the shaded cart, Sophia impulsively took her hand. "Angelica, I've never seen more incredible and exotic things than I have today. How can I ever thank you? I'm sure the sainted Virgin must rest often in these beautiful places. I do not doubt that she has heard my prayers, but I made healthy offerings at each altar just to make sure. "

Angelica hugged her and laughing softly said, "Sophia, we still have more shrines to pray at – the best is yet to come!" And they drove off gaily, having indeed enjoyed both visual and spiritual treats.

The cart clattered into the courtyard of La Martorana, where the abbess, a personal friend of Angelica's, waited calmly with two novices to welcome her guests. As introductions were made, Abbess Pace, who looked as peaceful as her name, escorted the small group into the church. The simplicity of the exterior and its bell tower contrasted markedly with the elaborate interior that made them gasp in amazement. Byzantine mosaics depicting Norman kings, delicate wood and marble columns painted with brilliant colors and everywhere – gold. It was like liquid sunshine pouring over them. The ethereal effect made Sophia almost run to the altar where gasping, she dropped to her knees along with everyone else behind her. The sun streamed in through etched windows, laving the altar in a heavenly light continually reflected by the interior splendor. The pilgrims, especially Sophia, lingered long there, and when the tired woman rose, her face was radiant. The obvious beauty of the shrine and the special tenderness shining in the face of the marble Virgin soaked the worshippers in love and compassion.

Sighing, they silently filed out the side door through a long passage into the convent where a simple yet delightful lunch was laid out for them. Fresh bread, wine, olives, cheese, figs, delicate lettuces laced with saffron and minced vegetables, together with small roasted pieces of meat, were on the table. To one side on an exquisitely carved display, alone as befitting its special status, was a plate of the nuns' famous almond pastries. The generous patronage provided without fail by Angelica every year ensured such a welcome at any time for her and any guests. Energized by the brilliance of the church and the delicious smells of the food, the pilgrims fell to and began exclaiming over what they had seen.

Unnoticed, Angelica and Abbess Pace withdrew to a small, austere chamber and sat talking quietly. Although this order had charge of the dazzling opulence in the sanctuary, the nuns' living and personal spaces were spare. A simple wooden bench and small table sat beneath a small window high on the wall that was, at the moment, illuminating a plain wooden cross on the opposite wall. There were neither hearth nor wall sconces for light. Angelica had been in this room many times, and felt its serenity wrap around her like swaddling clothes. Here she unburdened her heart regarding the last few days while the abbess listened quietly. When the two finished, the abbess, after holding Angelica's hands briefly in prayer, rose with her guest and returned to the pilgrims, inviting them to taste the convent's famous pastries.

Enthusiastically, every last crumb was devoured. So extravagant were the praises from her guests that finally the abbess had to hold up her hands, laughing, and protest for them to stop. With a chorus of goodbyes and thanks, Carlos and Perna, Sophia and Renata, blissfully made their way back to the courtyard and their horses. The guards, still licking their lips, had evidently had their repast too and were as satisfied as their patrons.

"Sophia, I'm sure you must be tired but we have two quick stops yet today. One is directly across the courtyard from us. Perhaps you noticed it as we came in. San Cataldo was originally built as the chapel of the palace of Maio of Bari, King William I's admiral." Everyone turned and noticed that its three dusky red domes mirrored those of San Giovanni.

Perna turned a perplexed glance to Angelica who, anticipating her question, nodded her head vigorously. "Yes, the Normans often used Moorish architects and incorporated Moorish style into their buildings. There were many more Muslims in Palermo at that time and, as you no doubt know, many of them were palace officials, such as Head of the Queen's Household or even Admiral, a Moorish term itself, yes? And of course, you know that Sicily was under Muslim rule for almost 200 years. It is beautiful and graceful, is it not? And colorful?"

Everyone agreed and trooped happily into the small church which, in contrast to *La Martorana*, was spare and unadorned, yet still pleased the group with its lovely lines and symmetry. After a short pause at the altar, the pilgrims crossed the courtyard thronged with people, helped the older women back into the cart and arranged themselves on their horses to set off once again. By this time, the languid afternoon sun was drooping. "Only one more stop today and then back for a long nap and supper," Angelica called out.

A short distance away, her guests were transported again into a garden filled with herbs, fountains, palm trees, roses, columbines, and neatly laid out vegetable plots. "This," said Angelic proudly, "is the Church of Sanitissima Trinita alla Magione. It belongs to the Teutonic Knights and is one of our most popular churches." Massive and awe-inspiring, the pilgrims respectfully made their way into the enormous, gloomy interior. Statutes and marble columns dominated, making the wayfarers feel small and insignificant. They could hear monastic chanting in the distance and a trace of incense floated through the air. The imposing nave pressed upon the pilgrims a mood of somber respect. They lingered here the least, but perhaps because of its size and grandeur, retained an impression of it in their memories long after they left Palermo.

Now her pilgrims were weary and sleepy. Angelica began to lead them home through another busy commercial and market section of Palermo. Checking on the women, she observed them to be actually napping with eyes closed inside the shaded cart. Impulsively, she decided on a slight detour at the Fondaco dei Catalani. Under the guise of buying wine for The Olive, Angelica glided into the owner's office, barely noticing a man loafing in the corner.

As she began to speak to the manager, a deep, slow voice was suddenly at her elbow. Startled, she looked up into the dark eyes of an imposing figure.

"Signora de Rogerio, I understand you have been asking about me. Let me introduce myself. I am Ferdinand de Francisco de Yrallia de Lerida, merchant of Barcelona and friend to kings and princes. Would you like to ask your questions in person?" And he smiled sardonically at her surprise and discomfort.

Angelica, initially panicky, rapidly controlled her face and her emotions. So *this* was the dangerous one. Well, he couldn't do anything to her in front of everyone here, and with her entourage waiting patiently, albeit almost unconsciously, outside. Reassured, she smiled slowly into his eyes, which widened with admiration at her quick control. "Signor de Lerida, I would very much like to sit down with you over a glass of wine. However, I have," she inclined her head towards the door, "a number of pilgrims with me, mostly ladies, and I must attend to their needs first. Perhaps you can suggest something?"

The merchant smiled like a barracuda. "Of course. Donato, please make our guests welcome." He snapped his fingers without looking at the hostel owner, who rushed around the counter past the two and ushered the sleepy and surprised pilgrims, stunned into momentary silence, into the shaded inner courtyard while rapidly calling to slaves and servants. "Bring cool water, fresh bread and fruit, some cheeses, olives, damp cloths for our guests to wash off the dust of the city! Hurry!"

As Donato took care of his impromptu guests, de Lerida offered his arm to Angelica, gesturing towards a private corner of the large, cool courtyard. Leaving her briefly seated under a large, fragrant lemon tree, he returned with chilled wine and fruit for their repast, then sat down uncomfortably close to her, smiling as he did so.

Angelica was thinking rapidly. Clearly he knew she had been asking about him. Should she stick to her story about buying goods for The Olive? Should she be bolder?

"Signor de Lerida, I have been making certain discreet, I hope," and at this she dimpled and smiled up at him, "inquiries, first about your goods for our hostel, The Olive. They are said to be of first rate quality and that impresses me. I am a *Catalana* by birth, as I'm sure you know, and I have a taste for some of the delicacies of my homeland. I also have a brother and sister-in-law who recently opened a tavern, a family business, and I was inquiring on their behalf as well." She glanced at him and he continued to look at her, his face expressionless. She fell silent, willing him to direct the conversation further so that she might know what tack to take.

The merchant obliged her by speaking in a low, sonorous voice. "Signora, I have heard your inquiries were of a more personal nature than wine and cheese. Forgive me, but I certainly have never made your acquaintance nor the acquaintance of your obviously esteemed husband," and here he gave a graceful little half-bow from the waist, "but since you are here now, my impetuous nature urges me to ask the true reason you have been asking about me?"

Angelica was taken aback by his directness, but being direct herself, briskly replied. "You may or may not know about some circumstances that have recently happened at The Leopard, my brother and sister-in-law's tavern in the Porta Patitellorum."

De Lerida raised an eyebrow and shrugged. She looked at him straightforwardly. "I will be frank, Signor. There have been two murders. My brother-in-law is falsely accused of one murder, and my family is determined to help him. Both men, we learned, had recent contact with you. Naturally, we are interested to know what your connections or your business may have been with them."

"And who are these men, Signora," he asked politely?

"They are – or were – Ludovico Stefani and Antonio de Paruta," replied Angelica. She waited, looking straight at him.

Amused by her blunt manner, Ferdinand kept his face blank. "Yes, I knew both of them slightly through my business partner, Simon de Paruta. Does that answer your question? In fact, I was thinking of going to see Simon later on today to offer my condolences for his nephew. I trust that would be proper, wouldn't you think?"

"I think your own conscience would be your guide, Signor de Lerida. Thank you for answering my question. Usually a gentleman's business connections would be of no interest to me, except for the unusual circumstances we now face. Do you understand?" and she lifted her golden eyes, unsmiling, to his face. It was an incomplete answer from an obviously secretive man, yet she dare not prod any further. She wanted to avoid drawing more attention to her family.

"Yes, I understand perfectly," he said coldly. "And now, may I escort you back to your group? And home safely?"

"Thank you, but we have our own escort. I appreciate your frankness." Angelica stood gracefully and walked over to her pilgrims, who were relaxing and chatting quietly on the other side of the courtyard. Speaking softly to them, they lazily began gathering their shawls, thanking Donato for his hospitality and pressing coins into his eager hand. She helped the very pregnant Sophia into the cart one last time, and as they rumbled slowly out of the cobblestone courtyard, her guards encircling the entourage, she glanced back. Ferdinand watched her, somewhat, she thought, like a lion watching its prey. She turned back to her group, leaving Ferdinand brooding under the lemon tree, thinking about murdered men and a lovely, golden-eyed woman.

CHAPTER 20

As the pilgrims filed back into The Olive, sleepy and sated, they encountered Pietro Manfredi sitting in front of the window to take the afternoon sun. He was silent and moody. Angelica glanced speculatively at the old crusader several times but he never noticed her or any of the others as they disembarked and entered the hostel. Best just to let him be, she thought.

Angelica and Raynaldus had had a long talk last night after he returned from Simon's, tired and anxious. Finding him in his study now, Angelica told him about her encounter with Ferdinand de Lerida. She decided not to say anything about her argument with Ysabella. Angelica had begun to feel very uneasy about the safety of her dear sister-in-law and her new business. After conferring hurriedly with Renata about the next day's plans and tonight's supper, Angelica slipped out of The Olive and hurried over to her old neighborhood in the Ruga Pisanorum.

Ysabella had gotten up early that day. She and William took Amodeus's breakfast to him, but for some reason, they were not allowed to stay and talk to him. She managed to tell him about Antonio but was unceremoniously shoved out by a yawning guard. As she angrily left, she glimpsed Amodeus's shocked face, and hurried home with her son. William, oblivious to his mother's anxiety, chattered all the way back to The Leopard, where he was summarily sent off to the kitchen to do chores. Larissa and Mario were already in the kitchen, sorting utensils and foodstuffs and beginning the day's cooking. Two slaves were cleaning the floors and the fireplace. As she continued to clean and inventory her supplies, Ysabella lost track of time. Her stomach finally reminded her that she had not fueled it. Was it really the middle of the afternoon? She hadn't heard the church bells at all! Where was her mind? She just sat down with a bowl of leftover soup when Uncle Leo strolled through the doorway.

"Ah, Ysabella. I have some business in the Great Market this afternoon. I have a few transactions to make, and we need some information, I think. Let me take William, will you? He's such good company." He ruffled the boy's hair as William jumped up and down in excitement. Grateful, Ysabella nodded and the two went happily out the door together discussing what they would be buying that day. As she focused on her son's face adoringly turned up to Leo's, who was listening gravely, she thought how lucky they were that Leo de Iannacio was a part of their lives.

Ysabella looked at the *buctarium* laid with dishes of food and was satisfied. She was determined even more to keep The Leopard open. The day had passed in a rush of cleaning and cooking and as the light began to fade, afternoon customers began to drift in. She had just set three mugs of ale before the cobbler and his assistants when the front door flew open, a slant of brilliant sunlight momentarily piercing the dimness. She spun around just in time to recognize Joanna, coming in smiling and talking of baking bread.

Both women bustled around the kitchen, gathering the flour and eggs to begin their task. After mixing and kneading and shaping in the warm room, both women were sweaty and sticky. "Let's sit down, Ysabella. I have something I need to say to you." Ysabella yawned and sat down at the huge table in the kitchen, absent-mindedly pushing little bits of flour and yeast around with her fingers. The silence stretched out like the loaves they were shaping. Surprised, Ysabella looked up to find Joanna staring at her disapprovingly.

"Ysabella, I know you've been under a terrible strain, and the neighborhood wants to protect you but several of the women were talking at the well this morning and well, you should know that some of them were really horrified at what you and Larissa did, going down to the port. They're wondering," pursing her lips, "if you're planning on doing anything else that is reckless and ill-considered." Ysabella's mouth dropped open. What?! The voice went on.

"And I'm just telling you, dear, that that ill-conceived plan of yours almost got not only you, but Larissa, killed! What are you thinking? We're respectable women. We don't sashay down to the port where questionable people are, not without our men anyway. I just thought you should know what they're saying, and that I agree with them. You must be more careful. Especially with Amodeus not here. Please … ". Her voice trailed off as she saw Ysabella's stricken face. Then she got up, awkwardly patted her on the shoulder, untied her apron, and left.

··········

William was having a wonder-filled time. Uncle Leo stopped for pastries at the bakery of Pino de Faccarella. The heavenly smells had overwhelmed him, and his shy paralysis caused both Pino and his wife to exchange smiles with Leo and give him a little extra, a sweet sesame seed bun filled with raisins and cinnamon. Deliriously happy, with sugar dripping down his chin, William walked with Leo to the Great Market, where Leo began hailing friends and discussing business and gossip. William wandered from stall to stall as he waited, greeting some vendors by their first names.

They all watched out for the scamp who escaped from home every chance he got to run to the market. He pestered all the merchants about their wares, from the exotic to the mundane. He simply couldn't get enough of the smells, colors, sounds and excitement that engulfed him at the bazaar. The great Arabic souk of several centuries ago had stood on this very spot. Even though most of the Arabic merchants had long ago left Palermo, there were still Muslims who lived in the city and visited the market frequently, merchants who still had vital and profitable contacts with Baghdad and even China, and who brought beautiful, foreign-looking ceramics, textiles and foods to the Sicilian capital. William often listened, mouth open, to the stories of one vendor, Salim, who sometimes gave him candied fruit made by his wife, and who told him wild tales of a sailor named Sinbad and the monsters and evildoers he fought.

William became absorbed at a woodworker's stall. An apprentice was fashioning a small wooden warhorse, prancing in its armor, and the young boy stood, fascinated, as the man's hands swiftly carved the delicate lines.

Looking up, he smiled, and offered the eager boy a small wooden sword. Delighted with the gift, William thrust and whooped in a poor imitation of a Roman soldier as the carver watched in amusement.

Spying something underneath the stall, William stooped to scoop up one particularly interesting shaving from the ground. Suddenly, a hand shot out, grabbing him around the mouth, and another hand grabbed his shirt. He was hauled behind the stall's awnings unnoticed by the apprentice who had gone back to his work.

Furiously, the boy began to struggle against the rough hands that held him fast, but he was pulled into a dark alley by two smelly, evil-looking men. The tall one, with lanky dark hair and bad breath, pushed him against a wall, uncoiling a rope obviously meant to tie him up. Terrified, the boy went limp, which resulted in his captor clutching him even more tightly. Stuffing a rag into the boy's mouth, the tall man swiftly tied his arms and legs, then scooped him up under his arm like a sack of potatoes and ran down the alley away from the busy market place. Scanning behind them, the men saw no one was following. They took a moment to catch their breath and to wrap the boy carefully in a large blanket. As they headed towards the Kalsa, a tangled warren of broken down buildings and wretched storefronts that had clearly seen better days, their burden could have been a pig or a kid headed to slaughter.

A short walk brought the trio to a nondescript building facing the harbor. Ducking hurriedly inside, they checked again to see if anyone had noticed. People in the lanes around them went about their own business and apparently had paid no attention to the men with a wiggling lump in their sack. Striding swiftly through to the back door, they trod up a narrow gangplank to a vessel moored at a nearby pier where they threw the boy into a small and windowless room, and slammed the door. The last thing the terrified boy heard was a bolt slamming home, leaving him in the dark.

Leo, ambling through the Great Market visiting old friends and asking for news about Lerida, eventually began to look around for William. It was getting on into the late afternoon and he really should get the boy home. He asked some of the merchants where the lad had gone, but all he received were shrugs or shakes of the head. Leo became concerned when his young charge's head hadn't soon popped up beside a stall, pestering someone or asking a thousand questions. Soon even the vendors realized that the boy who had scampered around only a short time ago had vanished, and as if in unison, most of the merchants silently left their shops and stalls and spread out over the labyrinth of twisting alleyways and narrow streets to look for the boy. When it finally became apparent that the boy had simply disappeared, Leo stood with his shocked companions in an uncomprehending helplessness. Salim, arousing the stricken man, fervently begged him to send a swift message to Raynaldus.

Ysabella did not immediately comprehend that something momentous had happened when Leo, Raynaldus, and Adam, followed by a small group of grim-faced merchants came in the door. She thought perhaps Raynaldus and Leo were bringing friends and business acquaintances to The Leopard for some supper and refreshments. Immediately, she bustled about, making her new customers comfortable. As she went to the storeroom for wine and beer, Raynaldus spoke softly to her and then disappeared with Leo and Adam into the back room. Surprised and curious, she turned over the crowd to Larissa and hurried after them.

"Raynaldus, you're so mysterious," she began, smiling.

"Ysabella, sit down," Raynaldus said gently. Then he and Leo told her about the afternoon's catastrophe.

Ysabella's mouth dropped open, and she turned to her brother-in-law. "You can't be serious! William is missing? Uncle Leo?" she screamed, eyes wide. She fell heavily into a chair as her hands fluttered up to cover her ears as if doing so would prevent any more bad news.

Leo knelt swiftly in front of her taking both her hands into his. "My dear," he whispered brokenly, "I'm so sorry – he was there one minute – I'm so sorry … " Ysabella's head dropped onto his shoulder and she began sobbing, seizing Leo's tunic spasmodically. Raynaldus paced the room angrily, trying to think.

He had been so worried about Ysabella's reaction that he had not thought of anything but telling her as soon as possible. That task accomplished, he now began to plot a way to find the boy. With his mind now on action, he asked Adam to send for the *magister platea*, the city official in charge of the Great Market, as well as the sheriff and the magistrate in charge of the quarter of the *Porta Patitellorum*. Adam left hurriedly, and Raynaldus motioned Leo away from the distraught woman.

"Ysabella, dearest, we need to think how to get your son back. We need to search – now – for him and bring him back home."

She lifted her reddened and tear-streaked face to him. "Why did they take him? Who could have done this?" she began angrily, spreading her hands on the table in front of her.

Raynaldus swiftly put his hand over hers, stopping her words. "Ysabella," he said carefully, staring into her panicked eyes, "perhaps you should come to stay with us for awhile. We don't know if this was some random snatching, or if it is connected somehow with the murders. We just don't know enough yet, but now, I'm really worried about you. So is Leo. Until the authorities find out why these men kidnapped William, and until they find him, you may be in danger. Please, come stay with us."

Ysabella sat very still, shocked at her brother-in-law's words and her son's disappearance. William was in danger! Drawing her hands into her lap, she plucked nervously at her dress, her hair partially covering her face, trying to comprehend. Her mind raced about how upside down their lives had suddenly become and not knowing why. Why was this happening! The immediacy of how precious her husband and son really were to her slammed into her brain. And she was afraid now. Really afraid. For Amodeus…for William…and for herself.

At first she had assumed that, as horrible as the murders were, they would find the killer or killers and the officials' mistake would be cleared up. But now it seemed that whoever was responsible might think nothing of killing her whole family. Amodeus should be here. She wanted to be smothered in his reassuring embrace and give him this burden. As she saw in her mind the dark, menacing cell of his confinement, there was a roaring in her ears and she seemed curiously disassociated from everyone. Woodenly, she rose, listlessly allowed Larissa to gather a few things, and went out the door with her family, still in a fog. Her lips moved, silently praying for her son's safety and an end to this surreal, unending nightmare.

At The Olive Angelica fussed over Ysabella and tried to make her comfortable. Ysabella kept screaming and crying. Who would take William? Why? Angelica finally gave her sister-in-law an herbal potion to help her sleep. She stayed until Ysabella drifted off, holding the work-worn hand and thinking. Tomorrow's planned excursion to Mount Pellegrino and the shrine of Santa Rosalia would have to be delayed. She stroked Ysabella's hair one more time and went downstairs to talk to Renata.

CHAPTER 21

William woke up shivering and hungry. His head hurt. Had they hit him and knocked him out? He couldn't remember. Everything happened so fast and his memory was fuzzy. He opened his eyes cautiously, afraid of who or what he might see. It was dark and as his vision began to adjust, he realized two things. First, he was alone. Secondly, the smelly bed that he was thrown onto was gently rocking. It seemed just like the time Uncle Leo and his friend, Josef the Jew, had taken him with them to finalize a business deal aboard a ship about to sail for Verona. That was it! He was on a boat! Were they leaving Palermo? Was he being sold into slavery? He had heard stories from Uncle Leo and the market vendors about young boys sold as slaves to the Saracens. Was that what was happening? He began to shake uncontrollably and tears slid silently out from under eyelids suddenly squeezed shut. As he struggled to control his tears, he heard slamming and thumping above him, and a loud male voice that was coming closer to his bed.

Abruptly the door was flung open and a man's silhouette loomed in the doorway. William sat up pushing backward against the rough wall. The man chuckled at the fear on his face, then tossed him some bread and cheese and a greasy leather flask. "Here," he said gruffly. "Eat that. Don't want you dyin' on us. No use to us that way." He then tossed a dirty blanket onto the bed, turned and stomped out, slamming the door and reinserting the spike that held it tightly closed.

William fell upon the food, and even though a day ago he would have thrown such rubbish to the dogs, he finished every scrap. He grimaced at the sour, watered wine in the flask but drained it as a man would in the desert. His hunger and thirst momentarily abated, he began looking around. There were no windows, but the gentle rocking made him sure he was on a boat. He sat for several moments paying attention to the languid rise and fall. He felt no sudden surge of motion or any waves buffeting the ship's skirting.

Perhaps they were not sailing or rowing, but moored to one place. Maybe they were still in Palermo and he could escape!

He leaped from the bed and began to explore his room. It seemed more like a large closet. Wooden planking, no windows, door stoutly locked from the outside. He began to stomp on each and every floorboard, testing the strength of the wood, but the planks resisted every effort. He then moved to the walls, with the same result. Dejected and tired again, he lay down on the bed, pulling the filthy blanket over him.

He must have fallen asleep because without warning a rough hand ripped the blanket off him and picked him up by his shirt. Frightened, the boy started howling, which ended abruptly when his holder casually slapped him across the mouth, growling at him to be quiet. William collapsed, frightened and hiccupping, as the man dragged him out of his prison and into another room. He tossed him onto the floor and when the boy looked up, he saw two men in front of him. One was well-dressed and tanned, silently observing the small bundle on the floor. The other was tall and lean, with dark, lank hair—the same man who had grabbed him at the market. A third man, bulky and bearded, stood in the shadows. William found himself staring at the eyes in the dark man's face, because one was blue and one was brown. Blinking, he sat up, rubbing his eyes.

The well-dressed man glanced at his companion. "Is this the right boy?" The other one nodded. "Then let's send a message. No more questions in the marketplace. No more of their amateur investigating. They keep on looking, the boy gets to take a trip to Araby and make new friends." They all laughed quietly, looking coldly down at the boy.

William glared up at him and then said fiercely, "Who are you? My uncle will put you in prison for this! He's important!"

Startled by the unexpected courage of the lad, both men grinned. "Well, boy, he'll have to find you first, won't he? I don't think he will!" drawled the man that William privately had labeled "the captain".

"But you show spunk, so I'll tell you what. You can remain in that little room untied. We'll give you food and drink. But if your family keeps looking for my friends here," and he turned to the two standing silently behind him, "well, you're going to take a little trip. It's all up to them, really, if you're going home or not."

William digested this quietly, staring around him. His mind began to race. How could he get away? He was only a small boy and there were three men, probably more. "Am I on a ship?" he asked hesitantly.

"Aye, you are," the captain said gravely. "They can search all Palermo and they won't find *you*!"

The captain turned toward the door and pulled a folded piece of paper from his vest. He shoved it into one of his companion's hand. "Leave him down here with some food. We have work to do. Deliver this to de Rogerio at The Olive. Leave it stuck on the front door with an old knife. They'll get the drift." The man with one blue eye nodded, and the trio all left the enclosure. As they opened the door, William caught a brief glimpse of blue sky and the shape of Mount Pellegrino, then the door slammed shut. He *was* still in Palermo. There was still hope.

....

Adam de Citella sat in his office with his sons and nephews. All of them were notaries and were gradually taking on more and more responsibilities in the very profitable family business that Adam started 30 years ago. The older man was grim and angry. The family had rarely seen him like this, but the thought that their favorite scamp had been snatched from them, and perhaps something worse, made them all gloomy and distraught.

Adam bellowed, "I want you to talk to every single vendor, every single merchant, every single shop owner. Find a description of whoever snatched our boy. Ask your questions under the guise of doing business--I don't want you to be obvious. And I want you to make it clear that everyone has to be silent on this! But I want it done and I want it done today. Meet me at The Olive tonight for supper." The younger men all nodded and left Adam sitting at his desk, drumming his fingers and looking out the window, wishing they had left this in the hands of the authorities.

Leo de Iannacio dragged himself into Adam's office and slumped onto the bench against the wall. He had aged ten years since yesterday. "Adam," he began, and then stopped.

Adam got up and put his hand on his friend's shoulder. "You couldn't know, Leo, that something like this would happen. Don't worry, we'll get him back. We'll get him back because these men really don't know who they're dealing with. They don't know who we know. They think we're just a bunch of fat, rich men without backbones. They'll find out they are very mistaken. Very."

Leo looked up and smiled. "Adam, if they only knew you 30 years ago! What a fierce man you were!"

"Yes, I was, Leo. Life here in Palermo has been sweet. Leaving Melfi was the best thing I ever did, but it was hard. Hard, and I saw cruel things after Manfred died. The Angevins were merciless. I found peace here. I found a wonderful woman, God rest her soul, and I have fine sons and daughters. But the de Rogerios are like family too, since you and I took them under our wings all those years ago. I'm not resting until I find that boy and whoever took him. And believe me, whoever took him will pay dearly." The old fierceness had obviously returned. The investigation, and the risk, had become too personal to stay out of the fray.

"Now, I think you and I have a few people we need to go see ourselves. Shall we?"

The two men walked out into the Porta Patitellorum towards the Kalsa and the port. As they walked along, Leo kicked distractedly at small stones in the road. Adam knew his friend wanted to say something so he waited patiently until Leo had formed his thoughts.

"Adam, I hate to bring up something distasteful. But did you draw up Amodeus and Ysabella's wedding contract and will?"

Surprised, Adam shook his head. "No. When they got married I was on the mainland on business. Salerno de Pellegrino did their contracts. Why?"

"Because, Adam, if this doesn't turn out the way we hope it does, Ysabella will need to make some decisions." Adam stopped in the street, eliciting a muffled curse from a man behind him. He looked at Leo, horrified. Leo looked him steadily in the eye and nodded.

"Yes, she will. Do you know when they got married whether they married under the *mos Latinorum* or the *mos Grecorum*? Couples in Palermo have such a choice, you know, and it all revolves around property dispersal."

Adam shook his head. "I don't know, Leo. Which one of us should talk to her?" Both men looked away, neither one wanting this depressing task.

Leo sighed. "I'll do it but Adam . . .," his voice trailed off miserably. "Yes, I know Leo." With nothing left to say, the two men left each other wrapped in his own thoughts.

....

Ysabella was pale, but firm when she woke up from her induced sleep and stumbled downstairs at The Olive. There was still a faint afterglow in the sky after the sunset, but clouds were massing on the horizon. She found Raynaldus and Angelica sipping cups of tea before the hearth in the kitchen. Despite the cook chopping onions for the night's meal, the entire hostel was eerily quiet.

"Have you found William yet?" Ysabella demanded, as if Raynaldus were shirking his duties by lazing in front of the fire. "Does Amodeus know?"

"Calm yourself, dear sister. Adam, Leo, and all the merchants are looking for William. We will find him" Raynaldus said grimly. "Amodeus may have heard something about this through the idle talk of his jailers—after all, the whole town probably knows by now—but no one has yet been to see him."

"I am not calm, and I will not pretend to be so! We're talking about my son, my only child," Ysabella retorted. She roughly swiped the back of her hand across her eyes to prevent the tears from falling and took two or three deep breaths, regaining a measure of composure. "Raynaldus, I know it's dark out but I will not rest until my husband knows. And I need to be the one to tell him. No one else. Either you come with me or I'll go alone. And then I must return to The Leopard. What if he comes home and no one is there?"

Raynaldus only grunted, swallowing hard. The last few days had turned their lovely Ysabella into a bearcat, he thought, and she would not hesitate to make good on her promise if he refused her. He was swathed in exhaustion but knew he would not truly rest even if he tried to sleep. Snapping his fingers and shouting for his menservants, he strode out the front door of The Olive. Grabbing hard onto Angelica's hand as she pressed a food packet into her arms, Ysabella took a random cloak from a peg near the door and followed slowly, fatigue and the remains of Angelica's sleeping potion clouding her consciousness.

They walked to the jail surrounded by watchful, armed retainers. Raynaldus was taking no chances now. He couldn't bear to look at his sister-in-law, but then, lost in her own thoughts and struggling with what to say to her husband, she barely noticed.

Raynaldus and Ysabella watched helplessly as Amodeus threw back his head and howled like a trapped animal when they told him William had been kidnapped.

"Why are they doing this to us?!" he screamed. "Who are these beasts? Why did they take my son?!" and he beat his fists against the cold stone walls until his hands were torn and bloody. Sobbing, he collapsed on the bench. Ysabella and Raynaldus, tears streaming down their faces, knelt beside him, Ysabella stroking his hair.

Amodeus's eyes ignited with a fierce light, but when he had no more fight left in him, they softened. "How many days have I been here helpless? They know I couldn't have killed Antonio. Get me out of here! I can't do anything to help you find my son by sitting here. Ysabella, my beautiful Ysabella, you're shouldering the burden of everything – investigating, taking care of the tavern, keeping us together …", his voice trailed off.

"And you, Raynaldus." Not wanting to discuss William yet, the horror still clamping on top of him, he hugged Ysabella and Raynaldus, tears in his eyes.

Raynaldus, swallowing hard, said gruffly, "Well, you'd do the same for me. We will have more to tell you tomorrow, but now I have to go. I have some people to talk to yet. I want you to eat, keep up your strength. Pray, brother, pray that we'll be successful soon. I know we're close." He gave a crooked smile to his brother and turned to call the guard.

Ysabella, her head still buried under Amodeus's armpit, hugged him fiercely, thinking she felt just as imprisoned as her husband. Then she turned to follow her brother-in-law. All three suddenly stared at each other, their love spilling out wordlessly like an undulating silk sheet. Raynaldus heard the key turn, cleared his throat, ushered Ysabella out before him and left Amodeus, who sat down shakily and slowly, between sobs, and began to eat the food they had brought him.

Nicolo popped his head inside the kitchen where his mother still sat before the hearth. Once he heard that, as usual, Ysabella had had her way and was going back to The Leopard after seeing Amodeus, he volunteered to make sure his father and aunt were safe and to escort them to The Leopard.

That headstrong woman, Angelica thought! I can't believe Raynaldus would let her go back! Of course, knowing her sister-in-law, what could he have done? He had come home very shaken himself. Angelica looked at her son speculatively. Since his friend Antonio was killed, he had been very quiet. Perhaps, like her, he needed something to do.

"All right, Nicolo, but be careful and make sure one or two of the guards stay there too. Don't let her stay alone. Larissa will be there, of course, but they aren't thinking of their own risk. In fact, you might want to stay there yourself, at least for tonight, to keep Ysabella company. You always were a favorite of hers."

Nicolo nodded, went out to the stables and saddled a horse. He thundered out of the small courtyard. He planned to do more than just check on his aunt, and he might need better transportation than his legs for that. Upon arriving at the tavern, he was met at the door by two armed men who demanded his name before they let him enter.

Nicolo had expected The Leopard to be dark and quiet. To his surprise, the tavern was still crowded, buzzing with chatter and the clatter of plates, bowls and utensils. The entire neighborhood had arrived determined to protect one of their own, and then stayed to eat and drink. Some of the men offered to sleep in the main room for her protection. Ysabella knew she had done the right thing by coming back. And although she tried not to show how desperately sick she was inside about her son and her husband, her anxiety flickered like the wings of a tiny butterfly behind her smiles and sallies. Some of the neighborhood women pushed her back onto her seat and took her place waiting the tables and shouting out the food orders as the owner sat gratefully, slowly sipping her wine and listening.

To her astonishment, the neighbors themselves had spread out over the city, asking friends and relatives to keep their eyes open for any sign of the young boy they considered their neighborhood mascot. Since he could walk, William had become a local favorite with his mischievous grin and pert forays through the streets with Uncle Leo or Nicolo and sometimes, to everyone's amusement, by himself. Everyone prayed that the boy would come to no harm.

Surprised by the activity, Nicolo hesitantly waded through the crowd to hug Ysabella, who hugged him back and smiled resignedly. "I can see you're not alone here, Aunt," making an attempt at humor. "Do you think you'll be safe here for awhile?" They both started laughing, twisting their heads at the throng of neighbors. "I brought my horse. Since you have so many protectors, I think I will ride through the port area and look for William. No, I don't expect to find him, but I just want to do something, you know?"

"Yes, I do know. My neighbors have made it quite clear that they won't leave me here alone and that they expect The Leopard to be open tonight. I think I'll be just fine, but please, Nicolo," she caught his hand, "be careful. I don't know who took William or why, but you could be in danger, too. Maybe we are all in danger, as your mother believes. I have to stay here, Nicolo. You understand--if William should come home....."

"Yes, Aunt, I understand, and I'll be careful. I'll come back here later and stay the night with you and Larissa. I promised my mother you wouldn't be alone." The young man patted his aunt's shoulder and made a silly little bow, then strode out the door with Ysabella looking fondly after him. After a brief moment of silence, the chatter picked up again and Ysabella was swept into the everyday cares of her neighbors and friends, silently appreciating the love and concern so evident in their faces and gestures, and their vain efforts to divert her.

Nicolo walked his horse down into the Kalsa, stopping appreciatively at side entrance of the vast and fragrant gardens of the Citadel, a massive fortress that complemented Mount Pellegrino across the harbor. Built by the last Emir of Palermo, it boasted a vast irrigation system that watered both the gardens and a private bath. Monks had taken over there and cultivated not only herbal medicines, but fruit orchards, vegetables and fragrant flowers. Nicolo always had thought of it as a peaceful oasis in the midst of the hustle and bustle of the busy commercial city, but clouds had moved across the island, and he could feel the dampness in the air. It would rain soon. Sighing, he moved on towards the port and found himself outside the office of the *magister portulano*. Hesitantly, he walked into the office of the master of the port, whom he had known since he was five years old.

"Nicolo!" a booming voice called out. He spun around and found himself face to face with the shrewd, friendly face of Francesco Ventimiglia, a close friend of his father's and the man to whom Ysabella and Larissa had spilled out their story of self-defense.

"Come in. Come in. Have some wine! I'm surprised to see you. What brings you down here so late? I was just about to go home myself."

The two stepped into Francesco's office and closed the door. While Francesco busied himself pouring wine for his guest, Nicolo tried to explain his presence. "I don't know why I ended up here, Signor Ventimiglia, but I have a question in the back of my head. I hope you won't think I'm foolish but ..." he trailed off, looking distressed.

Francesco inclined his head. "I know about the boy, Nicolo. I know you're all looking for him. I myself am keeping my eyes open for suspicious activities, so you let me know when you find him. I know your father will find him."

Nicolo looked down, then directly at Francesco, deciding to be blunt with his concerns. "If someone was kidnapping small boys to be sold as slaves, how would they get them out of Palermo?"

Francesco stared a moment at the young man thoughtfully before responding. "Well, there are several ways. We have a brisk slave trade here in Palermo, but as you know, it's generally a stopover either from North Africa, or from the East, or Genoa, where the slaves have been rounded up and collected. I don't approve of child slavery so I have tried to keep a very close eye for years on what goes on here regarding that. I mean, it's legal so my hands to some extent are tied, but I try to discourage that traffic where I can and see that the traders in children know they are unwelcome."

He frowned and put his long legs up on his desk, sipped some wine, and continued, "The slaves not sold here are moved out on ships. No question about that. We're an island, right? Some slaves are moved overland to Trapani where they work in the saltpans, and from there they may eventually be shipped to Genoa, Cyprus, sometimes Spain. Sometimes they are taken to Messina to be sold and whatever is left from that, to Malta or the Italian mainland to work in the mines until they die, mercifully. Children, now, that's a different story. They are usually shipped quickly to Genoa, then to the East. The Turks love their little eunuchs, you know, and pay high prices for the healthy and attractive ones." He sat silently while Nicolo struggled with images of William becoming a eunuch.

"I haven't seen any such ships lately. I know all the slavers and keep an eye on them. So far, the slaves I've seen moving in and out of here have been the usual – men and women. No children. I know just about every captain's ship in this harbor – big and small. Do you truly think William was taken for that purpose? No other boys were taken that I know of, so I thought William's disappearance had to do with the murders."

"That is the most likely theory, and we have no idea where they may have taken him, but we cannot afford to overlook any possibility."

"Then I would strongly suggest you get your father to go to the judges and have them authorize a ship-by-ship search for him. It's rarely done--you can see why--it's so time-consuming. But if you think he may be here, well, let's do it and see who and what we really have sitting out there in this harbor."

Nicolo's eyes widened and for the first time he felt some hope. "Signor Ventimiglia, might I take that suggestion to my father in writing from you? If I just go to him, he would certainly hesitate at such an undertaking."

"No need for that, son," said Raynaldus, as he stepped into the office. "Your man outside told me my son was in here with you, Francesco, and I hope you pardon my uninvited intrusion here."

Francesco rose and grasped Raynaldus's arm, smiling warmly at his friend. "It's hard to put one by your father, isn't it Nicolo?" he nodded.

"Well, I'm obviously not the only thinker in the family though, am I, Francesco?" Raynaldus shot back. He looked at his son with pride. "Right now Adam de Citella and his family are talking to all the merchants in the city that they can get hold of, and the city notary, Salerno de Pellegrino, is helping them. Between Adam and Salerno they draw up practically every contract in Palermo, not to mention having their fingers on the pulse of all kinds of business. I think by the end of the night, if we start this search of the ships immediately, a mouse won't be able to leave Palermo without us knowing about it."

Francesco nodded, crossed the room and opened the doors, shouting for his officers. Rapidly he gave the instructions to obtain warrants, and assemble men for the search. It was a large undertaking, and he gave detailed orders. Returning to the office, he told Raynaldus that he would begin assembling the men now, and if by chance everything was in place before they received the night judge's order to proceed, well, why waste time?

Raynaldus clasped his friend's shoulder for a long moment, turning his head so as not to show the tears that suddenly appeared. Francesco could not help but try to lift his friend's confidence.

"Raynaldus, don't worry, we'll find William and we'll also get to the bottom of this business with Amodeus. We know he didn't kill old Ludovico, and who knows who killed that snot Antonio – could have been anybody for that one. But we will get answers. Believe me, you have friends and we are all working on this." Raynaldus nodded appreciatively, unable to speak, and then put his arm around his son and left the little office. Nicolo waved his goodbye to maestro still beaming with gratitude.

"What a brilliant idea, son," Raynaldus began. Nicolo blushed. He hadn't really known why he had come to the port, but he was happy to be with his father, and he was happy just to be doing something. They both stood at the end of one of the long piers, gazing at the hundreds of ships in the harbor. Behind them they could hear Francesco bellowing commands and men running across squeaky planks and thudding through the dirt streets. Clearly the holiday season brought heightened activity in the port. The prospect of boarding all those ships one by one was daunting. There were so many! And who knew if William was on any of them? There was just as much possibility that they had thrown him over the rump of a horse like a sack of potatoes and left Palermo immediately, or had thrown him into some hovel in the warren of tenements that comprised most of the city. Perhaps in official correspondence the city was *Felicitas urbis Panormi*, the happy city of Palermo, but this evening it felt vast and threatening. As the first drops of rain grazed their cheeks, they did not envy the wet work of the men who would search the ships on their behalf.

"We should get out of this weather. Let's go back to The Leopard. Ysabella absolutely will not listen to me, so I may as well join the crowd and have something to eat. Were you planning to stay there this week, just to keep an eye on her and the tavern?" Nicolo nodded, and they both walked on, trailing Nicolo's horse behind them and talking, as fathers and sons do, about many things.

....

Nicolo and Raynaldus found most of their family eating quietly in a back room when they stepped into The Leopard. Obviously they were not the only ones worried about Ysabella. Mario hovered in the back, teetering anxiously from one foot to the other and blocking the doorway. When he saw Raynaldus enter, he beckoned insistently to have him follow to the end of the long counter where they were unlikely to be overheard. Mario's words rushed out in a harsh whisper. One of the neighbors had found the warning note fastened to the door. Mario took it but had been reluctant to hand it over to Ysabella. Now he pushed it into Raynaldus's hand as if the paper itself were cursed.

Raynaldus read the threats before silently slipping the note into his pocket and cautioned the man to tell no one. He needed to think about this. Thank God Ysabella hadn't seen it! On one hand, the boy was alive. That was good. He had to be close by for this note to be delivered so promptly. That was encouraging too. On the other hand, the paper just confirmed the real possibility of danger they had anticipated. Later, he would talk to Adam and Leo about it, but right now, he called over to his son who had been delayed by a curious crowd asking for news about William. Silently cherishing him, he put his arm around the young man's shoulder and squeezed it briefly. He looked up as the green door Ysabella so carefully painted to mark her own spot in the world swung open and saw Adam and his elder son enter. The four latecomers joined the others hoping for wine and warm food.

The baked octopus and roasted vegetables in cream sauce did not disappoint them. Once they told Leo and the others about the plan to search the ships, even in the rain, Ysabella thanked him sincerely. It was a great relief to have even a single hope to hang onto. Then she left the men alone, pulling Larissa and Mario back to their duties. The neighbors' efforts to run her business were greatly appreciated, but Ysabella could not let them stay away from their own homes and families.

Raynaldus and Adam were lingering over wine and talking in low tones. Nicolo had risen to follow the others back to the main room, but his father motioned to him to stay. Now he watched and listened silently, feeling as if he had just been elevated a notch in his father's esteem. Mario knocked softly on the doorjamb and allowed a nondescript man to enter the room. He stood before them, eyes averted, clutching a wet hat in his hands. Raynaldus thought he may have seen the man in the district before, but he did not know him. He gestured for the man to sit down.

The man was hesitant, but he did so. He looked tired and dirty; he was obviously a local tanner. The smell of the tannin and the myrtle leaves used to color and soften the leather, the bits of hair and leather clinging to the man's boots and clothing, were familiar to Raynaldus. Once he had left that business with Amodeus to purchase The Olive, it seemed like it took a month to wash the smell away.

"What is your name, sir? How may I help you?" Raynaldus inquired politely.

The man looked around carefully at the inquisitive faces and began to stammer so rapidly no one could understand him. At a kind nod from Adam, the man stopped, took a breath and lowered his voice to barely above a whisper. He continued more slowly. "I didn't think anything of it when I saw it, but now that the little boy's been taken and that conceited young dandy's been killed, well, I thought I'd better tell you. I talked it over with the wife and she made me come here. My name is Luco Dinocci."

Raynaldus and Adam leaned forward skeptically, trying not to appear too eager. Nicolo, Leo, and Adam's son all strained to hear the man's hushed voice from their corner.

"I don't know about old Ludovico and what happened to him. But when that young man was out in back, well, I had stepped outside to, you know, relieve myself." He looked down, embarrassed.

"I mean, it's just a little alleyway there. So, anyway, I was standing a ways down the alley when the door to the courtyard opened. I just thought it was someone else coming to join me, but it was Antonio. Suddenly someone rushed up and grabbed him as he tried to walk through the gate. He pushed Antonio back towards the tavern. No one spoke or screamed, so I ran to see what was going on. It looked like he used a knife to slit Antonio's throat. Then he dropped him right in the doorway there, taking that green cloak and wiping the knife across it. Mary forgive me, I just rushed back to the street so he wouldn't see me and blended in with the crowd. I saw him walk out of the alleyway, humming to himself, but by then there was no sign of a knife."

"Why didn't you come forward? Why are you only telling us this now?" Raynaldus exclaimed.

Dinocci lowered his head in shame. "I was afraid he saw me, and I didn't want to endanger myself or my family. For all I knew, he could follow me home!" He rose and spit quietly into a pail in the corner, feeling a little defiant at the accusations. "Besides, no one liked Antonio anyway. Good riddance, I say."

Adam and Raynaldus were astonished. Looking at each other but saying nothing, they gathered their thoughts and then asked quietly, "Do you remember what he looked like? Could you identify him?"

The tanner looked steadily at him. "You know, it was dark. There weren't no torches out in that *darbum* – it's a one-way alley. He wasn't from the neighborhood, I'll tell you that. I'd-a known that.

Different clothes. But I did see his face for a moment when he walked out of the alley. He stopped at the corner of the tavern and looked back over his shoulder. A light from the tavern shone on his face for a second. I think I'd know him again, but like I said, I don't know who he was, and he wasn't from the neighborhood."

Raynaldus leaped up excitedly, clapping Dinocci on the back. "Say nothing to anyone about this. Make sure your wife doesn't either. It could be dangerous for you. But Adam here is going to write down everything you saw. Describe his height, clothes, hair, face, as best you can, anything you can think of. Can you put your sign on it for us? For the magistrates?"

The man retorted proudly. "I can sign my name, sir. I can't read nor write, but I can sign my name."

Adam smiled, drew out a parchment and began to write. The others hovered, listening to each carefully asked question and answer. When Dinocci had signed his name and had been escorted to the door, Raynaldus drew a deep breath and went out into the tavern, looking for Ysabella. They had gotten some kind of break! Not much, but people were stepping up and that meant their questions and their networks were beginning to bear fruit!

CHAPTER 22

The food William got for his dinner was minimally better than the scraps they had given him earlier. His fear had not abated, but the tears seemed to be in check. He was fairly certain they wanted to sell him into slavery, and he would never see his mother or father again. But, as his mother was always saying, he was a clever boy. Could he find a way to escape? A clever boy would do that.

He ate slowly, thinking. He was on a ship, and that ship was apparently still in the harbor. He was in the hold. He wondered if that meant there would be a bigger space beyond his closet here. He needed to get into that bigger space. Maybe that would lead somewhere else and he could find an escape route. Putting aside a little food for later, he began again to test each and every plank in his tiny prison. Carefully, methodically, just as he would deploy his toy horses and knights on a play battleground, he looked over every inch. The heavy floor was solid. No amount of stomping or pounding would loosen even one rusty nail. Despairing, he sat back down to eat a little more and finish his water, his eyes roaming restlessly around the room.

Was that a chink of light in the corner between the two joined walls? Or was he tired and seeing things? He *was* tired – and scared. But with just a spark of renewed hope, he slid off the makeshift cot and crawled over to the corner. There *was* a faint glimmer of light! Something here wasn't straight! Maybe … He knelt down to examine the wood. It was difficult to see in the dark. They gave him no lamp, not even utensils to eat with. But yes, there was a sliver of light showing between the two walls. Gently, he began to test the wooden planks of siding that surrounded him. One was looser than the others! Pushing harder, he tried it again. It only budged minutely. Perplexed, he looked around for something to give him leverage. All he had was his wooden bowl that had held food. Wait! That wasn't all he had. Smiling in the dark, the small boy pulled out the little wooden sword he had been picking up at the woodworker's stall just before he was grabbed. He had gripped it fiercely when he was snatched thinking he could use it as a means of self defense, but the two men wrapped him up so snuggly that he had never had the chance to use it.

"Please God," he prayed silently. "Let this work. Help me." He had never prayed much. A typical little boy, he had preferred to finger the things in his pocket or imagine great battles in his head whenever his mother made him go to church. But some of the catechism had apparently sunk in unbidden, because now he prayed earnestly.

Grasping the small wooden sword in his hand, he stuck the tip into the slit between the two boards and pushed. He felt the opening widening just a bit. If the toy was solid enough not to break, he could maybe—just maybe—pry the loose board apart from its neighbor. At first the work was slow and tedious. His meager strength did not seem to make much headway. Sweating and shaking after what seemed like several hours, the almost exhausted boy heard a small crack as if the butcher's cart rolled over a stick in the street. A rather generous sliver of wood gave way, much to William's excitement, and he could see more light. Did anyone else hear it? Was his captor just outside?

Although he impulsively wanted to kick the board loose and try to squirm through, William sat back and rested on his heels. He thought of his mother but then pushed his rising tears down. Setting aside his diminutive pry bar, the boy felt the aches in his arms subside. He lay down awkwardly in the narrow space to peer through the opening. Nothing moved. He could not hear anyone breathing or snoring. He thought the light might be from a lantern on the other side of the room, but from this angle, he couldn't see more than a foot or two above the floor.

He turned over and gazed upward into the darkness as his breathing steadied from his labors. He reached out to grasp the flask of water, but only a few drops trickled into his mouth when he upended it. Now he wished he hadn't eaten every last crumb of his bread and drained the water earlier. He was hungry again, and he needed a burst of energy. Well, nothing to be done about that, he thought, and tired, sore and afraid, he resolutely turned himself around in the corner.

This time he pushed against the board with his feet. He grunted and strained as hard as he could. Another crack—louder this time! Surely someone could hear that, even above the everyday creaking noises made by a ship swaying in the water. He waited, expecting loud voices or thudding treads on the stairs to erupt at any moment. Nothing. Was he truly alone?

One more shove and he had just enough room between the planks to squirm through. But through to where? He peered out again. The slit of light had grown only slightly bigger and not any brighter than it was. Dark, hulking forms crowded the sides of his little opening. Were they barrels, amphorae, piles of extra sails? Did it matter? He had to get out, find another hiding place in the bigger room, and replace the board he had cracked open so that—hopefully--they wouldn't immediately see how he had escaped. Maybe he could find another hiding place and sneak up the stairs to the deck after dark.

Carefully, with the board still attached by a few splinters to its partner, William wriggled head first into the hole. A jagged edge caught on his shirt and jerked him back. A stab of fear returned, but he gulped it down and set about patiently working the cloth loose. He was able to squeeze his right arm through in front of him, whimpering out loud as the splintered board scraped across the skin. He reached out into the darkness, feeling around his hatch for anything that might crash to the floor if he pushed all the way through. He touched something coarse but pliable. Splaying his fingers, he groped the unseen object. Cargo? He grabbed onto the rough outer cover, feeling small kernels inside. Ah, a grain sack, just like the ones in the storeroom at The Leopard.

The sack must be resting on the floor, he reasoned, a solid floor. He wouldn't fall into a deeper hole if he continued. Gritting his teeth now and clutching his life-saving toy sword with his left hand, he slowly pulled himself through, holding onto the sack for leverage. He allowed himself a big smile as he again caught his breath. So there!

But he was hunched up in a very small space between very large, heavy sacks. There was little room to maneuver and even less to turn around and bend the broken board back into place. He sat awkwardly for a moment, and thought. He had come this far and was determined not have wasted all that effort. Crammed against the lumpy sacks, he soon smiled again. His little sword! What a weapon it had become! Squirming his arm close to his chest into just the right position, he thrust the point forward into the bag, forcing a small hole in the coarse cloth. He kept working the sword up and down, side to side, until the hole became large enough for a few kernels to spill out. The bag leaked slowly at first, but as William rocked against it and pulled at the edges of the opening, the grain ran out in a steady stream.

Finally he could push himself far enough into the sack to turn around. Tiredly, he tried to carefully rearrange the cracked wood over the opening. He could see it wasn't perfect--some of the splinters were gone--but he did the best he could. Then with the last of his strength, he climbed up the sack, more grain spilling beneath his feet. On top of the sack at last, he gave a last shove and the sack plopped against the splintered board, covering his escape hatch just like the rock that sealed Jesus' tomb. He would rest here for just a minute, he thought, before finding a way out. He closed his eyes and began to give thanks.

A roaring voice panicked him. "Where is that brat? How did he get out? Did you leave the door unlocked? Did someone get in here? FIND HIM!" And the sound of the wooden bowl crashing against the door--or someone's head--followed. William started up, his heart hammering. How long had he slept? They might find him any minute! He had to hide somewhere! Staring wildly around, he forced himself to sit until his eyes could make out the dim shapes looming around him that he had seen earlier. Not much else. Was he in the main cargo hold? He would not be lost among these grain sacks for long, but right now he was hidden from view by the door of his cell that had been flung open. His captor stomped around in the cell throwing covers from the bed and looking beneath the hard planks of the little cot, words of rage echoing in the small space.

William had only a few seconds to move. He slid down the sack to the floor and fell to his hands and knees, the tiny wheat kernels digging into his palms. It might be better to explore this way instead of standing up where he might hit his head on some unseen beam or become an easy target. He scrabbled through the dark interior heading towards the very darkest corner he could find. Doors were slamming, feet were pounding. He had to get out of sight. Or get off the ship. Anything so that they didn't find him again.

The dark, lanky man who had been with the Captain screamed for light and a ship's boy in a tattered blue caftan, not much older than William, ran down the stairs with a lantern. The man grabbed the lantern shoving the boy aside. He stood in the center of the chamber and shone the light from one wall to the next trying to catch a glimpse of William's blond head. He lurched forward when he saw movement against the far wall, but it was only a rat scurrying back to its nest.

William was wedged between the side of the ship and several coils of heavy rope stored in one corner. The light glinted off the spilled grain and danced across the rope's surface, but did not penetrate the darkness beneath. With the illumination from the lantern, William could see more of his surroundings. A barrel stood underneath a small window. A narrow wooden staircase fastened by ropes to the low ceiling led upward.

That must lead up to the deck, William thought. I'm not sure it's a good time to try that! Otherwise, the hold, while big, was almost empty. They must have already unloaded their cargo. Wonder what it was, he thought to himself.

After staring around once more and seeing nothing, the man kicked the cabin boy toward the stairs and climbed up behind him cursing and blustering. He called for extra men to search the hold. More noise and shouting above made William even more nervous and frightened; he had only seconds to move. Not stopping to make a plan or think things through, he sprang from his place of safety and clambered unsteadily onto the top of the barrel to reach the window. The empty barrel rocked dangerously threatening to send him scudding across the floor right back into the hands of his kidnappers. He clawed at the window's rusty latch and had just managed to unlock it when the shouting from above intensified. They were coming. He had no time. Teetering on the rim of the barrel, William snatched up the lid and slid down inside, pulling the lid awkwardly back over him.

"Check down in the hold! Move every sack and every barrel. Check every damn inch of this ship! Now! Or ..." and the snarled threat went unheard as footsteps stampeded down the rungs of the stairway and thudded into the hold. The captain, the dark man, and three others burst into the hold, each gripping a lantern, brightening the entire space at once.

"Check those sacks! No, not in them, idiot! He wouldn't be IN them, check around them! See how the grain has been spilled."

Two sailors skidded over the kernels on the floor to move the sacks, and as they did so, a chunk of wood clattered down. "Look! Captain! Look! The board – this is how he escaped!"

"Let me see," roared the leader. "He has to be here somewhere! Wait! Who opened that porthole?" Silence.

"He must have gone out the window and climbed up the ropes. He's somewhere up on deck! Find him!" And the whole group charged back up the stairs.

"Spread out! Find him!" Feet rumbled right and left from the hold, voices calling to one another.

William trembled violently inside the barrel. Would they come back? Would they look inside the barrel? What should he do? Cautiously he popped the barrel lid up with his head, the white knuckles of both hands latched to the rim. Luckily, his desperate move had plopped him head first into a barrel full of rags! Now what? He quickly lifted himself up and out, laying the lid to one side. All the commotion for the moment seemed to be higher up and on the other side of the ship. If he could just make it up the stairs!

William crept to the narrow stairs and looked up. A few stars were just twinkling to life in the narrow width of dusky sky that he could see.

"Search that hold again!" the captain screamed, closer this time. Other raised voices reverberated in response.

Oh no! He was trapped! He had been so close to escape but was now forced to hide again. He dove underneath the staircase just as someone's foot crashed down onto the first riser. More men poured down the staircase and into the hold.

The captain's bellows above were fainter as he again moved away from the open trap door. The commotion was here in the hold as men overturned the barrel, lugged the coils of rope from their corner and thrust iron staves into every dark space. When all their backs were turned at once, William made his decision. Move now! He scampered up the stairs and found himself—magically—alone. He was on top, on deck!

Forgetting his wounds, his exhaustion, William crawled quietly on his hands and knees to the rail. He fully expected to be plucked up by a giant hand, but as he looked hurriedly left and right, he saw no one. At the rail he looked at the dark water far below him. Must be 100 feet down, he thought, and another mile to the pilings of the pier! He shuddered and hesitated, but he also saw the lights of Palermo beckoning. One of those lights would be The Leopard—home, his mother. No time to be a coward, he said to himself.

William swung over the railing and lowered himself until his arms were stretched out like a prisoner on the rack. Still clinging, trembling, to the lip of the railing, he heard voices and feet coming towards him. It was now or never. He clamped his legs tightly together, pointed his toes, took a deep breath, and let go. As he knifed down into the cold water, his pursuers ran up from the hold yelling and jostling. Their shouting covered the sound of his splash, and William let himself sink into the water like a cannonball for a few more seconds before he naturally began swimming. Bumping into the ship, he flailed around blindly until he managed a finger hold on the side of the vessel. He poked his head out of the water, spitting and gulping the salty air. The sounds of cursing and utter chaos reigned above. Looking around to get his bearings, he took a deep breath and slid underwater towards the lights of the city. How could they know that he had been swimming in Palermo's Papireto River since he was a baby? Please God, let him make it!

CHAPTER 23

Ysabella was arranging plates of food and snacks at the *bucterium* near the kitchen when Raynaldus followed the tanner out of the back room. She looked weary. The strain was telling on her, Raynaldus thought. God's eyes, it was telling on them all. He called her name quietly as he cleared his throat. She glanced up, automatically smiling as he approached. Angelica had been right. Raynaldus looked drained too, but there was a hint of a smile on his face.

He leaned over the counter and told her what the tanner had seen. Her mouth dropped open momentarily, and then she smiled a real smile at Raynaldus. "Raynaldus, we're starting to get somewhere! People are beginning to come to us!" She clenched her fists fiercely and pounded lightly on the counter. "Someone will come with information about Ludovico, too. I know it! Something that will help Amodeus!"

Raynaldus ran his fingers distractedly through his hair and cleared his throat. "I think so, Ysabella, I think so. We have everyone looking for William, and we may have a few clues, but another issue remains. We need to get to the bottom of Amodeus's animosity towards Ludovico. We need to get that out of him, no matter what. Otherwise, the magistrates will, and it won't be pretty how they do it. Nor will be the consequences if he refuses to speak."

Ysabella nodded mutely. She had begged her husband to tell them, but hestubbornly refused. What was he hiding? Raynaldus thought for a moment before saying, "You seem to have plenty of people here for protection. Nicolo will stay until, well, until he comes home. I'm taking Leo now and going to the jail. We'll get the story out of him if we have to beat him over the head ourselves."

He walked away from the counter, thinking already how to approach his stubborn little brother, and looking around for Leo.

Ysabella ran after him. "Raynaldus! Take some food to him, please? Some sweets, some cheese, a loaf of fresh bread." She choked on her renewed hope and whirled around to prepare the package.

Raynaldus spotted Leo across the room, talking and drinking wine with Josef the Jew. Approaching the men, Raynaldus beckoned silently to Leo and nodded a greeting to Josef. Josef nodded in kind and ambled out of the tavern. Raynaldus laid out his errand. "Leo, we need to get to the bottom of whatever it is that Amodeus hated about Ludovico. We're getting some witnesses to come forward so we will need to be prepared. And it's time he talked. I'm not leaving that jail until he tells us. Will you come with me?"

"Yes, Raynaldus, it's time. Let's go." Accompanied by several servants with torches and weapons, the two men strode into the night, determined once and for all to get some answers from Amodeus.

....

The rusty clink of the chain falling away made Amodeus glance up expectantly as his visitors stepped into the gloomy cell. Raynaldus took the torch from his servant and dismissed him. He searched his brother's face as though the answers he wanted would be written there, but instead, he was shocked at the changed man before him. Paler, thinner, the normal brightness of his eyes now shaded. Why hadn't he seen this before?

Raynaldus and Leo put down the basket of food, gesturing to it wordlessly. Amodeus shook his head. Raynaldus began pacing, but after a turn or two across the tiny enclosure, stopped directly in front of his brother.

"Amodeus, you must tell us why you hated Ludovico. It is critical to your case. I'm not leaving until you do." Amodeus, who had grown increasingly perplexed as his brother paced around, now growled in disgust and turned his face away.

Raynaldus sat down on the bench beside him, folded his arms and waited. Leo did the same, pulling a small knife and a piece of wood out of his pocket. Silent moments passed. Leo whittled at the wood and Raynaldus stared at the floor. It became clear to Amodeus that what his brother said was true--they weren't leaving until he told them. Resigned, he cleared his throat and began to speak barely above a whisper, hesitating after every sentence.

"It was right before the fire. I was what, five? Six? Ludovico came into the shop. I was playing behind the myrtle bales. I don't think anyone knew I was there. Only our mother was in the room, but it was obvious he had come to see her. He didn't ask for Father. It also seemed, although I was so young ..." and his voice trailed off.

"Well, that they knew each other. I don't know, it seemed, they knew each other well." He was silent for a few minutes. Raynaldus and Leo waited patiently.

"I don't remember what they talked about, but Mother was quiet and firm. Ludovico began to get excited, to wave his arms about and talk louder. His face got redder. He was getting angry. Mother seemed calm, but her eyes narrowed and I think she was getting angry too. Then she said something that made him crazy. He began smashing a bench against the wall. My mother screamed, and soon slaves and then Father came running into the shop from the back. Ludovico glared at each of them, purple-faced, then spun on his heel and left. I was terrified, but I couldn't move from my spot."

Amodeus slumped into the corner, staring down at the floor, his eyes filled with grief as he continued. "Our parents sent the slaves back to work and went into the side garden speaking to each other in very restrained tones, gritting their teeth. I crept to the window trying to hear, but all I could make out were a few words. Mother told Father that before she met him, she and Ludovico had, well, had a relationship. That's all I remember! I was so shocked. I had such an idyllic picture of our family, like little ones often do, but then I imagined horrible things would happen. And they did!

"The next evening…Well, you know the rest. The fire burned down the shop and our parents with it. I'm still convinced that Ludovico had something to do with it! I know he killed them! Yes, I hated that monster then, and I hated him up until he died in the street! You should have seen him that afternoon! I just didn't understand how anyone could do something like that, or how I as a little child could say anything about what I saw. I know he did it! I just could never prove it!" and his head fell into his hands and he began to sob.

Raynaldus was stunned. He had never heard this story, never. He had never suspected any relationship between Ludovico and their mother. He looked at Leo in amazement, feeling so helpless and guilty that his brother could not tell him about this dark secret.

Leo frowned, glaring at Amodeus. He leaned over and shook the young man's shoulder, hard. "Look at me, Amodeus. Look at me! You foolish boy. Ludovico had nothing to do with that fire. After he made a fool of himself at your shop, he came running to me. He was livid about your mother's rejection and threatened all sorts of things, but your mother was happy with your father, they had a family. I managed to calm him a little and convince him that he needed to leave your family alone. I suggested that he leave town for a while until he could resolve his feelings. He left that afternoon, vowing never to speak to either your mother or your father ever again. He didn't return for a month. When I told him about the fire, his shock was unmistakable. He didn't have a clue about it. He knew nothing! And you've been blaming him all these years, and letting it eat away at you needlessly! Wake up! He didn't know anything." Leo dropped his trembling hand from Amodeus's shoulder and left the cell, leaving the brothers alone.

Amodeus was in shock. He stared down at his hands, appalled, not daring to look at his brother. He felt Raynaldus's weight beside him on the bench, then a hand on his knee. Amodeus glanced up, eyes filled with shame and anger. Raynaldus peered at him, still shaken by the story that had gushed out like a torrent. "I knew there had to be a reason, Amodeus. Why didn't you tell me? After all these years we have been together, I had no idea. I feel like I failed you. We've always been so close." He bowed his head with grief, thinking of the canker that had been gnawing away inside of his carefree, laughing brother.

Amodeus choked, "I couldn't tell you. I was so scared that I didn't know what to do. Then as I got older, I began to doubt what I saw, and I worried that if you ever learned about it, you would have this hatred inside you, too. Or maybe you would do something to Ludovico. I never was sure of what I thought or felt. I just knew he was there and suddenly, our mother and father were dead."

It was Amodeus's turn to pace about his cell. Turning to Raynaldus, he spread his shaking hands out in front of him. "I was wrong, Raynaldus. I was wrong. I thought sometimes I was sinful too, for thinking it, but it had just settled inside me like a stone and I couldn't dislodge it. Like an old ragged pair of boots I couldn't throw away. I just hung on to it. I tried to have nothing to do with the old man, and I could barely stomach that Ysabella and Joanna were so close, but Raynaldus, I didn't kill him. It happened just like I said. He was lying in the street, robbed and dead by the time I found him."

Raynaldus looked up quickly. "I know, brother, I know. I know you would never kill someone in cold blood. I know that. Now I know why you disliked him so much, but don't you see? That dislike was widely known and weighs heavily against you. When the story comes out--and it will, it must--it will seem like a motive. If people say, 'well, why did he wait so many years?' the magistrates can argue that you impulsively seized the opportunity. You are known to be rash at times, that's something they will point out. We have to work quickly now, but don't worry. We're beginning to get some information. People have seen things. We have leads to follow and the whole community is looking for your son."

CHAPTER 24

Pietro Manfredi sat in the anteroom of the Archbishop's palace, waiting patiently. All soldiers knew how to wait. They did more waiting than fighting. Tiro, the Archbishop's secretary, was curious. This dusty old man who didn't look important clearly was important to the Archbishop. His lord's face, normally so controlled, had turned ashen when Tiro brought in his name.

The Archbishop declared, "I want everyone who has business here today to be taken care of quickly! Tell Signor Manfredi he will be the last one, but assure him that he will be seen."

Tiro had never seen the Archbishop process so many people and their petty claims or complaints so fast. Usually he was calm, methodical. Today he was almost frenzied, although if one didn't know him well, it wouldn't have been obvious. Now the last of the common petitioners was inside and the next audience would be with this mysterious stranger, this Pietro Manfredi. What would they talk about?

"Tiro! Show this gentleman out and give my instructions to the sergeant-at-arms. Go with him. Leave me with Signor Manfredi." Tiro raised an eyebrow and the Archbishop gave a minute shake of his head.

"No, leave us completely alone."

Tiro bowed his head in acquiescence, disappointed that his burning curiosity was not to be satisfied this afternoon. He took the commoner by the arm and moved him through the doorway, at the same time gesturing for Pietro Manfredi to enter the Archbishop's private office. He closed the massive doors softly behind the two men, and lingered in the hall a moment before relaying instructions as he was told.

Pietro, having steeled himself to come face to face with Roberto Scarani, now a primate of the church, found himself alone in the sumptuous chambers. White and red marble ran in detailed geometric patterns across the floor and gilded columns rose next to a large, bright window overlooking the palace gardens. A crucifix nearly as large as that hanging in the public sanctuary below looked down on the office and all business conducted there as a silent reminder of God's presence. Bookcases packed with tomes and papers lined the eastern wall behind a massive table delicately carved with fruits, vines, and the figures of saints. Despite the luxurious surroundings, it was a simple space, befitting the simple man Pietro had known all those years ago. So deep into his memories of that last day he had seen his friend and companion, Pietro failed to hear the quiet approach of the Archbishop of Palermo.

"Pietro. I have prayed for this day. You can't know how much," said a low voice.

Pietro froze in place, mixed emotions fighting over his usually stoic face. "As have I, Roberto," he said, dropping to one knee to kiss the ring of office now worn by his former friend. Roberto gently took Pietro's hand and raised him to his feet, laughing at the obedient gesture. Now in their fifties, the two men stared at each other curiously, taking in the details with which age and time had cloaked them.

The archbishop gestured to a table by the window set with food and drink. The men sat down and were silent for a moment.

Then Pietro, looking directly at the priest, said slowly, "Roberto, I have come to Palermo to ask God's forgiveness for everything I did in the Holy Land – and afterwards – and you should know that I bear no malice towards you, or even Simon or Ludovico, even though Ludovico almost killed me. I'm sure you thought he had, or you would not have left me there."

Roberto nodded, itching to ask questions but restraining himself as it was clear Pietro was not finished.

"I've searched my soul and even though I prayed to be able to forgive you, it really wasn't until I met my wife that I found out what love and forgiveness were. My wife, though, has now died, and my daughter…" he smiled as the archbishop started. "Yes, I have a lovely daughter, but she is happily married in Blois and after my lord died, I didn't really feel needed there. I wrote to my brother, with whom I hadn't been in touch for years and, to my relief and surprise, he immediately wrote to me and told me to come back to Trapani to live with him and his family. I accepted the offer and learned they were coming here to go on a pilgrimage.

"I decided that I would accompany them and offer what little protection this old body can still perform, but I would do my own personal pilgrimage. Now here I am. I happened to first see Ludovico at the tavern the night he was murdered. I was stunned. Then I saw you at Ludovico's funeral Mass, and I can't tell you what a shock it was to see you, well, officiating. I had no idea where you were, or even if you were still alive. I've walked and thought and now, well, here I am. I am not here to wreak vengeance or tell the world our sad little story. I just wanted you to know that I've changed since that time, I hope for the better. If you care to tell it, I'd like to hear your story."

For the first time in a long time, Pietro let out a belly laugh. "You, a Prince of the Church! Who would have thought?"

Laughter came into Roberto's eyes and he, too, smiled. He grasped his old companion's hand impulsively. "For years I've wondered about you. I'm humbled that you do not hate me--that you are here in forgiveness and not revenge. Let me tell you that that event also changed my life – all our lives.

"Simon and Ludovico went to Acre on the camels we took. I turned back to Jerusalem. I was horrified, afraid, and ashamed. I didn't really know what to do, and I think I tried to return to the

Holy City to kill myself in combat. But what happened was something very different. I took food and water and began walking. Simon and Ludovico begged me not to do it, but I was driven by some irresistible compulsion. I was so preoccupied with my thoughts that I never even heard them coming. A small band of horsemen. Thinking they were Saracens, I fell to my knees and simply waited for justice. Instead, they were Hospitallers on patrol.

"They were amazed to find a crusader out in the middle of nowhere. Too ashamed to lead them back to the caravan, I made up a story – I forget what now – and agreed to go with them. They had moved their operations to Lydda, a town between Jerusalem and the coast which the Emperor Frederick II had regained in the Treaty of Jaffa. It was a half-day's ride from where they found me to sanctuary. I was exhausted, dehydrated, wounded and sick of spirit. During my recovery the Master of the Order himself nursed my wounds and we had many talks. I unburdened myself to him, the only man who has ever heard my complete confession of what happened to you – to us – that day. I will never forget the compassion in his eyes the night he gave me absolution. It came with a price, however. I took vows and became a knight monk in the Hospitallers. I planned to live and die in the Holy Land as part of my penance. My new patron, however, had other plans."

Pietro listened, enthralled. The closeness he felt toward this man almost 40 years ago now came flooding back from a place in his heart that he had sealed off and never thought to re-open. He listened as Roberto described how his patron had taught him to read and write. He became fluent in Latin, Arabic, Syriac and Italian. He learned French and German from his brother Hospitallers. He learned Greek from a tutor in Cyprus. He fought less and less and studied more and more.

One day his patron called him to his side to say, "Roberto, I am dying. I have one more thing I must ask of you. You must leave here. This is not for you. Your skills, your duty lies in Rome. You have valuable knowledge about the Holy Land, how to fight in it, how to live in it. More importantly, though, you know what true repentance is. Go to that hotbed of intrigue and deceit – and by your example and education, your own personal knowledge and experience, show them the True Way."

"My friend, my dear long-lost friend," Roberto continued, "I cannot pretend that I have succeeded at the task he gave me, but every day, every day, I have tried." With tears in his eyes, he fumbled to open his cassock, showing an astonished Pietro his ongoing penance--a rough hair shirt with small clots of old and new dried blood dotting its surface underneath his magnificent robes. "I have worn this every day since I took my vows in Lydda, in memory of you," he said simply.

Neither man said anything for a long while. Roberto then cleared his throat and, wiping his eyes, said softly, "Pietro, I need to ask you something." Pietro nodded, still overwhelmed by this entire encounter. "I felt for old times that I needed to say goodbye to Ludovico in my own way. I did so, publicly and privately. But my friend, did you kill him?"

Pietro started but replied in a hushed voice. "No. For years I wanted to, but that wasn't why I came to Palermo. No. I must admit the old hatred flared when I first saw him, but I walked away from him. I found myself in a beautiful little church and prayed. God answered my prayers. My anger melted, my desire for revenge went away, and this time, I don't know why and I certainly know nothing about God's grace and how He works, but this time, it did not come back. And I knew that my prayers for love and forgiveness had been answered. I don't know who killed Ludovico or why, but I'm determined to find out. Would you help me?"

Roberto nodded. "For 38 years I have prayed for the chance to speak to you again. And now, let us talk about Ludovico and Simon." And the two men, clasping each other's shoulders, walked out into the sunlit garden behind the palace and continued talking.

CHAPTER 25

Ferdinand de Lerida made his way slowly to Simon de Paruta's
house. This time he had bathed and dressed in his usual elegant
finery. Winding his way through the noisy Ruga Miney, he passed
moneychangers sitting on benches under makeshift porticos,
counting out foreign coins and putting them into various bags.
High end *botegas* displayed luxury fabrics, rare spices, expensive
jewelry – all were busy, peppered with the wrangling and
bargaining of merchants in Italian dialects, mongrel Latin, French,
and even his native Catalan. Occasional greetings called out to
him were answered with a desultory wave of his hand. He was
thinking hard about his business with Simon.

Ferdinand felt the need to stop and clear his head. Clucking to his
stallion, he turned into the large, well-kept courtyard of Palermo's
famous tavern owned by the Teutonic Knights, The Lumia.
Tossing his reins to the stable boy who had quickly appeared,
Ferdinand entered the noisy main room and from a corner table
where he sat alone, ordered a small pitcher of wine. The comely
serving girl flirted with teasing dark eyes, but it was like talking to
a stone. Ignoring her, he thought about Simon, the lovely
Catalana, and the two murders. Were those incidents attracting too
much attention to Simon or to their activities together? So far, he
had kept a low profile in Palermo. He was known only as a rich
Catalan merchant within the higher echelons of the capital's
business circles. He came and went as he pleased, and no one
noticed. Now people were looking at him more closely, more
closely than he cared for. Hmmm, what to do?

Ferdinand left The Lumia and clattered into Simon de Paruta's
courtyard on his black stallion. Even though the two deaths were
advantageous to his mission from the standpoint of disposing of
two garrulous, perhaps too knowledgeable people, they were—
nonetheless--drawing too much attention to him, and therefore to
his and Simon's secret activities. Simon was clearly getting sicker
and would likely die soon. It was time, perhaps, for Ferdinand to

cultivate some of his other contacts and cut Simon loose. Things were getting too chaotic. He was sure Simon would understand. Preoccupied with his thoughts, he barely noticed Venutus standing subserviently, waiting to usher him into the house.

"Lord," Venutus intoned.

Startled, Ferdinand looked up angrily, slapping his gloves against his thigh. "Do you have to be so sly?" he asked testily. "I didn't even know you were you there."

Venutus smiled deprecatingly and bowed his head, turning to lead him down the hallway. Irritated, Ferdinand watched him retreat and wished he could look down at the man's face, intimidating him with his stare as he usually did with people. Unfortunately, they were about the same height, so Ferdinand simply followed him seething into Simon's study.

"Simon. How are we today?" he said briskly, noting his host's pallor and the tremor of his hands. He sniffed at the musty odor of disease that enveloped the entire room, then plunged in decisively, barely acknowledging Simon's cold nod.

"Yes, we should talk, don't you think? In light of..." expressively waving his hands and waiting impatiently for Venutus to leave. Bowing himself out and smiling to himself as he closed the door, Venutus almost ran over Mateo hovering outside.

"Forgive me, Master," he said cautiously.

"Venutus, I don't like that man," Mateo said decisively.

"Neither do I," Venutus responded quietly. "But your uncle does business with him, so there it is. Now, can I do something for you? What do you need?" And he drew the young man off towards the garden and away from the study. They both sat down on a bench in the warm sunshine, Venutus waiting patiently while Mateo gathered his thoughts.

"Venutus, I want to tell Uncle Simon something, but I'm not sure it's important. And Venutus," he whispered, "I really miss my brother."

Venutus laid a sympathetic hand on the boy's shoulder, his mouth twisting in unseen scorn as he thought briefly about the dead youth who had been nothing but cruel and contemptuous to him. "I understand. Perhaps you could tell me, and I could just mention this to your uncle in a casual way. Would you like me to do that?"

"Yes. That would be so kind of you. I don't want to bother him, but I don't know what to do. Would you speak to him for me?" Venutus nodded and Mateo proceeded to pour out his puzzlement over the four men who had the strange medallions. Mateo went on to say that he had poured out his thoughts to Nicolo, as well. Venutus froze, listening to the boy's prattle. He was just about to speak when Ferdinand's voice echoed loudly down the hallway and his rapid exit interrupted their talk.

"Would you excuse me for a moment, Master Mateo, so that I may see to your uncle?" Mateo nodded and Venutus rapidly walked into Simon's study.

"Lord?" he said tentatively to Simon's slumped back.

"Venutus, get me some wine, would you?" As his valet busied himself to the task, Simon informed him of the purpose of Ferdinand's visit. "He thinks we should set aside our activities for awhile to avoid drawing unwanted attention. These murders have everyone poking around, and he doesn't like being in the middle of it. Venutus, I hope these killings are solved. I don't like any threads left hanging. I can't really say I miss Antonio – I don't, frankly – or Ludovico either. But it's unsettling and it does put the spotlight on us."

Venutus murmured agreeably and handed his master a tooled pewter goblet of wine. Clearing his throat, he asked, "Lord, do you think perhaps Signor de Lerida had something to do with the murders?"

Simon turned around to accept the wine and looked directly into his valet's eyes. "Of course, Venutus, don't you? Oh, by the way, did you hear that the de Rogerio brat has been kidnapped? Apparently some slaver grabbed him and he may already be in Tunis. What do you think about that? Raynaldus is livid, so he won't rest until he finds his nephew or the men responsible. It is an interesting development, and clearly connected to their little amateur investigation, wouldn't you say?"

Venutus could only agree. "Someone must think they know too much."

·········

William's arms felt like dead tree limbs. He always thought he could swim all day, but this was different than playing, and he never had to deal with tides or currents. He was hungry, cold and worn out, but he knew this was his only chance for escape. He could still hear angry shouting and swearing behind him. He headed for the nearest boat, a tall caravel that loomed out of the water like a mountain with lights on the mast and stern. There were men moving about. Determinedly, the boy put his last exhausted effort out and numbly swam for a thick anchor line that he barely made out against the feeble lights of the ship. It seemed to take hours, but finally his icy fingers grasped the slippery fat line.

Clutching at the slimy hemp, he almost went under again as his hold slid off. Sputtering, he came back up floundering and gasping. He threw his whole arm around the anchor line, slowly moving his legs to keep afloat. He rested his head against it. What should he do? What if the men on this boat were like the ones on the last one? Would they want to do the same things to him? Were they slavers? Or pirates? Would he be safe? He wasn't sure he had another escape in him. He was cold, hungry, terrified and exhausted.

With one arm around the anchor line, he floated for a few moments, trying to think. What would Nicolo do? Uncle Leo? They would tell him to find someone in charge. That's it. Find someone in charge. In a minute. He had just closed his eyes to concentrate when his decision was made for him.

"Captain!" a hoarse voice bawled. "Something's on the anchor line! Look!"

Suddenly William found himself looking up into a dozen peering eyes staring curiously at him. Afraid, he froze but then, almost without realizing it, he yelled, "I'm William! Help me!" He watched their jaws drop, and some men began grinning.

"Well, William, we'll get you!" And just like that, they hauled him up like a fish with a grappling hook and a net. And just like a fish he flopped onto the deck, shivering and shaking.

A large hand picked him up by the waist of his pants. "Well, who are you?"growled a husky voice. The men began snickering, and the captain started laughing too.

"William, right? So, William, out for a swim? Any particular reason?" Everyone except the boy chuckled and stomped their feet in appreciation of the man's wit.

Irritated, the boy snapped, "I'm hungry and wet and cold. And my uncles and my mother are looking for me. And I want to go home!" He burst into tears.

The captain's eyebrows shot up in surprise and then he grinned. "Well, we can fix some of that, boy." Casually he tossed the wet boy over his shoulder like a sandbag and went below deck into the galley.

"Cook!" he roared. "We have a guest! A boy dolphin, swimming around the harbor! Get him something to eat!" Some of the sailors crowded down after their captain, curious, while others returned to their business.

The warmth of the kitchen seeped into the young boy and he began to regain his composure. "You aren't slavers, are you?" he piped up.

The captain frowned down at him and grunted, "Why are you asking? Are you someone's slave? Cause if you are, you're going right back to your master. We don't harbor runaways." The cluster of men began murmuring and looking at each other.

"No!" quivered William. "I was kidnapped and I live in Palermo and my name is William de Rogerio, and I live at The Leopard, that's in the Porta Patitellorum, and my uncle is an important man. He's Uncle Raynaldus and my mother is Ysabella and she's beautiful. A very bad man snatched me at the Great Market when I was with Uncle Leo. He's important too." He paused to collect his thoughts and also to attack a very tasty smelling bowl of stew that the cook had pushed in front of him. With the rough blanket the sailors threw around his shoulders and the hot food, he began to feel warm again.

"Huh. Lot of important men in your family," snickered one sailor.

The captain smiled, looked around, "Naturally. Kind of like mine." They all guffawed as he hunkered down on his haunches next to the ravenous boy inhaling his food. "Boy, what were you doing in the water?"

William slurped the rest of his stew, and sighing, began to tell his story. The men around him shifted their feet, listening with narrowed eyes, sometimes rolling their eyes. When he described his escape, the captain, who had remained silent, nodded slowly. "Well, William, think you can point out what ship you escaped from?"

The boy bobbed his head, "I think so, sir." The man easily picked him up and brought him above deck, with his men trailing behind him like curious ducks.

The captain set him down and his first mate sidled up to him. "Whatcha think, captain?" he said.

"Well, he don't talk like a slave. He speaks like a gentleman. He don't act like a slave either. He's got spunk. And if half that story's true, he's a smart one. Let's test it out. Get in the dinghy and row over to the Maestro Portulano. There's something going around about searching the ships. It has to be important if they're willing to search all the ones in the harbor. Just maybe… We're not leaving until tomorrow anyway." The captain signalled two men to accompany the mate, and they slid down the side of the ship and took off rowing their little craft toward shore.

The captain turned back to the boy. "Look around, boy. What ship out there kidnapped you?"

William peered through slats and over the top edge of the deck rail. Slowly he walked down the side of the vessel and then crossed over to the other side. "I think there, sir. Although I didn't get much time to look around a whole lot once I got out of the hold."

The captain smirked in the dark and looked out towards the distant ship moored at the mouth of Palermo's harbor. He could see through his glass that there was a great deal of activity aboard, unusual at this time of night. Lots of lights too, scurrying around like will o'wisps.

"Hmmm, maybe. Well, boy, I'm no slaver. Don't believe in it. Especially little ones. But we'll wait until Giacomo gets back from the Maestro's office. Then we'll see." He looked down at William to see what effect his words had had.

Reassured, the boy smiled and said, "Can I have some more food?"

Several hours later, the boy was curled up on a bench in the galley wrapped in a blanket and sated at last. Three men returned to the boat with the mate and boarded the ship to speak with the captain.

"I am Francesco Ventimiglia, *Maestro Portulano*, and I'm looking for a small boy by the name of William. I know him, so don't try any tricks." The men with him were silent, but armed to the teeth and alert.

The captain backed away a few steps and then swept his arm in a welcoming gesture down into the galley. "Have a look, Maestro. He's in there sleeping. We fed him and warmed him up. Hope he's who you're looking for." They all clattered down into the galley and found William on his back, snoring quietly.

"That's him," Francesco said quietly. "I can't tell you how grateful we are." After Francesco heard what William had told the captain, he called softly to one of his men, muttered some instructions, and went on deck where the captain pointed out the vessel.

"Captain, come back with me and get your very substantial reward. Also, may I enlist some of your men for a boarding party?" Keeping his face blank, the captain nodded, chose half a dozen men and together they all returned to the port with a small sleeping boy who didn't wake up once.

CHAPTER 26

Raynaldus walked thoughtfully down the cobblestoned street to The Olive, his menservants striding a few paces behind and one ahead with the *lampada* to light the way. He thought mournfully of the secret his brother had been harboring for so long. And although the fact that his mother and Ludovico had once loved each other stunned him, he was grateful that Leo set both of them straight about the fire that had killed his parents and set Amodeus on a path of resentment and hatred. If that story had gotten out, there would have been a motive to kill.

Raynaldus turned into the entrance to The Olive and noticed how unusually lit up the hostel was, even though it was nighttime and they had guests. Puzzled, he stepped into the main *salon* where he saw Angelica sitting across the table from a strange man. As soon as they heard his footsteps, both leaped up, with Angelica throwing herself at him, hugging him and smiling. "Raynaldus! They found William! He's safe! He's at the office of the *maestro portulano*!"

He smiled broadly and hugged her back. "That's wonderful! We have to let Ysabella know immediately." He gave instructions to two men who left instantly for The Leopard. Striding across the room, he grasped the shoulder of the messenger asking him for all the details. As the rescue was recounted with all three laughing and exclaiming, they sat down to savor the first good news in days, sharing a glass of wine.

Ysabella listened to Raynaldus's message and burst into tears. Joanna, who had come to support her friend, beamed with gratitude, her eyes glistening. Larissa and Mario whooped and laughed, hugging each other. Nicolo put his arms around his aunt, and she leaned against his chest crying quietly with gratitude. Soon she would have her son back. Now all she had to do was get Amodeus back and her life would be complete again. Although, really, nothing would ever be quite the same, she thought.

Adam de Citella finished his notes and wandered out of the back room. Hearing the good news, he beamed just like everyone else. "When will he be coming home? Is the *maestro* keeping him overnight for questions? Should we go there? What did he say?" Adam grasped the messenger's shoulder with urgency.

The messenger shook his head regretfully. "I don't know anything about that. Master Raynaldus didn't say, and I didn't think to ask. If you would like to accompany me back to The Olive, perhaps the *maestro's* man is still there." They all nodded excitedly and snatching up cloaks and hats, left the cleaning for tomorrow, and rushed out the door, chattering happily on their way to The Olive. Tonight they would celebrate!

Ysabella rushed in just after the *magister portulano* himself. "Where is he? William!"

A small torpedo launched itself at her yelling, "Mama! Mama! Some bad men grabbed me and put me on a ship and …"

The rest was lost as Ysabella clutched him frantically and swung him up off the floor and sobbed incoherent murmurings against the boy's head. A babble of talk exploded in the room. The pilgrims, awakened by the noise and laughter, joined the family in The Olive's huge *cantina* to listen wide-eyed to the exciting conclusion of William's adventure. They had never envisioned such a drama unfolding on a simple pilgrimage! Angelica and Renata happily swooped back and forth from the kitchen and the pantry as they served wine and small fried pieces of meats and vegetables, cheese and fruit.

Although Ysabella could hardly bear to let go of him, William was scooped up by the various men and made to repeat his story again. Ecstatic to be back with his family and flushed with pride at his escape, the boy began gesturing and talking.

Angelica hugged her sister-in-law fiercely. "I told you we'd find him. He gave Francesco a description of the men who held him.

But more importantly, Francesco led a boarding party onto that very ship and captured the captain and crew, including the man who kidnapped William! Francesco says the man also confessed to being one of the thieves that night who robbed Ludovico! He confirmed that Ludovico was already dead when they robbed him. Ysabella, that means Amodeus can go free!"

Ysabella began sobbing. Her son was returned to her, and now her husband would be coming home too. Grateful tears cascaded down her face as she shrank onto a bench, both laughing and crying with relief. Angelica cried with her and Renata, watching their intimacy and envying it, smiled broadly.

A banging on the table made the babble slowly cease. Raynaldus loudly asked for everyone's attention. Next to him, Francesco, smiling but grave, surveyed the room. Ysabella ran to Raynaldus and hugged him tightly. Smiling, he stroked her hair, but beckoned Angelica to take her. He cleared his throat and began to speak.

"I know all of you think this means Amodeus will be freed!" Everyone nodded and there was murmuring all around. Ysabella, watching his grave expression, frowned.

"Ysabella, I wanted to tell you privately, but everyone here may as well know." Now he had their attention; absolute silence fell in the room.

"Francesco and I have been talking. Yes, the thief admitted he robbed Ludovico that night. He says Ludovico was already dead. We found Ludovico's medallion on him, too, so he confirms that part of Amodeus's story. But the problem is, neither he nor his companion saw who killed him. He said an arm shot out of the alley and dragged Ludovico into it. They heard some small noise and then saw Ludovico slumped over. They waited for a few minutes, afraid, but when nothing happened, they ran over to the body. The killer was gone." Voices spiraled upwards in expressions of disbelief and anger.

Raynaldus raised his voice slightly. "That still leaves the mystery of who killed him and who killed Antonio. We know Amodeus is innocent, but we already knew that! So this is the plan. Our killer is still loose. We keep the thief in jail. Francesco and I think that Amodeus should stay there as well." He put up his hands in front of him to ward off the shouts and questions that hammered him. He couldn't look at Ysabella, who had grabbed Angelica's hands and stared at him, astonished.

"Quiet! Please! Listen to me!" He took a deep breath.

"If Amodeus stays in jail, the killer will think the magistrates still have their designated murderer. If they let him go, the killer will see that we know something and either flee or hide. And at this point, everyone," he raised his voice again as exclamations and objections were shouted, "at this point, we have no clues that lead to his identity. Maybe the medallions will provide a lead, we don't know. For right now, we hope this plan with result in him exposing himself." For the moment, Raynaldus and Adam preferred to keep the tanner's information secret. Who knew if even here someone might inadvertently say something that certain ears shouldn't hear?

"Francesco and I are going to talk to the sheriff tomorrow morning. We're sure he will go along with this plan. We'll move Amodeus to better accommodations, and he'll be treated much better, but to outsiders it will look as if the officials have made up their mind. We'll obviously tell Amodeus, but I do ask that no one in this room, and I mean no one, says a word to anyone."

He turned to Francesco. They whispered a few words together, at the conclusion of which Francesco nodded and marched out the door. Ysabella, still in shock, sat down abruptly. Angelica was confused, but put her arms around her sister-in-law and murmured in her ear, "Dearest, please. Trust Raynaldus. He knows what he's doing."

Raynaldus appeared before them. He squatted down and took Ysabella's hands. "Think about this. We need to find the killer. If we let Amodeus out, the killer will know he is not safe. We don't know why Ludovico or Antonio was killed, but we need to find out in case he kills or wants to kill, again. Who would be next? We do have one clue to investigate, but only we can know that. We hope it will lead to solving this. Please trust me just a little longer."

Ysabella was trembling. She stared into Raynaldus' worried eyes and said firmly, "Yes, Raynaldus. I do trust you. You've done so much already. I'll trust you this time too."

Raynaldus swallowed hard and hugged her, then stood up briskly. "You yourself have brought about a good deal of this. You've done things no woman should have to do. You and Larissa have put yourselves in danger, and you've suffered through your son's kidnapping. It's more than most women could tolerate."

Ysabella absently patted Angelica's comforting hand on her knee. "We will see this through, Raynaldus. We will. I'm just so grateful that Amodeus will be safe. But if the thieves didn't kill Ludovico, then his death and Antonio's must be connected." The others nodded, but none of them knew what that connection could be.

Renata began to carry the leftover food and drink scattered throughout the room into the kitchen. William's return and Amodeus's exoneration were wonderful news. But still, who could have killed Antonio? She shivered wondering what may have happened if he hadn't, merciful Mary, thrown her over. If she were still with him, would she be dead too? Immersed in these thoughts, she didn't hear someone come into the kitchen behind her.

"Here, Renata, I brought the rest of the plates and glasses," Nicolo's voice penetrated her concentration.

She started abruptly before realizing who it was, turned and smiled. "Thank you, Nicolo."

Nicolo stared at her for a moment, caught by her beauty, then turned and walked out. This was no time to think about girls, but her face and her thick, dark hair! Renata smiled secretly after him.

She had noticed Nicolo, too. What a lovely family this was, she thought. It was so easy to talk to Angelica, and Raynaldus had shown himself to be a man of integrity. She liked Ysabella tremendously, too. Even William's antics didn't make her too crazy. If only she could stay here instead of returning to Trapani. She sighed, turning back to the sink. Only a few more days in Palermo. Sophia had to rest, but when she had completed her devotions and felt strong enough, she wanted to go home before the baby came. Well, Renata thought, she would try to relish every moment! Washing the dishes and plates, she regretted that she would have to go.

CHAPTER 27

Ysabella sat at The Leopard drumming her fingers on the *buctarium*. What were the missing pieces? Who was doing this? Frowning, she put her head in her hands and groaned, but the pressures of the day took precedence over her confusion. Calling to Larissa, she went to check what she had in her storeroom. She needed to open the tavern shortly and Mario was already clattering around the kitchen, carving the meat to be cooked and cleaning the fish to be steamed.

"Mistress, it's very dark in here," Larissa said cautiously as they stood just inside the storeroom.

"Yes, too dark," Ysabella replied absently. "Even though I know the room now like the back of my hand, not everyone does. And if we send someone like Nicolo back here for something, we can't have them falling all over the place? What do you suggest?" She turned back to look at Larissa, who narrowed her eyes thinking.

"Well, what about a small bowl of oil hanging right inside the door, maybe, with floating bits of candles? No one, after all, would come in here without a torch or candle, light of some sort anyway. They could just reach over, light the little lamp and see their way in."

"Good idea, Larissa! It's simple and thrifty. Let's do it now before we forget." And the two women ran off to gather the necessary items. Once they carefully placed the bowl of oil, Ysabella shut the door, then opened it, stepped inside with a candle and lit the candlewicks. The light cast a soft glow throughout the neatly ordered storeroom. Both women smiled with pride, thinking 'another small task accomplished' and went off to oversee the night's cooking. Always so much to think about. Maybe, Ysabella thought, maybe I'll just sleep late tomorrow morning.

"Mama! Mama!" William shouted as he ran down the stairs from his room. "Those bad men are in jail, and I am here with you!" Ysabella and Larissa both hurried to meet him. Ysabella swept him into her arms and buried her face in his neck. She still couldn't bear to let him out of her sight, but she knew he still had to identify the men that took him. It would provide more clues to the murder and may help to free Amodeus, but she wondered when all this would end so that they could get back to a normal life. In fact, she thought dazedly, I can't even remember what normal is any more. Burying those thoughts, she looked up at Leo who had arrived to take the boy to the port.

"Leo, would you like some cool fruit juice or a glass of wine?"

"No, thank you, Ysabella. There are two men here, one in the back and one in the front. They're armed and here to protect you and William. You might give them something to eat and drink a little later on. I'm going down to the market to take care of some business, but I'll be back soon. I just brought this for William. A man cannot be without a sword when there are villains around." The old man handed William the wooden toy and walked briskly out the door.

"William, Leo will be back soon to take you to the port. In the meantime, you either stay inside here with Mario or Larissa and me, or you go outside and make sure – do you hear me? – make sure you stay where Uncle Raynaldus's manservant can see you."

"Yes, Mama," the boy promised solemnly. After seeing those men again, he wanted no more adventures for the day. He was still thinking about what could have happened to him, and he was still frightened. He withdrew to the courtyard taking his protective toy with him. Nicolo was coming over later to show him how to use it. Things had certainly changed since his father was taken. He began playing quietly. Inside, he could hear Ysabella and Larissa direct the servants and slaves as they readied The Leopard for business.

CHAPTER 28

Angelica gathered her pilgrims together in the courtyard in the soft light of early morning, quietly consulting the kitchen women over food baskets and provisions for the day's excursion. Sleepy but excited, Sophia lumbered down the stairs of The Olive and clambered awkwardly into the canopied cart, helped by Renata and Carlo. Today they were going to pray before Santa Rosalia on Monte Pellegrino! It would be an all-day excursion because of the distance and the slow pace they would be forced to take, but everyone was wound up with anticipation. They would be treated to more exotic sights in Palermo, and at the end of their climb, they would enjoy breathtaking views of the city and the whole *Conca d'Oro* from the heights of the towering peak.

Impatiently the mules and horses stamped their feet and tossed their heads, anxious like their passengers to be off and moving. Angelica and Renata mounted their palfreys, walked them to the head of the small company, and smiled broadly at each other in anticipation of the day's adventures. Last night's news had lifted a dark curtain from everyone's mood.

The only person missing from the outing was Pietro, who was already mysteriously gone, but only Carlo fretted about his behavior. As the company began to move out, the guards closed protectively around them. Since their pace was to be basically at a walk, Angelica had chosen a route through the city different from what her guests had seen previously. As usual, she had an itinerary carefully thought out with rest stops and shady places to eat and drink.

She took them directly past the looming cathedral and out the ancient *Porta Carini*, and then turned towards an area created by the Caliphate to house Saracen soldiers and slaves. Now the Seralcadi district was a fashionable and rich area. They carefully threaded their way through walled, perfumed gardens, well-tended orchards, water mills and imposing residences. She planned to stop at Leo de Iannacio's tavern for refreshments and a short rest in his large and lovely courtyard.

Meanwhile, another cavalcade was making its exhausted way to the port. A short but bloody fight had erupted last night on the ship boarded by the soldiers of the *Maestro Portulano*. Surprised and angry at the intrusion, the ship's captain fought to the death. Most of the others, however, had been taken alive and were being transported to Francesco Ventimiglia's holding cells for questioning. It was only a matter of time, Francisco hoped, until he found who had paid to kidnap William and why.

But one man had escaped in the confusion. The crafty rogue slithered down into a small rowboat as soon as the fighting began. Panting, frightened, constantly looking over his shoulder, the fleeing thief rowed in a frenzy. He saw they were pursuing him and redoubled his efforts. He didn't have far to go, and he was confident he wouldn't be caught, but did they know where he was going or whom he needed to see? He only knew that his information had better reach his paymaster first or else he was a dead man.

Frantically he rowed the last few strokes and leaped upon the pier near *La Catena*, the seaside church where the massive port chains were kept. Under cover of darkness, he stashed the boat under the dock and in knee-deep water, waded to shore. Time to confess the bad news.

Quickly he made his way to the squalid tavern to wait for his patron. Cold and wet, he slunk into the dilapidated room and hunched in front of the meager fire trying to dry off. Slowly the warmth seeped into him and he dozed spasmodically, afraid of what the morning would bring.

....

William's dark thoughts had subsided as he played in the morning sun. He was now accompanying his Uncle Leo and Uncle Raynaldus to the port to identify the captured men. He knew exactly what they looked like. Chattering like a monkey and waving his wooden sword, he acted almost as he did every day. Leo marveled at the buoyancy of youth. How quickly William seemed to recover from a terrifying experience! Not only did he seem to be his usual bouncy self, but Ysabella had confided that the boy had slept like a log all through the night. Not one nightmare!

Although today he was more watchful, William's curiosity was still unquenchable. He begged to stop and inspect the merchants' stalls that held dyestuffs, cloth, herbs, and toys. Especially prevalent near the port were the food stalls, and the boy peered from the saddle at the catches of the day – swordfish, eels, sea urchins and tuna, as well as the signature sardines that were part of Palermo's daily fare. Fresh fruits and vegetables were alluringly displayed and tied bunches of flowers - roses, jasmine, and lilies, madder and daffodils were set out to attract the perfumers and dyers. This time, Raynaldus shook his head at William's repeated pleas to stop, and they continued on to the office of Francesco Ventimiglia.

Tying their horses in the already bustling courtyard of the master of the port, Raynaldus and Leo each took one of William's hands, silently agreeing that the boy would not be lost this time, and guided him into the official's anteroom. Francesco Ventimiglia marched out of his office and running his hand through his thick black hair, gestured the group to enter. He looked as though he had not slept and was wearing the same doublet Raynaldus saw last night. Lined up on one side of the officer were several men, bloody, bruised, angry and shackled.

William paled as he saw them. Perhaps he wasn't so unaffected as Leo supposed. The master of the port smiled, resembling a predator as he narrowly looked from the boy to the bound men. The men shuffled and tried to fade into the wall. Trembling, William tugged at Raynaldus's hand and whispered to him. Raynaldus listened with grave attention and then, ruffling his nephew's hair, handed him over to Leo who solemnly escorted him from the room. Francesco and Raynaldus looked at each other knowingly, and both men cleared their throats as they closed the door and began to question the prisoners.

CHAPTER 29

Angelica and her troupe crowded eagerly into Leo de Iannacio's tavern on the broad *platea,* or boulevard, of the Seralcadio. It was sheltered from the sun and weather by a tall, wooden colonnade whose roof was cleverly carved and painted. All along the road, the group had marveled at the lovely stone facades of expensive residences, the shaded porticos and stalls, and the orchards and gardens of what was once, during Islamic times, the quarter of the slaves. Angelica was telling her entourage the history of the quarter and how it had been the home to palace slaves as well as to other high-ranking Muslim officials of King Roger's court in Norman times. She pointed out the traditional features of Islamic architecture that the Seralcadio retained and was known for – shady trees, pleasure parks, plentiful fountains, gardens, orchards, and numerous public baths.

As she talked she ushered them into the cool, spacious tavern, greeting Leo's manager familiarly. "Iacobus, how are you?" she said graciously. "You can see we have some hungry and thirsty pilgrims here. What are you serving today?" He led them into the shaded courtyard to a table surrounded by jasmine and lavender, putting jugs filled with cool water and fruit juice before them.

Sophia was uncustomarily quiet. Today she was even more uncomfortable than usual, but because she was looking forward to praying at the shrine of Santa Rosalia, she said nothing. Carlo asked her several times how she felt, but she simply smiled and patted his hand. Angelica announced that, as her own home was not far from here, she would walk over and bring back her two girls to accompany them up Monte Pellegrino. All the pilgrims waved at her and nodded, continuing to chat and relax.

Assuring that Iacobus provided them with food and drink, she took her leave and walked up the familiar boulevard accompanied by a manservant. Nodding and waving at friends and acquaintances, Angelica strolled through her neighborhood. After a few blocks she turned into a smaller street and into a multi-story imposing residence shaded by large myrtle trees.

"Mama! Mama!" screamed her two daughters as they ran to meet her.

"Beatrice! Matilda!" Angelica hugged her daughters and stroked their cheeks. She drew them to her. "How would you like to go with me to the shrine of Santa Rosalia today with our guests from The Olive? Would you like that?" Excited cries and dancing answered her and she laughed.

"Well then, let's get you ready. Everyone is over at Uncle Leo's tavern waiting on us, so hurry. Have you eaten, my pets?" she asked solicitously as all three, arms entwined, moved off to get ready.

Angelica thought how precious they were and how frightened and angry she would be if someone had tried to take her girls. She was spending too much time away from her daughters, and they were beginning to resent it. She couldn't wait until Raynaldus found another hostel manager. Well, she thought, soon. And today, we'll all be together. She turned as the girls squealed and argued about what they would wear for their outing.

Hair brushed, faces scrubbed and wearing fresh dresses, Angelica and her daughters returned to Leo's tavern and walked into the back courtyard. There she found her guests relaxing in the shade and discussing what they had already seen of Palermo's nouveau riche quarter. Evidently the prosperity impressed them, Angelica thought with amusement, but in a more sober vein, acknowledged that it was something she had taken for granted for quite awhile. But Amodeus's arrest and William's kidnapping had forced her to take another look at what was important--Nicolo and her girls, and Raynaldus. How radically their lives would change if something happened to her husband or her children! She needed to remember that as they approached the shrine. She would pray not only for

Sophia's wish to be granted, but that her own family would continue to be safe in these worrisome times.

Shaking these somber thoughts off with a toss of her head, Angelica greeted the pilgrims, pausing with each one to ask what they had eaten and explain what their next stop would be. Everyone stood, stretched, and strolled singly or in pairs towards the patiently waiting animals. Iacobus waved goodbye and thanked Angelica for bringing him customers. Smiling and energized, Angelica herded her group towards the cart, putting her daughters in with Sophia to distract her from her growing discomfort. I have to say this for her, Angelica thought admiringly, she may prattle on and on but she certainly is a plucky one, visiting these shrines so close to delivery. She thought back on her own pregnancies realizing how coddled she was, and glad of it. She didn't think she would have undertaken such a journey! Sophia must want a boy very badly.

Thinking about that, she turned to find Renata bending over her younger daughter, Beatrice, telling her a story about Trapani and weaving roses into her hair. She had made an instant friend. Angelica reflected on how much Renata had changed in the last few days, from a sullen, self-centered beauty to a confident, caring young lady. Her brief involvement with Antonio and his subsequent death had made her reevaluate her own actions and their consequences. It had been an instructive time for everyone, Angelica thought, in more ways than one.

Merging their animals and the cart into the heavy traffic of the Seralcadio, the group made their way through the *Porta St. Georgio* to the base of the wide pathway leading up Monte Pellegrino. To their right they enjoyed a harbor view dotted with steeples of numerous churches and the open squares surrounding them. To their left were tidy fields where workers moved through, cultivating crops or tending animals. White, fluffy clouds skittered overhead as a light breeze ruffled their clothes and the horses' manes. It was a warm, lovely day typical of the Sicilian spring, perfect for making a pilgrimage to Santa Rosalia. Even Sophia's discomfort seemed to be momentarily alleviated as the entire party paused, enjoying the breeze, the sunshine and the views.

Walking their horses through an orange grove, the little procession followed the winding path higher and higher until they could glimpse the buildings and ever-present vendors' stalls in front of the shrine itself. Angelica began to explain the origin of the saint, a young aristocratic Norman girl who, 200 years ago, had fled to the mountain cave for solitude, and who had died here after caring for the sick and the poor. To everyone's astonishment, her body had remained undecayed after her death. When people began to report miracles after her interment, it wasn't long before a shrine and sainthood followed.

Santa Rosalia was a perpetual favorite, a kind, loving spirit to whom women of all ranks appealed to for help. It was an added attraction that her shrine, built into a large, dark cavern, remained cool in the fierce Sicilian summer and warm during the mild winters, providing a welcome respite from the stultifying sounds and smells of a large, crowded, commercial city. The commanding views from atop Monte Pellegrino added to a festive, picnic atmosphere that every pilgrimage to the saint seemed to embrace.

Working their way through cajoling vendors, praying visitors, and gossiping women refreshing themselves at roadside stands, Angelica directed the little group to a grassy spot near the shrine. Angelica murmured to a manservant to water and feed the animals, and she and Renata helped a groaning Sophia out of the cart.

Tottering towards the shrine and flanked by Perna and Renata, she slowly climbed the stone stairs worn uneven by thousands of hopeful feet. Angelica's young daughters ran up and down the stairs while their mother lingered outside, enjoying the fresh air. When she straightened up and hushed Beatrice and Matilda to lead them quietly towards the shrine, a piercing shriek rent the air, echoing weirdly throughout the cave. Angelica snatched her daughters to her in fear but quickly realized what it was. She gathered her skirts and raced into the shrine, the girls running after her.

Sophia was lying to one side, imploring Santa Rosalia to give her a boy NOW. The saint, enclosed in a glass case and lying serenely unaware of Sophia's agony, seemed to smile faintly.

Angelica gasped, "Sophia's baby is coming!"

She scurried to summon the saint's nuns, but having heard the cry, they were already running into the cave. Calmly observing the situation at a glance, an older nun patted a frantic Renata and consulted with Perna, who had taken immediate control. With the men's assistance, the sobbing Sophia was rolled gently onto a blanket and carried to the domiciliary at the side of the shrine. As the nuns bustled to set up the birthing stool, heat water and review their stock of herbs and medicines, Perna pulled a reluctant Renata through the door but waved away Angelica and her daughters.

Angelica, no stranger to childbirth, sat quietly in the shrine savoring the quiet and keeping watch on her children. Eventually the girls tired of staring at the dead saint and curled up on each side of their mother, falling asleep. Despite the occasional moans and whimpers from the nearby chamber and the muted prayers of the saint's supplicants, Angelica herself followed the girls' lead and dozed off.

The afternoon droned on. Novices collected donations and made the sign of the cross over the visitors who came and went. Beggars were sent away with a piece of bread and a prayer, and the usual traffic of the day had no idea of the pending delivery. Carlo found a purveyor of religious trinkets to pass the time with, and the guards played dice under the shade of a rock wall.

Suddenly Angelica snapped open her eyes at a faint but familiar sound. A baby wailing! Her daughters rubbing their eyes and yawning beside her, Angelica hastily pushed them in front of her to the small building where Sophia had been hidden away. At the same time, Renata and the old nun appeared with broad smiles lifting their faces. Renata ran to her. "Angelica, the prayers have worked. Mother has a son! A baby boy! A healthy baby boy!"

"Never underestimate the power of prayer! Or being close to a saint!" laughed Angelica. Everyone joined in, realizing that Sophia had gotten about as near to Santa Rosalia as she possibly could have. She had clearly received a powerful dose of heavenly grace.

Carlo hurried over and he clapped his handswhen he heard the news.

"Arturo will be thrilled," he laughed. He peered towards the building hoping to see his wife emerge, but when she did not, he strolled down to one of the stalls for fruit juice and a melon slice to celebrate.

The old nun arranged for the mother and newborn to remain at the convent for several days while she could regain her strength. The others left to return to The Olive in festive spirits with hearts full of thanks. What a wonderful ending to the day today, Angelica thought, as she led her tired pilgrims down the mount towards home. Almost as good as yesterday's, when they had found William.

CHAPTER 30

Angelica led her weary pilgrims through the gate at the tip of the Cassaro that broadened into the *Platea Marmorea.* The party's earlier chatter and enthusiasm had waned, and they traveled now consumed in their own private thoughts. The stink of the tanning district crept over the thoroughfare and settled in their nostrils like a fog. The guards parted the way ahead of them and followed behind the cart, still alert for danger.

What a day! Thank God, we're almost home she thought tiredly, brushing a stray lock of hair from her face. Beside her, Renata quietly sat on her palfrey, walking it sedately down the familiar street, her face in shadows beneath a broad-brimmed hat. What was she thinking, Angelica wondered. How would her life be now that her mother had the baby boy she had wanted for so long? Lately Renata had discarded her headstrong ways and seemed to settle right into the rhythms of The Olive. Angelica had noticed Nicolo's interest in the girl, but also his reticence. A sudden surge of love for her son filled her soul. Sophia's should turn out so well, she thought proudly. The boy sometimes enjoyed carousing and mischief a little too much, but truly, she had faith in his good heart and common sense. 'I think he will turn into the kind of man his father is,' she thought.

As they neared The Olive, traffic became more congested, and when they turned into the street leading to the hostel, she saw that the gates were open and her courtyard bloomed like a rose garden. A retinue of guards wearing the Archbishop's insignia and bold, red silks crowded the cobblestone enclosure. What in the world? She glanced at Renata, whose face was as astounded as her own. Stableboys came running to take the horses and assist the guests. Angelica's hope for a few moments of solitude vanished on this sea of red. Brushing the dust from her clothes, she made her way slowly through the guards to the main room, and Renata followed.

Sitting at a table were Pietro Manfredi and the Archbishop of Palermo, chatting away and drinking wine like old friends! Open-mouthed, she and Renata hastily stepped forward to the table, knelt before the Archbishop and stared stupified at the floor. The conversation interrupted, the Archbishop quickly asked them to rise and spoke simply.

"Signora and signorina, please. I am Roberto de Scarani, and Pietro Manfredi and I are old friends. Thank you for providing such hospitality so that we could remember old times together in private." Wide-eyed, Angelica rose, now really curious about the nondescript old crusader. Gathering her wits, she curtsied and asked if they needed more refreshments.

"No, thank you," the Archbishop replied. "But I would like a private room where Pietro and I could talk with your husband, Leo de Iannacio and Adam de Citella, if that would be convenient. Could you ask them to attend us here?"

"Yes, Your Excellency. We will prepare a room immediately," she murmured and backed out of their presence. Angelica had no idea why her husband would be meeting with these men, but she snapped her fingers, summoning a young boy whom she instructed to quickly find the three men in question. "And take a horse! Hurry!"

She propelled Renata into the kitchen. "Renata, prepare the small room off the garden for the Archbishop and Signor Manfredi. Make sure they have cold water, wine, fruit, bread and cheese."

Renata nodded and began to hurry off. "And Renata! Make sure the Archbishop's men are given food and drink as well. We don't want His Excellency to hear that his men were left hungry and irritable."

Renata nodded again and whirled to do as she was bid. Turning back to the Archbishop Angelica led them down a short hallway and threw open the doors to a small sunlit room facing the garden.

The men nodded and strolled to the window, speaking in low tones. A lemon tree shaded a corner just outside the window and lavender and yellow jasmine swayed lazily in the breeze. Angelica was satisfied that this pleasant space was restful for them.

She turned again to Carlo and Perna, still brushing themselves off in the courtyard and glancing curiously at the red-clad throng. They had not caught sight of Angelica's prominent guest, and she didn't bother to explain. In the farthest corner of the main salon, servants hurriedly set out platters of cheese and cups of cold water to refresh them. As they became preoccupied with reliving their day, Angelica ran upstairs to clean up and change her clothes. Just as she was finishing, she heard pounding hooves and saw her husband, Adam and Leo hurriedly dismounting. Taking a deep breath, Angelica stepped into the salon and deftly greeted the men.

"Angelica, what is going on?" asked Raynaldus. "Whose guards are outside?"

"Husband, Leo, Adam, follow me, please," she smiled mysteriously. They followed her down the hall to a closed door. Pausing before the door, she said softly, "The Archbishop of Palermo is here with Pietro Manfredi."

Savoring their look of utter astonishment, she knocked lightly on the door and opened it, gliding into the room and saying in a low, pleasant voice, "Gentlemen, are you comfortable?" As Pietro and Roberto turned towards the newcomers, nodding and smiling to Angelica, the three men strode into the room and knelt before the prelate.

"No, please, no ceremony here *maestri*. Raynaldus, Adam, Leo – we have been acquainted with each other for a long time. My friend, Pietro, has brought to my attention some business that we all seem to have in common. Shall we sit down? Let's discuss this."

Angelica swept out and closed the door gently. Leaning for a moment against the lintel, she exhaled noisily with a profound sense of confusion and amazement. Renata appeared at the end of the hallway and together the two women disappeared into the kitchen, discussing the new development in low but animated voices.

Raynaldus, Adam and Leo listened intently as the Archbishop unfolded the story of his past. As the churchman talked, Pietro's attention drifted. He stared at Angelica's thriving garden as his mind floated through the past. He refocused his attention just as his friend was finishing the stunning tale. He noticed Raynaldus staring intensely at him before shifting his attention back to the Archbishop. Caught off guard, Pietro thought about how Raynaldus had continued to question him about Ludovico. Despite their adversarial relationship, Pietro had a feeling that he and Raynaldus were alike in a number of ways, particularly in their determination to finish whatever it was they started. Smiling to himself, Pietro admitted that he liked Raynaldus, and the other two as well. Now that they were all on the same side ...

Roberto ended his story and, for a moment, there was a profound silence in the room. Obviously all three men were deeply moved. Roberto himself, after the reunion and after telling twice in one day what he had held in for so long, sat back in his chair, worn out by emotions from the past. Trained so long to hold in his passions, Roberto had not expected to be so exhausted and yet exhilarated.

"So now, my friends," Roberto continued after a long pause, "you can see why I am interested to find Ludovico's killer, and Antonio de Paruta's as well. And what I don't like is that Ferdinand de Lerida is mixed up in this because this is the crux of it… This must go no further than this room." He looked at each man sternly. Pietro, Raynaldus, Adam and Leo, although somewhat puzzled, nodded their silence. "Because this may involve treason."

No one moved. Everyone knew the penalty for treason was death, and not a quick one either. If one wasn't noble, death would be prolonged and agonizing. Raynaldus glanced at Adam and Leo. Leo was frowning but caught his friend's glance and nodded slightly.

Adam, in his usual forthright manner, looked at neither man but directly at the Archbishop. "I think I may speak for all of us, Your Excellency. You have our word nothing of this will be spoken outside this room, but I am confused. Your story makes it clear that all four of you – yourself, Simon, Ludovico and Pietro here – have shared a past, but what does that have to do with treason or with our investigation?"

Roberto replied briskly. "You probably think that Ferdinand de Lerida is simply a Catalan merchant. Certainly he is that, but we also know him as a spy for the King of Aragon. And possibly, Simon de Paruta is his partner in treasonous activities. It seems they are reporting back to Aragon the strength and disposition of Charles' military troops I have found out that they are especially interested in the warship being built in Trapani.

"I want to put all my cards on the table here and now. I have no love for King Charles. I am a Sicilian through and through and have always put Sicily first in my heart and even, if I can, in my politics. However, the King is the King. If there is to be war between Aragon and Sicily, so be it. I would prefer to have Sicily rule Sicily and not an outsider, but that never does seem to happen, does it? Therefore, we have to be careful. Also, my true master is the Pope, who is a firm ally of Charles and encouraged him to fight for Sicily in the first place. His Holiness also hopes, as you know, to eventually return Sicily to the status of a papal fief as it was during Norman rule. This is a cat and mouse game and we could get caught in the middle. So let's air our political views first, and then decide what steps are to be taken in this murder investigation. So far, it looks like Ferdinand de Lerida, with or without Simon de Paruta's knowledge, may have killed two men – two Sicilian men-- and that we cannot let go unpunished."

Adam spoke up then. "If this Ferdinand is a lackey of Peter of Aragon, then we have to be careful, especially when King Charles is about to launch an invasion of Byzantium. That would leave Sicily wide open for Aragon, and any excuse might do for an invasion. Falsely accusing a nobleman high in the favor of Aragon could precipitate a carefully engineered conflict."

The Archbishop nodded and looked around the table, discerning agreement with Adam's words.

Adam slowly resumed. "I, also, am a Sicilian patriot. I do not like Charles or any Frenchmen, but I do like the law and order he has established. Increased trade comes with safer seas. As long as he is king uncontested, I will support him. On the other hand, he has appointed multitudes of French and Provencal magistrates to the detriment of our learned and experienced Sicilians. And there is a question of remaining an uncontested king. The problem, as you know, is that Constance, Peter's queen, is our beloved Manfred's daughter, a direct descendant of our last Sicilian king. Should there be a war, many Sicilians would fight for Manfred's daughter and against Charles, no matter how he has increased trade. It would turn into a very bloody civil war. My personal preference is to support a Sicilian even if she is a woman. We will at least have more influence in running our own lives. Aragon would have to establish his court in Palermo. Many people resent that Charles's court sits in Naples, because many political positions – and the influence of those positions - are geographically removed from our people. I think, Your Excellency, this about sums up everyone's feelings in this room about Charles."

Roberto smiled and looked around the table. All the men nodded soberly, looking directly at the Archbishop. These were men, he thought, that he could work with. Hard working, sober, patriotic, law-abiding but decisive. They would be loyal to Sicily. This was something to remember. "So, if this Spaniard is the killer, what would you gentlemen propose?"

Everyone looked at Raynaldus, who cleared his throat and putting his elbows on the table said bluntly, "We get at him through Simon de Paruta. We know Simon is his business partner. It's odd that Antonio was one of the murder victims, but I've been thinking about that. It's no secret that Simon was trying to involve Antonio more in the business, but of course we all also know what a wastrel that young man was and how Simon was getting more and more disgusted with him. Indiscreet. Actually rather stupid. Not at all like Mateo, whom, I understand, Simon is very fond of. I can't believe that Simon had his nephew killed, but I do know he has grown increasingly to dislike him. My son, Nicolo, has told me that Antonio's position with Simon was becoming more and more precarious because of his gambling debts and whoring. Perhaps Simon manipulated Ferdinand into doing the deed, or Ferdinand himself decided on it. But Simon is sick, and perhaps we can use that to pressure him. He also, I think, wants to protect Mateo. Finally, it has occurred to me that every time we seem to be getting close and talk to Simon, something happens, like William's kidnapping. How can that be a coincidence?"

Raynaldus could always put two and two together, Leo thought. A plan of going to Simon seemed logical. And anything, he thought grimly, was better than sitting around waiting for Amodeus to hang. Still--was his old acquaintance and some time business partner so cold as to murder his own flesh and blood? Something in this was not right. He could only hope that the wily Simon could shed some light on this whole business.

CHAPTER 31

The escaped kidnapper in the tavern was still dozing in front of the fire when a touch on his arm made his eyes blink open. Starting, he turned his head and saw his master in a hooded cloak standing thoughtfully in profile in front of the fire, warming his hands. Earlier the man had positioned himself to see everyone coming or going from the front door or the alleyway; but somehow, he had fallen asleep, a dangerous thing to do in this place.

Without looking directly at him, his master asked in a mildly irritated tone, "What happened?"

After his employee stammered out his story, he fell silent, fearful of what would happen and now tensely alert. Still turned sideways to him, his master said brusquely, "This is unfortunate. But for now, stay here today and do nothing. They'll be searching for you. I'll find a safe place for you." And then he slid from the room as silently as he had arrived.

The kidnapper breathed a sigh of relief. He had been terrified to confront the man and explain the loss of the boy, but now, reassured, he stood up, stretched, and thanked St. Jude. He called for another flagon of ale before he stumbled down the corridor to relieve himself outside near the sheep pen. The last thing he saw before he died was a smelly wooden enclosure and a serene cerulean sky.

....

Adam and Leo hurried over to the *maestro's* jail at the port. A thought flitted through Leo's head that if they didn't get some helpful information, Ysabella would take on the task herself, and that would embarrass all the men involved. She was certainly showing a resolve and toughness no one knew she had.

At the old crusader's suggestion, they also brought along a well-muscled young servant who was totally trustworthy. The *maestro portulano* had imprisoned the ringleaders of the kidnapping plot who were identified by the boy, but separated them from each other for interrogation purposes. Although children, usually orphans or street urchins, were kidnapped every day for the slave trade, this deliberate kidnapping of the taverner's son was something darker. God's teeth, he thought, the boy could have been sold to some heathen camel driver! Well, he was as interested in the truth as his visitors.

They entered a small dank cell where a dark-haired, lean man was huddled on a grimy blanket, a chain tethering one foot to the wall. As he looked up, Leo was startled to see one eye was blue was one was brown. They hauled him brutally to his feet.

"Why'd you kidnap the boy and whose orders were you following?" Adam began roughly. Sullenly, the man looked down to the ground, then looked up and snarled. Glancing at the manservant, Leo nodded. The man stepped forward and nonchalantly punched the ruffian in the kidneys, dropping the fellow to his knees.

"Oooph! Stop it!" but before he could say anything else, a hobnailed boot caught the side of his face, and the dark-haired man sprawled gasping on the cold stone floor as blood slowly pooled underneath him. Oh *cocca*, he thought to himself, these old men mean business. "Wait! Wait!" He spit out a tooth and sat up dizzily. Adam stared impassively down at him. He was fully prepared to torture this man to get whatever he needed. This was a matter of *famiglia*. No mercy to be shown here. The kidnapper stared up at Adam and read his eyes. No point in not telling them – he was sure the name he knew was a fake anyway.

"A man in a tavern, the one in the Kalsa near the Whore's Den," he said, still spitting out blood. "It's called the Maltese Cross. He said his name was Ferdinand Valletta. I can describe him. I'm sure it's a false name, but I can describe him." Leo nodded and held up his hand. He then asked the *maestro* for a more private place to hear the story. A guard unchained the prisoner and led him and Leo to a back room where the man began to talk.

Half an hour later, Leo and Adam returned to The Olive where Raynaldus and Pietro were making plans to go to Simon's house. As they opened the door, they could see Ysabella pacing the room at a little distance from the two others. Their entrance distracted her for only a moment, and the relentless pacing began again. A disgruntled scowl on her face erupted as Raynaldus chastened her.

"No, you cannot go to Simon's house, Ysabella. Pietro and I will do that. The old man would never talk of business matters in front of a woman."

"But Amodeus is MY husband!" she retorted. "And it was MY son who nearly lost his life. I need to find the truth."

"Calm yourself, my dear," murmured Leo as he took her hand and guided her to a chair. "Perhaps we have a little information that will help us. Adam and I have been to the port." Everyone's ears perked up. Ysabella was furious at being treated like a child, but she bit her tongue. She wanted to hear what Adam and Leo had found out.

"The prisoner said there is a man they call "The Master" because he has hired them often to do this kind of work. He pays well and calls himself Ferdinand Valletta, although the prisoner – and we, for that matter – are sure it's a false name."

Raynaldus glanced around the table. "Could this be a coincidence, really? Ferdinand? Is the trail leading back to Ferdinand de Lerida again?"

"Don't be so naïve, brother," Ysabella barked. "A man with a false name would just as soon have two, three, or a dozen false names. Go on, Leo. Describe this mysterious devil."

"Well," Leo hesitated, "we have no guarantee that the description is accurate. The sailor claims to have seen the man only once, although if we find the other man who escaped, we might learn more."

"Just tell us what he said," Ysabella snapped impatiently.

"Yes, yes, he is described as tall, muscular, well spoken, brown eyes, dark hair. Short, trimmed beard. Always wears a hooded cloak and dresses conservatively, not flashy. A man of few words, but always has lots of coins. Ruthless. Rumor says he's killed people himself although no one has ever witnessed it. Most often meets at a tavern called the Maltese Cross. Some have tried to follow him to see where he goes but one ended up dead and the others simply lost him. Does that sound like our Catàlan?"

"Hmmmm. Yes. Could be, but still awfully vague. Nothing to distinguish him – no scars, no wounds, anything like that?"

"Not that the man could remember."

"Sounds like half the men we know," Ysabella grumbled. I'll just go back to The Leopard and lock up any man with a hooded tunic and mud-spattered boots in the storeroom." The fury that had propelled her earlier pacing was spent, and they were no closer to a solution.

CHAPTER 32

Raynaldus cleared his throat again. "All right, It's time to have a talk with Simon. We'll bring you any information we get, Ysabella. I'll leave you to your business. Nicolo can't be running your place by himself."

The four men left The Olive, walking the short distance towards Simon de Paruta's *palazzo*. Outside the gated courtyard, they paused, glanced at each other, and reaffirmed the approach to the old merchant that they had discussed together.

Raynaldus put his hand on Pietro Manfredi's shoulder. "Simon is not aware that you have returned. I think, my friend, you might go first. This is no time to be delicate."

Pietro grimaced but nodded. "I think you're right," he said, and led his friends through the opened gate and marched across the courtyard. Before they reached the door, Venutus opened it, courteously standing aside to let the men enter the cool marbled vestibule.

"Venutus, would you please tell your master we would like to speak with him again?" said Raynaldus.

Venutus bowed his head, studying Pietro through his lashes. 'Who was he?' Venutus wondered as he made his way to Simon's study.

"Master, Raynaldus de Rogerio, Adam de Citella, Leo de Iannacio and an unknown gentleman who is armed are here to see you."

Simon had been nodding over an account book, but the numbers were swimming before his eyes. His hair was untidy and his eyes were bloodshot. A carafe of wine sat at his elbow and a dram or two had been poured into a glass. Simon had barely been able to pull himself together to deal with Antonio's funeral arrangements, and since then, he was failing even faster. He wasn't thinking clearly about his business affairs and could hardly remember things. He was lethargic and perpetually cross.

"No, Venutus. I will not see them. I feel horrible today," he bellowed with surprising resolve. "They just want to pester me about the murders, and I have nothing more to say. Tell them to go away. Tell them I died--anything. God knows that's coming soon enough." He glared at Venutus threateningly.

Venutus's brown eyes were compassionate, but he was resolute and used to dealing with Simon's moods. "Master, may I suggest that you agree to meet with them? They'll only return if you send them away now and may even be more troublesome if it looks like you have no interest in solving your own nephew's murder."

"Hmmph," Simon growled. "I see your point. This will be tedious, I'm sure, but let's get it over with. Show them in; bring the usual refreshments. And stay in the room--I might need you."

"Yes, lord," Venutus said with satisfaction. "Perhaps they will explain their progress in the investigation." Venutus then smoothed the old man's hair and propped him up a little straighter with damask pillows before ushering the guests into the study.

As they had planned, Pietro tramped in first, laying his broadsword carefully on Simon's desk, the gleaming medallion on its hilt winking directly at Simon like an evil eye.

Simon looked up to greet them and suddenly, his mouth refused to work. A long silence was broken only by Simon's ragged gasps. He splayed one hand out on the desk, another clutching his chest. He was unable to take his eyes off Pietro, who stared down at him impassively. Alarmed, Venutus rushed towards his master but Simon angrily waved him off, trembling. The other men stood quietly behind Pietro, observing Simon's reaction.

"So, Simon, you old bastard, I take it you are surprised to see me," rumbled Pietro. The other men crowded into the room and surrounded Simon, curious and wary. "Alive, that is."

Simon nodded weakly. "What happened to you, Pietro, after … " he waved his hand, still transfixed at the sight of his old comrade.

"Yes, well," Pietro said briskly. "Let me tell you the rest of the story." And he casually poured himself a glass of wine as he thought about what he would say.

"After Ludovico tried to kill me, and did kill the boy, I lay there for. I think, hours. I don't know. I was only half conscious--in and out. I heard voices off and on, but far away as if I were at the bottom of a well. Then someone turned me over. I gripped the man's arm with what little strength I had, afraid that his sword or knife would finish me off. I looked into a dark face with hazel eyes. He said something in French and looked me over in a curious, gentle way. I don't remember anything more until that evening. I didn't know what day it was. I woke up, there was a fire, men, Christian men with horses and armor. Dusty and tired, but they were trying to feed me sort of broth. They had bound my wound and somehow stopped the bleeding. All I could do was to turn my head slightly.

"It's a long story, but the gist of it was that I was rescued by John, Count of Blois, who was returning from that debacle in Jerusalem. He took me to France, and I became his man. I married, had a daughter, and actually, Simon, I had a relatively happy life there. But my wife died, my daughter married and then, my master, a man I had grown close to, became deathly ill. I decided to return to Sicily, to see my brother, to maybe even find some peace from that year of slaughter--innocent people, often. You know; you were there.

"When I began to regain my strength, I swore I would exact revenge on the *friends* who stabbed me and left me for dead. I wanted to kill you or maybe just wound you and leave you for dead like you did me. But as the years went on, and I found my Juliana, and my daughter was growing up, I felt that hatred leave me, bit by bit. Now, I just want peace and quiet. I'm old. My bones hurt when I get up every morning. Hatred takes a lot of energy, and I need to conserve my energy for more constructive things. Like living with my brother in peace, playing with his children and grandchildren, maybe breeding horses, even making peace with you and Roberto." The very room seemed to breathe carefully as each man in it contemplated the word "peace."

Pietro paused, and Simon looked slowly around the room. "Then what do you want from me?" he asked.

Pietro sat down, leaned back, his eyes never leaving his old acquaintance. "It's a little matter of treason, Simon, a little matter of treason. Yes, and murder, too."

Simon sagged back, mouth agape. "But what do you mean …?

"Simon, I had a long talk with the Archbishop yesterday. You know our old companion, Roberto? He told me many interesting things." He paused delicately. "We know about the relationship you have with Ferdinand de Lerida. We know he isn't a simple, wealthy, Catalan merchant. We know you have committed treason. Charles will not like that, Simon. He's very touchy about those things. So, let's talk about Ferdinand, and then let's talk about murder - Ludovico, your nephew. Charles is also very prickly about people who kill his subjects. That takes away from the tax base, you know." The men around him stood silently staring at Simon. Their stares felt like the weight of a thousand pieces of lead pressing in on him.

"No! I didn't kill anyone! Are you crazy?" Then he saw Pietro's cynical expression. "Our past, Pietro, well, is past. It was so long ago! And I thought you were dead! I would never have left you if I thought you were alive! No, I didn't like Ludovico – he had become a drunk and just a sloppy … and I didn't like my nephew either! Everyone knows that! But I didn't …"

The men advanced towards the desk and glared mercilessly at the shaking merchant. Venutus stood frozen, unable to move. Simon closed his eyes and grimaced before giving a gasp and slumping over his desk.

Venutus rushed to his master's side pushing the visitors back toward the door. "Master! Master!" He took the collapsed man in his arms, but there was a horrible gurgling sound and Simon was dead.

CHAPTER 33

Back at The Olive Raynaldus gloomily played with a cluster of grapes.

"He didn't confess. He knew he was near the end, anyway. He'd been sick for a long time. We knew about his treason, and he had confronted Pietro and his dark secret. He had nothing to lose by admitting to those murders. But he didn't. We can't be sure he was responsible." He turned to the rest of the group.

"I don't think he did it either," said Leo quietly. "We still have a murderer out there. But what can the link be between Ludovico and Antonio, if not for Simon? And no one has tried to kill Simon, so what is the killer's motive?" He raised a questioning eyebrow.

Pietro was sitting by the herb-scented window. Feeling the question more than hearing it, with a small wave of his hand he turned and said, "No, I don't think Simon had those men killed. Even when that – incident – happened with the four of us, I never got a sense he was a killer. He wanted to manage things, to be smarter than the rest of us, and he was a good soldier, but he killed only in self-defense or in a battle. Regardless, these murders have something to do with him because he's the connection between the two. I just can't figure it out." He shrugged, irritated.

Leo had an idea. "The thief's description was not very helpful, but he would, of course, know his 'Master', as he calls him, if he saw him again. Can we arrange for this man to somehow see Ferdinand de Lerida and identify him?"

Adam nodded. "That seems like the best way to do it. We'll just take him out of the cell and somehow get him to a place where de Lerida is. We just need to plan a chance encounter."

Adam looked around and saw various degrees of assent. "Really, where else can we go with this?"

Mateo ran into the garden sobbing. First his brother, who was his best friend, then his Uncle Simon, who had become like a father to him. Fighting back tears, he pounded his fist on a gnarled old fig tree, thinking furiously. Hearing someone behind him, he whirled around. Venutus was watching him sympathetically. The servant cleared his throat. "Lord, we need to sit down with the Archbishop and talk about your uncle's various, um, activities. And we do need to get papers organized and your inheritance legally filed with the court. Tiresome things, yes, I'm sorry to intrude on your grief, but …"

Mateo nodded stiffly, still unused to his new title. Thank God Venutus was here! He had always been here, and Mateo knew he needed someone comforting and familiar to rely on right now.

"Venutus, thank you for being here. You will stay, won't you? I … I need your help."

Venutus smiled. "Absolutely, Lord. I will always be here. I owe your uncle a debt of gratitude I can repay only by serving him, and now you, to the best of my ability." His secret smirk could not be seen as he bowed his head to the young man.

··········

"Raynaldus, are you out of your mind? You want to bring that…that kidnapper and thief to our tavern?!" Ysabella stamped her foot angrily, glaring at her brother-in-law, hands on her hips. Angelica hovered in the background with a cleaning rag in her hand, nervously watching her two favorite people go head to head.

Raynaldus held up his hands as if to dodge a blow. "Dearest sister, we need him to identify the one they call "The Master". We don't know who it is. I'm positive that Simon didn't murder Ludovico or Antonio, so the killer/kidnapper is still out there. Please, I beg you. He's the only one who can help move us forward. It may be Ferdinand, although I'm not sure how we would get Ferdinand de

Lerida here to The Leopard. Plenty of men would be here to protect you and William. Think about it, please!" He sat down abruptly, staring up at his angry sister-in-law. Ysabella only stamped her foot and stalked off into the kitchen.

Twenty minutes later, Ysabella clomped back into the main room and slammed her hand down on the table where Raynaldus and Angelica were talking quietly. Raynaldus' face twitched as he tried to remain impassive. "All right," Ysabella snapped. "Bring him here. But you'd better have plenty of men around, if nothing else, to protect him from me!" Abruptly she hugged Angelica, burying her face in Angelica's dark tresses. "I don't have any better idea," she said more quietly as she straightened up and walked upstairs.

As she slowly climbed the steps, her mind wandered back to the opening night at The Leopard. Everyone had been so happy, expectant. She had been so proud! What did the priest say about pride going before a fall? Well, this was some fall. And it began with Antonio and Ludovico's ugly little spat. Then Antonio's murder. Suddenly, her eyes grew big as she remembered something. Excitedly, she ran back down the stairs. Raynaldus and Angelica had been joined by Leo and Adam, but she skipped over the usual greetings.

"Raynaldus, I have an idea—two, in fact--and listen before you say anything. It seems that this is the most logical way to get that man here. Raynaldus, you and Angelica own The Olive, Amodeus and I own The Leopard. Let's say our wine vendor has disappeared and we need more supplies quickly. Lerida will remember Angelica, I'm sure, from their little talk at the *Fondaco dei Catalani*. And we have been told his ships have just come in, so he will have plenty of good Spanish wine to sell us. Let's lure him here with the promise of business, but of course," she smiled mischievously, "he'll really want to see Angelica." She glanced nervously at her sister-in-law, who stared back at her open-mouthed.

Raynaldus said appreciatively, "You've come up with a good plan, Ysabella. Who do you think is more appropriate to approach this man, Leo and me or you and Angelica?"

"You men are too official and he would smell a trap. I think Angelica and I should do this, and we'll send a messenger asking him to come to The Leopard tonight. Having met the unforgettable Angelica," she turned and winked playfully at her sister-in-law, "he would be intrigued, if nothing else. And he seems to be conceited enough to think that perhaps Angelica is attracted to him, too. I'm counting on his pride. That's how we'll get him here."

Angelica began to laugh and nodded emphatically. "I think Ysabella's right, don't you?"

"Now," Ysabella continued briskly. "My second idea is this. That tanner--the one who came to you and Adam after Antonio was killed and said he saw someone outside the tavern. Bring him here too. If we have two people identifying him, all the better." She glanced at her family for confirmation.

The men all nodded. Leo smiled to himself. Clever girl, that one. Always had been but she's so lovely men rarely notice how quick she is. Only Raynaldus was a little uncomfortable, but he had to admit the idea was sound and would probably work.

Adam elbowed him slyly and leaned over to whisper loudly, "Let's face it. Your wife is a lot more attractive than you are, you know!" At that, everyone laughed, enjoying the little joke and Raynaldus's discomfiture.

Ysabella fetched paper and ink. Sitting at the tavern counter, Angelica wrote a short note to the merchant and showed it to her companion. Ysabella read over it twice before suggesting a few changes. When the note was finalized, Angelica called one of the slaves to take the note to the fondaco.

"Well, we'll know soon if he'll come. I asked him to arrive here early this evening just as the dinner crowd starts to come in. It will be noisy so the extra men will not be as noticeable, and we can have them playing dice or whatever in the back. It will give us time to get that thief in here. And Raynaldus, that is your job!" Angelica and Ysabella traded a look of quiet satisfaction as everyone went to do their bidding.

··········

"Wine? They need wine? Hmmm." Ferdinand sat at a table in the *fondaco* remembering his visit with the lovely Angelica de Rogerio. He had been charmed by her. That she was another man's wife didn't even enter his head. He was also confident that she had been fascinated by him, as, he thought modestly, what woman wouldn't be? Without turning around, he called abruptly for paper and pen, which materialized at his elbow. Quickly he scratched a reply for the slave to return with to The Leopard. Yes, it might prove to be a remarkable evening.

"He's coming, Ysabella! Tonight. He'll be here a little later than we planned, but then, the more people here the better. We must get ready to meet with him. We need to be alluring, but modest. After all, we are married women. We only need to keep him distracted long enough to let that mangy dog get a look at him."

They both started laughing. "I think," Ysabella said mockingly, "that we won't have any problem doing that."

CHAPTER 34

Nicolo and Renata were kept busy attending to the pilgrims at The Olive. Sophia especially needed special foods and rest while she nursed her baby and recovered from childbirth. Angelica, distracted by Ysabella's investigation and the upward spiraling of events, almost unthinkingly handed over a great deal of The Olive's management into Renata's inexperienced, but surprisingly capable hands.

Renata, a forgotten daughter with no particular skills, was emerging as a clever manager. She began to show a deep interest, as well, in the large herb garden Angelica kept at the rear of the hostel. Initially she was interested only for the extra relish such herbs could provide in the dishes she prepared, but eventually she learned to love the garden work for the relaxation it offered. She found after a busy day that she loved to sit near the lavender, gently inhaling its soothing fragrance.

She and Maria, Angelica's head cook, were concocting a new chicken dish when Nicolo walked into the large kitchen. Two enormous fig trees hung over the door and shaded the kitchen from the hot Sicilian sun. Even so, a small portico just outside the kitchen door was for the cooking grills, so that kept most of the heat out of the main room.

"Maria, in Trapani we have tons of sea salt, which I think might help this chicken. At home we stuff it with tarragon, basil, thyme, salt, oregano and sometimes a little pepper and cinnamon, although those two are so expensive!' She rolled her eyes and Maria laughed.

"Well Renata, the mistress keeps a close eye on our kitchen expenses! You can tell that herb garden saves us from buying inferior spices from some of those rascally merchants. Nothing but the best for the mistress! But then again, we work hard for it. That garden needs constant tending and she herself is usually out there in it. But with all that's been going on," she waved a hand with a herb-encrusted spoon, "it's a Godsend you're here. I see you've been going out there every day weeding and picking. Bless you."

The cook prattled on. "Who would have thought that the Archbishop of Palermo would come here? Goodness! What will happen next?! And poor Master Amodeus! Still in that filthy jail! And Lord Antonio, girl, you are well out of that one, bless his soul, don't mean to speak ill of the dead, but really, Renata, you deserve so much better!" The two chattered on about people, spices, and cooking as Nicolo watched unobserved.

Of course he had noticed Renata the first day she walked through the door, but she was Antonio's love interest. Then, unsure because of her beauty, he avoided her. But in the few days since then (was it only five days ago?) with the crazy murders, William's kidnapping, the astonishing secret of the Crusaders, Sophia's giving birth at the shrine, Renata had almost unobtrusively taken over The Olive. Angelica had other things on her mind, acting as the pilgrim's city guide and protecting her sister-in-law. Although Aunt Ysabella certainly didn't seem to need much protection these days, he thought laughingly. He and Renata had been thrown together constantly as his parents struggled to keep the maelstrom of Amodeus and Ysabella's events from drowning all of them. To say it had been an exciting week was definitely an understatement.

Renata absently flicked a lock of hair behind her ears, listening intently to Maria's instructions on stuffing her bird. Glancing up, she saw Nicolo lounging in the doorway and smiled broadly. Nicolo grinned at her and slouched into the kitchen. "Can I help?" he asked. Maria glanced up affectionately. She adored Nicolo and the feeling was returned heartily. She was like a second mother to him, sneaking him treats when he was little and, as he grew older, sending him on all kinds of errands into the exciting world of Palermo's markets.

"Yes, you can help," she said. "Get some more wood for the grills, and make sure the main salon tables are wiped off. We just fed some of those hungry pilgrims and I can't remember if I cleaned the tables or not."

He smiled and nodded and as he walked past them to get wood, Renata gave him another lovely smile. God, she was beautiful. His heart hammering, he allowed himself to put aside thoughts of the current insanity around them and slip into daydreams.

Maria watched happily as Renata's eyes followed Nicolo out the door. Lord, when that girl had first walked through the doors of the hostel (had it only been a few days ago?) she was sullen, proud, snappish. Antonio's death had really shaken her, and being around the mistress-- a beauty herself but smart and kind--was just the balm for someone like Renata. Running a big hostel like The Olive AND her own household, Angelica was a model of efficiency, and still had time for her loved ones, Raynaldus and Amodeus and Ysabella and William, not to mention her own daughters. No, Renata could have certainly turned to worse models than her own mistress. Maria began to tell her stories of Nicolo when he was young, to Renata's not very secret delight.

....

"Stop pacing!" Angelica grunted. "How much leather do you want to wear off those slippers?"

Ysabella rolled her eyes at those comments but obediently flopped down on the bed and sighed. Ysabella's room above the tavern was softly lit by the late afternoon sun. A sharp shaft of sunlight pierced the seemingly tranquil area like the rising anxiety in Ysabella's throat. They could hear Mario and Larissa chatting and laughing over the evening's preparations, the pots and serving spoons clanking as they bustled around the kitchen. An inviting aroma of fish poached in wine was creeping up the stairs along with other delicious odors. A couple of early customers were already in the dice room.

Angelica sat on the bed and beckoned. Ysabella sat up and turned around like a child as Angelica began to pull an ivory comb through her tangled tresses. "Ouch!" yelled Ysabella. "Don't pull so hard. Angelica, I'm so worried about tonight. For Amodeus' sake, I hope this will end our nightmare, but what if it doesn't? What if this Catalan isn't the one? We have no other ideas, really."

"No need to worry. We'll find the real killer, whether it's Lerida or not. And now we have the Archbishop's resources, too. Wasn't that a surprise of all surprises?!! That dusty, crusty old crusader--I never gave him a second glance!"

"Raynaldus and Leo have been truly steadfast during our troubles. Even Adam seems more agreeable to our investigation. Amodeus may not realize how well he is loved by his friends and family, but as soon as he is home, I'll make sure he hears about all of it. And I want him home! Too many days have passed without him. What if we can't free him in time? We've presented the evidence to the sheriff. He knows Amodeus didn't kill Ludovico or Antonio but it was so obvious," she paused, trembling, gathered herself, "that if we don't find the real killer, he'll take Amodeus just so he can have someone to hang." She glared fiercely into the mirror, her anger again beginning to overcome her fear.

"I can only imagine," whispered Angelica, feeling Ysabella's pain.

"So", shoving the grim thoughts to the back of her mind, "MAYBE I should forego the ribbons and cover my hair. I can't look like a common harbor strumpet. But you've seen this man. What will encourage him to take us seriously?"

"Yes, I have seen him. He is arrogant and smug, obviously used to getting what he wants. He'll come here for his own purposes, you know. His agent really handles the trading and he probably wouldn't actually transact business with us. Don't forget, he also fancies himself a ladies' man. I think you must look your very best. God will forgive a little seductiveness when it is used for a good cause, so the ribbons must show." Angelica laced the lavender bodice, placing a knee in the small of her sister-in-law's back in an effort to pull the strings tighter.

"How do you expect me to breathe?" Ysabella grumbled.

Angelica pushed her away and spun her around, satisfied, then sat on the bed, blowing a strand of hair away from her face. "That color just makes your eyes leap out of your face. The purple gossamer cascading from the top of your head is perfect, and so is the ivory comb. You look much more like an angel than a tavern keeper. I say show off those golden locks and purple ribbons!"

Ysabella smiled at herself in the mirror wearing her favorite bodice and ribbons. Then with a pang, she thought how Amodeus would have loved to see her tonight. He could barely keep his hands off her when she wore this. Well, hopefully soon he would be standing in front of her again and when he was, going down to the tavern would be the last thing on her mind.

"I've always been careful about my reputation, Angelica, but tonight, I don't care! We'll let them wait a little longer," Ysabella responded. "Now sit down so I can return the favor and fix your hair just right."

Angelica had dressed modestly as a married woman and mother of three children should. Childbearing had not left her flabby and pear-shaped as it did so many others. Tonight her burgundy surcote was snug enough to suggest her feminine curves without being brazen. The sleeves of the rose-colored gown were pleated and embroidered in the latest fashion, hinting at her financial and social status. She sat calmly as Ysabella wound a gauzy scarf threaded with gold through her dark tresses. The satiny sparkle of the scarf, together with heavy gold and garnet earrings, made Angelica's lioness eyes glitter and teased out the mahogany highlights in her hair.

Angelica stood up and swirled around laughing. "Well, dear sister, we are quite a pair tonight, aren't we?" But just as quickly her face turned somber. "I hope this ends tonight, Ysabella."

"Yes", Ysabella said gravely. "I want Amodeus home. I want us to be normal again. I don't want to have to be afraid for my son."

"The group downstairs is waiting. Raynaldus told me extra men from the Archbishop's guard will be disguised as neighbors playing dice, and no one could keep the old crusader away once he heard the plan. He clearly knows how to handle a sword and seems to have his own score to settle with Lerida."

Biting her upper lip a little, Ysabella summoned her resolve and led her sister-in-law to the stairs. As the hems of their dresses appeared, everyone in the tavern looked up. Carefully the two women glided down the steps and walked into the main salon. There wasn't a man present who didn't catch his breath.

My god, thought Raynaldus, I forget how incredibly beautiful my wife is. And that whoreson will be ogling her tonight! As if reading his thoughts, Adam put a sympathetic hand on his arm, getting only a glower for his efforts. Adam could hardly resist grinning. Yes, the women were quite lovely. What a contrast! Ysabella's honey colored hair and violet eyes with Angelica's smoldering golden eyes framed by her dark hair and cloth of gold scarf. Beautiful women.

Let's hope it works, Leo was thinking.

CHAPTER 35

Larissa bustled out of the kitchen wiping her hands on the corner of her apron and watched the women descend. "I thought it got kind of quiet out here," she announced, breaking the spell that had fallen over the crowd. Everyone laughed heartily and turned back to what they were doing.

Larissa inhaled noisily as she stared at the two women. "Well, I guess you won't be in the kitchen tonight, will you?" she said merrily and darted back to taste the fish and add a little more wine and cardamom.

Ysabella and Angelica chuckled too, catching each other's eyes in sidelong glances. "I think we must look all right," Ysabella whispered, and Angelica laughed out loud. The tavern was filling slowly with customers. Neighbors and well-wishers who loyally supported "The Cause," as they privately called the investigations among themselves, drifted in, and The Leopard was soon bustling with noisy patrons.

Ysabella tied on a long apron and became absorbed in filling flagons of ale and opening bottles of wine. She slipped so easily back into her duties as tavern-keeper that her previous anxiety faded from her thoughts and her careful attention to her appearance was forgotten altogether. She walked up to Raynaldus. "Is our tanner here?" she asked.

Raynaldus nodded shortly, inclining his head towards some men in the corner. "He's over there. Just be sure this Ferdinand character passes very close to him. Don't be in the back room with him too long either. Or I'm coming in."

Ysabella chuckled to herself. Raynaldus – so protective! So bristly! She cut her eye towards Angelica, who was also smiling over her husband's comments, and then they both took a deep breath, remembering the gravity of their little theatrical tonight.

They swept behind the long counter to wait. A hum of activity escalated as patrons and protectors fell into their normal activities. Within a short time, a commotion outside told them their man had arrived.

The door thumped open and in strode Ferdinand, trailed by several men. Conversations paused briefly as people stared, but they soon resumed their meals and chatter. Ferdinand paused on the threshold, scanning the tavern. His eyes widened a bit as the two women swept regally toward him, smiling and gesturing. "Welcome to my humble tavern, Senor de Lerida," murmured Ysabella. Angelica nodded serenely, noting the impression they had made on Ferdinand that his face could not conceal.

Walking slowly towards the fireplace near the tanner's table, both women turned with their backs to the fire.

Ysabella swept an arm towards the large room. "This, Signor, is The Leopard. It is not nearly so large as my sister's establishment, The Olive," and she put her arm lovingly around Angelica's waist, "but we do a brisk business. As I'm sure Angelica's note mentioned, our wine vendor has disappeared, and we need supplies, and we need them now." She dimpled and turned her head slightly towards the back of the tavern, allowing Ferdinand to savor her delicate profile.

"Ladies, may we discuss this business in a more private venue?" he asked politely. Ysabella nodded her head and both women swayed towards the back of the tavern towards a private room with Ferdinand trailing appreciatively in their wake. For once, his usual alertness momentarily deserted him.

After the women and Ferdinand had disappeared down the back hallway, the tanner slid over to Raynaldus's table. "That is not the man I saw. I'm positive," the tanner whispered. "Same height and a beard, but the facial features are different. And I think the man I saw was a little more slender. No, that's not the one I saw in the alley."

Raynaldus sighed, slapped the man on the back and pushed a small beaker of wine in front of him as thanks. The tanner nodded and returned to conversing with his companions.

Raynaldus went over to a corner table where the kidnapper sat with a guard, his leg irons hardly noticeable. "Well?" The man just shook his head. Now what, thought Raynaldus, as he made his way towards the back of the tavern to interrupt a womanizer ogling his wife.

....

Angelica, Renata and Nicolo met Ysabella the next morning outside the gate of The Olive after their morning chores. As the women smoothed their dresses and patted their hair, they contemplated last night's adventure with Ferdinand. The evening had given the women plenty to laugh over this morning. The business ended swiftly with contracts for wine to be delivered the following day. Ysabella and Angelica had been amusing everyone with their description of their encounter, especially when Raynaldus had burst into the room and curtly introduced himself.

But now they had a more sobering duty to perform. They were going to give their formal condolences to Mateo de Paruta. The women could not imagine the plight of the boy, a friend of Nicolo's, being surrounded now only by servants. As they walked through the Cassaro down the wide boulevard that led to Simon's palace, the din of hawkers, storekeepers, merchants, and preachers went almost unnoticed. Angelica and Ysabella murmured about Mateo's loss of his brother and uncle and wondered if he would go to live with his mother. Behind them strolled Renata and Nicolo, enjoying each other's company and equally oblivious to the noise around them.

The warm Sicilian sunshine glinted off Renata's hair, making Nicolo notice its richness and sheen. Although he kept up a stream of conversation with his companion, pointing out an exotic parrot, an interesting shop and other sights of Palermo, all he could think was 'she'll be leaving soon'. Will I ever see her again? What would my mother think? His gaze rested on his mother and aunt walking ahead of him, their heads together. Renata certainly was no sheltered virgin. If he expressed an interest in her, would his parents consider her soiled goods?

The small group approached the de Paruta palazzo, noticing a restive stallion with black and gold harness being brought to the front door. They watched as Ferdinand de Lerida stepped outside, talking over his shoulder to Venutus. Ferdinand was frowning and gesturing, Venutus calmly listening. Why, I never noticed how tall Venutus is, thought Ysabella, surprised. He's the same height as Ferdinand, who is a tall man. She couldn't help but exchange a quick smirk with Angelica thinking about Ferdinand at The Leopard last night.

Angelica coughed delicately. At the sight of new visitors, Venutus gracefully skirted around Ferdinand and his horse and gave a small bow, leaving the Catalan in mid-sentence. Ferdinand snapped his head around, grimacing, only to see Angelica and Ysabella smiling up at him.

"Signoras! Such an unexpected pleasure!" and he swept off his hat, bowing low over their hands.

"Yes, Signor de Lerida, for us as well," Angelica purred. "Such a sad occasion that brings us here."

Turning to Venutus, she murmured the purpose of their visit softly to him. He inclined his head and moved ahead of her into the house. Ferdinand paused, collecting his thoughts. He had almost forgotten about poor dead Simon. Good grief, these women together were really spectacular but still, they were only women and he had business to attend to. Hopefully, that idiot servant of Simon's would remember his instructions.

"A pleasure last night, to be sure," he smiled, teeth as white as chalk. "I will personally oversee the wine delivery to your establishments today," and, he thought, I will get a good look at The Olive. The Catalana might be more well off than she let on. Just something to tuck away in his store of information….

When Renata and Nicolo joined them, the women bade Ferdinand a soft farewell and followed Venutus into the vestibule. As the valet turned to tell them that Mateo was in the garden, light from the doorway illuminated his figure. Ysabella thought absently how well-trimmed his beard looked, and how muscular he was. God's eyes, she thought, it's as if I never saw him when I was here! I'm probably noticing him because he'll be all Mateo has as he grows into a young man. And with that thought, she looked Venutus full in the face with an interest that startled him.

Momentarily confused, Venutus froze. Ysabella smiled, then asked softly, "May we go through to the garden, Venutus?" Mateo was sitting slumped on a bench next to a shady palm tree. As all four began murmuring sympathies, Mateo gave himself up to their kindness with relief.

…………..

Ysabella, Larissa and Mario all stretched their backs after mopping the tavern floor. After Ysabella returned from their errand of mercy she had needed physical activity. She changed into her everyday work clothes, donned a smock and began to clean. "Every time we do this job, mistress," Larissa began, "I thank the saints that you had the sense to insist on a tile floor and not all those filthy stinky rushes." Mario murmured something agreeable and went out back to relieve himself.

Ysabella walked over to the bar. Pulling out some glasses and a small *botti* of wine, she poured out three drinks. At the table she lapsed into silence and stared into the bottom of the cup. Larissa watched her mute friend and could see that something was cooking in the woman's head. Suddenly, Ysabella raised her head, cleared her throat and smiled broadly at her friend. Oh no, thought Larissa, here we go again. She has another idea. I hope it won't kill us this time. Eyes narrowed, she waited for Ysabella to speak.

"I know this is a long shot, Larissa," Ysabella started. "But I keep thinking that all this chaos revolves around Simon de Paruta. Yes, I know he's dead, but somehow…" She snapped her fingers, jumped up and called for a slave. "Please find Raynaldus for me and ask him to come here as soon as possible. He should bring Adam de Citella with him. I have something urgent to discuss with them." The boy nodded and ran out the door.

Curious, Larissa waited for an explanation. But none was forthcoming, because Ysabella had run upstairs to change her clothes.

CHAPTER 36

"I still don't quite understand what you want me to do, Ysabella," Raynaldus said impatiently. "We have the resources of the Archbishop of Palermo working with us now. What more can we do?"

"Please, Raynaldus, just listen. You know that Simon's estate is a valuable one--extremely complicated, yes?" Raynaldus nodded, still not understanding. "And Adam, you drew up Simon's will years ago, right?" The old notary agreed, mystified. "Well, I think you and Adam need to go to Mateo de Paruta and explain some of the finer points of inheritance to him. And I think you should take the tanner with you as some sort of associate. And when you're being served refreshments, I think you should casually mention that William's kidnapper is in jail with Amodeus."

"I don't know what this has to do with anything," Raynaldus began but stopped abruptly as Ysabella imperiously held up her hand.

"Please, brother, please trust me. It may come to nothing. I'm not sure my idea is important, but let's see what happens after your visit. You have to talk to him about these things anyway, do you not?"

Raynaldus and Adam traded skeptical looks, but Adam shrugged and agreed.

"Let's go, Raynaldus. She won't rest until we do it. I have no idea what she thinks will happen, but the sooner we do it, the better it will be." Adam then turned back to Ysabella.

"I guess you have convinced me, Ysabella," he said. He had feared from the beginning that their activities would only draw unwanted scrutiny from Charles' officials, but now he was contradicting his oldest friend and offering Ysabella support she had not expected.

"Ysabella's the only one thinking about this night and day, and if she has a plan, I am willing to go along. What's one more visit?" Ysabella shot the old notary a grateful look, but Raynaldus glared at him. Adam sent the slave boy to fetch the tanner.

"The days are passing and we still have no murderer. Amodeus may hang, and I am swimming in confusion," Ysabella pleaded. "This is my last hope, and if you won't help me, I'll go there myself. I can find another plausible reason to call on Mateo."

Raynaldus stared at her speculatively. There was no doubt Ysabella had become the driving force of the investigation. Her ideas and her boldness had amazed everyone, including, he thought wryly, Ysabella herself. She had become more assertive and confident, and, he thought with surprise, he trusted her instincts. She was shrewd, something he hadn't given her credit for before.

"Well, sister, I will do as you ask. You've pointed the way all through this horrible mess, so I can't doubt you now."

Ysabella's eyes moistened. Praise from Raynaldus was rare. She covered his fingers with hers and huskily murmured, "Thank you, Raynaldus. Thank you." Overcome, she leaped up and began furiously sweeping her clean tile floor.

The two men rose and walked out the door discussing what items they would review with the young heir. The tanner waited in the street, as surprised by his summons as the others.

"I'll send you a message as soon as we're done," Adam called out over his shoulder.

Larissa watched as Ysabella stopped sweeping and leaned against the *bucterium*, absently polishing the long counter with a cloth.

"Ysabella, are you going to tell me what you think is going to happen?"

"It's so far-fetched, Larissa. It may mean nothing. No, this time I think I'll keep it to myself." Ysabella moved off into the kitchen leaving Larissa to finish her wine alone.

…………..

Raynaldus, Adam and the tanner walked through the broad, smooth avenue that led to the Cassaro. Not knowing what they might encounter, they had decided to have two armed escorts accompany them. They tactfully had asked the tanner to change into clean clothes so he would fit in with their entourage and not smell like blood and carcasses. Suitably attired, no one would even notice him. As they approached Simon's *palazzo,* Adam took the tanner's arm and whispered to him. Nervously, the tanner nodded. He rarely went through this aristocratic section of Palermo. He didn't shop here. He attended church in his parish and the Great Market was in the opposite direction, as was the port where he bought fresh fish. This was a new world to him, of privilege, silks and satins. He stayed close to Raynaldus as the magistrate strode through the palace gates as naturally as he stepped into The Leopard.

A manservant greeted them at the door where Raynaldus brusquely stated their business. They were ushered into the garden while the servant went to find Mateo. Venutus appeared as if conjured up by a magician, murmuring greetings. Adam took an unobtrusive step backward so the tanner could get a clear view, but just then Venutus turned around and went back into the palace.

"I'm not sure," the tanner whispered. "His build is the same but he turned around before I could see his face." Raynaldus began pacing, and Adam nervously licked his lips.

"God's teeth," muttered Raynaldus. "Usually the man is hovering like a vulture, now he's vanished." Adam merely nodded. The man would show himself soon, he thought, if only to hear their conversation.

A few dark clouds scuttled over the garden as they waited. When Mateo arrived, he raised an eyebrow towards the armed escort. "Do you need weapons to talk to me now, Raynaldus?" he asked playfully.

"No, no, of course not; but the family has been threatened, so we travel in packs these days. May they wait in the hall until we're finished? I'm assuming we can do this in your study?" Raynaldus smiled thinly, and gestured for the tanner to stay with the guard.

"Of course, follow me." Mateo led the men into the cool, tiled manse.

"Well, Mateo, I truly appreciate that you're willing to listen to some of these very dry matters after such terrible losses."

Mateo sat tiredly with Adam and Raynaldus. He nodded his head. "I need to understand these things, even though right now I don't feel like looking at papers or doing anything connected with Uncle Simon's business."

The boy swallowed, and the men felt sympathy for the young man who was struggling to be strong. The door to the study opened before they started on business, and Raynaldus inhaled the aroma of fresh, warm bread. He watched Venutus smoothly begin to set up a side table with wine, fresh bread and cheese so that the three men could serve themselves at leisure. Then he turned to Mateo and casually said, "Well, did I tell you that we may be coming to a resolution of this whole sorry affair?"

Mateo sat up straighter, his eyes brightening. "No, Master Raynaldus, how is that?"

"We managed to catch William's kidnapper the night that William was returned. He is in jail with Amodeus. So many things have happened that I swear I can't keep it all straight."

"You didn't tell me about this," Mateo breathed, smiling. "Will he talk? Is he talking?"

"Yes, we're getting information out of him. I'm confident it will lead to something. But let's move on. How about some cheese, some bread, a little wine? Perhaps we can get through some of our tedious business."

Mateo nodded, and the three men stood and walked over to the inviting table Venutus had laid out. As he absently thanked his steward, Mateo was startled to notice Venutus clenching and unclenching his hands. Then he remembered how much Venutus had been involved in the cloth business. I shall have to keep him informed of what's going on, Mateo thought. I've been thoughtless, thinking only of myself. He did love my uncle. And he smiled at his valet, but Venutus for once failed to see it.

CHAPTER 37

One look at the tanner's face in the hallway after their meeting had been enough. Adam smoothly took him aside as Raynaldus lingered to explain something technical to Mateo and instructed him to go directly home without speaking to anyone. He dispatched one armed man to The Olive, another to The Leopard, and one to get the sheriff.

Ysabella was still cleaning The Leopard as though possessed when the messenger confirmed her suspicions. "Larissa! Listen! It was Venutus the tanner saw in the alley. I really noticed his appearance when we went to see Mateo, but the idea that he could be responsible was just too outlandish to voice aloud. But now he can be arrested. My husband will be free! He's coming home, Larissa! I have to tell William. Where is that child of mine? Have you seen him?"

"He went to The Olive with Nicolo." Ysabella nodded gratefully. No more kidnappings, no more murders. The authorities would get what they needed out of Venutus. She could relax now. They were safe and Amodeus would be coming home!

"I heard what you said, mistress," Mario said coming out of the kitchen, "But it may not be over yet. Master Raynaldus told me earlier to be sure everyone goes to The Olive. We will have to lock up for one night at least."

"But they'll arrest Venutus right away, I'm sure. Why do we have to leave?"

"Lady, who knows where his minions are lurking, or if they are already planning to harm you?" Mario answered roughly.

"Master Raynaldus is playing it safe. Let's go." He crossed his arms over his chest and scowled at her, letting her know he would not take no for an answer.

Ysabella looked around The Leopard, noting the many tasks left undone despite her day's work, and sighed. Clearly no one would let her stay behind. She threw a kerchief over her hair and followed them out the door.

…………..

When Ysabella woke to church bells the next morning, it was a sunny Easter morning. She lay in the soft folds of the bedding a few more minutes before opening one eye like a wary cat. A pool of golden light lay below the arched window. I must have been exhausted to sleep so late, she thought. Where is everyone? And why is it so quiet? William, if no one else, should have been looking for me. Oh, of course--I'm not too important compared to the distractions that Nicolo provides.

A shiver ran through her as her toes touched the cool tiles. It was going to be a glorious day, she knew. Amodeus will be home today, now that we led the sheriff to the real murderer. Bless our friend, the tanner! Dear Tomaso will have free wine at The Leopard for some time to come. Amodeus will be surprised when he sees how well we have managed on our own. Suddenly her serenity and hopefulness crumbled at her feet. Amodeus will be home today! TODAY! We left The Leopard in such a rush last night....He can't come home to unswept floors and dirty dishes. I have work to do!

Pulling her clogs on as she flew down the stairs, Ysabella called out for Larissa. The whole house was silent. No clatter from the kitchen. No hum of conversation in the dining hall. Not even the whinny of horses in the stable. She was obviously alone. Then she stopped in her tracks, remembering it was Easter morning. Everyone must have gone to Mass already, she thought. Well, that explained it. Odd they let me sleep through Mass, though, but I can't wait for them to return. Larissa and Mario will go back to The Leopard right after the final blessings, but I can start on the chores without them. Mary, forgive me, but I will have to delay my duties to Jesus until evening prayers.

The latch on the door moved just as she reached for it, and she found herself clutching only air. A sudden fear rose in her throat, and she took a step backward nearly falling over her own feet. A tall, armed man stepped across the threshold and grabbed at her arm to prevent her fall.

"There, now. Are you alright? I heard you calling, mistress. Mistress Angelica asked me to wait until you had awakened. They all went to Mass."

"My, you startled me!" Ysabella stammered, regaining her balance. "Yes, I heard the church bells. Please tell my sister-in-law I have gone to The Leopard."

"But she said you weren't to leave The Olive until they return from church. She said to tell you."

"Nonsense. She knows my husband is returning today. She'll understand. You just wait here and be sure The Olive is secure while they are away. They arrested our murderer, so I'm perfectly safe."

Later on, the guard would remember her confidence as he watched her hurry from the gates.

. . . .

"What do you mean you didn't arrest him?" Leo shouted at the sheriff about the same time as Ysabella unlocked the green door to her own establishment across town.

"We have a witness who identified him, and he saw him with that green cloak Antonio always wore! Are you leaving a murderer on the street to terrorize honest citizens?" And he ranted on, knowing he was losing control.

The sheriff watched him, amused. "We don't know that. I will question him again, of course, when some of my men have returned. Maybe this afternoon....But last night your comrades pulled me away from my supper with a beautiful woman for nothing. This Venutus explained his presence around The Leopard that night. There was nothing more to be done. Quit playing at investigation, old man. You have no evidence of anything. And remember, there were two murders. I have a sweet little pigeon in my coop already. At least one murder is solved."

"We brought you evidence. We have witnesses. We have shown the two deaths are connected." He could hold his tongue no more. "By convicting the wrong man you save yourself the trouble of actually earning your pay. You Angevins are all alike. You use any excuse to grind us under your thumbs in the guise of 'law and order.' My family remains at risk and you do nothing. I will make sure the Archbishop and the King know of your negligence in this matter."

"Treasonous words do not serve your cause. Get out before I hang you as well. I'll take it from here."

Leo was horrified. He ran to The Olive, determined to hear directly from Raynaldus what that lying weasel could have said to avoid arrest. Raynaldus….Why had Raynaldus not taken action when the sheriff refused? He could have placed a temporary guard on the palazzo. He could have squeezed a confession out of Venutus himself. He could have done…well, *something*! Now Ysabella and William were in even greater danger. Maybe they all were!

Leo rushed through the gate at The Olive calling loudly for Raynaldus. He made it across the threshold into the silent foyer before the guard caught at his sleeve.

"The Master is not here, sir. He did not return last night."

"What? Didn't return? Where is he? Angelica! Where is Angelica and…and where are the others?"

"They all went to hear the Archbishop say Easter Mass at the Cathedral. That pilgrim woman with the new baby was going on and on about baptizing the bawling creature on Easter Sunday. Some sort of sign, she said."

Gesturing wildly, Leo grabbed the man's arm. "Forget the pilgrims, man. Where is Raynaldus?"

The guard took his time in answering. "Mistress had a message last night that he had gone to see the Archbishop. Can't imagine they would talk all night, though. It is passing strange he didn't come home."

"Don't be ridiculous." Leo gripped the man's forearm with a fury that finally conveyed his urgency. "Listen to me. That madman of a sheriff did not arrest the murderer. The family could be in danger. Get as many armed men as possible. Hire some if you must. I will cover the expense. Send them to the church to protect the family, especially Ysabella and William. And find Raynaldus!"

"But, sire, Mistress said…." the man grunted.

"Do as I say, and do it now! Don't you understand? They may be in danger. I need to see a magistrate about that sheriff. This is outrageous!" Leo dashed out of the courtyard of The Olive, infused with anger and panic.

The Archbishop was just finishing the benediction when the guard from The Olive and two other hired men halted outside the main doors of the Cathedral. They noticed Renata, her mother, and her still-howling baby brother leave with the first worshippers almost before the last 'Amen', but the others were apparently delayed in the crush of people around them. Now that religious obligations were fulfilled, a holiday mood encouraged folks to chat with their friends, and take the time to admire the Cathedral's precious icons and statuettes.

Had the guard not noticed the golden netting Angelica wore over her hair when she left The Olive, he wouldn't have seen her sheparding her daughters through the crowd. The gold shimmered over her dark tresses like sunlight filtering through a forest. Nicolo and Pietro strolled out soon after, but Raynaldus still had not joined his family. Angelica, a bit blinded by the bright sunshine after the dim interior of the nave, stopped to speak to her daughters. Beatrice tried so hard to look grown up and confident among all these strangers, but Matilda still clung to mother's hand. The girl yelped in surprise when a hand reaching to grasp Angelica's arm brushed across her cheek.

"My lady," the guard stammered, still struck by the oddities of the day's events, "Master Leo sent me to protect you and to find Master Raynaldus. He said you are in danger. Do you know where your husband is?"

"No, I do not, but why would we be in danger? And who sent you?"

"It was Signor Leo, madam. He was very agitated when he arrived at the hostel, and then he ran off again to find a magistrate. Just like Mistress Ysabella did earlier."

"Ysabella? What do you mean? You were to have her wait until we returned. Are you unable to follow simple instructions?"

"I tried, mistress, but she wouldn't wait. I could not forcibly restrain her. She said you would understand and she would be safe at The Leopard."

"Yes, but now you say we are not safe. Did Signor Leo explain his reasons?"

"He said the sheriff was an arrogant madman and the murderer was not arrested. I don't really know who he meant."

Angelica snapped to attention, quickly grasping the man's meaning even if he did not. With everything that had happened this week, her family easily could be in danger. An image suddenly flooded her mind—Raynaldus, blood-covered, lying in some rat-infested alley. Was that why he did not join them at Mass? Was he already dead?

"Mama, what is it?" Matilda squeaked. She was beginning to cry.

A grim determination pushed away the gruesome thoughts of her husband as Angelica looked down at her daughter's frightened face and tried to smile. "It will be all right, my dear, but we must hurry home. I will buy you the sweets I promised tomorrow."

Members of her household, her pilgrims, and Ysabella's servants were all loitering out of earshot. She could not let them suspect any danger. She turned to the guard. "Gather everyone together in one group and take them back to The Olive, but say nothing. I will follow close on with Nicolo and Signor Manfredi. They will protect me."

Pietro had noticed the hushed conversation and instinctively went to Angelica's side.

"What now, madam? How may I help?" She rapidly told Pietro what had happened.

Assuming a natural authority out of old habit he gave pointed instructions to Nicolo and the guard. He placed a hand on Angelica's shoulder as if to guide her along with the group, but she stood rooted to the spot and looked at him imploringly.

"Signor Pietro," she said, her voice cracking with anxiety, "Despite my instructions, Ysabella returned to The Leopard alone this morning. She may not know that Venutus is still free. Please go to her. She needs protection much more than the rest of us."

"I will protect her as if she were my own daughter."

CHAPTER 38

Pietro took two strides down the side street, and then stopped for a moment wondering what a murderer might do. Venutus wouldn't bother Ysabella; he had to get out of town. He wouldn't have time to go to The Leopard. Where would he be? Of course, getting whatever he could lay his hands on and a horse – somewhere he wouldn't be questioned and would still have authority. He would be at Simon's.

Bellowing for The Olive's guardsmen, he instructed one to run to The Leopard, just in case.

"You," he snapped to the tallest one, "you come with me." And he took off running with the surprised man at his heels.

Both men skidded into the courtyard, Pietro already assessing the surroundings. It was eerily quiet. No servants bustling or sounds of activity. Probably all at Easter mass with their families.

Shoving his companion forward he whispered, "Go around to the garden and enter the *palazzo* through the kitchen. Be quiet and careful. If you see Venutus, shout." The man nodded and slipped away.

Cautiously Pietro crept through the front door. Unlocked, hmm. Cocking his head, he listened intently. Nothing. He glided through the hallway and headed for Simon's study but stopped. He heard voices. Or one voice – low and angry. Who was in there? Where was Mateo? Cautiously he stepped forward. As he approached the door, slightly ajar, he heard Raynaldus – snarling. Raynaldus? The quiet, sober, always-in-control merchant and politician? Unsheathing his sword, he slowly pushed the door wider. His jaw dropped.

Venutus was breathing heavily and backed against the wall, holding his side with bloodstained fingers, glaring at the man in front of him. "Don't think this flesh wound will stop me, Raynaldus. I've killed many men, and I'll kill you. Get out of my way."

"No you won't, *bastardo*. You're already skewered, just like the pig you are. Didn't expect that from me, did you? You think I'm afraid of you? Remember what I used to be? A tanner, well, technically, a butcher. A butcher of animals. Animals like you. You let my wife and my sister-in-law parade like whores in front of that Catalan. You kidnapped my nephew – my nephew!" he screamed suddenly. "And my brother! Locked up! Almost hanged! My FAMILY, you swine!"

Pietro, frozen, couldn't move. Venutus gasped and coughed, dribbling blood down his chin.

"You put my whole family in danger, and for what? Money! We didn't do anything to you! Oh no, you're going nowhere, and you won't be terrorizing anyone else either."

Venutus glowered and lunged. Before Pietro could move, Raynaldus neatly sidestepped the desperate move and again thrust his butcher's knife deep into the heart cavity under the ribs. Grunting, he ripped upwards.

Cords standing out on his neck, Venutus screamed, spat at his attacker, and fell to the floor making incoherent whimpers. A bloody hand clutched at Raynaldus's ankle. Impassively, Raynaldus kicked the wounded man in the face with his boot toe, then bent down and yanked his head up by the hair.

"Nooooo ..." and Raynaldus the butcher cut his throat.

....

Ysabella worked in a light-hearted mood, eagerly anticipating Amodeus's return. She hauled the water, cleaned the fireplace, swept the main room, scrubbed the tables and put everything in its place by the time the bells all over town rang again announcing the conclusion of services. As soon as the pea soup delicately flavored with bits of ham—one of Amodeus's favorites---was on the hearth, she would have a few moments to wash up. She wanted to look her best when he walked in the door. She especially wanted him to see her draped in the lavender silk scarf he had given her a few months before this nightmare began.

Ysabella was still focused on her soup when Amodeus, followed by Leo and Adam, ran through the door of The Leopard calling her name. Excited, she raced out to meet him. Her rather smelly man shoved his way through the family and neighbors who had poured into the tavern after him, all patting his back and trying to shake his hand. Amodeus burst into her sight, and overcome with emotion, knelt before her and clutched her in his arms. He seized her so tightly that she could scarcely breathe, but she had no complaints. He buried his face in her hair muttering her name.

"Amodeus! Amodeus!" she sobbed. Finally, he was safe, and they were together.

"Wine for everyone!" Amodeus called after another murmured exchange with his wife.

"What kind of host would I be to forget refreshment for my visitors? We have reason to celebrate."

Nicolo, William, and the others now crowded around the freed man. William clung to his father, yelling in his ear.

Mario and Larissa quickly tied smocks over their church clothes and carried in wine and spice cakes as if they were serving royalty. Bread, fruit and olives were placed on the sideboard within easy reach. The best glasses were unearthed from a rear cupboard and passed around to all. Laughter and congratulations spread among them in a universal release of tension. And suddenly, the tavern was alive with laughing, happy neighbors all crowding in around Ysabella and Amodeus.

Ysabella happily clutched her husband's arm. "Now that I have you back, I'm not leaving your side. But what happened? Didn't Raynaldus escort you home? Where is he?"

"I'm here," Raynaldus answered, striding in the door with the old Crusader.

"Venutus was apprehended at Simon's house," signaling Pietro with a nod, "and I'll tell you the rest later. First I want to hear how you figured it out."

"Just where were you, Raynaldus?" Leo butted in before she could respond. "You were away from The Olive all night. I worried that we would have another corpse."

"Someone must have been looking after me," he quipped, glancing upwards. "After Venutus managed to sweet-talk the sheriff last night, I hurried directly to our friend, the Archbishop, hoping he would have more information we could use. His men were ferreting out the details of Simon's spying, but they had found nothing to implicate our culprit. We talked all night, examining every possible solution, even up to the moment he had to conduct Mass this morning. He was going to give me letters to appeal to Charles himself, so I waited in his chambers until the service was over. I sent word to Angelica last night, and I knew she would arrange for the guards."

"I acted as you instructed," Angelica answered, "but by the time your messenger arrived, Ysabella was asleep. I knew how much the chaos this week had taken out of her, so I didn't have the heart to wake her with more bad news. I chose to leave her abed this morning, too. Mea culpa."

Raynaldus cleared his throat to start again. "Venutus told the sheriff that Simon had ordered Antonio to stay in the palazzo after Ludovico's murder. Even Mateo confirmed that. So when they found him missing, Simon sent Venutus to bring him back. He decided Antonio might be with Nicolo, so he went to The Leopard, but didn't find him. He explained that he took Antonio's green cloak when he left the house since it was getting colder and Antonio had left without it."

"No! No!" Ysabella nearly shouted. A little color had returned to her cheeks. "I distinctly remember Antonio wearing the cloak when he came through the door. It was so noticeable. Didn't you tell the sheriff that?"

"Of course, but there was no way to prove it. Venutus's alibi was at least plausible, so the sheriff refused to hold him."

Angelica squeezed onto the bench and patted Ysabella's shoulder. "Ysabella, you are really the hero of this whole thing. None of us even thought of Venutus. I still don't understand how you thought of him." Everyone impatiently waited to hear her story.

"Do you remember, Angelica, when we went over the Simon's house to comfort Mateo? You went inside to speak to some of the servants, and Mateo and I were in the garden talking. He was so alone, you know, he was just pouring out his heart. And he told me several things about Venutus. He told me Venutus was so loyal because Simon had saved his father from ruin. Simon had come to rely more and more on Venutus and thought of him almost as family. Mateo said Venutus showed him a letter Simon had written giving Venutus everything if anything happened to the boys. Who knows if Simon really wrote such a thing? And it wasn't formally part of the will you drew up for him, Adam. Well, Venutus began acting like he was already head of the family, making decisions, spending money, and so on. Mateo disagreed with him about most of that, so he was worried. I just comforted the boy as best I could. I knew Adam and Raynaldus would see that Mateo got his full inheritance.

"I had nearly forgotten about his stories until I saw Venutus standing next to that despicable Ferdinand de Lerida. I noticed how much they looked alike, although Venutus was a bit taller. Their beards were similar. That got me thinking, and I remembered everything Mateo had told me. I was suspicious of the man, but I wasn't rushing into another fiasco like we had with Lerida. I just kept it to myself for a while. I couldn't imagine that Mateo really had any idea that Simon was spying for Aragon, but the oh-so-loyal Venutus had to be right in the thick of it. Simon couldn't leave the house, and Lerida wasn't in Palermo often, so he had to use Venutus or other intermediaries. I mean, it wasn't all love and devotion, certainly."

She paused to sample the bread and fruit, and she was surprised to find out how hungry she was. She was still chewing on an apricot when she went on. "I guessed that Ludovico must have been involved, too. He was always under Simon's thumb, and according to Joanna, he was acting very strangely lately. We all saw what a hothead he could be when he was drunk. What if he knew something and had to be silenced before he spilled it to the wrong people? And then it got back to Simon that Antonio had been following Ferdinand, so suddenly he might have been a liability. Venutus was always lurking about, so I'm sure he knew those two felt Antonio was a risk." She paused again to stuff some grapes into her mouth. No one else had said a word.

"I could believe that Simon ordered the murder of Ludovico--he saw him just as an old drunk no one would miss--but I couldn't believe he wanted Antonio dead, even though he despised him. The key is that regardless of Antonio's risk to the spies' plot, he was also a liability for Venutus. Venutus hated Antonio, and he wanted to be rich. Only Venutus knew how close to death's door Simon really was. Venutus was afraid he might be out on his ear when Simon died – Antonio would probably see to that!

"So when that stupid sheriff arrested Amodeus for Ludovico's murder, Venutus saw his chance to lay the blame on us; to have the authorities and everyone else think it had something to do with The Leopard. All Venutus had to do then was follow Antonio to The Leopard one night and do exactly what he had done to Ludovico. He made it seem like The Leopard was a den of murderers or something. Worst of all, even though Venutus didn't plan it that way, Amodeus ended up being the murder suspect. I couldn't just sit and do nothing because it wasn't true, and he could have died because of it!"

The tale concluded, Amodeus looked at his wife with both devotion and a new respect. Despite the impulsive mistakes he had heard about, she took charge like a ship's captain and had everyone running the length and breadth of the city, all the while running the business and earning the respect of the neighborhood.

"You saved yourself from killers and kidnappers. Let's toast our family's protector once more," he said, pride beaming from his face.

"Then I think it's time to ask you to leave. We need rest, and," he said ruefully, "I need a bath." Ysabella nodded vigorously and everyone laughed.

"I will never take my family, my love, or my good fortune for granted again. And I'm sure Ysabella would agree with me."

"Yes, husband. We are so lucky, aren't we?" Clinging to her husband, she smiled gratefully at Angelica, Raynaldus and the throng around her.

Amodeus turned to his brother. They stared at each other with a new appreciation, and Raynaldus stepped forward to hug his younger sibling for a long moment. Amodeus said, "Tell me, Raynaldus. Who apprehended Venutus and where was he?"

"Oh, Pietro and I will tell that story another time. It's complicated. But right now, I'd say he's definitely in custody and no threat to anyone." He and Pietro exchanged a sly grin and the topic slipped by as everyone began laughing and talking again.

One by one, the family filed by Amodeus and Ysabella, kissing her forehead, clasping his hands in theirs, or muttering a blessing or two. Pietro knelt and pressed her hand to his lips as if she were a countess. Even skeptical Adam warmly gripped Amodeus's hand, saying he had known all along that Ysabella would triumph.

Angelica lingered a few more minutes. "I have chores in the morning, but I'll be here to check on you as soon as our little group of pilgrims leaves for home. They will have some hair-raising stories to tell in Trapani—about Sophia getting a boy child, the four Crusaders and the gold medallions, the Archbishop saying the funeral Mass for Ludovico, not to mention two murders and how you solved them! I have a feeling all those stories will live for years. I miss you terribly at The Olive, but you have a new life here. Renata has proved most useful at the hostel, and did I tell you—she convinced me and her mother to let her stay in Palermo?"

The exhaustion of total relief had swept over Ysabella, but at this news she perked up. She clapped her hands and hugged her sister-in-law. "That's good news, Angelica! I hope that doesn't mean we'll see less of Nicolo!" The women winked at each other.

"Well, I thought I would be in charge here when I left The Olive," Amodeus announced, "but now I see that with Ysabella at the helm, The Leopard can't fail. Since our opening night was so rudely interrupted, I think we should have another one. Don't you, *mia cara*?" Ysabella only rolled her eyes.

THE END
....

Book Two of the Vespers Trilogy will be available in 2013

BOOK 2 EXCERPT

PROLOGUE – FEBRUARY 20, 1282

In the end, he was murdered because he hesitated. Roberto de Scarani, Archbishop of Palermo, traveled to the famous monastery of La Cava located in the misty mountains of Capua at the request of his dying friend, Abbot Catapanus Marino. He heard the abbot's gasping last words with escalating horror and wished he had never come, or come too late. The abbot pressed an old, creased page into the trembling Archbishop's hand, then wheezing softly, joined the long line of heavenly shepherds.

Roberto – former Crusader, Church prelate, international ambassador – had seen and heard many things in his 57 years, but this terrified him. This affected dynasties – of the Mediterranean and as far as Western Europe and England! He didn't want to know this thing.

Tiro, his faithful Greek secretary, found him slumped in a chair, head in hands, brow furrowed. Assuming it was grief for his old friend, Tiro clucked around him, tempting his master with bits of fruit, sweets, some wine. Roberto ignored it all. Tiro was perplexed, he had never seen the Archbishop, usually so decisive, so energetic, like this. "More wine, Tiro," he snapped.

When he returned, Roberto was sealing up a letter. "I'm going to the chapel to pray. We're leaving tonight," he said abruptly to his surprised secretary.

"Yes, Your Excellency," Tiro hesitated. "Will we not be staying for the Abbot's funeral?"

"No, we ride tonight. Pack my things. You, me and three guards. The rest of the entourage can follow after the funeral." Bowing, Tiro backed out and rapidly began issuing orders.

The Archbishop made his way to the chapel. Before entering, he spoke briefly to a young monk, who bowed and hurried towards the stable. The Archbishop entered the chapel, fell on his knees before the altar and began praying. Intent on his prayers, he never heard the footsteps and barely felt the blows.

As he lay dying in a widening pool of blood, the Archbishop's fading thought was *Pietro, my old friend, do not fail me.*

The assassin stole out of the monastery, satisfied The Secret had been kept. The Archbishop had found out from that foolish old abbot, but it had ended there. All the Episcopal messengers were accounted for, along with the Greek secretary. He had sent no letters, no messages.

He was positive. When the Archbishop died, The Secret died with him. His mistress would be very pleased.

MAP NOTES

The map of medieval Palermo in this book was originally drawn by Franco D'Angelo of Palermo, Sicily. With his permission, we have added a few landmarks, fictional and otherwise, that help the reader identify places in the story.

In 1281 Palermo had five quarters: the Cassaro, the Albergharia, the Seralcadio, the Kalsa and the Porta Patitellorum. The Cassaro was the oldest quarter inhabited by the Romans and Byzantines and was also the highest topographically. It is surrounded by two rivers in a wishbone configuration and bisected by the Via Marmora. Although the medieval map shows an axis street across the lower half of the Cassaro, no such street actually existed in 1281. The newest quarter, the Porta Patitellorum, is where The Leopard and the Great Market are. This quarter is named for the *patitelli*, who made *patiti,* sandals of leather and wood.

The two rivers no longer exist in modern Palermo and therefore, the Admiral's Bridge, an 11th century elegant construction, sits in a park with grass underneath as opposed to water.

The port, called La Cala, was also configured differently than present day Palermo. It curled in towards Piazza Marina in the shape of a comma; land which was later filled in beginning in the 14th century.

Most of the major churches in *Murder at the Leopard* still exist in Palermo. The Archbishop's Palace, which the story has put in its present site across from the Cathedral, was actually on the north side of the Cathedral on today's Via Incoronazione.

We have tried to accurately place the Fondaco dei Catalani, Great Market, and the Synagogue using scholarly sources. But since there are no addresses in the medieval world, the placement of The Leopard and La Lumia, Palermo's largest tavern owned by the

Teutonic Knights, is total guesswork. As stated before, The Olive and Simon's house are fictional constructs.

The second book mentions the last surviving mosque in Palermo in the Forum Sarracenorum, which was confirmed by Hugo Falcandus in the 12th century. Again, we have tried to place it as accurately as possible using scholarly sources.

MAPS

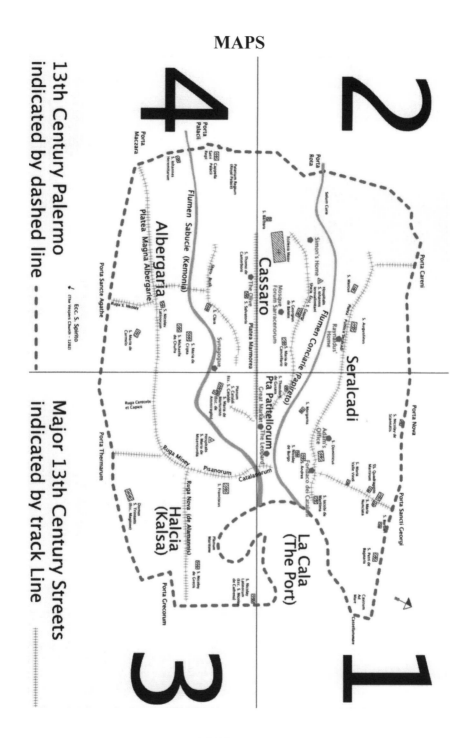

13th Century Palermo
indicated by dashed line - - - - - - -

Major 13th Century Streets
indicated by track Line ++++++++++++

297 | P a g e

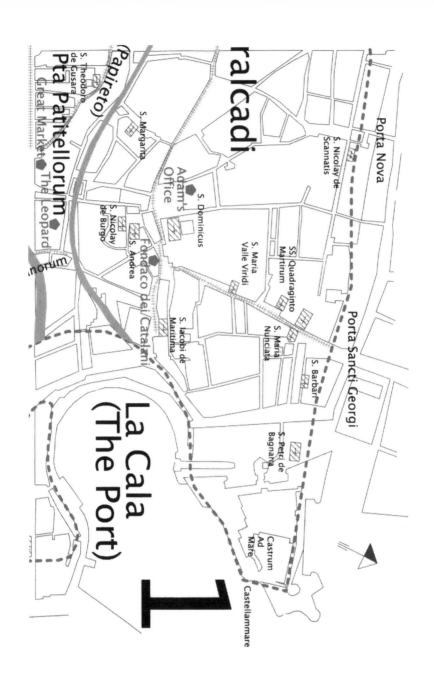

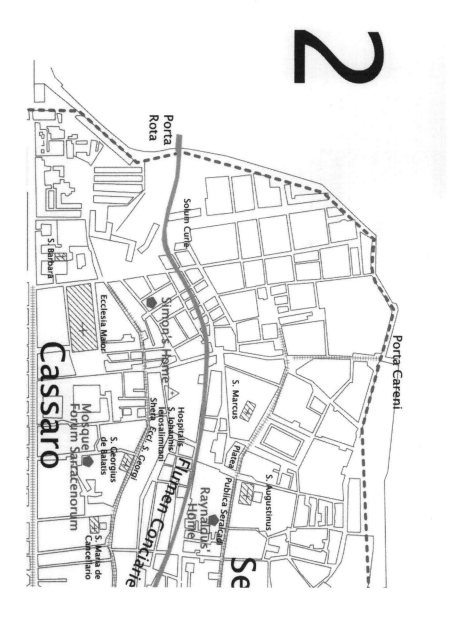

2

Porta
Rota

Solum Curie

S. Barbara

Ecclesia Maior

Simon's Home

Cassaro

Mosque
Forum Sarracenorum

S. Georgius
de Balatis

Shera

Ecc. S. Georgi

Hospitalis
S. Johannis
Ieiosalimitani

S. Maria de
Cancellario

Flumen Conciarie

S. Marcus

Platea
Publica Seralcadi

Raynaldus'
Home

S. Augustinus

Porta Cafeni

Se

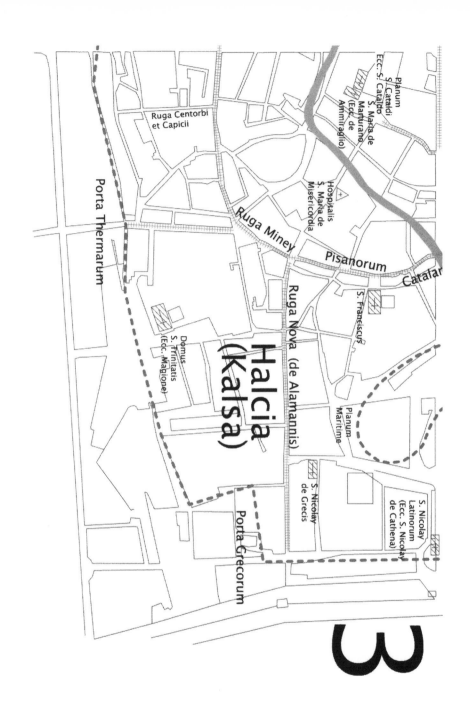

Porta Thermarum

Ruga Centorbi
et Capicii

Planum
S. Cataldi
Ecc. S. Cataldo

S. Maria de
Marturana
(Ecc. de
Ammiraglio)

Ruga Miney

Hospitalis
S. Maria de
Misericordia

Pisanorum

Catalan

S. Franciscus

Domus
S. Trinitatis
(Ecc. Magione)

Ruga Nova (de Alamannis)

Halcia
(Kalsa)

Planum
Maritime

S. Nicolay
de Grecis

S. Nicolay
Latinorum
(Ecc. S. Nicolay
de Cathena)

Porta Grecorum

3

4

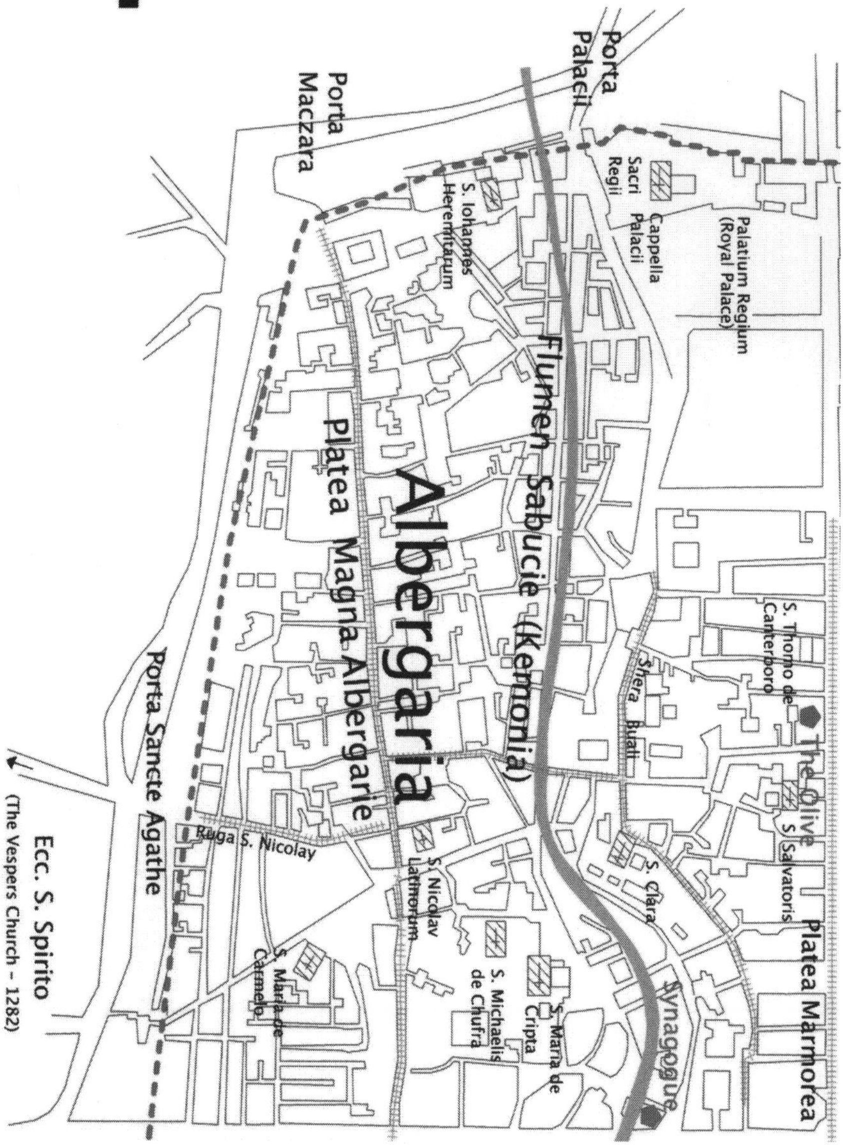
Porta Palacii
Porta Maczarara
Palatium Regium (Royal Palace)
Cappella Palacii
Sacri Regii
S. Iohannes Heremitarum
Flumen Sabucie (Kemonia)
Albergaria
Platea Magna Albergarie
S. Thomo de Canterboro
Shera Bucli
The Olive
S. Salvatoris
Platea Marmorea
S. Clara
Synagogue
S. Maria de Cripta
S. Michaelis de Chufra
S. Nicolav Latinorum
S. Maria de Carmelo
Ruga S. Nicolay
Porta Sancte Agathe
Ecc. S. Spirito
(The Vespers Church - 1282)

GLOSSARY

Asr - Period of day for Muslim prayer – afternoon

Buctarium - Small room with a counter usually for food presentation

Cambiatori - Money changers who dealt locally, such as loans, deposits, bills of exchange, money changing. Leo de Iannacio was often described as such a man.

Casa - A house, usually two stories

Casalina - Tiny house, usually one room

Conciatores - Tanners, such as Ysabella's family and the de Rogerio brothers' family

Contrada - A parish

Darbum - Arabic word for a dead end alley

Dhuhr - Period of day for Muslim prayer – noon

Duchena - Bench outside a house or shop that was covered, often used as a small area to set up goods

Ecclesia - Latin for church

Fajr - Period of day for Muslim prayer – near dawn (see also, dhuhr, asr, maghrib and isha'a

Fideiussore - A guarantor in a contract who stands surety

Flumen - A river

Fondaco - Inn or hostel for lodging, commerce and/or storage depot for goods; a Western term employed by Latin speakers; see also funduq

Forum Sarracenorum - A forum is a public place, a plaza or piazza; this would be the public place of the Saracens

Fundaco - See the above "fondaco" but this term also referred to a warehouse used to store goods; other terms for warehouses in the sources are a paratore or magazine

Fundacarius - Warehouse manager

Funduk - Islamic inn or hostel for lodging, commerce and/or storage depot for goods; an Arabic term usually owned by the ruler as opposed to a private commercial space

Hospicium - Large mansion or palace, often a complex of buildings, sometimes referred to as a hospicium domorum. These complexes usually had courtyards, gardens and interconnected real estate.

Isha'a - Period of day for Muslim prayer – nightfall

Iurati - Elected municipal officials like Raynaldus de Rogerio

Macello della Iudayce - The Jewish market

Maestro Portulano – Master of the Port; harbormaster

Maghrib - Period of day for Muslim prayer at sunset

Magister de Platea - a city magistrate comparable to a modern city department of Streets & Sanitation - he is in charge of the main boulevard traversing that quarter and its maintenance, cleanliness and garbage pickup

Magnum Macellum - The Great Market where, among other things, meat was sold to the residents

Penne - Wings of a house

Planum - An empty space within the city

Platea - The great avenue running through each quarter of the city, paved or cobbled and often shaded. They intersected the main piazze of the city and ended and/or began at one or more of the main gates.

Porta - A gate, such as the Porta Palacium where the pilgrims enter Palermo

Ruga - A street

Shera - A small street

Solerata - Upper story of a house

Syri - An honorary term meaning "great merchant"

Tenimentum domorum - A tenement of houses, it is somewhat like a modern large apartment building with an internal courtyard and usually on a main street or platea. Raynaldus de Rogerio lives in such a complex in the Seralcadio.

Terrene - Ground floor of a house

Vanella - An alley, different from a darbum by its open-ended character

CAST OF CHARACTERS
THE VESPERS SERIES

Baroness de Caltagirone - Wealthy, aristocratic widow in Palermo; old friend of Ferdinand de Lerida

Adam de Citella - Prominent notary of Palermo; he and his sons close to the de Rogerio family

Leo de Iannacio - Close friend ("uncle") of the de Rogerio Family; citizen of Palermo, older, wealthy merchant

Josef the Jew - Resident of Palermo, de Lerida's business manager

Ferinand de Lerida - Devoted courtier of King Peter of Aragon; the King's Assassin; poses as a Catalan merchant selling luxury goods

Julianna Manfredi - Pietro's dead wife

Pietro Manfredi - Former crusader, military man of the Count of Blois, returning home to Trapani; brother to Carlo

Arturo Pandolfo - Sophia's husband

Carlo Manfredi - Pietro's brother, who still lives in Trapani

Perna Manfredi - Carlo's wife, a midwife

Renata Pandolfo - Sulky beautiful 14 year old daughter of Sophia and Arturo

Sophia Pandolfo - Very pregnant wife of Arturo; making a Pilgrimage to Palermo to pray for a son

Antonio de Paruta - Oldest nephew of Simon, 17 years old

Angelica de Rogerio - Wife of Raynaldus; 32 years old, daughter of a Catalan merchant; manages The Olive

Amodeus de Rogerio - Orphaned at an early age; Amodeus is 35 and younger brother of Raynaldus

Beatrice de Rogerio - Young daughter of Raynaldus and Angelica

Matilda de Rogerio - Young daughter of Raynaldus and Angelica

Matteo de Paruta - Nephew of Simon and adoring younger brother of Antonio, 14 years old

Nicolo de Rogerio - Oldest child and son of Raynaldus and Angelica, about 17

Raynaldus de Rogerio - Orphaned at an early age; Raynaldus is 40 and older brother of Amodeus

Simon de Paruta - Former Crusader, patriarch and uncle of Antonio and Matteo

William de Rogerio - Eight year old son of Ysabella and Amodeus

Ysabella de Rogerio - Wife of Amodeus; 27 years old, a tanner's daughter; Amodeus and Ysabella own The Leopard, a tavern

Roberto de Scarani - Archbishop of Palermo, former Crusader

Joanna Stefani - Long suffering wife of Ludovico; dear friend and neighbor of Ysabella

Ludovico Stefani - Spice merchant, drunk, first victim, former Crusader

Larissa and Mario - Trusted servants/neighbors, a married couple who work at The Leopard

Venutus - Faithful, lifelong retainer of Simon's

THE VESPERS IN A NUTSHELL

PART I – 1282-1302

Approximately a half mile southeast of the old city walls of Palermo is the small Church of the Holy Spirit built in 1177 by Walter Ophamil, the English Archbishop of Palermo. It was the custom of that church to hold a festival on Easter Monday. On Easter Monday, March 30, 1282, the usual Vespers service was held. Before the service, people gathered in the square to gossip and sing. A group of French officials who had been drinking entered the square, ignoring the usual hostility of the Sicilians to their oppressors. A young Angevin officer named Drouet dragged a married woman from the crowd and began harassing her. This outraged her husband, who pulled out a knife and stabbed Drouet to death. Instantly, the small group of Frenchmen were surrounded and massacred by the Sicilians. Not one survived. As the bell rang for Vespers, messengers spread throughout Palermo, then Sicily, calling for an uprising against the Angevins.

Palermo immediately filled with angry men who poured into houses, inns and streets, killing anyone French – men, women and children. Sicilian girls who had married Frenchmen were killed with their husbands. By the next morning, approximately 2,000 men and women were dead and the rebels were in complete control of Palermo. The Angevin flag was torn down and Palermo declared itself a commune. Eventually, the entire island followed suit. Appeals to the Papacy for protection were ignored, and in desperation the Sicilians turned to the Peter, the King of Aragon, whose wife, Constance, was the daughter of Manfred, illegitimate son of Frederick II. King Peter agreed to help against his enemy, Charles of Anjou and on August 30, 1282, landed at Trapani with his army. By October 1282, the Sicilian and Aragonese forces had expelled the Angevins from the island.

Charles of Anjou, about to launch his attack on Constantinople, was in Naples when he learned of the massacre at Palermo. He was furious to postpone his Byzantine expedition for something he incorrectly thought was a local flare-up. Charles made a long list of reforms to appease the Sicilians, but it was too little, too late. He immediately enlisted help from his papal ally. Pope Martin excommunicated Peter of Aragon in November of 1282 and on January 13, 1283 called for a Crusade against Peter, his Sicilian rebels and anyone who helped them. Participants would receive the same privileges as crusaders in the Holy Land. Two years later, on January 7, 1285, Charles of Anjou died at Foggia. He never returned to Sicily after the Vespers and never left for Constantinople. Pope Martin and King Peter died later on the same year.

The 1295 Treaty of Agnani produced conditions that led to Sicilian violence and decline in the coming decades. The Treaty of Agnani was a defensive pact made between the Aragonese and the Pope. Growing Aragonese hegemony made the Angevins, French and papal forces uneasy. Boniface VIII called for a crusade against Catalonia which belonged to Aragon, laid an interdict upon it and excommunicated the King of Aragon. In the face of such united force, the King of Aragon renounced his claim to Sicily in order to keep his Iberian empire. His younger brother, Frederick (soon to be Frederick III) refused to give up his governorship of Sicily and crowned himself King of Sicily with the enthusiastic support of the Sicilians. Fighting continued for seven more years, after which the 1302 Peace of Caltabellotta was finally made.

PART II – 1302-1337

The Peace of Caltabellotta in 1302 temporarily halted the fighting between the Angevins and the Sicilians. The illusion of family was fostered by two marriages that took place between the Aragonese royal house and the Angevins. The Peace, however, stipulated that upon the death of Frederick III, the island would revert to the Angevins. Frederick III ended up ruling for 41 years but the constant expectation of an earlier demise and a return to Angevin control fostered violent factions and a hoarding of capital.

In 1311, several events coalesced to renew the violence. The Angevins formed an alliance with Genoa to invade Sicily to retake southern Italian peninsular lands still under Sicilian control. Sicily's famous Catalan Company had already crossed over to Greece and taken over a great deal of territory. Henry VII, Holy Roman Emperor, was crowned in Rome the same year and decided to retake the Italian peninsula for himself. Sicily became his ally to rid herself permanently of the Angevin threat. The Angevins, seeing themselves surrounded on the north by the Holy Roman Empire, on the south by the Sicilians, in the west by the Catalan/Aragonese empire and in the east by the Catalan/Sicilian hegemony, attacked. Henry VII's unexpected death in 1314 left the Sicilians badly exposed. Committed to the cause, however, they continued to pour money, men and materials into the alliance. By 1318 the first complaints were raised about debts and war expenses and by 1321 a severe demographic and economic declined began, along with renewed Angevin invasions. War devastated the crops and brought the feudal barons into urban centers in an effort to keep their profits and their power. Gangs of armed thugs began to roam Palermo. By 1328 urban riots were common and by 1329 the blood vendetta between the two great feudal families of the Ventimiglia and the Chiaromonte escalated into a full-scale civil war.

Palermo was the largest and most important city in Sicily at this time. It was a royal administrative center and a commercial hub. But foreign and civil wars kept it in turmoil, causing people to flee into the city, creating even more chaos. By the end of Frederick's reign in 1337, Sicily had been depopulated by war and financially drained.

Made in the USA
San Bernardino, CA
28 August 2013